The Rancher's
Christmas Song

Also available from RaeAnne Thayne

Haven Point

Serenity Harbor
Snowfall on Haven Point
Riverbend Road
Evergreen Springs
Redemption Bay
Snow Angel Cove

Hope's Crossing

Wild Iris Ridge
Christmas in Snowflake Canyon
Willowleaf Lane
Currant Creek Valley
Sweet Laurel Falls
Woodrose Mountain
Blackberry Summer

The Cowboys of Cold Creek

The Holiday Gift
A Cold Creek Christmas Story
The Christmas Ranch
A Cold Creek Christmas Surprise
A Cold Creek Noel
A Cold Creek Reunion
Christmas in Cold Creek
A Cold Creek Baby
A Cold Creek Secret
A Cold Creek Holiday
A Cold Creek Homecoming
The Cowboy's Christmas Miracle

For a complete list of books by RaeAnne Thayne,
please visit www.raeannethayne.com.

NEW YORK TIMES BESTSELLING AUTHOR

RAEANNE THAYNE

The Rancher's
Christmas Song

CONTENTS

CONTENTS

The Rancher's Christmas Song

Dear Reader,

This is my sixteenth book in the overarching Cowboys of Cold Creek series (which is really a collection of various miniseries within a series). Every time I tell myself I'm done with the series, I come up with one more idea, another character I can't leave hanging. The moment I introduced Ella Baker in last year's *The Holiday Gift*, I knew I would have to tell her story. She played an important role in that book by helping the hero and heroine finally come together, but in the process, Ella ended up with her heart bruised. I couldn't let that be the end of things for her! I'm thrilled to have the chance to give the earnest and caring music teacher her own happy ending with sexy rancher Beckett McKinley—and his unruly twin boys!

Every time I return to Pine Gulch, I feel like I'm back among friends. Thank you for coming along!

Wishing you all the most joyous of holidays!

RaeAnne

To my dad, Elden Robinson,
who loved Westerns and cowboy music and
who made the best popcorn west of the Mississippi.
I miss you more than words can say.

Chapter One

The twin terrors were at it again.

Ella Baker watched two seven-year-old tornadoes, otherwise known as Trevor and Colter McKinley, chase each other behind the stage curtains at the Pine Gulch Community Center.

In the half hour since they arrived at the community center with their father, they had spilled a water pitcher, knocked down a life-size cardboard Santa and broken three ornaments on the big Christmas tree in the corner.

Now they were racing around on the stage where tonight's featured act was set to perform within the next half hour.

She would have to do something. As organizer and general show-runner of this fund-raising event for the school's underfinanced music program, it was her responsibility to make sure everyone had a good time. People's wallets tended to open a little wider when they were happy, comfortable and well fed. A gang of half-pint miscreants had the potential to ruin the evening for everyone.

She had tried to talk to them. As usual, the twins had offered her their angelic, gap-toothed smiles and had promised to behave, then moments later she saw them converge with four other boys to start playing this impromptu game of tag on the stage.

In order to tame these particular wild beasts, she was going to have to talk to someone in authority. She gave a last-ditch, desperate look around. As she had suspected, neither their uncle nor their great uncle was in sight. That left only one person who might have any chance of corralling these two little dynamos.

Their father.

Ella's stomach quivered. She did *not* enjoy talking to Beck McKinley and avoided it as much as possible.

The man made her so ridiculously nervous. He always treated her with careful politeness, but she could never read the expression on his features. Every time she spoke with him—which was more often than she liked, considering his ranch was next door to her father's—she always felt like she came out of the encounter sounding like a babbling fool.

Okay, yes. She was attracted to him, and had been since she moved back to Pine Gulch. What woman wouldn't be? Big, tough, gorgeous, with a slow smile that could charm even the most hardened heart.

She didn't *want* to be so drawn to him, especially when he hadn't once shown a glimmer of interest in return. He made her feel like she was an awkward teenager back in private school in Boston, holding up the wall at her first coed dance.

She wasn't. She was a twenty-seven-year-old professional in charge of generating funds for a cause she cared about. Sexy or not, Beck had to corral his sons before they ruined the entire evening.

Time to just suck it up and take care of business. She was a grown-up and could handle talking to anyone, even big, tough, stern-faced ranchers who made her feel like she didn't belong in Pine Gulch.

It wasn't hard to find Beck McKinley. He towered about four inches taller than the crowd of ranchers he stood among.

She sucked in a steadying breath and made her way toward

the group, trying to figure out a polite way to tell him his sons were causing trouble again.

She wasn't completely surprised to find her father was part of the group around Beck. They were not only copresidents of the local cattle growers association this year, but her father also idolized the man. As far as Curt Baker was concerned, Beck McKinley was all three wise men rolled into one. Her father still relied heavily on Beck for help—more so in the last few years, as his Parkinson's disease grew more pronounced and his limitations more frustrating.

At least her father was sitting down, leaning slightly forward with his trembling hands crossed in front of him atop the cane she had insisted he bring.

He barely looked at her, too engrossed in the conversation about cattle prices and feed shortages.

She waited until the conversation lagged before stepping into the group. She was unwilling to call out the rancher over his troublemaking twins in front of all the others.

"Beckett. May I have a brief word?"

His eyebrows rose and he blinked in surprise a few times. "Sure. Excuse me, gentlemen."

Aware of curious gazes following them, Ella led Beck a short distance from his peers.

"Is there a problem?" he asked.

She pointed toward the pack of wild boys on the stage, who were chasing each other between the curtains. "Your sons are at it again."

His gaze followed her gesture and he grimaced. "I see half a dozen boys up there. Last I checked, only two of those are mine."

"Colter and Trevor are the ringleaders. You know they are. They're always the ones who come up with the mischief and convince the others to go along."

"They're natural leaders. Are you suggesting I try to put the brakes on that?"

His boys were adorable, she had to admit, but they were the bane of her existence as the music teacher at Pine Gulch Elementary School. They couldn't sit still for more than a few minutes at a time and were constantly talking to each other as well as the rest of the students in their class.

"You could try to channel it into more positive ways."

This wasn't the first time she had made this suggestion to him and she was fairly certain she wasn't the only educator to have done so. Trevor and Colter had been causing problems at Pine Gulch Elementary School since kindergarten.

"They're boys. They've got energy. It comes with the package."

She completely agreed. That was one of the reasons she incorporated movement in her music lessons with all of her students this age. All children—but especially boys, she had noticed—couldn't sit still for long hours at a time and it was cruel to expect it of them.

She was a trained educator and understood that, but she also expected that excess energy to be contained when necessary and redirected into proper behavior.

"Our performers will be taking the stage soon. Please, can you do something with the boys? I can just picture them accidentally ripping down the curtains or messing with the lights before we can even begin."

Beck glanced at his boys, then back down at her. His strong jaw tightened, and in his eyes, she saw a flash of something she couldn't read.

She didn't need to interpret it. She was fairly certain she knew what he thought of her. Like her father, Beck thought she was a soft, useless city girl.

Both of them were wrong about her, but nothing she did seemed to convince them otherwise. As far as her father was concerned, she belonged in Boston or New York, where she could attend the symphony, the ballet, art gallery openings.

Since the moment she'd arrived here with her suitcases a little more than a year ago, Curt had been trying relentlessly to convince her to go back to Boston with her mother and stepfather and the cultured life they had.

Beck seemed to share her father's views. He never seemed to want to give her the time of day and always seemed in a big hurry to escape her presence.

Whatever his true opinion, he always treated her with stiff courtesy. She would give him that. Beck McKinley was never rude to anybody—probably one of the reasons all the other ranchers seemed to cluster around the man in public. Everybody seemed to respect his opinion and want to know what he had to say about things.

The only thing she wanted from him right now was to keep his boys from ruining the night.

"I'll talk to the parents of the other boys, too. I'm just asking if you'll please try to round up Colter and Trevor and have them take their seats. I'll be introducing our performers in a moment and I would like people to focus on what they came for, instead of how many straws Colter can stick up his nose."

He unbent enough to offer that rare, delicious smile. It appeared for only a moment. His cheeks creased and his eyes sparkled and his entire face looked even more gorgeous. "Good point, I suppose. The answer is five, in case you wanted to know. I'll grab them. Sorry they caused a ruckus."

"Thank you," she said, then walked away before she was tempted to make another joke, if only to see if he would offer up that smile again.

Better to quit while she was ahead, especially since her brain was now struggling to put together any words at all.

Beck watched Ella Baker walk away, her skirt swishing and her boot heels clicking on the old wooden floor of the community center.

He had the same reaction to her that he always did—sheer, wild hunger.

Something about that sleek blond hair and her almond-shaped eyes and the soft, kissable mouth did it to him. Every. Single. Time.

What was the *matter* with him? Why did he have to be drawn to the one woman in town who was totally wrong for him?

Ella wore tailored skirts and suede boots that probably cost as much as a hand-tooled saddle. She was always perfectly put together, from the top of her sleek blond hair to the sexy but completely impractical shoes she always wore.

When he was around her, he always felt exactly like what he was—a rough-edged cowboy.

Can you at least pretend you have a little culture? Do you have any idea how hard it is to be married to someone who doesn't know Manet from Monet?

Though it had been four years since she died—and five since she had lived with him and the twins—Stephanie's words and others she had uttered like them seemed to echo through his memory. They had lost their sting over the years, but, boy, had they burned at the time.

He sighed. Though the two had similar blue-blood backgrounds and educations, Ella Baker looked nothing like his late wife. Stephanie had been tall, statuesque, with red hair she had passed on to their sons. Ella was slim, petite and looked like an exotic blonde fairy.

Neither of them fit in here, though he had to admit Ella tried a hell of a lot harder than Stephanie ever had. She had organized this event, hadn't she?

He should probably stop staring at her. He would. Any moment now.

Why did she have to be so damn beautiful, bright and cheerful and smiling? Every time he saw her, it was like looking into the sun.

He finally forced himself to look away so he could do as she asked, quite justifiably. He should have been keeping a better eye on the boys from the beginning, but he'd been sucked into a conversation about a new ranching technique his friend Justin Hartford was trying and lost track of them.

As he made his way through the crowd, smiling at neighbors and friends, he was aware of how alone he was. He had been bringing the boys to these community things by himself for nearly five years now. He could hardly believe it.

He was ready to get out there and date again. The boys had somehow turned seven, though he had no idea how that happened.

The truth was, he was lonely. He missed having someone special in his life. He was tired of only having his uncle and his brothers to talk to.

Heaven knows, he was really tired of sleeping alone.

When he did jump back into that whole dating arena, though, he was fairly sure it wouldn't be with a soft, delicate music teacher who didn't know a mecate from a bosal.

It might be easier to remember that if the woman wasn't so darned pretty.

In short order, he found the boys on the stage and convinced all of them it was time to find their parents and take their seats, then led his own twins out of trouble.

"Hey, Dad. Guess what Thomas said?" Colter asked, as they were making their way through the crowd.

"What's that, son?" He couldn't begin to guess what another seven-year-old might pass along—and was a little afraid to ask.

"His dog is gonna have puppies right before Christmas. Can we get one? Can we?"

He did his best not to roll his eyes at the idea. "Thomas and his family have a miniature Yorkie that's no bigger than my hand. I'm not sure a little dog like that would like living on a big ranch like ours with all our horses and cattle. Besides, we've already got three dogs. And one of those is going to have her own puppies any day now."

"Yeah, but they're *your* dogs. And you always tell us they're not pets, they're working dogs," Trevor said.

"And you told us we probably can't keep any of Sal's puppies," Colter added. "We want a puppy of our very own."

Like they didn't have enough going right now. He was not only running his horse and cattle ranch, the Broken Arrow, but also helping out Curt Baker at his place as much as possible. He had help from his brother and uncle, yeah—on the ranch and with the boys. He still missed his longtime housekeeper and nanny, Judy Miller, who was having double–knee replacement and would be out for six months.

Adding a little indoor puppy into the chaos of their life right now was completely unthinkable.

"I don't think that's going to happen," he said firmly but gently.

"Maybe Santa Claus will bring us one," Colter said, nudging his brother.

At seven, the boys were pretty close to understanding the truth about Santa Claus, though they had never come right out and told them. Every once in a while he thought they might know, but were just trying to hang on to the magic as long as possible. He was okay with that. Life would be full of enough disappointments.

He was saved from having to answer them by the sight of beautiful Ella Baker approaching the microphone.

"Hey! There's Miss Baker," Trevor said, loudly enough that she heard and looked in their direction.

Though families had been encouraged to attend the event and it was far from a formal concert, Beck was still embarrassed by the outburst.

"Shh," he said to the boys. "This is a time to listen, not talk."

"Like church?" Colter asked, with some measure of distrust.

"Sort of." *But more fun*, he thought, though of course he couldn't say to impressionable boys.

Trevor and Colter settled into their seats and Beck watched as Ella took the microphone. He figured he could watch her here without guilt, since everyone else's eyes were on her, too.

"Welcome, everyone, to this fund-raiser for the music program at the elementary and middle schools. By your presence here, it's clear you feel strongly about supporting the continued success of music education in our schools. As you know, programs like ours are constantly under the budget knife. Through your generous donations, we can continue the effort to teach music to the children of Pine Gulch. At this time, it's my great pleasure to introduce our special guests, all the way from northern Montana. Please join me in welcoming J. D. Wyatt and his Warbling Wranglers."

The introduction was met with a huge round of applause for the cowboy singers. Beck settled into his chair and prepared to savor the entertainment—and prayed it could keep his wild boys' attention.

He shouldn't have worried. An hour later, the band wrapped up with a crowd-pleasing, toe-tapping version of "Jingle Bell Rock" that had people getting up to dance in the aisle and in front of the small stage.

His twins had been utterly enthralled, from the first notes to the final chord.

"That was awesome!" Colter exclaimed.

"Yeah!" His twin glowed, as well. "Hey, Dad! Can we take fiddle lessons?"

Over the summer, they had wanted to learn to play the guitar. Now they wanted to learn the violin. Tomorrow, who knows, they might be asking for accordion lessons.

"I don't know. We'll have to see," he said.

Before the twins could press him, Ella Baker returned to the mic stand.

"Thank you all again for your support. Please remember all proceeds from ticket sales for tonight's performance, as well as our silent auction, will go toward funding music in the schools. Also, please don't forget tomorrow will be the first rehearsal for the Christmas show and dinner put on by the children of our community for our beloved senior citizens at The Christmas Ranch in Cold Creek Canyon. This isn't connected to the school and is completely voluntary. Any students ages four to sixteen are encouraged to join us."

"Hey. That's us!" Trevor said.

"Can we do it, Dad?" Colter asked, with the same pleading look on his face he wore when asking for a second scoop of ice cream. "We wanted to last year, remember? Only you said we couldn't because we were going to visit our Grandma Martin."

That had been a short-lived visit with Stephanie's mother in Connecticut, who had thought she would enjoy taking the boys into the city over the holidays and showing off her grandsons to her friends. After three days, she had called him to pick up the boys ahead of schedule, sounding ages older than she had days earlier. She hadn't called again this year.

"Can we?" Trevor persisted.

Beck didn't know how to answer as items on his massive to-do list seemed to circle around him like buzzards on a carcass. He had so much to do this time of year and didn't know how he could run the boys to and from the rehearsals at The Christmas Ranch, which was a good fifteen minutes away.

On the other hand, Ella Baker lived just next door. Maybe he could work something out with her to give the boys a ride.

Of course, that meant he would have to talk to her again, though. He did his best to avoid situations that put them into closer proximity, where he might be tempted to do something stupid.

Like ask her out.

"Please," Colter begged.

This was a good cause, a chance to reinforce to them the importance of helping others. The holiday show had become a high point to many of the senior citizens in town, and they looked forward to it all year. If the twins wanted to do it, how could he possibly refuse?

"We'll see," he hedged, not quite ready to commit.

"You always say that," Trevor said. "How come we never really *see* anything after you say we will?"

"Good question. Maybe someday, I'll answer it. We'll have to see."

The boys laughed, as he hoped, and were distracted by their friend Thomas—he, of the tiny puppies—who came over to talk to them.

"Are you gonna do the Christmas show? My mom said I could, if I wanted."

"We want to," Trevor said, with another cajoling look at Beck.

"Maybe we can have a band," Thomas said. "I'll be J.D. and you can be the Warbling Wranglers."

As they squabbled good-naturedly about which of them would make the better lead singer, Beck listened to them with a sense of resignation. If they really wanted to be in the Christmas program, he would have to figure out a way to make it happen—even if it meant talking to Ella Baker again.

The thought filled him with far more anticipation than he knew was good for him.

Chapter Two

"What a fantastic event!" Faith Brannon squeezed Ella's hand. "I haven't enjoyed a concert so much in a long time."

"Maybe that's because you never go out," Faith's younger sister, Celeste, said with a laugh.

"Newlyweds. What are you going to do?" Hope, the third Nichols sister, winked at their group of friends.

Ella had to laugh, even as she was aware of a little pang. Faith had married her neighbor, Chase Brannon, about four months earlier, in a lovely wedding in the big reception hall of The Christmas Ranch.

It had been lovely and understated, since it was a second marriage for both, but there hadn't been a dry eye in the hall. They seemed so in love and so deserving of happiness.

Ella had managed to smile all evening long. She considered that quite an accomplishment, considering once upon a time, she had completely made a fool of herself over the groom. When she first moved to Pine Gulch, she'd had a gigantic crush on Chase and had all but thrown herself at him, with no clue that he had adored Faith forever and had just been biding his time until she came to terms with her husband's premature death.

Ella had almost gotten over her embarrassment about events of the previous Christmas. It might have been easier to avoid the happy couple altogether except the Nichols sisters—all married now and with different surnames but still "the Nichols sisters" to just about everyone in town—had become some of her dearest friends.

They were warm and kind and always went out of their way to include her in activities.

"You did a great job of organizing," Hope said now. "I couldn't believe all the people who showed up. I met a couple earlier who drove all the way up from Utah because they love J.D. and his Wranglers. I hope you raked in the dough."

"Everyone has been generous," she said. "We should have enough to purchase the new piano we need in the elementary school with plenty left over for sheet music at the middle school."

She still didn't think it was right that the art and music programs had to struggle so much to make ends meet in this rural school system. Judging by tonight, though, many members of the community seemed to agree with her that it should be a priority and had donated accordingly.

"It was a great community event. What a great turnout!"

"Just think." Hope grinned. "We get to turn around and do this again in a few weeks at The Christmas Ranch."

Faith made a face. "You wouldn't believe how many people have brought up that Christmas program to me tonight, and I'm not even involved in the show!"

"You're a Nichols, though, which makes you one of the co-queens of Christmas, like it or not," Ella said.

The Nichols family had been running The Christmas Ranch—a holiday-themed attraction filled with sleigh rides, a life-size Christmas village and even their own herd of reindeer—for many years. It was enormously successful and at-tracted visitors from around the region.

The popularity of the venue had grown exponentially in the last few years because of the hard work of the sisters.

A few years earlier, they had come up with the idea of pro-viding a free catered dinner and holiday-themed show presented by area children as a gift to the local senior citizens and the event had become legendary in the community.

"We are so lucky that you've agreed to help us again this year," Celeste said now to Ella.

"Are you kidding? I've been looking forward to it all year."

The event—more like an old-fashioned variety show—wasn't professionally staged, by any means. Rehearsals didn't even start until a few weeks before the performance and there were no auditions and few soloists, but the children had fun doing it and the attendees enjoyed every moment.

The previous year's performance had been a wonderful grow-ing experience for Ella, serving as an icebreaker of sorts to help her get to know the local children better.

She hoped this year would only build on that success.

"Wait until you see some of the songs we have planned. It's going to knock your socks off," she said.

"How can you be so excited about wrestling seventy school-children already on a Christmas sugar high?" Faith shook her head. "You must be crazy."

"The very best kind of crazy," Celeste said with a smile.

"You fit right in with the rest of us," Hope assured her, then changed the subject. "Hey, did you see that good-looking guy who came in with Nate and Emery Cavazos? His name is Jess Saddler and he's temporarily staying at their cabins. Em said he's single and looking to move in and open a sporting goods store in town. He's cute, isn't he?"

She followed the direction of Hope's gaze and discovered a man she didn't know speaking with Nate and Emery, as well as Caroline and Wade Dalton. Hope was right, he was great-looking, with an outdoorsy tan and well-styled, sun-streaked hair that looked as if it had never seen a Stetson.

He also had that overchiseled look of people who earned their strength at the gym instead of through hard, productive manual labor.

"I suppose."

"You should go introduce yourself," Hope suggested, ignoring the sudden frown from both of her sisters.

"Why?" Ella asked, suspicious.

Hope's innocent shrug didn't fool her. "He's single. You're single. Em said he seems like a great guy and, I don't know, I thought maybe the two of you would hit it off."

"Are you matchmaking for me?"

"Do you want me to?" Hope asked eagerly.

Did she? She wasn't sure how to answer. Yes, she was lonely. It was tough to be a single woman in this family-oriented community, where everyone seemed paired up. There weren't very many eligible men to even date and she often felt isolated and alone.

She wasn't sure how she felt about being the latest pity project of her friends. Did she seem desperate to them?

That was an uncomfortable thought.

"I don't need a matchmaker. I'm fine," she told Hope. "Even if I met the right guy today, I'm not sure I would have time for him, between working at two schools, doing music therapy at the senior citizen center and taking my dad to doctor appointments."

"When you care about a man, you make time," Celeste said.

"I don't think the guy is going anywhere. After Christmas, you should think about it," Hope added.

"Maybe." She could only hope a bland nonanswer would be enough for them.

Hope looked disappointed but was distracted when another neighbor came up and asked her a question about a private company party scheduled the following week at The Christmas Ranch.

While she was occupied, Faith turned to Ella with a frown on her soft, pretty features.

"It sounds like you have too much on your plate," Faith said. "Now I feel guilty we roped you into doing the Christmas show again."

"You didn't rope me into anything," she assured her. "I meant what I said. I've been looking forward to it."

"When will you have time to breathe?"

She didn't mind being busy and loved teaching music. It had been her passion through her teen years and pursuing a career in music therapy was a natural fit. She had loved her job before she came here, working at a school for students with developmental disabilities, but there was nothing like that here in this small corner of southeastern Idaho. Teaching music in the schools was the next best thing. She had to do something with her time, especially considering her father continued being completely stubborn and unreasonable about letting her take over the ranch.

She was busy. She just wasn't *that* busy.

"If you want the truth," she admitted, "I may have slightly exaggerated my overloaded schedule to keep Hope from making me her next project."

Faith looked amused. "Very wise move on your part."

"Don't get me wrong. It's sweet of her and everything. It's just…"

"You don't have to explain to me. I totally get it."

"I'm just not looking for a male right now."

"Too bad. Looks like a couple of cute ones are headed this way."

She followed Faith's gaze to find the twin terrors barreling straight toward her at full speed. To her relief, they managed to stop inches from knocking her and Faith over like bowling pins.

"Hey, Miss Baker. Miss Baker! Guess what?"

The boys' faces were both covered in chocolate, a fairly solid clue that they'd been raiding the refreshments table. How many cookies had they consumed between the pair of them? Not her problem, she supposed. Their father could deal with their upset stomachs and sugar overload.

"What's that, Trevor?" She directed her question to the one who had spoken.

He hid a grin behind his hand. "I'm not Trevor. I'm Colter."

"Are you sure?" She raised an eyebrow.

He giggled. "How come we can never fool you? You're right. I'm Trevor."

The boys were the most identical twins Ella had ever seen and they delighted in playing those kind of switch-up games with the faculty and staff at the elementary school. From the first time they met, though, Ella had never struggled to tell them apart. Colter had a slightly deeper cleft in his chin and Trevor had a few more freckles.

"Guess what?" Colter finished his brother's sentence. "We're gonna be in your Christmas show."

Beside her, Faith gave a small but audible groan that completely mirrored Ella's sudden panic.

On the heels of that initial reaction, she felt suddenly protective of the boys, defensive on their behalf. It really wasn't their fault they misbehaved. None of it was malicious. They were high-spirited in the first place and had a father who seemed more interested in taking over her father's ranch than teaching his two boys to behave like little gentlemen.

But then, she might be a tad biased against the man. Every time she offered to do something to help Curtis, her father was quick to tell her Beck would take care of it.

"Is that right?" she asked. The show was open to any children who wanted to participate, with no auditions and guaranteed parts for all. They wouldn't win any talent competitions, but she considered the flaws and scenery mishaps all part of the charm.

"Our dad said *we'll see*," Colter informed her. "Sometimes

that means no, but then I heard him asking your dad if he thought you might be able to give us a ride to and from practice on the days no one from the ranch could do it."

Her jaw tightened. The nerve of the arrogant rancher, to go to her father instead of asking her directly, as if Curt had any control over the matter.

"And what did my father say?"

"We didn't hear," Trevor confessed. "But can you?"

Their ranch was right next door to the Baker's Dozen. It would be no great hardship for her to accommodate the McKinleys and transport the twins if they wanted to participate, but it would be nice if Beck could be bothered asking her himself.

"I'll have to talk to your father first," she hedged.

The boys seemed to take her equivocation as the next best thing to a done deal.

"This will be fun," Colter said, showing off his gap-toothed grin. "We're gonna be the best singers you ever saw."

To reinforce the point, Trevor launched into a loud version of "Rudolph the Red-Nosed Reindeer" and his brother joined in. They actually had surprisingly good singing voices. She'd noticed that before during music class at school—though it was hard to confirm that now when they were singing at the tops of their lungs.

They were drawing attention, she saw. The cute guy with Em and Nate was looking this way and so was Beck McKinley.

Ella flushed, envisioning the nightmare of trying to keep the boys from trying to ride the reindeer at The Christmas Ranch, or from knocking down the gigantic sixteen-foot-tall tree inside the St. Nicholas Lodge.

"You can be in the show on one condition," she said, using her best teacher's voice.

"What's that?" Colter asked warily.

"Children of all ages will be participating, even some kindergarten students and first graders. They're going to need someone to set a good example about how to listen and pay attention. They'll be watching you. Can you show them the correct way to behave?"

"Yeah!" Trevor exclaimed. "We can be quiet as dead mice."

That was pretty darn quiet—and she would believe *that* when she saw it.

"We can be the goodest kids in the whole place," Colter said. "You'll see, Miss Baker. You won't even know we're there, except when we're singing."

"Yeah. You'll see," Trevor said. "Thanks, Miss Baker. Come on, Colt. Let's go tell Thomas." In a blink, the two of them raced off as quickly as they had appeared by her side.

"Those boys are quite a pair, aren't they?" Faith said, watching after them with a rather bemused look on her features.

Ella was again aware of that protective impulse, the urge to defend them. Yes, they could be exhausting but she secretly admired their take-no-prisoners enthusiasm for life.

"They're good boys. Just a little energetic."

"You can say that again. They're a handful. I suppose it's only to be expected, though." Faith paused, her expression pensive. "You know, I thought for sure Beck would send them off to live with family after their mother left. I mean, here was this tough, macho rancher trying to run his place while also dealing with a couple of boys still in diapers. The twins couldn't have been more than two."

"So young? How could a mother leave her babies?"

"Yeah. I wanted to chase after her and smack her hard for leaving a good man like Beck, but he would never let anybody say a bad word about her. The only thing he ever said to me was that Stephanie was struggling with some mental health issues and needed a little time to get her head on straight. I think she had some postpartum depression and it probably didn't help that she didn't have a lot of friends here. We tried, but she wasn't really very approachable."

Faith made a face. "That sounds harsh, doesn't it? That's not what I mean. She was just not from around here."

"Neither am I," Ella pointed out.

"Yes, but you don't constantly remind us of how much better things were back east."

Because they weren't. Oh, she missed plenty of things about her life there, mostly friends and neighbors and really good clam chowder, but she had always felt as if she had a foothold in two places—her mother's upper-crust Beacon Hill society and her father's rough-and-rugged Idaho ranch.

"Anyway, she left to get her head on straight when the boys were about two and I can't imagine how hard it must have been for Beck on his own. A year later, Stephanie died of a drug overdose back east."

"Oh, how sad. Those poor boys."

"I know. Heartbreaking. Her parents are high-powered doctors. They fought for custody of the boys and I think it got pretty ugly for a while, but Beck wouldn't hear of it. He's a good dad. Why would any judge take the boys away from father and the only home they've ever known and give them to a couple of strangers?"

"He strikes me as a man who holds on to what he considers his."

"That might have been part of it. But the truth is, Beckett adores his boys. You should have seen him, driving to cattle sales and the feed store with two toddlers strapped in their car seats in the crew cab of his pickup truck."

Her heart seemed to sigh at the picture. She could see it entirely too clearly, the big, tough rancher and his adorable carbon-copy twins.

"He's a good man," Faith said. "A woman could do far worse than Beckett McKinley. If you're ever crazy enough to let Hope fix you up, you shouldn't discount Beck on account of those wild boys of his."

That wouldn't be the only reason she could never look seriously at Beck, if she was in the market for a man—which she so totally wasn't. For one thing, she became nervous and tongue-tied around him and couldn't seem to string together two coherent thoughts. For another, the man clearly didn't like her. He treated her with a cool politeness made all the more striking when she saw his warm, friendly demeanor around others. And, finally, she was more than a little jealous of his close relationship with her father. Curt treated his neighboring rancher like the son he'd never had, trusting him with far more responsibility than he would ever consider giving his own daughter. How could she ever get past that?

She was saved from having to answer when Faith's husband, Chase, came over with Faith's daughter and son in tow.

Chase smiled at Ella and she tried to ignore the awkwardness as she greeted him. This was all she wanted. A nice man who didn't make her nervous. Was that too much to ask?

"Mom, can we go?" Louisa said. "I still have math homework to finish."

"We're probably the only parents here whose kids are begging to leave so they can get back to homework," Chase said with a grin.

"Thanks again for the great show, Ella," Faith said. "We'll see you tomorrow. Now that we've been warned the McKinley twins are coming, we'll make sure you have reinforcements at practice tomorrow."

She could handle the twins. Their father was another story.

As much as he enjoyed hanging out with other ranchers, shooting the, er, shinola, as his dad used to call it, Beck decided it was time to head out. It was past the boys' bedtime and their bus would be coming early.

"Gentlemen, it's been a pleasure but I need to call it a night," he said.

There were more than a few good-hearted groans of disappointment.

He loved the supportive ranching community here in Pine Gulch. Friends and neighbors came through for each other in times of need. He couldn't count the number of guys who had stepped in to help him after his father died. When Stephanie left, he had needed help again until he could find a good nanny and more than one neighbor had come over without being asked to lend a hand on the ranch.

The Broken Arrow would have gone under without their aid and he knew he could never repay them. The only thing he could do now was help out himself where he could.

As Beck waved goodbye and headed away from the group, he saw Curt Baker climb to his feet with the aid of his cane and follow after him. Beck slowed his steps so the older man could catch up.

"Thanks again for stepping in today and helping Manny unload the feed shipment."

"Glad I could help," he answered.

It was true. He admired Curt and owed the man. After Beckett's father died, Curt had been the first neighbor to step in and help him figure out what he was doing on the ranch. Now the tables were turned. Curt's Parkinson's disease limited his ability to care for his own holdings. He had reduced his herd significantly and brought in more help, but still struggled to take care of the day-to-day tasks involved in running a cattle ranch.

He had actually talked Curt into running with him to be copresidents of the local cattle growers association. It wasn't a tough job and gave Curt something else to focus on besides his health issues.

"Have you thought more on what we talked about over lunch?"

As if he could think about anything else. As much as he enjoyed cowboy folk songs, he'd had a hard time focusing on anything but Curt's stunning proposal that afternoon.

"You love the Baker's Dozen," he said. "There's no rush to sell it now, is there?"

Curt was quiet. "I'm not getting better. We both know that.

There's only one direction this damn disease will go and that's south."

Parkinson's really sucked.

"I'm not in a hurry to sell. So far Manny and the other ranch hands are keeping things going—with help from you and Jax, of course—but you and I both know it's only a matter of time before I'll have to sell. I want to make sure I have things lined up ahead of time. Just wanted to plant the seed."

That little seed had certainly taken root. Hell, it was spreading like snakeweed.

The Broken Arrow was doing better than Beck ever dreamed, especially since he and his brother, Jax, had shifted so many of their resources to breeding exceptional cattle horses. They still ran about 500 cow-calf pair, but right now half the ranch's revenue was coming from the equine side of the business.

He would love the chance to expand his operation into the Baker's Dozen acreage, which had prime water rights along with it. He wasn't trying to build an empire here, but he had two boys to consider, as well as Jax. Though his brother seemed happy to play the field, someday that might change and he might want to settle down and become a family man.

Beck needed to make sure the Broken Arrow could support him, if that time came. It made perfect sense to grow his own operation into the adjacent property. It would be a big financial reach, but after several record-breaking years, he had the reserves to handle it.

"How does Ella feel about this?" he asked.

Curt shrugged. "What's not to like? You take over the work and we have money in the bank. She'll be fine. She could go back to Boston and not have to worry about me."

He wasn't sure he agreed with Curt's assessment of the Ella factor. Yeah, she didn't know anything about ranching and had only lived here with her father for a little longer than a year, but Ella was stubborn. She adored her father and had moved here to help him, though Curt seemed reluctant to lean on her too much.

"Anyway, we can worry about that later," Curt said. "My priority is to make sure I sell the land to someone who's actually going to ranch it, not turn it into condominiums. I've seen what you've done with the Broken Arrow since your father died and I have no doubt you'd give the same care to the Baker's Dozen."

"I appreciate that."

"No need to decide anything right now. We have plenty of time."

"You've given me a lot to chew on."

"That was my intent," Curt said. "Still need me to talk to Ella about taking your boys to the music thingy tomorrow?"

He winced, embarrassed that he'd even brought it up earlier. He was a grown man. He could talk to her himself, even if the woman did make him feel like he'd just been kicked by a horse, breathless and stupid and slow.

"I'll do it," he said. "I actually have a few things in town so should be able to take them tomorrow. When I get the chance, I'll try to talk to her then about future rehearsals."

He wasn't sure why his boys were so set on being in this Christmas program, but they were funny kids, with their own independent minds. He had always had the philosophy that he would try to support them in anything they tried. Basketball, soccer, after-school science clubs. Whatever.

Even when it meant he had to talk to Ella Baker.

Chapter Three

"Trevor. Colter. That's the last time I'm going to ask you. Please stop making silly noises. If you keep interrupting, we won't make it through all the songs we need to practice."

The twins gave Ella matching guilty looks. "Sorry, Miss Baker," Colter said.

"We'll be good. We promise," his brother added.

Somehow she was having a hard time believing that, especially given their track record in general and this practice in particular. After a full day of school, they were having a tough time sitting still and staying focused for the rehearsals, as she had fully expected.

She felt totally inadequate to deal with them on a December afternoon when they wanted to be running around outside, throwing snowballs and building snow forts.

Would it distract everyone too much if she had them stand up and do jumping jacks for a minute? She decided it was worth a try. Sometimes a little burst of energy could do wonders for focus.

"Okay, speed workout. Everyone. How many elf jumping jacks can you do in one minute? Count to yourself. Go."

She timed them on her phone and by the end the children were all laughing and trying to outdo each other.

"Excellent. Okay, now close your eyes and we'll do one more moment of deep breathing. That's it. Perfect."

That seemed to refocus everyone and they made it through nearly every number without further incident, until the last one, "Away in a Manger."

The song sounded lovely, with all the children singing in tune and even enunciating the words—until the last line of the third verse, when Trevor started making noises like a certain explosive bodily function, which made the entire back row dissolve into laughter.

By the time they finished the ninety-minute rehearsal, though, she felt as wrung out as a dirty mitten left in the snow.

As soon as parents started arriving for their children, Hope popped in from the office of The Christmas Ranch with a mug of hot chocolate, which she thrust out to Ella.

"Here you go. Extra snowflake marshmallows. You deserve it. You survived the first rehearsal. It's all uphill from here."

"I hope so," she muttered. "Today was a bit of a disaster."

"I saw Beck's boys giving you a rough time," Hope said, her voice sympathetic.

"You could say that. It must be tough on them, coming straight from school to here."

Eight rehearsals. That's all they had. She could handle that, couldn't she?

"Do you need me to find more people to help you?"

She considered, then shook her head. "I think we should be okay with the two teenagers who volunteered. Everyone is so busy this time of year. I hate to add one more thing to someone else's plate."

"Because your schedule is so free and easy over the next few weeks, right?"

Hope had a point. Between the Christmas show, the care center where she volunteered and the two schools where she worked, Ella had concerts or rehearsals every single day be-tween now and Christmas.

"At least I'm not a bestselling illustrator who also happens to be in charge of the number-one holiday attraction for hun-dreds of miles around."

"Lucky you," Hope said with a grin. "Want to trade?"

"Not a chance."

Hope wouldn't trade her life, either, Ella knew. She loved creating the Sparkle the Reindeer books, which had become a worldwide sensation over the last few years. She also adored running the ranch with her husband, Rafe, and raising their beautiful son.

"Let me know if you change your mind about needing more help," Hope said.

"I will."

After Hope headed away, Ella started cleaning up the mess of paper wrappers and leftover sheet music the children had left behind. She was gathering up her own things when a couple of boys trotted out of the gift shop.

Colter and Trevor. Was she supposed to be giving them a ride? Beck hadn't called her. He hadn't said a word to her about it. Had he just assumed she would do it without being asked?

That didn't really seem like something Beck would do. More likely, there was a miscommunication.

"Do you need me to call your dad to let him know we're done with rehearsal?"

Colter gave an exasperated sigh. "We told him and told him about it last night and this morning at breakfast. We took a note to school so we could ride a different bus here, then our dad was supposed to come get us when practice was done. I don't know where he is."

"Maybe we'll have to sleep here tonight," Trevor said. "I call under the Christmas tree!"

"You're not sleeping here tonight. I can give you a ride, but I need to talk to your dad first to make sure he's not on his way and just running late. I wouldn't want us to cross paths."

At least he hadn't just assumed she could take care of it. Slightly mollified, she pulled her phone out of her pocket. "Do you know his number?"

The boys each recited a different number, argued for a few moments, then appeared to come to a consensus.

She punched in the numbers they gave her without much confidence she would actually be connected to Beck, but to her surprise he answered.

"Broken Arrow," he said, with a brusqueness she should have expected, especially considering he probably didn't recognize her phone number.

Those two simple words in his deep, sexy voice seemed to shiver down her spine as if he'd trailed a finger down it.

"Beckett, this is Ella Baker. I was wondering…that is, your sons were wondering, uh, are you coming to pick them up?"

Darn it, she *hated* being so tongue-tied around the man. She had all the poise and grace of a lumbering steer.

There was a long, awkward pause, then he swore. He quickly amended it. "Uh, shoot. I totally forgot about that. What time is rehearsal done?"

"About twenty minutes ago," she answered, letting a bit of tartness creep into her voice.

He sighed. "I've got the vet here looking at a sick horse. We're going to be another ten minutes or so, then I'll have to clean up a bit. Can you give me a half hour?"

He still couldn't seem to bring himself to ask for her help. Stubborn man. She glanced over at the boys, who were admiring the giant Christmas tree in the lodge. She wasn't sure she had the physical or mental capacity to keep them entertained and out of trouble for another half hour.

"I can give them a ride home, if you would like. It's an easy stop on my way back to the Baker's Dozen."

"Could you? That would be a big help. Thank you." The relief in his voice was palpable.

"You're welcome. Do you want me to drop them at the barn or the house?"

"The horse barn, if you don't mind. That's where I'm working."

She was suddenly having second thoughts, not sure she was ready to see him two days in a row.

"All right. We'll see you shortly, then."

"Thank you," he said again.

She managed to round up the boys in the nick of time, seconds before they were about to test how strong the garland over the mantel was by taking turns dangling from it.

How had Beck's house not burned down to the ground by now, with these two mischievous boys around?

"Why are you driving us home?" Colter asked when they had their seat belts on in her back seat. "Where's our dad?"

"He's taking care of a sick horse, he said. The vet's there with him and they lost track of time."

"That's Frisco. He was our mom's horse, but he's probably gonna die soon."

She wasn't sure how to reply to that, especially when he spoke in a matter-of-fact way. "I'm sorry."

"He's really old and too ornery for us to ride. He bites. Dad says he better not catch us near him," Trevor said.

She shivered, then hoped they couldn't see. She had to get over her fear of horses, darn it. After more than a year in horse and cattle country, she thought she would be past it—but then, twenty years hadn't made a difference, so why should the past year enact some miraculous change?

"You better do what he says."

"We don't want to ride that grumpy thing, anyway," Trevor said. "Why would we? We both have our own horses. Mine is named Oreo and Colt's is named Blackjack."

"Do you have a horse, Miss Baker?"

She remembered a sweet little roan mare she had adored more than anything in the world.

"I used to, when I was your age. Her name was Ruby. But I haven't been on a horse in a long, long time. We don't have any horses on the Baker's Dozen."

In one bold sweep, her dad had gotten rid of them all twenty years ago, even though he had loved to ride, too. Thinking about it always made her sad.

"You could come ride our horses. We have like a million of them."

Familiar fear sidled up to her and said hello. "That's nice of you, Colter, but I don't know how to ride anymore. It's been a very long time since I've been in a saddle."

"We could teach you again," Trevor offered, with a sweet willingness that touched something deep inside. "I bet you'd pick it up again easy."

For a moment, she was very tempted by the offer but she would have to get past her phobia first. "That's very kind of you," she said, and left it at that. The boys didn't need to know about her issues.

"Hey, you know how to sing, right?" Colter said suddenly, changing the subject.

Considering she had one degree in music therapy and another in music education, she hoped so. "Yes. That is certainly something I do know how to do."

"And you play the guitar. You do it in school sometimes."

And the piano, violin and most other stringed instruments. "That's right."

"Could you teach us how to play a song?" Colter asked.

"And how to sing it, too?" Trevor said.

She glanced in her rearview mirror at their faces, earnestly eager. "Does either of you know how to play the guitar?"

"We both do, kind of," Colter said. "Uncle Dan taught us a couple chords last summer but then he said he wouldn't teach us anymore because we played too hard and broke all the strings on his guitar."

"Oh, dear."

These boys didn't do anything half-heartedly. She secretly hoped they would continue to be all-in as they grew up—with a little self-restraint when it was necessary, anyway.

"But we would never do that to your guitar, if you let us practice on it," he assured her with a grave solemnity that almost made her smile.

"We promise," his twin said. "We would be super careful."

She couldn't believe she would even entertain the idea for a moment, but she couldn't deny she was curious about the request. "What song are you trying to learn how to play and sing?"

"It's a good one. 'Christmas for the Cowboy.' Have you heard that one?"

"I'm not sure."

"It's about this cowboy and he has to work on Christmas Eve and ride his horse in the snow and stuff," Trevor informed her.

"He's real mad about it, and thinks it's not fair and he wants to be inside where it's warm, then the animals help him remember that Christmas is about peace on earth and stuff."

"And baby Jesus and wise men and shepherds," Trevor added.

"That sounds like a good one."

She combed through her memory bank but wasn't sure if she had ever heard it.

"It's our dad's favorite Christmas song in the whole wide world. He hums it all the time and keeps the CD in his pickup truck."

"Do you know who sings it?" she asked. It would be much easier to track down the guitar chords if she could at least have that much info.

The boys named a country music group whose name she recognized. She wasn't very familiar with their body of work.

"So can you teach us?" Colter asked as they neared the turn-off for the Broken Arrow. "It has to be with the guitar, too."

"Please?" Trevor asked. "Pretty please with Skittles on top?"

Well, she did like Skittles. She hid a smile. "Why is this so important to you? Why do you want to learn the song so badly?"

As she glanced in the rearview mirror, she saw the boys exchange looks. She had noticed before they did that quite often, as if passing along some nonverbal, invisible, twin communication that only they understood.

"It's for our dad," Trevor finally said. "He works hard all the time and takes care of us and stuff and we never have a good present to give him at Christmas."

"Except things we make in school, and that's usually just dumb crap," Colter said. "Pictures and clay bowls and stuff."

Ella had a feeling the art teacher she shared a classroom with probably wouldn't appreciate that particularly blunt assessment.

"When we went to bed last night after the concert, we decided we should learn that song and play it for our dad because he loves it so much, but we don't know the right words. We always sing it wrong."

"Hey, maybe after we learn it, we could play and sing it in the Christmas program," Colter said.

"Yeah," Trevor said, "Like that guy and his wranglers last night."

She didn't know how to respond, afraid to give the boys false hope. She didn't even know what song they were talking about, let alone whether it was appropriate for a Christmas program designed for senior citizens.

"I'm afraid I'm not familiar with that song—" she began.

"You could learn it, couldn't you?" Colter said.

"It's probably not even too hard."

As she turned into the ranch, they passed a large pasture containing about a dozen horses. Two of them cantered over to the fence line, then raced along beside her SUV, their manes and tails flying out behind them.

She felt the familiar panic, but something else, a long-buried regret for what she had lost.

"If I can find the song and agree to teach you, I need something from the two of you in return."

"Let me guess. You want us to quit messing around at rehearsal." Colter said this in the same resigned tone someone might use after being told they faced an IRS audit.

"Absolutely. That's one of my conditions. You told me you could behave, but today wasn't a very good example of that. I need to be able to trust you to keep your word."

"Sorry, Miss Baker."

"We'll do better, we promise."

How many times had the boys uttered those very same words to one voice of authority or other? No doubt they always meant it, but something told her they would follow through this time. It touched her heart that they wanted to give this gift to their father, who had sacrificed and struggled and refused to give up custody after their mother died.

She wanted to help them give something back to him—and she wanted something in return, something that made her palms suddenly feel sweaty on the steering wheel.

"That is one of my conditions. And I'm very firm about it."

She paused, sucked in a breath, then let it out in a rush and spoke quickly before she could change her mind.

"I also have one more condition."

"What?" Trevor asked.

Her heart was pounding so hard, she could barely hear herself think. This was foolish. Why did she think two seven-year-old boys could help her overcome something she had struggled with for twenty years?

"You said you could teach me how to ride horses again. I would like that, very much. I told you it's been a long time since I've been on a horse. I...miss it."

More than she had even dared acknowledge to herself.

Once, horses had been her passion. She had dreamed about them, talked about them, drew pictures of them, even during the months when she was living in Boston during the ten months out of the year her mother had custody of her. It used to drive Elizabeth crazy.

Everything had changed when she was eight.

"You really can't ride?" Trevor said. "You said that before but I didn't think you meant it. You're a grown-up."

These boys probably spent more time in the saddle than out of it. She had seen them before as she was driving by the ranch, racing across the field and looking utterly carefree. Until now, Ella hadn't realized how very much she had envied them.

"Not everyone is as lucky as you two," she said as she pulled up to the large red indoor horse barn and arena. "I learned how to ride when I was a child, but then I had a bad fall and it's been...hard for me ever since."

Hard was an understatement. What she didn't tell the boys was that she had a completely reasonable terror of horses.

She had been only a year older than the boys, on a visit here with her father. Her sweet little Ruby had been nursing an injury so she had insisted to her father she could handle one of the other geldings on a ride with him along their favorite trail. The horse had been jittery, though, and had ended up being spooked by a snake on the trail just as they were crossing a rocky slope.

Not only had she fallen from the horse, but she had also tumbled thirty feet down the mountainside.

After being airlifted to Idaho Falls, she had ended up in a medically induced coma, with a head injury, several broken vertebrae and a crushed leg. She had spent months in the hospital and rehab clinics. Even after extensive therapy, she still limped when she was tired.

Her injuries had marked the final death knell to the marriage her parents had tried for years to patch back together. They had been separated on and off most of her childhood before then. After her riding accident, her mother completely refused to send her to the ranch.

The custody battle had been epic. In the process, a great gulf had widened between her and her father, one that she was still trying to bridge, twenty years later.

If she could only learn to ride, conquer her fear, perhaps Curt Baker wouldn't continue to see her as a fragile doll who needed to be protected at all costs.

"I know the basics," she told the boys now. "I just need some pointers. It's a fair trade, don't you think? I teach you a few chords on the guitar and you let me practice riding horses."

The boys exchanged looks, their foreheads furrowed as they considered her request. She caught some furtive whispers but couldn't hear what they said.

While she waited for them to decide, Ella wondered if she was crazy. She couldn't believe she was actually considering this. What could these boys teach her, really? She was about to tell them she had changed her mind about the riding lessons but would still teach them the song when Trevor spoke for both of them.

"Sure. We could do that. When do you want to practice? How about Saturday?"

"We can't!" Trevor said to his brother. "We have practice Saturday, remember?"

"Oh, yeah. But maybe in the afternoon, when we're done."

Why was she even considering throwing one more thing into her packed schedule? She couldn't do it. Ella wiped her sweaty palms on her skirt. "We can forget this. It was a silly idea."

"Why?" Trevor asked, his features confused. "We want you to teach us how to play and sing a song for our dad's Christmas present and you want to learn how to ride a horse better so you don't fall off. We can teach each other."

"It will be fun. You'll see. And maybe you could even buy one of our dad's horses after you learn how to ride again."

That was pushing things. Maybe she first ought to see if she could spend five minutes around horses without having a panic attack.

"So can you come Saturday afternoon?" Trevor asked.

"Our dad won't be home, so that would be good. Then he won't need to know why we're teaching you how to ride horses. Because otherwise, we'd have to tell him it's a trade. That would ruin the surprise."

"I...think I can come Saturday." Oh, she was crazy.

"Yay! This will be fun. You'll see."

She wasn't so sure. Before she could come up with an answer, the door to the barn opened and Beck came striding out with that loose-limbed, sexy walk she always tried—and failed—to ignore.

He had someone else with him. Ben Caldwell, she realized, the veterinarian in town whose wife, Caidy, had a magical singing voice. She barely noticed the other man, too busy trying not to stare at Beckett.

Her hands felt clammy again as she opened her car door, but this time she knew it wasn't horses making her nervous.

Chapter Four

"You know, it might be time to say goodbye."

Ben Caldwell spoke gently as he ran a calming hand down Frisco's neck. "He's tired, he's cranky, he can't see and he's half-lame. I can keep coming out here and you can keep on paying me, but eventually I'm going to run out of things I can do to help him feel better."

Beckett was aware of a familiar ache in his gut. He knew it would be soon but didn't like to think about it. "I know. Not yet, though."

The vet nodded his understanding but that didn't make Beck feel any less stupid. No doubt Dr. Caldwell wondered why he had such a soft spot for this horse that nobody had been able to ride for five years. Frisco had always been bad-tempered and high-spirited, but somehow Stephanie had loved him, anyway. Beck wasn't quite ready to say goodbye yet.

He shook the vet's hand. "Thanks, Ben. I appreciate you coming by."

"You got it."

Sal, one of Beck's border collies, waddled over to them, panting a welcome. The veterinarian scratched her under the chin and gently patted her side.

"She hasn't had those pups yet."

"Any day now. We're on puppy watch."

"You'll call me if she has any troubles, right?"

"You know it."

He had great respect for Ben. Though Beck hadn't been too sure about the city vet when the man moved to town a handful of years ago, Dr. Caldwell had proved himself over and over. He'd also married a friend of his, Caidy Bowman, who had gone to school with Beck.

They were finishing up with Frisco when he heard a vehicle pull up outside. Beck's heartbeat accelerated, much to his chagrin.

"You expecting somebody?" Ben asked.

"That would be Ella Baker. I, uh, forgot to pick the boys up from rehearsal at The Christmas Ranch and she was nice enough to bring them home for me."

"That Christmas program is all the buzz at my place, too," Ben said. "My kids can't wait."

Ben had been a widower with two children, a boy and a girl, when he moved to town. Beck sometimes had Ben's daughter babysit the twins in a pinch.

The two men walked outside and Beck was again aware of his pulse in his ears. This was so stupid, that he couldn't manage to stop staring at Ella as she climbed out of her SUV.

Ben sent him a sidelong look and Beck really hoped the man didn't notice his ridiculous reaction.

"I'll get out of your way," Ben said. "Think about what I said."

"I will. Thanks again."

Ella and the boys both waved at the veterinarian as they climbed out of her vehicle.

"Hey, Dad! Hey!" His boys rushed over to him, arms wide, and he hugged them, wondering if there would ever come a time in his life when they didn't feel like the best damn thing that had ever happened to him.

He doubted it. He couldn't even imagine how much poorer his life would be without Trevor and Colter. Whenever he was tempted to regret his ill-conceived marriage, he only had to hug his boys and remember that all the rest of the mess and ugliness had been worth it.

"Hey, guys. How was practice? Did you behave yourselves?"

"Um, sure," Colter said.

"Kind of," his brother hedged.

Which meant not at all. He winced.

"We're gonna do better," Colter assured him. "We promised Miss Baker. Me and Trevor thought maybe we could run around the building three times before we go inside to practice, to get our energy out."

"That sounds like a plan."

It was a strategy he sometimes employed when they struggled to focus on homework at night, taking them on a good walk around the ranch so they could focus better.

"I'm starving," Trevor said. "Can I have a cheese stick?"

"Me, too!" Colter said.

"Yeah. You know where they are."

The boys ran into the barn, heading for the fridge inside the office, where he kept a few snacks.

He turned to her. Like his father always said, better to eat crow when it was fresh. It tasted better hot and was much easier to swallow.

"How big of an apology do I owe you for the boys' behavior?"

To his surprise, she smiled, something she didn't do around him very often. For some reason, the woman didn't seem to like him very much.

"On a scale of one to ten?" she asked. "Probably a seven."

"I'm going to take that as a win."

Her smile widened. It made her whole face glow. With a few snowflakes falling in her hair and the slanted afternoon sun hitting her just right, the universe seemed to be making it impossible for him to look away.

"It's hard for two seven-year-old boys to be in school all day, then take a long bus ride, then have to sit and behave for another hour and a half," she said. "I understand that. They have energy to burn and need somewhere to put it. Today was hard because there was a lot of sitting around while we practiced songs. Things won't be as crazy for our next practice, I'm sure."

"It really does help if they can work out a little energy."

"We did elf jumping jacks. You're right, things were better after that."

She paused, her smile sliding away. He had the feeling she was uncomfortable about something. Or maybe he was the only uncomfortable one here.

"Do you need me to give the boys a ride to the rest of our practices?" she finally asked. "I can take them with me to The Christmas Ranch after school and bring them back here when practice is over."

Her generous offer startled him. The night before, he had wanted to ask her the same thing, but in the light of day, the request had seemed entirely too presumptuous.

"Are you sure that wouldn't be a problem?"

"You're right next door. It's only five minutes out of my way, to bring them up here to the house. I don't mind, really."

"That's very gracious of you. If you're sure it won't be an inconvenience, I would appreciate it."

"I don't mind. I should warn you, they might be a little later coming home than some of the other children, since I have to straighten up our rehearsal space after we're done. Perhaps they can help me put away chairs after practice."

"Absolutely. They're good boys and will work hard, as long as they have a little direction."

The wind was kicking up, blowing down out of the foothills with that peculiar smell of an approaching storm. She shivered a little and he felt bad for keeping her standing out here. He could have invited her inside the horse barn, at least.

"I really do appreciate it," he said, feeling as big and rough and awkward as he always did around her soft, graceful beauty. "To be honest, I wasn't sure how I would juggle everything this week. I'm supposed to be going out of town tomorrow until Monday to look at a couple of horses and I hate complicating the boys' schedule more than I have to for Uncle Dan and Jax."

"No problem."

"Thanks. I owe you one."

"You do," she answered firmly. "And here's how you can pay me back. We're signing up drivers for the night of the show to pick up some of the senior citizens who don't like driving in the snow. Add your name to the list and we can be even."

That would be no hardship for him. It would take up one evening of his life and he could fit a half-dozen senior citizens in his crew cab pickup.

"Sure. I can do that."

"Okay. Deal."

To his surprise, she thrust out her hand to seal the agreement, as if they were bartering cattle or signing a treaty. After a beat, he took it. Her fingers were cool, small, smooth, and he didn't want to let go. He was stunned by his urge to tug her against him and kiss that soft, sweet mouth.

He came to his senses just an instant before he might have acted on the impulse and released her fingers. He saw confusion cloud her gaze but something else, too. A little spark of awareness he instantly recognized.

"I need to, that is, I have to...my dad will be waiting for me."

"Give my best regards to Curt," he said.

The words were a mistake. He knew it as soon as he spoke them. Her mouth tightened and that little glimmer of awareness disappeared, crowded out by something that looked like resentment.

"I'll do that, though I'm sure he already knows he has your best regards," she said stiffly. "The feeling is mutual, I'm sure."

He frowned, again feeling awkward and not sure what he should say. Yes, he and her father got along well. He respected Curt, enjoyed the man's company, and was grateful he was in a position to help him. Why did that bother her?

Did she know Curt had offered to sell him the ranch?

He was hesitant to ask, for reasons he couldn't have defined.

"I should go. It's been a long day. I'll bring the boys back from practice tomorrow and take care of Saturday, too."

"Sounds good. I won't be here, but Jax and Dan will be."

She nodded and climbed into her SUV in her fancy leather boots and slim skirt.

He watched her drive away for much longer than he should have, wondering why he felt so awkward around her. Everyone in town seemed to like Ella. Though she had moved back only a year ago, she had somehow managed to fuse herself into the fabric of this small Idaho community.

He liked her, too. That was a big part of the problem. He couldn't be around her without wondering if her skin was as soft as it looked, her hair as silky, her mouth as delicious.

He had to get over this stupid attraction, but he had no idea how.

He was so busy watching after her taillights, he didn't notice the boys had come out until Trevor spoke.

"Hey, Dad. What are you lookin' at?" his son asked.

"Is it a wolf?" Colter vibrated with excitement at the idea. They had driven up to Yellowstone for the weekend a month ago and had seen four of them loping along the Lamar Valley road. Since then, the boys had been fascinated with the idea of wolves, especially after Beck explained the Pine Gulch area was part of the larger far-ranging territory of the various Yellowstone packs.

"Nope. No wolves," he said now. "I'm just enjoying the sight of our pretty ranch."

His sons stood beside him, gazing at the ranch along with him.

This was what should matter to him, passing on a legacy for these boys. He had worked his ass off to bring the Broken Arrow ranch back from the brink since his father died a decade ago. The ranch was thriving now, producing fine cattle and the best quarter-horse stock in the entire region.

He intended to do his best to protect that legacy for his boys and for his younger brother, so he could have something more than bills and barren acreage to give them after he was gone.

He would build on it, too, when he had the chance. Any smart man would take any opportunity to expand his holdings. Beck couldn't let anything stand in the way, especially not a pretty city girl who wore completely impractical boots and made him think things he knew he shouldn't.

Ella's pulse was still racing uncomfortably as she drove the short distance between his ranch and the Baker's Dozen.

Why, oh, why did Beck McKinley have to be so darned gorgeous? She didn't know how it was possible, but he seemed to get better looking every time she saw him.

This crush was becoming ridiculous. She felt like a giddy girl who had never talked to a man before. Completely untrue. She'd been engaged once, for heaven's sake, to a junior partner in her stepfather's law practice.

Okay, she had been engaged for a month. That counted, right?

On paper, Devin had been ideal. Handsome, earnest, ambitious. They enjoyed the same activities, listened to the same music, shared the same friends. She had known him since third grade and dated him all through college. Her mother and stepfather adored him and everyone said they made a perfect couple.

He proposed on her twenty-sixth birthday, with a ring that had been gorgeous and showy. Shortly afterward, they had started planning their wedding.

Well, her mother had started planning her wedding.

Ella's job in the process appeared to consist of leafing through bridal magazines and nodding her head when her mother made suggestion after suggestion about venues and catering companies and dress shops.

Three weeks into her engagement, she found out her father had Parkinson's. Not from Curt, of course. That would have been too straightforward. No, his longtime housekeeper, Alina, wife to his longtime foreman, Manny Guzman, called to let her know he had fallen again. That was a news flash to her, since she didn't know he had fallen before.

After some probing, she learned Curt had been diagnosed a year earlier and had kept it from her. Apparently he had balance issues and had fallen a few times before, requiring help from one of the hands to get back up.

This time, his fall had been more serious, resulting in a broken hip. She had taken leave from her job and immediately caught a flight to Idaho the next day, which hadn't made Devin very happy. After two weeks of him pleading with her to come back, she realized to her chagrin that she didn't want to go back—and worse, that she had barely given the man second thought.

She didn't love him. How could she possibly merge her life with someone she didn't love? It wasn't worth it, only to make her mother happy.

Ella had flown back to Boston, returned his ring and ended the engagement. He hadn't been heartbroken, which only seemed to reinforce her realization that theirs had been a relationship borne out of convenience and familiarity.

They would have been content together. She wanted to think so, anyway, but she wasn't sure they would have been truly happy.

Devin had never once made her insides feel as if a hundred butterflies were doing an Irish step dance. Not like...

She shied away from the thought. Yes, Beck was hot. Yes, she was attracted to him and he left her giddy and breathless. So what?

She didn't *want* to be attracted to him. It was pathetic, really, especially when it was clear the man thought she was useless out here in ranching country.

Join the crowd, she wanted to tell him. He and her father ought to form a club.

Oh, wait. They already had formed a mutual admiration society that completely excluded her.

She sighed, frustrated all over again at her stubborn father, who couldn't see that she was capable of so much more than he believed.

A blue pickup truck was parked in front of the Baker's Dozen ranch house as Ella pulled up, and she made a face. She recognized the truck as belonging to Chris Soldado, the physical and occupational therapist who came to the house twice a month to work with her dad, both for his ongoing recovery from the broken hip and to help him retain as much use of his limbs as possible as his Parkinson's progressed.

He must be working after-hours. She grimaced at the prospect. His visits always left Curt sore and cranky. More sore and cranky than usual, anyway.

As she let herself in, she found Chris Soldado and her father in the great room. Her father was leaning heavily on his cane while Chris seemed to be putting equipment back into his bag. Chris was a great guy who had been coming a couple times a month for as long as she had been back in Pine Gulch. He was firm but compassionate with Curt and didn't let him get away with much.

"Hi, Chris," she said with a smile.

"Hey there, Ella," he said. He gave her a flirtatious smile in return. "I'm just on my way out. I was telling your dad, he needs to be doing these exercises on his own, every day. That's the best way to retain as much mobility as he can for as long as possible. Make sure of it, okay?"

She tried to nag, but it usually only ended up frustrating both of them. "I'll do that. Thanks."

"This will probably be my last visit for this year. I'll see you in January, Mr. Baker."

Her father made a face but nodded. He looked tired, his features lined with strain.

She let the therapist out, then returned back to her dad and kissed him on the cheek. He needed to shave, something she knew was difficult for him with the trembling of his hands. That was one more area where he didn't want her help.

Maybe she ought to ask Beck to help Curt shave, since he was so good at everything else.

She sighed. "How was your day?"

"I just had physical therapy and that was a high point."

Oh, she missed the kind, loving father of her childhood. Big, hale, hearty. Wonderful.

He was still wonderful, she reminded herself. She just had to work through the occasionally unpleasant bits to get there.

"How about yours?" he asked, which she appreciated. He didn't always think to ask. "You're late getting home, aren't you?"

"Yes. Remember, I told you I would be late for the next few weeks. We had our first practice for the Christmas pageant."

"Oh, right. It slipped my mind during the torture session. How did it go?"

"Good, for the most part. The McKinley twins caused a bit of trouble but nothing I couldn't handle."

"Those boys are rascals," Curt said, but she heard clear admiration in his voice. "Alina left shepherd's pie. She said we just had to bake it but after Chris showed up, I forgot to turn on the oven."

"I can do that. Let me help you to your chair."

"No. I'm fine. If I sit in that recliner, I'll just fall asleep like an old man. I'll come in the kitchen with you."

That was an unexpected gift, as well. She decided to savor the small victories as she led the way to the kitchen. She fussed until he sat on one of the kitchen chairs, then she poured him a glass of water before turning on the oven and pulling out the potato-topped casserole that had always been a favorite of her father.

"So tell me what those twins were up to today," he said. Curt always seemed to get a kick out of Beck's boys and their hijinks.

"Nothing too egregious."

While she made a salad and set the table, she told him stories about the boys. He laughed heartily when she mentioned the bodily noises during "Away in a Manger" and about them trying to hang from the garland, and she was suddenly grateful beyond measure for those twins and their energy, and for providing this lighthearted moment she could share with the father she loved.

Chapter Five

"That was excellent. Really excellent," Ella said, praising the two little cowboys seated at a table in the classroom she shared with the part-time art teacher.

She had arranged for Trevor and Colter to stay after school for a half hour so they could rehearse the cowboy ballad they wanted to sing for their father. She would drive them out to The Christmas Ranch when they were finished.

This had been the most logical rehearsal spot, even if the walls were currently adorned with collage after collage of grinning Santas made out of dry macaroni and cotton-puff beards.

Fortunately, all those Santas checking to see whether they were naughty or nice didn't seem to bother Trevor and Colter McKinley.

"We sound good enough to be on the radio, huh?" Trevor said.

She envied their sheer confidence, even as it made her smile. "Definitely," she answered. "You picked up the words and melody of the chorus perfectly. Why don't we try the whole thing from the beginning? Straighten up in your seat, now. You'll sing your best if your lungs have room to expand and they can't do that when you're all hunched over."

The boys sat up straight and straightened their collars as if they were preparing to take the stage at the Vienna opera house. She smiled, completely charmed by them. If she wasn't careful, these two troublemakers would worm their way right into her heart.

"Okay. Hit it," Colter said.

"Please," his twin added conscientiously.

They had decided that because of time constraints, it would be better if she just accompanied them so they didn't have to learn the words to the song and the unfamiliar guitar chords at the same time. She played the music she had found, the first gentle notes of the Christmas song.

The boys sang the lines in unison, their voices clear and pure and quite lovely. Their voices blended perfectly. She could only imagine how good it would sound if they could learn a little harmony.

They could work on that. For now, she wanted to focus on making sure they knew the words and phrasing of the song.

"That sounded really great," she said, after they went through the song four more times in a row.

"Our dad's going to love it," Trevor declared.

"I'm sure you're right." She glanced at the clock. "We had better run or we'll be late for practice with the rest of the children. We can run through the song a few more times on the way."

They grabbed their coats and yanked on backpacks while she prepared to close up the classroom.

"We'll meet you by the office," Colter said. Before she could call them back, they headed out of the classroom. She locked the door and was about to follow after when the fifth-grade teacher from across the hall opened her own door.

"Was that really the McKinley twin terrors I heard in here?" Susan Black looked flabbergasted.

"Yes. They asked me to help them prepare a song they could perform as a gift to their father for Christmas."

The older woman shook her head. "How did you get them to sit still long enough to even learn a line? I think I may seriously have to think about retirement before those two hit fifth grade."

"They like to sing. Sometimes it's just a matter of finding the right switch."

"You've got the magic touch, I guess."

She had no idea why the boys were beginning to respond to her, she thought as she walked toward the office, but she wasn't about to jinx things by questioning it too much.

The boys were waiting impatiently for her and raced ahead when she opened the outside door. They found her SUV in the nearly empty parking lot immediately—no surprise, as she'd given them a ride just the day before.

"Thanks again for helping us," Trevor said when they were safely seat-belted in the back and she was on her way.

"It's my pleasure," she told them.

"Are you still coming tomorrow to ride horses?"

That panic shivered through her and she almost told them to forget about that part of the deal. Two things stopped her. They were proud little cowboys and she sensed they wouldn't appreciate being beholden to her for anything. And second, she knew she couldn't give in to her fear or it would control the rest of her life.

"Are you sure it's okay with your dad?" She couldn't quite keep the trepidation from her voice.

"He won't care and he's gonna be gone, anyway."

"Oh, right. He's looking at a couple of horses."

"Yep. We talked to our uncle Jax and he said he can help us saddle up the easiest horse on the ranch for you."

"That's Creampuff," Colter said. "She's a big softie."

"You'll like her," Trevor assured her. "Even though she likes to wander out when she gets the chance, Dad says he could put a kitten on her back and she'd never knock it off."

"Sounds perfect for me, then," Ella said, trying not to show her nervousness.

"Great. So just wear stuff you can ride in tomorrow. Boots and jeans. You know. Not teacher clothes."

Apparently they didn't approve of her favorite green wool sweater set and dressy dove-gray slacks.

"Got it. I'll see if I can find something a little more appropriate," she said.

"It will be fun. You'll see," Colter said.

She had serious reservations, but tried to swallow them down as they arrived at The Christmas Ranch for rehearsal.

First things first. She had to make it through two more practices before she could have time to worry about her upcoming horseback-riding lesson.

"We were good today, don't you think?"

After rehearsal on Saturday, Ella glanced in the rearview mirror at the two boys sitting in her back seat.

"You really were." She had to hope they didn't hear the note of wonder in her voice. "And yesterday, too. You paid attention, you stayed in your seats, you didn't distract your neighbors. Good job, guys."

"Told you we could be. It wasn't even that hard. We just had to pretend we were dead mice."

"Dead mice who could still sing," Trevor added.

Ella tried to hide her smile. "Whatever you did, it worked perfectly. Let's see if we can do it again next week, through the rest of the rehearsals we have left until the show."

"We will be," Trevor said. "We promised you, and our dad says a man's word is his wand."

It took her a second to fit the pieces together. "I think he probably said bond. That means a commitment."

"Oh, yeah. That was it. A man's word is his bond."

That sounded like something Beckett McKinley would say to his sons.

He was a good father. The boys were high-strung, but their hearts were in the right place. They were working hard to prepare a Christmas gift for their father and that day she had also watched them show great kindness to Taft Bowman's stepdaughter, who had Down syndrome and some developmental delays. She was older than they were by a few years but they still seemed to have appointed themselves her champion.

She should tell Beckett what good young men he was raising. Something told her he didn't hear that very often.

She pushed away thoughts of the man, grateful at least that she wouldn't have to see him today. She was stressed enough about riding the horses. She didn't need to add any additional anxiety into the mix.

As she drove up the snow-packed road to the ranch house, those same horses that had greeted them the first time she brought the boys home raced alongside her SUV, a beautiful but terrifying sight in the afternoon sunlight.

She wouldn't be riding one of those energetic creatures. She would be riding a horse named Creampuff. How scary could something named Creampuff really be?

Terrifying enough that she felt as if her heart was going to pound out of her chest. She let out a breath. Why was she putting herself through this, again? It wouldn't make any difference with Curt. Her father loved her but he couldn't see her as anything but fragile, delicate, someone to be protected at all costs.

She pushed away the thought. This wasn't for her father. She needed to ride again for *herself*. She needed to prove to herself she could do it, that she could overcome her fears and finally tackle this anxiety. The opportunity had presented itself through these twins and she couldn't afford to miss it.

"Where should I park?" she asked as she approached the buildings clustered around the ranch house. "Where do you think we will be having this lesson?"

"Uncle Jax said we could use the riding barn. He said he would have Creampuff all ready for you. But then Uncle Dan made us promise we'd stop at the house first to grab some lunch and put on our boots."

"That sounds like a good idea. I need to change my clothes, anyway."

Despite the boys' fashion advice, Ella had worn a skirt and sweater to the Saturday rehearsal, as if preparing for a day at school. It seemed silly in retrospect, but she hadn't wanted to appear in jeans. In her experience, she tended to command more respect with her students when she was a little dressed up.

Her riding clothes were packed into a small bag on the passenger seat beside her, but she hadn't given much practical thought to when and where she would actually change into them. She should have had the foresight to do it at The Christmas Ranch before they left.

They directed her where to park and she pulled her SUV into a driveway in back of the house. The boys led the way inside, straight to the kitchen.

They found Daniel McKinley, Beck's uncle, wearing an apron and loading dishes into the dishwasher.

"There you two are. Howdy, Miss Baker."

She smiled at him. As always, she was delighted by his old-fashioned, courteous nature and ready smile.

He was quite a charmer in his day, she had heard—a bachelor cowboy who cut a broad swath through the female population of the county. Now he was over seventy with a bad back and struggled almost as much as her father to get around these days.

"You ready for your riding lesson?" Dan asked, offering her a smile that still held plenty of charm.

Would she ever be? "Yes," she lied. "I can't wait."

"These boys will get you up on a horse, you wait and see. Best little cowboys I ever did see. They'll have you barrel racing in the rodeo by summer."

That was far beyond what she even wanted to attempt. She could only pray she would be able to stay in the saddle.

"I'm makin' sandwiches, if you want one," he offered. "Nothing grand, just grilled ham and cheese. It's one of the four things I know how to cook."

"What are the other three?" she asked, genuinely curious.

"Coffee, hot dogs and quesadillas. As long as I'm only making them with cheese and salsa. Oh, I can do scrambled eggs, too, if you've got a hankering."

She had to smile, completely enchanted by him. "I'm great with a ham sandwich. Thanks so much for offering."

"It's no trouble. Just as easy to make four sandwiches as it is three, I suspect."

"I appreciate it, anyway. May I help you?"

"You can help me by sitting down and relaxing. Something tells me you don't do enough of that, Miz Baker."

True enough, especially the last month. She would have time to rest after the holidays.

"If it's all right with you, I would like to find somewhere to change into more appropriate clothing for a riding lesson."

"You can use Beck's bedroom. First door on the right."

She instantly wanted to protest. Was there really nowhere else in this big, beautiful log house for her to change, besides Beckett McKinley's bedroom? She didn't want to know where he slept, where he dressed, where he probably walked around in his briefs.

She let out a breath, aware that she would sound completely ridiculous if she raised a single irrational objection to his suggestion.

Nothing left but to accept with grace, she decided. "That sounds good. I'll change my clothes and then come help you with lunch."

He pointed her on her way, his leathery features split into a smile. Unlike her father, Dan McKinley still appeared to have a healthy appetite. He limped around the kitchen but other than that, his skin was firm and pink instead of the sallow tones her father sometimes had.

Curt had probably lost twenty pounds in the months she

had been back in Pine Gulch. He was still large-framed, but his clothing all sat loosely on him these days and he wore suspenders to keep up his pants.

It made her sad to see the comparison between the two men, though she reminded herself she couldn't change the course of her father's disease. She could only try to make his world as comfortable and accessible as possible.

She gripped her tote bag and hurried down the hall lined with beautiful western artwork, highlighted by tasteful inset lighting.

As she might have expected, judging by the rest of the house, Beck's bedroom was gorgeous, spacious and comfortable, with a river-rock fireplace in one corner and expansive windows that looked over both his ranch and her father's. It was dominated by a massive log bed, neatly made, with a masculine comforter in tones of dark blue and green.

The room smelled of him, of sagebrush and leather and rainy summer afternoons in the mountains.

She inhaled deeply and felt something visceral and raw spring to life inside her. Oh. She wanted to stand right here and just savor it.

That bed. Her imagination suddenly seemed entirely too vivid. A snowy night and the two of them tangled together under that soft blanket, with all those hard muscles hers alone to explore.

"Snap out of it," she ordered herself, just seconds before she would have pulled his pillow up to her face to inhale.

Good grief. She didn't come here to moon over Beck. She was here to conquer her fears and tackle something that terrified her.

Okay, he terrified her, too. But this was about horseback riding.

With renewed determination, she quickly kicked off her dressy boots and slipped down her skirt, then pulled on her favorite weathered jeans.

Her Christmas sweater with the reindeer and sleigh had been fun for the kids during rehearsal for the program, but would be too bulky and uncomfortable under her coat while she was riding.

She started to pull it over her head but the textured heavy yarn that was part of the design tangled in one of the combs she'd used to pull her hair back. Shoot. If she tugged it too hard, she would rip the sweater and ruin it. She didn't want that. It was one of her favorites, a gift from a friend in Boston.

With her hands above her head and the sweater covering her face, she tried to extricate the design from her hair comb when suddenly she heard the door open.

Panic burst through her and she almost crossed her arms over her chest. At the last minute, she remembered she still had on the plain white T-shirt she wore underneath the sweater.

"Who's there?" she demanded, her face buried in sweater.

"Beck McKinley," a deep voice drawled. "I believe I should be the one asking questions, Miss Baker. It's my bedroom, after all, and to be perfectly honest, I can't begin to guess what you might be doing in it."

She closed her eyes, wishing she could disappear. She should have known. Who else would it be? Wasn't that just the way her luck went? The one person she didn't want to see would, of course, be the one who stumbled in on an embarrassing moment.

She would have far preferred his brother, Jax, who flirted with everyone and could be handled simply by flirting right back.

She ought to just yank down the sweater and rip it, but she couldn't quite bring herself to do that.

"I'm sorry. Your uncle told me I could use your room to change into riding clothes. Didn't he tell you?"

"I haven't talked to Dan since breakfast. I've been holed up in my office on the other side of the house all morning. Riding clothes, Ella?"

She did *not* want to have this conversation with him with her sweater tangled around her head. The only bright spot in this entire miserable predicament was that she was wearing a T-shirt underneath the sweater. She couldn't imagine how mortifying if he had walked in on her in only her bra.

"It's a long story. I can tell you, but would you help me with my sweater first?"

After a pregnant pause, he finally spoke. "Uh, what seems to be the trouble?"

His voice had an odd, strangled note to it. Was he laughing at her? Where she couldn't see him, she couldn't be quite sure. "It's stuck in my hair comb. I don't want to rip the sweater—or yank out my hair, for that matter."

He was silent, then she felt the air stir as he moved closer. The scent of him was stronger now, masculine and outdoorsy, and everything inside her sighed a welcome.

He stood close enough that she could feel the heat radiating from him. She caught her breath, torn between a completely prurient desire for the moment to last at least a little longer and a wild hope that the humiliation of being caught in this position would be over quickly.

"Hold still," he said. Was his voice deeper than usual? She couldn't quite tell. She did know it sent tiny delicious shivers down her spine.

"You've really done a job here," he said after a moment.

"I know. I'm not quite sure how it tangled so badly."

She would have to breathe soon or she was likely to pass out. She forced herself to inhale one breath and then another until she felt a little less light-headed.

"Almost there," he said, his big hands in her hair, then a moment later she felt a tug and the sweater slipped all the way over her head.

"There you go."

"Thank you." She wanted to disappear, to dive under that great big log bed and hide away. Instead, she forced her mouth into a casual smile. "These Christmas sweaters can be dangerous. Who knew?"

She was blushing. She could feel her face heat and wondered

if he noticed. This certainly counted among the most embarrassing moments of her life.

"Want to explain again what you're doing in my bedroom, tangled up in your clothes?" he asked.

She frowned at his deliberately risqué interpretation of something that had been innocent. Mostly.

There *had* been that secret moment when she had closed her eyes and imagined being here with him under that soft quilt, but he had no way of knowing that.

She folded up her sweater, wondering if she would ever be able to look the man in the eye again.

"It's a long story. Your sons offered to teach me how to ride horses."

"Trevor and Colter."

She finally gathered the courage to lift her gaze to his. "Do you have any other sons?"

"No. Two are enough, thanks. Why would Trevor and Colter offer to teach you how to ride horses?"

She suddenly didn't know how to answer that. He couldn't know the boys wanted to surprise him with a special song for Christmas, that they were bartering services. Telling him about it would completely ruin the surprise, and she wasn't about to do that to the boys, especially after they were trying so hard to uphold their side of the bargain.

"I guess they felt sorry for me when I told them I couldn't ride. I may have let slip at some point that I'm a little…nervous around horses and I would like to get over it."

He raised an eyebrow. "Let me get this straight. You're nervous around horses, but somehow you thought two seven-year-old boys could help you get over your fear?"

Okay, it sounded ridiculous when he said it like that. What had seemed like a good idea at the time now seemed nothing short of foolish.

"Why not? They're excellent riders and their enthusiasm is…contagious."

"Like chicken pox."

"Something like that." She forced a smile. "They aren't afraid to tell everyone what good riders they are. I figured it couldn't hurt to see if some of that enthusiasm might rub off on me."

It sounded silly in retrospect, but there was nothing she could do about that at this point. The deal had been struck and she didn't want to hurt the boys by pulling out of the arrangement now, when they were so excited to teach her.

Beck continued to watch her with a baffled look on his features. What was he even doing there? She thought he was supposed to be out of town this weekend.

"If you would rather I didn't go riding with them, I understand. I should have asked you first. The boys and I talked about it yesterday after practice. They told me you wouldn't be here but that Dan said it was okay. I guess I assumed perhaps he would talk to you. I don't want to cause trouble, though. If you don't want me here, I can grab my Christmas sweater and go home."

She wouldn't blame the man if he threw her off his ranch. Without telling him about the deal she and the boys struck, she sounded completely irrational.

"No. It's fine. We have a couple of really gentle horses that are good for beginners."

She released the breath she hadn't realized she'd been holding. He didn't *sound* like he thought she was crazy.

"The boys promised me a horse named Creampuff. I like the sound of that name, if she lives up to it."

"That's just the horse I would have suggested. She's about as mellow as it gets."

"Sounds perfect. Thank you."

He tilted his head and studied her. "You can ride our sweet Creampuff on one condition."

"What's that?" she asked, suddenly wary at the look in his eyes.

"You let *me*, not the twins, give you riding lessons."

She instantly remembered standing close to him and the shivery little ache that had spread through her. The more time she spent with Beckett McKinley, the more chance she had of making a complete idiot of herself over him.

"That's completely not necessary," she said quickly. "I'm sure the boys and I will be fine."

"First lesson of horses, you can't be sure of anything. Even the most gentle horse can sometimes be unpredictable. I would hate for something to happen to you." He cleared his throat. "Just like I would hate for something to happen to *anyone* on my ranch, riding one of my horses."

Naturally, he wasn't worrying about her in particular. She told herself that little ache under her breastbone was a hunger pang, nothing more. It certainly wouldn't have been disappointment.

What exactly would riding lessons from Beckett McKinley entail? Did she want to find out?

"The boys were looking forward to teaching me." She tried one last time.

"They can still take the lead and give you some pointers. It will be a good experience for them, actually. I'm sure you've found that teachers often learn more than their students about a subject matter. It's good for them to think about the fundamentals of something that by now seems instinctive to them."

She would have to agree. Teaching someone else how to play a particular instrument always reminded her of the basics.

"They can take the lead but I would feel better if I could be there to keep an eye on things, just in case."

She told herself she didn't want his eyes—or anything else—on her. But what choice did she have? It was his ranch, his sons, his horses.

"I thought you were supposed to be out of town, buying horses."

She didn't want to tell him that she would never have agreed to come here for these lessons if she thought she would run into him. If she had known he would end up finding her half-dressed in his bedroom with a sweater tangled in her hair, she would have locked herself in her own bedroom at the Baker's Dozen.

"Plans changed. We found the horses we needed early on and agreed to a fair price with the owner, so we didn't need to stay for the entire sale. We came back last night."

No doubt that defined most of Beck's life. He made a decision early and then went for it. That was probably fine when it came to horses, but not so good when he made a snap decision about her and couldn't seem to see beyond it.

"You thought I was gone."

"The boys said something about it. I would never have come to your bedroom to change my clothes if I thought there was any chance you could be here to run into me."

"Were you hoping to avoid me?"

"Don't be silly," she snapped. "Why would I need to avoid you?"

He didn't answer, only raised an eyebrow.

Before she could think of a way to answer, she heard one of the twins from outside. It sounded like Trevor, but their voices were so similar, it was tough to tell them apart when she couldn't see them.

"Miss Ella? Is everything okay? Our sandwiches are all done but Uncle Dan says we have to wait for you so we can eat. He said that's the polite thing to do when you have guests."

He sounded so disgusted, she had to smile. "It is customary, yes."

"How much longer is it gonna take you to get dressed?"

He didn't say it outright, but the implication was clear. *What the Sam Hill is taking you so blasted long?*

"I'm ready now. I'm coming," she called, before turning back to Beck. "I'm sorry you were dragged into this when you probably had other things to do this afternoon. I'll make some excuse to the boys, tell them I changed my mind or something."

"Why would you go and do that, especially after we went

to all the trouble to get you extricated from your Christmas sweater?"

The man had a point. Something told her she wouldn't be able to wriggle out of these lessons like she had eventually done with her sweater. She was stuck, so she might as well make the best of it.

Chapter Six

After she left, Beck released his breath, then inhaled deeply. The scent of her still filled his bedroom—peaches and cinnamon, a combination that made his mouth water.

How did Ella Baker manage to twist him into a dozen crazy knots every time he was with her? He felt as trussed up as a calf at a roping competition.

He closed his eyes, reliving how stunned he had been to walk into his own bedroom and discover her standing there, half-dressed, like all his illicit fantasies come true.

Okay, she hadn't really been half-dressed. She had been wearing a plain T-shirt, but he wasn't sure if she was aware it had ridden up with the sweater, revealing about three inches of bare, creamy abdomen.

At the sight of that little strip of skin, his stupid brain had taken him in all sorts of unruly directions. He had wanted to kiss that patch of skin, to slide off the rest of her clothes, to toss her down on his bed and spend the rest of the day tangled under the quilt with her.

Man, he had it bad.

He opened his eyes as the magnitude of what he had consented to do loomed suddenly as large as the Tetons outside his windows.

Riding lessons. How in the world was he supposed to give the woman riding lessons, when he couldn't stop thinking about all the inappropriate things he would much rather teach her instead?

And what on earth were his boys thinking, to invite her here without talking to him first? He sighed. Those two rascals had the funniest, most convoluted thought processes, especially when they had their minds set on a project. He supposed he should be happy they liked their music teacher enough to want to help her.

Wasn't that what the holidays were all about? Helping others? He didn't see how he could object, really.

She *did* have a phobia about horses. A fairly serious one. He had seen it for himself one day over the summer, when he had been repairing a fence line between the two ranches. Because it had been a lovely July morning, he'd chosen to ride Ace on a trail that connected the two ranches, to the spot that needed repair. He had been minding his own business, enjoying the splendor of the day, when Ella had suddenly jogged into sight on the trail ahead of him, listening to music through earbuds and wearing shorts that showed off her tanned legs.

She hadn't noticed him at first, probably because of the music. When she spotted him and Ace, she had jumped a mile and had scrambled onto a rock beside the trail to let him pass. He had stopped to greet her—the polite thing to do between neighbors—but she hadn't seemed at all in the mood to chat.

He thought it was because she didn't like him. Now he wondered if it had more to do with her aversion to horses.

He wasn't sure if he and the boys could do anything to help that kind of phobia, but he suddenly wanted to try. He would like to be able to give her this. It was a small thing, only a few hours out of his life, but if he could help her get over her fear of horses, he might feel a little less guilty about taking up Curt on his offer to buy the Baker's Dozen.

It only took a few moments for him to realize the task of helping Ella conquer her fear of horses might be slightly harder than he suspected.

"Nothing to be afraid of." He kept his voice calm, slow, just as he would do to a spooked mare. "Creampuff is as easy and gentle as her name. She's not going to hurt you, I promise. It's not in her nature."

"I'm not afraid," she said, which was an outright lie. Her body betrayed her. She trembled, muscles poised as if she was ready to bolt.

"Sure. I believe you," he said, his voice soothing.

Her nervousness temporarily lifted long enough for her to glare at him. "You don't have to patronize me," she said stiffly. "It must be obvious I'm terrified. I don't want to be, but I am."

"You don't have to be afraid, Miss Ella," Colter told her with an earnest look. "Creampuff is so lazy, she only moves every other Sunday. That's what Dad says, anyway."

"Good thing today is Saturday, then," she said, with a slight smile.

"Exactly," Trevor said. "Why don't you start by making friends with her? Dad keeps crab apples in the barn for her, since that's her favorite treat."

That was a good idea to break the ice between her and the horse, one he should have thought of himself. His boys were smart little caballeros.

"Colt, why don't you grab a couple? You remember how to open the box?"

"Yep." Colter headed over to the metal box containing the treat. "We had to put a latch on it after Creampuff here learned how to lift the lid and help herself."

"Did she?" Ella's voice was faint, as if coming from the other side of the barn.

"She would eat those until she's sick, unless we put a few obstacles in her way," Beck answered, still in that calming voice. "Here you are. Give her this, nice and slow."

He handed her a crab apple. "Put it on your palm, not your fingers." He probably shouldn't tell her that if she wasn't careful, Creampuff might munch on her fingers by mistake.

"There. She likes you," he said when the horse lipped the apple from her palm. He also didn't mention that Creampuff would take a crab apple from just about anybody or anything. She had no scruples when it came to her treats.

"How about another?" he asked. Without waiting for an answer, he handed her a second crab apple. She put it on her palm herself and actually smiled a little this time when Creampuff snatched it away before she could even thrust her hand out all the way.

"Now pet her," Trevor suggested. "She likes it when you scratch along her neck. Yep, like that."

"You must think I'm the world's biggest scaredy-cat."

His boys didn't say anything. Though no one could ever call them well-mannered, precisely, sometimes they could be surprisingly polite. This was one of those times. They looked at each other but chose to remain silent rather than agree with her.

"I don't think you're a scaredy-cat," Beck said quietly. "I think something terrible must have happened to you on a horse."

She sent him a swift look, and he could see the truth of his words reflected in the haunted shadows in her gaze. "How did you know? Did my father tell you?"

It didn't exactly take a crack detective to figure it out. She wasn't just nervous, she was petrified.

This hadn't been a good idea. He didn't like seeing her so upset.

"You don't have to do this, you know. There's no law that says you have to ride horses around here."

She was silent, petting the horse. He was happy to see her hands weren't trembling quite as much as they had earlier.

"You might not find it in any Pine Gulch city code," she said after a moment, "but it's one of those unwritten societal laws, understood by everyone who lives here. You have to know your way around horses if you want to truly fit in around here."

He opened his mouth to argue with her, then closed it again. There might be a kernel of truth to what she said, at least in some circles. He had a feeling Curt Baker saw things that way. He was an old-school rancher, through and through. Funny that Curt himself didn't ride, either. Beck had to wonder if that had something to do with whatever had happened to Ella.

"I've always figured most rules were made just so folks could figure out a creative way to break them. Really, Ella. Don't torture yourself. It's not worth it"

She gazed at him, eyes wide as if she didn't expect understanding from him. Her surprise made him squirm. What? He could be as sensitive as the next guy.

She looked at him, then at Creampuff. As he watched, determination flooded those blue eyes.

"I want to do this. I can't let my fear of something that happened when I was eight years old control the rest of my life," she said. "I've given it too much power already."

Eight years old. He tried to picture her, pigtailed and cute and blonde, with that little hint of freckles. What had frightened her so badly?

Whatever it was, he respected the hell out of her for her courage in confronting it.

"Okay, then." His voice came out more gruffly than usual. "Now that you've made friends with Creampuff here, I guess it's time to climb on. When you're ready, I'll give you a hand."

Her hands clenched into fists at her side then unclenched and she nodded. "I'm ready."

Filled with admiration—not to mention this blasted attraction he didn't want—he helped her hold on to the saddle horn and put her boot in the stirrup, then gave her a lift into the saddle.

She held tight to the horn. "I forgot how far off the ground I can feel on the back of a horse."

The twins had mounted by themselves and rode their horses closer to her. "It's great, isn't it?" Trevor said with a grin. "I feel about eight feet tall when I'm on Oreo."

She seemed to be close to hyperventilating. They couldn't have that. He stepped closer and kept his voice low and calming.

"Just hold on to the reins. I've hooked a lead line here and I'm just going to walk you around the training arena a bit, until you feel more comfortable."

"You won't let go?" Her panic was palpable.

He gave her a reassuring smile. "I promise. You got this."

As he led her around the small arena where they held horse auctions and worked to train horses in bad weather, he kept talking in that slow voice about nothing, really. The year he constructed this building, the other barn that was built by his great-grandfather, the house his grandfather had added.

The boys could never have handled this level of fear. He was deeply grateful that his schedule had worked out so he could be here to help her through this.

"You're doing great," he said after about fifteen minutes, when she seemed to have relaxed a little and her features no longer looked so pinched and pale. "You ready to take the reins on your own now?"

"Do I have to?" she asked ruefully. "I was just beginning to breathe again."

He tried to hide his smile. She had grit. He'd give her that. "You don't have to, but you'll never really get a feel for riding a horse until you're the one in command."

She released a heavy sigh. "I suppose you're right. Okay. You can let go."

He twisted the lead line onto the saddle horn and stood by her thigh. "Here are a few basics. Sit up tall, creating a nice, straight line from shoulders to hips. Don't hold the reins taut, just relax them in your hands, and use the least amount of pressure you can to get the horse to do what you want. It's all about pressure and release. The moment she starts doing what you want, going where you want, you let off the pressure."

He went over a few other basic commands but he could see Ella was starting to glaze over.

For all her complacency, Creampuff was a very well-trained horse. She tended to know what her rider wanted before the rider did.

"You got this," he repeated, then stood back to watch.

Ella sat atop the motionless horse for a long moment, then— just as he was about to step in and give Creampuff a verbal command—Ella gave the perfect amount of pressure with her knees into her sides to get her moving.

Though her movements were awkward and stiff, she had obviously been on a horse before. He was a fairly decent teacher but not *that* good that she could instantly pick it up. No, he had a feeling it was more a case of muscle memory. Ella held the reins in the best position and didn't yank them, but instead used slow, steady movements.

She had done this before. Even if it was a long time ago, something inside her remembered.

Colter and Trevor watched from the back of their horses. "You're doing great," Trevor called.

"Keep it up," his brother said. "Way to go, Miss Ella. You'll be riding the rodeo before you know it."

Ella's visible shudder at the suggestion might have made him smile under other circumstances, if he wasn't so worried about her.

"You *are* doing great," he called. "Now see if you can get her to go a little faster."

"Why on earth would I do that? I don't *want* her to go faster."

He tipped his hat back. "Okay. Take it slow and steady. Nothing wrong with that."

She kept going another twenty minutes, taking the horse around the arena several times, then practicing bringing her a stop again before urging her forward once more. By the time they were done and she rode to a stop in front of him, she looked exhausted but beautifully triumphant.

"You ready to call it a day?"

"Yes. I think so."

He reached up a hand to help her and as she slid off the horse and to the ground, he tried not to notice how wonderful her soft curves felt against him. He was quick to let go when her boots hit the dirt floor.

"How was it?" he asked.

"Not as difficult as I expected, actually." She looked surprised and rather pleased at that discovery. "You were right. Creampuff really is a sweetheart."

"She does live up to her name, doesn't she?" He gave the old horse an appreciative pat as the twins rode up and dismounted.

"You did super good," Colter said.

"Yeah," his brother agreed. "You hardly even bounced around in the saddle."

"I hate to admit it, but there is a certain part of me that would disagree with you right now," Ella said, rubbing the back pocket of her jeans.

The boys giggled while Beck did his best not to shift his gaze to that particular portion of her anatomy.

"Boys, can you take care of the horses? Miss Baker's, too."

The twins had been brushing down their horses since they were old enough to ride. They led the horses away and he turned to Ella, though he kept one eye on the boys, across the arena, as they scrambled to take off saddles and hackamores. They didn't need direct supervision but he still liked to monitor things in case they had trouble.

"That was some good, hard work. A lesson like that deserves a beer. Or at least a soda."

"I wouldn't mind some water," she said.

"I don't doubt it. Overcoming your fear is thirsty business."

In the harsh lights of the indoor arena, her color rose and she looked down.

"Hey. I meant that with upmost respect," he assured her. He led the way into the corner that functioned as the office out here. He reached into the fridge and pulled out a water bottle for her, a beer for him.

"You really did work hard. I could tell it wasn't easy for you."

She sighed and took a healthy swallow from the bottle. A few little droplets clung to her lips from the bottle's mouth and he had to fight the urge to press his own lips there.

"It's so stupid," she said, frustration simmering in her voice. "I don't know why I can't get past it."

"Want to tell me about it?"

She looked at the horses, then back at him with a helpless sort of look. "Not really. But I suppose you have the right to know, especially after all your help this afternoon."

"I don't know about that. But I'd like to hear, if you want to tell me."

She took another swallow and he had the feeling she was biding time as much as slaking her thirst. "You know I didn't grow up on the Baker's Dozen."

Considering he had lived next to Curt his whole life and only saw Ella a few memorable times over the years, until she moved back to Pine Gulch, he was aware of that fact. "I did. I gather your parents were divorced."

"Yes. Eventually. They were separated on and off through most of my early childhood. They would try to make it work for a month or two, usually for my sake, then things would go south and my mom would pack us up and move back to Boston."

"That must have been tough."

"Yes. I adored my father and I always loved coming out to the ranch, even when it was just for a short visit. My favorite times were the summers, when I could be here for weeks at a time. Back in Boston, I dreamed about horses all the time. In the pictures I've seen of my bedroom, there are dozens of pictures on the wall of horses I had either drawn myself or cut out of old ranch magazines I took back with me. I loved to ride. At least that's what they tell me."

That struck him as an odd way to phrase things, but she continued before he could ask what she meant.

"I was three the first time my dad put me on a horse. I don't have a memory of it. Or anything else before I was eight years old."

That seemed awfully late for a first memory.

"Eight? Why eight?"

She looked down at her water bottle with a faraway expression. When she looked back up at him, her expression was bleak.

"That's the year I died."

Chapter Seven

Died? What the hell was that supposed to mean? Shock tangled his tongue, but even if it hadn't, he would have had no idea how to respond.

"I know. That sounds ridiculous and melodramatic," she said, her expression rueful. "But it's the truth. I was dead for about five minutes before they could get my heart started again."

She spoke in a matter-of-fact way, but her hands trembled again, as they had when she first faced the horse arena.

"You were eight? What happened?"

She watched the boys as they competently brushed down the horses. "My mom and I were both here that summer. It was the last time my parents tried to reconcile, I guess, though they didn't tell me that was why we had come back to the ranch. They had been separated on and off most of my life, but neither of them could ever bring themselves to file for divorce. I don't know why but they couldn't seem to take that final step."

"Were you happy about it? About your parents trying to reconcile?"

"I wish I could tell you. Apparently I wanted nothing more

than to live here permanently. According to my mom, all I talked about whenever we were in Boston was living here in Pine Gulch and having my own horse and riding whenever I wanted. I think she resented how much I loved the ranch, if you want the truth. She never did."

Yet one more thing he had in common with Curt Baker. The man had never come right out and said it, but Beck had guessed as much.

What was wrong with these Pine Gulch men who insisted on marrying completely inappropriate women who couldn't wait to leave?

"We had only been back about three weeks when I took out a new horse," Ella went on. "I was with my dad and we were just riding above the ranch, nothing too strenuous, but apparently a snake slithered across the trail and spooked the horse and I fell—not just off the horse but about twenty feet down a rocky slope. I ended up with multiple injuries."

His blood ran cold as he pictured it. "You stopped breathing, you said?"

"Yes. My father was right there and he managed to do CPR to eventually restart my heart. I was airlifted to the hospital in Idaho Falls, and then to the regional children's hospital in Salt Lake City."

"How long were you there?"

"Two months. Seven surgeries. I was in a medically induced coma for weeks while the swelling from the brain injury went down. When I came out of it, there was obvious damage. I didn't remember anything. Not just the accident, but everything that happened before. Total blank slate. I had to relearn how to walk, talk, use a fork. Everything. I still have no memory of what happened the first eight years of my life, only from pictures and what my parents have told me."

He shook his head, trying to imagine how tough that must have been, to lose eight years of her life. He glanced at the boys, who were just finishing up with Creampuff. She was only a little older than they were and had to relearn everything.

No wonder she had been terrified of horses! He wasn't sure he ever would have had the guts to get back on.

"I just have one question."

"What's that?"

His jaw clenched. "Why in *blazes* did you get back on a horse today, after everything you've been through? I would think any sane woman would try to stay as far away as possible from something that's caused so much suffering."

She looked pensive, her fingers curled around the water bottle. "Today wasn't about the horses, Beck. It was about me." She paused. "I keep thinking that if I learn how to ride again, I'll find some piece of me I lost when I was eight."

He couldn't believe Curt had never told him about Ella's accident. Maybe that explained why the man didn't have any horses on the Baker's Dozen. He knew some ranchers thought they were too much trouble and not worth the effort, preferring ATVs and utility vehicles to a good cattle horse. He had always assumed Curt was one of them.

"I guess your parents didn't get back together."

She gave a short laugh. "You could say that. My mother would have been happy if I never came back to Pine Gulch. She blamed my father, said Curt deliberately put me on a horse that wasn't appropriate for an eight-year-old girl with limited experience who wasn't the expert rider she thought she was. She filed for divorce while I was still in the hospital."

How had that impacted Ella? Did she blame herself for her parents' divorce? Did she wonder if they would have been able to finally piece things together, if not for her fall?

He couldn't help seeing her with new compassion and found himself impressed all over again at the courage it must have taken her today to climb up on Creampuff.

"For the first few years after the divorce, she made my dad fly out to Boston for visits, which he hated. They were awkward, tense episodes that weren't comfortable for either of us. When I got older, after the dust from their custody battle settled, I insisted on coming out as often as I could. My dad refused to let me get on a horse. To reduce temptation, he sold them all, even though it was something he always loved. That was a tough pill for me to swallow, but Curt said my mom wouldn't let me come back to the ranch if she found out I had gone riding again. He wasn't wrong, actually."

He couldn't imagine that kind of animosity. Beck's own parents had been happily married until his father's untimely death, even with his mom's rheumatoid arthritis, which limited what she could do around the ranch. His dad had been a loving caretaker as far back as Beck could remember, one of the things he respected most about him.

After his father died, Beck's mother had moved to Florida to be closer to her sister. She was doing well there, though he missed her. She and the boys talked via Skype every Sunday evening.

"I can't believe I didn't know this about you," he finally said.

She made a wry face. "It's not like I go around introducing myself to people by telling them that I spent several weeks in a medically induced coma after falling off a horse."

"But my family lived next door to yours. I should have known. I would have been, what, eleven or twelve? That's old enough to be aware of what's going on in my own community."

On the other hand, Curt Baker had always been a little removed from the greater Pine Gulch society. Beck's parents may well have known and may have mentioned it to him, but since he didn't know Ella personally back then and she was several years younger—and a girl, to boot—he wasn't sure it would have had much impact on him.

"It doesn't matter," she said. "It was a long time ago. Almost twenty years. The doctors all said it was a miracle that I made it through without much lasting damage."

"Nothing?"

"My leg aches in bad weather and I still limp a bit when I'm tired. To be totally honest, I do have the occasional memory lapse. I call it a glitch. Every once in a while, I forget a word that's pretty basic."

"Everybody does that."

"That's what I tell myself. I'm lucky. It could have been much worse."

"It doesn't sound like nothing. It sounds like you've been through hell. Nobody would blame you for never getting on a horse again, Ella. Like I said, it's really not necessary out here. There are plenty of people in Pine Gulch who've never been on a horse yet somehow still manage to live good, productive lives."

She was quiet, her features pensive. "I hate being afraid," she finally said. "Especially of something I once loved."

He had to respect that. "I'm not sure you can force yourself to the other side of a perfectly justifiable fear, simply through willpower."

"Maybe not completely," she acknowledged. "I'm okay with that. Still, I'd like to see if I can regain a little of that passion I once had."

He wanted that for her, too. In that moment, Beck resolved to do whatever he could to help her. "In that case, you'd better come back tomorrow for a second lesson. One hour in a horse arena on the back of a narcoleptic nag like Creampuff isn't enough to inspire passion in anyone."

"I don't know about that. I enjoyed myself far more than I expected."

"Come back tomorrow. Let's see if you can enjoy it even more."

"I could do that." She considered. "It would actually be good timing. Some friends are taking my father to a cowboy poetry event in Idaho Falls and they're supposed to be gone most of the day."

"You're a grown woman, Ella. He can't stop you from riding now, even if he wanted to."

"I know. I usually make him a nice dinner on Sunday afternoons after church. Since he'll be gone, I won't have to do that—or explain why I'm leaving or where I'm going."

"Great. You can just come straight here after church, then. You might as well stay for dinner. We'll probably grill steaks. It's just as easy to toss another one on the coals."

He wasn't sure why he extended the invitation. By her expression, it was clear she was as shocked as he was by it.

"I… Thank you. That would be nice. I'll bring a salad and rolls and some kind of dessert."

"You don't have to do that, but I'm sure the boys would enjoy it."

His side dishes usually consisted of baked potatoes or instant rice.

"Enjoy what?" Trevor asked. They had apparently finished with the horses, who were all fed and watered and turned out to pasture.

"Miss Baker is going to come for another riding lesson tomorrow. I invited her to have dinner with us, too."

"Yay!" Trevor exclaimed.

Colter, he noticed with sudden trepidation, was giving the two of them a speculative look that left Beck more than a little uncomfortable.

What was going through the kid's mind? Beck wasn't sure he wanted to know—any more than he wanted to examine his own thoughts, at least about Ella Baker.

She wasn't sure she should be doing this.

Even as she loaded food into her SUV in preparation for driving back to the Broken Arrow, Ella was filled with misgivings.

She still had no idea what had prompted Beck to issue this unexpected invitation to dinner and a second riding lesson. Maybe pity. He *had* invited her right after she spilled her entire pathetic story to the man, after all.

More puzzling than his invitation had been how quickly she accepted it, without really thinking things through.

She should have refused. As much as she might have wanted another lesson, another chance to recapture the joy she had once known while riding, she was beginning to think it might not be a good idea to spend more time with Beckett and his boys.

The lesson the day before had eroded her defenses, left her far too open and vulnerable to him. She rarely talked about her accident, even with close friends. It was a part of her, yes, but something that happened so long ago, it hardly seemed relevant to the woman she had become—except as it pertained to her lingering fear of horses.

Why had she confided in Beckett McKinley, of all people?

He had been so patient with her during the lesson and, dare she say, even kind. It was a side of him she wasn't used to seeing. She could admit, she found it wildly appealing.

She wished she could have been able to tell what had been running through his mind when she told him what had happened so long ago. No such luck. The man was still a mystery to her. Every time she thought she had him figured out, he did something to toss all her preconceptions out the window.

This invitation for dinner, for instance. It would have been kind enough to simply invite her over for the lesson. Why add dinner into the mix?

Maybe he just felt sorry for her. The poor, pathetic girl who had nearly died not far from here.

She sighed and climbed into the SUV. She didn't like that idea. But what else could it be?

Though she was tempted to call off the whole thing, she made herself drive through the lightly falling snow to the nearby ranch.

The snowflakes looked lovely as they twirled out of the sky against the pine trees that bordered the road. The perfect holiday scene—except this was her second winter in southern Idaho and she knew the winters here could be anything but idyllic.

Oh, she hoped the weather cooperated for the Christmas program the following week. The children had already worked so hard to learn the songs and would be putting in a full week of intense rehearsals. She hated to think of all their effort being wasted because bad weather kept people away.

That was a hazard of living here, she supposed. You just had to keep your fingers crossed and learn how to take what comes.

Her stomach knotted with nerves as she drove under the Broken Arrow arch, which also had their brand burned into it. She had seen the McKinley men only hours ago at church. Beck had looked big and tough and handsome in his bolo tie and western-cut suit and the boys had looked just as handsome in clean white shirts and similar bolo ties.

They had come in late, hair still wet and Trevor's shirt buttoned wrong, and had waved so enthusiastically at her as they took their seats that Celeste Delaney beside her had whispered a teasing comment about the McKinley twin terrors having a crush on her.

She hadn't responded, even though she wanted to tell Celeste they weren't terrors. They were sweet, good-hearted boys who happened to have a little more energy than most.

She wasn't sure how her feelings for the boys had shifted so abruptly after only a few encounters. A week ago, she would have been one of those rolling her eyes at their antics. Now she saw them through a new filter of affection and even tenderness.

Mostly, they needed a little more direction and restraint in their lives.

She pulled up to the ranch house, her pulse abnormally loud in her ears, aware it wasn't the horse riding that made her nervous this time, but the idea of spending an afternoon with Beck and his adorable sons.

It was too late to back out now, she told herself, as she headed up the porch steps and rang the doorbell. They were planning on her.

Colter answered before the doorbell even stopped echoing through the house.

"Hey, Miss Ella!" he exclaimed, giving her that irresistible gap-toothed grin. "Guess what? Our dog is having puppies, *right now.*"

"Is that right?"

"Yeah. She's down in the barn. Dad says we can go down to see her again after you get here."

Beck walked into the foyer in time to hear his son's announcement. He looked gorgeous and relaxed in jeans and a casual collared navy shirt that made his eyes gleam an even deeper blue.

"More excitement than you were probably expecting on a quiet Sunday afternoon."

As if she needed more excitement than the anticipation bubbling through her all morning at the idea of spending the afternoon with him and his boys.

"I would love to see the puppies, if you don't think the mother would mind."

"This is her fifth litter. At this point, I don't think she would care if the high school marching band came through during labor."

She couldn't hide her smile at that image. For a moment, something hot and glittery flashed in Beck's expression as he gazed down at her. Her resident butterfly friends danced harder in her stomach.

He seemed to have lost his cool politeness toward her and she didn't know whether to be relieved or terrified.

She was already ridiculously attracted to him, on a purely physical level. She would be in serious trouble if she actually *liked* him, too.

Something told her it was a little too late for caution now.

After a moment, he cleared his throat. "We can take a look on our way down to the horse barn."

"Sounds good. I have a salad that needs to go in the refrigerator and rolls that will need to continue rising. Mind if I put them in your kitchen first?"

"If it means fresh rolls, you can do anything you want."

Ella was quite certain he didn't mean the words in any suggestible way. That didn't stop her imagination from going a little wild for just a moment, until she reined it back with much more pressure than she would ever have used on Creampuff.

"This way," he said.

She followed him into his updated kitchen, with its stainless appliances and granite countertops.

The day before, when she'd eaten lunch here, she had observed that this was obviously a household of men. The kitchen wasn't messy, exactly, but it was more cluttered than she personally would have found comfortable. The sink had dishes left over from breakfast, and some kind of dried substance, likely from an overflowing pasta pot, covered one of the burners.

Just like the day before, she had a strong impulse to dig in and go to work cleaning things up, but she had to remind herself that wasn't her bailiwick. She was only there for dinner and another riding lesson.

"Sorry about the mess in here." Beck looked a little uncomfortable. "Until a few months ago, we had a nanny-slash-housekeeper, but she was having some health problems so had to take a break. My brother and uncle and I have been trading off household responsibilities until I can find someone new and I'm afraid none of us is very good at it."

The picture touched her, three men working together to take care of these twin boys. She remembered Faith telling her Beck had refused to give his in-laws custody, though the boys had only been toddlers.

Ella was aware of a small, soft warmth fluttering to life in her chest.

"It's a lovely home," she murmured. "I can tell the boys are very happy here."

He offered that rare smile again and for a moment, she felt

as if that warmth was swirling between the two of them, urging them inexorably closer.

"I should put this in the refrigerator," she said quickly, holding out the bowl containing the green salad she had made.

"Let me make a little room." He moved a few things around, leaving her a space amongst a few leftover containers and a half-empty case of beer.

"Now I only need a warm spot for the rolls to rise. Any suggestions?"

"Judy, our old housekeeper, always used the laundry room."

"That works."

He led the way to a large combined mudroom and laundry room. There were two washers and dryers in the space and both were going, sending out humid heat that would be perfect for her wrap-covered rolls.

"Judy always used that shelf up there. It's a little high for you to reach, I can put them up there for you."

"Looks like a perfect spot. Thanks." She handed him the jelly-roll pan of dough balls. Their fingers touched as he took it from her and a shiver rippled over her.

She thought his gaze sharpened but she couldn't be sure. Oh, she hoped he didn't notice her unwilling reaction.

He took the pan but simply held it for a long moment as the tension seemed to thicken between them. He looked as if he had something he wanted to say and even opened his mouth, but the boys burst into the laundry room before he could.

Ella told herself she was relieved.

"Let's go! We want to see the puppies!" Colter said, voice brimming with excitement.

Beck finally looked away to focus on his sons. "We're coming. Grab your coats while you're in here."

The boys complied and Beck finally slid the pan of rolls onto the high shelf, where the warmth would help them rise more quickly.

"How long until they're ready to bake?"

"I pulled the dough out of the freezer, so it will need to thaw as well as rise. Probably about ninety minutes."

Her dad loved homemade rolls, but it was too much trouble to do very often for only the two of them, so she had started making a big batch every month and freezing the dough.

"That should be about perfect to give us time to see the puppies and ride for a while, if you're still up for it."

"I'm here, aren't I?" she said wryly. "I'm ready."

"Excellent. Let's go."

The twins led the way outside, chattering to each other about Christmas vacation and a school field trip during the upcoming week to The Christmas Ranch, where they both planned to visit Sparkle, the famous reindeer immortalized in books as well as onscreen in an animated movie.

She would have thought their daily rehearsals at the ranch were sufficient holiday cheer, but apparently not.

By default, she and Beckett fell behind the boys a little.

"How's your dad?" Beck said. "I haven't seen him for a few days."

She sighed with remembered frustration. Curt was having a hard time accepting his limitations. That morning, before he left for the cowboy poetry event, she had caught him trying to put up a stepladder to fix a lightbulb that had gone out in their great room. The man had poor balance on solid ground, forget about eight feet up in the air on a wobbly ladder.

"Stubborn as ever," she answered. "I'm beginning to think it must be something in the water up here."

He laughed, the sound rich and deep in the cold December air. "You might be right about that. I've got two boys drinking that same water and they could write the book on stubborn."

He definitely had his hands full with those twins. She had a feeling things weren't going to get easier as they hit their preteen and teenage years.

"Anyway, your dad might be stubborn but he's a good man. After my dad died when I was still too young to know what the hell I was doing here on the ranch, Curt took me under his wing. I learned more from him those first few months than my whole twenty-three years before that."

She hadn't realized his father died when Beck was so young. Sympathy for him helped mute the sting of hearing her father had been willing to help a neighbor learn the ropes of ranching. Too bad he wouldn't do the same thing for his own daughter.

"What happened to your father?"

"One of those freak things. Doctors figured it was a brain aneurysm. He was out on a tractor, perfectly fine one minute, the next he was gone. I'd always planned to take over the Broken Arrow from him, since neither of my brothers was much interested in running the place."

"Jax works here, doesn't he?"

"Yeah, but it took him a while to figure out what he wanted to do. I'm still not convinced his heart's in it, but it's tough to tell with Jax. I always knew I wanted to run the ranch, I just didn't expect to do it so early."

"I'm sorry. That must have been tough on you."

"At first, but good neighbors like Curt stepped in to help me figure things out."

"I'm glad my dad was here for you," she said softly. "And now you're helping him in return."

Beck shrugged, looking embarrassed. "I'm not doing much. I'm glad I can help."

He stopped in front of a different barn than the larger, more modern facility where they had ridden the day before. "Here we are. Guys, remember what I told you. We can watch, if we do it quietly so we don't distract Sal while she's taking care of her puppies."

"We remember," Trevor said solemnly. The boys tiptoed into the barn—which wasn't particularly effective, since they were both wearing cowboy boots.

She followed, not sure what to expect. The barn was warmer

than she might have thought, and smelled of straw and old wood and the earthy smells she associated with a ranch.

Beck led the way to a wooden stall about halfway back. She peered over the railing to where a mostly black border collie lay on her side on a blanket that had been spread over the straw.

She looked exhausted, poor thing, as her litter suckled for nourishment.

"They look like little rats," Trevor whispered.

"Beautiful little rats," his brother said loyally, which made Ella smile.

The puppies were small, eyes still closed. They made little whiny noises as they ate.

"Is that all of them, girl?" Beck asked in a low voice. "Looks like she might be done. How many do you count?"

"Seven," Colter said, moving his finger in the air to mark each one. "No, eight."

"Good job, Sal," Beck said softly. The tired mother gave a half-hearted tail wag before returning to care for her litter.

They all watched the little creatures with fascination for a few more moments. It was an unexpectedly intimate moment, standing there by the wooden stall beside Beck and his boys, almost like they were a family unit.

They most definitely weren't, she reminded herself. That sort of thinking could get her into all kinds of trouble.

"We should probably let her rest now," Beck said eventually.

"Will they all be okay out here?" Trevor asked. "It's cold outside."

"But warm in here. Sal and the puppies have everything they need here—warm, soft blankets, with plenty for Sal to eat and drink. My guess is, she'll probably want to sleep for a week after having eight puppies."

"What will you do with them all?" Ella asked.

"I'll probably keep a couple to train, then sell the others. Sal has champion bloodlines and the sire does, too. Those are going to be some excellent cow dogs."

He glanced down at her. "You ready to ride again?"

"I am," she admitted. "Believe it or not, I'm actually looking forward to it."

He gave her a full-on, high-octane smile that turned her insides to rich, gooey honey.

"That is an excellent sign, Miss Baker. Watch and see. We'll make a horsewoman out of you yet."

She didn't share his confidence—but as long as she no longer had panic attacks when she came within a hundred feet of a horse, she would consider these few days to be worth it.

Chapter Eight

An hour later, she managed to pull Creampuff to a stop squarely in front of the spot at the railing where Beck had stood for the last hour, offering advice and encouragement during the lesson.

"Good girl," she said, patting the horse's withers.

"Wait, was that an actual smile?" he teased. "If I didn't know better, I might think you're enjoying yourself."

"You might be right. I think I've almost stopped shaking. That's a good sign, isn't it?"

"An excellent one." He offered an encouraging smile. "On a day when it's not so cold, you should come out to take a trail ride above the house. It's slow going in the snow, but worth it for the views."

A few days earlier, the very idea would have sent her into a panic attack. Her accident had happened in those very foothills and while she didn't remember it, the specter of what had happened there still loomed large in her subconscious.

The fact that she could even consider such an outing was amazing progress. She shifted in the saddle, satisfaction bubbling through her. She had done it, survived another riding lesson, and had actually begun to enjoy the adventure.

Oh, she had missed this. She really did feel as if she was rediscovering a part of herself that had been buried under the rubble of her accident.

Trevor rode up on his big horse, so loose and comfortable that he seemed to be part of the horse. "Is it time for dinner yet? I'm starving."

"Me, too," his brother said, joining the group.

"I guess that's up to our guest," Beck said. "What do you say, Ella? Want to keep riding or would you like to stop for chow?"

"Let's eat, before you guys start chewing the leather reins."

The boys giggled with delight at her lame joke and warmth soaked through her. There was something so *joyful* about being able to make a child laugh. She had never realized that until going to work in music therapy.

"Chew the reins," Trevor said, shaking his head. "That would taste gross!"

"Yeah, steaks would be much better, all the way around," Beck said. "Why don't you boys take care of the horses and put them up while Miss Baker and I start dinner?"

She slid down without assistance. "I would like to help with the horses, actually. If I intend to start riding again, I need to relearn how to care for them."

His eyes warmed with approval. "Good point. It should only take the four of us a few moments. Boys, let's show Miss Baker how it's done."

Beck couldn't remember the last time he had enjoyed an afternoon so much.

He was growing increasingly intrigued with Ella Baker, forced to completely reevaluate his preconceptions of her as just one more city girl who didn't belong.

She had far more grit than he ever would have believed a few days earlier. Most women who had gone through an ordeal like hers would have stayed as far away as possible from something that represented the trauma they had endured.

Not Ella.

When they had first come into the stables, he had seen how nervous she was. Her small, curvy frame had been trembling slightly as he helped her mount Creampuff, her features pale and set.

It had concerned him a little, especially after she seemed to have enjoyed it the day before. He supposed he should have anticipated her reaction. She had spent many years being afraid of horses, for legitimate reasons. He couldn't expect that to go away overnight, simply because she had an enjoyable experience on an easy mount.

He shouldn't have worried. Within a few moments, she had warmed to it again. After only a few moments, she had visibly relaxed, and by the end of the hour, she had been laughing.

Would she be afraid the next time? For her sake, he hoped she didn't have to fight that battle each time she wanted to ride a horse—though he had to admire the sheer guts she showed by putting herself through it. In his experience, few people demonstrated that kind of raw courage.

He liked her.

Entirely too much.

He frowned at the thought as he hung up the tack on the well-organized pegs. It was hard *not* to like her. She was kind to his sons, she had given up her life back east to come back and care for her father, and she had more courage than most people he'd ever met.

If he wasn't careful, he would do something really stupid, like fall hard for her.

He jerked his mind away from that dangerous possibility. He couldn't. She might be pretty and smart and courageous, but that didn't make her right for him. He would do well to remember she was a city girl. Like her own mother, like Stephanie. Ella was cultured, sophisticated, not the sort of woman who would be comfortable wearing jeans and boots and listening to old Johnny Cash songs.

The thought depressed him more than it should.

They could be friends, though. Nothing wrong with that. A guy couldn't have too many friends, right?

"Everybody ready to go get some food, now that we've all taken care of the horses?" he asked, forcing a note of cheerfulness he didn't feel into his voice.

"Me!" his twins said in unison. Ella smiled and the impact of it was like standing in the middle of a sunbeam.

"We should probably check on the puppies one more time before we head up to the house, if you don't mind," he said.

"Do you seriously think I would mind being able to see those cute puppies again?"

"Good point," he admitted.

The temperature had dropped several degrees by the time they walked outside toward the barn where he had set up Sal for her first few weeks postdelivery. His instincts, honed from years of working the land, warned him they would have snow before morning.

As they trudged through the snow already on the ground from previous storms, he went through his mental weather-preparedness checklist. It wasn't all that lengthy. From his father, he'd learned the important lesson that it was better to ready things well in advance. The Broken Arrow was always set up to deal with bad weather, which made it much easier for this particular ranch owner to sleep at night.

When he wasn't having completely inappropriate dreams about his lovely neighbor, anyway.

In contrast to the gathering storm, the old barn was warm and cozy, a refuge from the Idaho winter.

Sal and her puppies were all sleeping when they peered over the top railing of the stall. Despite Colter's and Trevor's careful effort to tiptoe in on their cowboy boots, Sal must have sensed them. She opened one eye but closed it quickly, busy with the task of keeping eight puppies fed and alive.

Without being asked, Trevor and Colter filled her water and added a bit more food to her bowl. They were such good boys. Yeah, they could be rambunctious at times, but beneath all that energy, they were turning into helpful, compassionate young men.

He couldn't have asked for more.

"She looks exhausted, poor thing," Ella said beside him, her expression soft and sympathetic.

"She's a good mom. She'll be okay after a little rest."

"Until she has eight wriggling puppies climbing all over her."

He grinned. "Shh. Don't say that too loudly or she might decide to hightail it out of here before we get to that point. I don't particularly fancy hand-feeding eight puppies."

"Would she do that?" Ella asked, plainly concerned.

"I'm teasing," he assured her. "Sal knows what to do."

They watched the puppies for a few more moments in silence before he ushered everyone back out into the cold.

"Race you," Trevor said to his brother and the two of them rushed away through the gathering darkness.

"I wish I had even a tiny portion of their energy," Ella said with a sigh.

"Right?"

She shook her head. "How do you keep up with them?"

"Who says I do? There have been more than a few nights when I fall asleep reading to them and only wake up when the book falls to the floor."

She smiled, probably thinking he was kidding. He only wished he were.

"They're good boys. You know that, right?"

He was touched that her thoughts so clearly echoed his own from a few moments earlier. "I do. Once in a while I forget. Like whenever I go to their parent-teacher conferences and hear the litany of classroom complaints. I have to remind myself I wasn't the most patient student, either, yet somehow I still managed to graduate from high school *and* college. My senior year, I was running the ranch, too, and taking night classes."

"It must be challenging on your own."

"Sometimes," he admitted. "There are days I feel like throwing in the parenting towel before we even finish breakfast. It's hard and frustrating and relentless. Each decision I make in the day has to focus on the boys' welfare first. Every other priority is a distant second."

"I can't even imagine." In the fading afternoon light, her features looked soft and so lovely, he had a hard time looking away.

"I'm not really alone, though. Until a few months ago, we had Judy to help us. She did all the heavy lifting when it came to the logistics of caring for the boys when they were smaller."

"You must miss her terribly."

"Definitely. She had been a huge part of our lives since the boys were small. Judy was just about the only mother figure they had. They don't seem to remember their mother much."

"How old were they when she…left?"

He hated thinking about Stephanie and all the mistakes he had made.

"Barely two," he said, his voice pitched low even though the boys had already made it inside.

"She had terrible clinical and postpartum depression as well as anxiety—made harder because, as it turns out, she hated living on a ranch. She missed her family, her friends, the excitement of her life back east."

Their marriage had been an epic mistake from the beginning. He thought they could make a go of things, though now that idea seemed laughable. Still, they had been wildly in love at first. After only a few fiery months, reality had begun to sink in that maybe they couldn't manage to reconcile their differences and then Stephanie found out she was pregnant.

She had cried and cried. He should have clued in to the challenges ahead when he saw her reaction. As for Beck, he had been scared witless one moment, filled with jubilation the next. He had asked her to marry him and it had taken another three months of discussions—and the revelation through her first ultrasound that her pregnancy would provide a double blessing—before she agreed.

Things only went downhill from there, unfortunately. She had struggled fiercely with postpartum depression and hadn't really bonded with the twins. Even before she left to find help, he and the series of nannies he hired until they found Judy had been the ones getting up at night with them, making sure they were fed, providing the cuddles and the love their mother couldn't.

"That must have been tough," Ella said softly.

For both of them. Stephanie had been a mess emotionally and mentally and he had hated knowing he couldn't fix things for her.

"She stuck it out as long as she could, until both of us realized things weren't getting better. She needed help, more help than she could find here. Her parents are both doctors and had connections back east so they wanted her to get help there. It was always supposed to be temporary but the weeks turned into months and then a year. *Soon*, she kept telling me. Just another month and she would be ready to come back."

He sighed as the tough memories flooded back. "Eighteen months after she left, she died from a prescription-drug overdose. Doctors said it was probably accidental."

That *probably* always pissed him off. Even the smallest chance that Stephanie might have deliberately chosen to leave the two cutest kids on the planet just about broke his heart.

Something of his emotions must have shown on his features. Ella made a small sound, her own expression deeply distressed.

"Oh, Beck. I'm so sorry."

"I am, too—for the boys' sake, anyway. They're doing okay, though. They ask about her once in a while, but not so much anymore. They don't remember her. They were only toddlers when she left. They ask after Judy far more often than they do their mother."

"I'm sorry," she said again.

"I don't know why I told you all that," he said. What was it about Ella that compelled him to share details of his life he usually preferred to keep to himself? There was something about her that drew him to her, something more than her pretty eyes and her soft, delicate features.

He liked her. Plain and simple. It had been a long time since he felt these soft, seductive feelings for a woman.

Not that he planned to do a damn thing about it—except spill all his dirty laundry, apparently.

"You're cold. I'm sorry I kept you out here so long."

"I'm not cold," she protested. "Only sad that any woman could deliberately choose to walk away from such amazing boys and—and you."

Was it his imagination or did she blush when she said that? His interest sharpened. Again, he was aware of the tug and pull of attraction between them.

He wanted desperately to kiss her. He ached with it, the hunger to pull her close and brush his lips across hers, gently at first and then, if she didn't push him away, with a little more intensity.

He caught his breath and inclined his head slightly. Her eyes went wide and she swallowed. He thought she might have even leaned toward him, but at the last moment, before he would have taken that chance, the back door opened.

"Hey, what are you still doing out here?" Trevor asked.

He couldn't very well tell his son he was just about to try to steal a kiss. Trevor didn't give him a chance to answer, anyway, before he went on.

"Hey, can Colter and me watch a Christmas show before dinner?" Trevor asked.

After mentally scrambling for a second, Beck did his best to shift back into father mode. It took great effort, especially when all he wanted to do was grab Ella close and explore that delicious-looking mouth until they were both breathless.

He cleared his throat. "You know the rule. The TV can come on when chores are done."

"They are. I just took the garbage out and Colt finished putting away the dishes in the dishwasher."

He couldn't ask for more than that. "Fine. One show. Fair warning, dinner shouldn't take long. You might have to stop the show in the middle, if the food is ready before the show is over."

"Okay." Trevor beamed, then hurried back inside to tell his brother the good news, leaving Beckett along with Ella and this awkwardness that seemed to have suddenly blossomed between them.

"Ella…"

She didn't quite meet his gaze. "Your boys are hungry. We should probably take care of that."

He was hungry, too, but the choice T-bones he had been marinating all afternoon wouldn't slake this particular appetite.

She was right, though. The boys needed to eat—and he needed to do all he could to regain a little common sense when it came to Ella Baker.

Forty-five minutes later, nerves still shimmied through her from that intense moment on Beck's back step.

Had he really tried to kiss her?

She couldn't be completely sure but was about 95 percent certain. The vibe had certainly been there, crackling through the air between them.

She had done her best to ignore it through dinner, but couldn't seem to stop staring at his mouth at odd, random moments.

She caught herself at it again and jerked her gaze away quickly, setting her napkin beside her plate and leaning back in her chair.

"That was truly delicious," she said, trying for a casual tone.

"I'm not exaggerating when I say that was probably the best steak I've ever had. What do you use for a marinade?"

"Nothing too complicated—soy sauce, honey, a little bit of ground black pepper and a splash of olive oil."

"Sometimes the simple things are the best. Thank you again for inviting me to dinner."

"I didn't do anything but grill some steaks and toss a couple of potatoes in the oven to bake. You provided everything else. I should be thanking *you*. Those rolls were little yeasty bites of heaven."

The description pleased her. Why was it so much more fun to cook when people appreciated the effort?

"We're done," Colter announced. "Can we go back and finish our show?"

"Yeah," Trevor chimed in. "The Abominable Snowman guy was just learning how to walk with one foot in front of the other. That's our favorite part."

Ella had to smile, since that had always been her own favorite part of that particular Christmas special.

"Clear your plates first. You can take our guest's, as well, if she's finished."

"I am, thank you."

"Do you want to watch the rest of the show with us?" Trevor asked.

Though the earnestness behind the request touched, Ella glanced at her watch. How had the entire day slipped away?

"Thank you, but it's later than I thought. I should go. I hate to eat and run, but I should probably be home before my father arrives back at the ranch. Sometimes he needs help getting out of his coat and boots."

By the understanding she glimpsed in his gaze, she understood that Beck knew as well as she did that the word *sometimes* was unnecessary. Curt might refuse to admit it, but he *always* needed help. His limitations were growing all the time, something that made her heart hurt whenever she thought about it.

"Let me hurry and wash the salad bowl and the pan you baked the rolls in, so you can take them home clean."

"Unnecessary. I have other dirty dishes at home I still need to wash. I can easily throw these in with them."

He looked as if he wanted to argue but held his tongue.

"Guys," he said instead to his sons, "can you tell Miss Baker thanks for joining us today?"

"Thanks, Miss Baker," they said in unison, something they did often. She wasn't sure they were even aware of it.

"I'm the one who must thank you for the wonderful day. I'm so grateful to you for sharing your puppies with me and for helping me with my riding lessons again. I owe you. I mean it."

The boys nudged each other, hiding their matching grins that indicated they knew exactly what she meant, that she would in turn help them practice the song for their father before the show the following week.

"You're welcome," Trevor said.

"See you tomorrow. At practice," Colter added, with such a pointed, obvious look, it was a wonder Beckett didn't immediately catch on that something else was going on.

She followed Beck from the dining room to the kitchen. Despite her protests, he ended up washing the pan she had used for the rolls as well as the now-empty salad bowl.

She finally gave up arguing with him about it and picked up a dish towel instead. "While we're at it, we might as well finish cleaning your kitchen. I can spare a few more moments."

This time, he was the one who looked as if he wanted to argue, but after a moment, he shrugged.

She was right, it only took them a few moments. She found the domesticity of the scene dangerously seductive, the two of them working together in the kitchen while the sounds of the Christmas show filtered in from the television that was in a nearby room.

"It really was a great steak," she told him again.

"Thanks. I don't have many specialties in the kitchen, so I'm pretty proud of the few I can claim."

"With reason."

He tossed a spatula in the rinse water and she pulled it out to dry.

"One of the toughest things about us men being on our own now that Judy is gone is figuring out the food thing all the time. She used to leave food in the fridge for us to heat up, but now Jax and Dan and I have to take turns. I think the boys are getting a little tired of burgers and steaks, but that's mostly what I'm good at."

"I hear you. My problem is the opposite. I would like to cook other things, but my dad's a cattleman through and through. Red meat is about all he ever wants, though Manny Guzman's wife prepares meals for us a few times a week and she likes to slip in some chicken dishes here and there."

"You take good care of your father," he said, his voice slightly gruff.

She could feel her cheeks heat at the unexpected praise. "Whether he wants me to or not. He's constantly telling me he doesn't need my help, that I should go back to Boston. That's where my mother lives with her second husband."

"Why don't you?"

She wasn't sure she could articulate all the reasons. "I love my dad. He needs help, no matter what he says, and I'm in a position to offer that help. He doesn't have anyone else. Not really."

She shrugged. "Anyway, I like it here. The people are kind and my job is tremendously rewarding. It hasn't been a sacrifice."

He said nothing, just continued washing the last few dishes, then let the water out of the sink while she wiped down the countertops.

"That should do it," he said when she finished. "Thanks for your help. I've got to say, the kitchen looks better than it has in weeks. None of us enjoys the cleanup portion of the program. That's probably obvious."

"It wasn't bad," she assured him. "You know, even if you don't hire another full-time housekeeper, you could still have someone come in a couple times a week to straighten up for you."

"That would certainly help. Know of anyone looking for a job?"

"Not off the top of my head, but I can ask around." She glanced at the clock on the microwave. "And now I really do have to go. Dad expected he would be home in about a half hour from now. If he makes it home ahead of me, he's going to worry about where I am."

"I'll grab your coat."

He brought it in from the mudroom and helped her into it, which only seemed to heighten her awareness of the heat and that delicious outdoorsy scent that clung to him.

"Thanks again," she said, then reached for her dishes. He beat her to it, picking them up and heading for the door.

"What are you doing?"

"I'll walk you out. Even we Idaho cowboys learn a few manners from our mamas."

"I never said otherwise, did I?"

"No. You didn't," he said gruffly.

Who had? His troubled wife? The thought left her sad.

The storm hadn't started yet. Though it still smelled like impending snow, the clouds had even cleared a little, revealing a few glittery expanses of night sky.

"Oh," she exclaimed, craning her neck. "Look at all those stars. It always takes my breath away."

"Yeah, it's one of the best things about living out here, where we don't have much light pollution."

"A few times when I came here over the summers, my dad would wake me in the middle of the night so we could drive into the mountains to see the meteor shower."

"The Perseids. I do the same thing with the boys. Every August, we take a trail ride up into the hills above the ranch and spread our sleeping bags out under the stars to watch the show."

There was another image that charmed her, the picture of this big, tough cowboy taking his young twin sons camping to show them nature's fireworks show. "That sounds lovely."

"We've got another meteor shower this week. You should check it out."

"Thanks, but I think I'll pass on anything that involves sleeping out under the stars in December."

He smiled as they reached her SUV. She opened the rear door and he slid the pan and bowl inside, then stepped forward to open her door for her.

"Good night," she said. "Thank you again for a lovely afternoon."

"It was my pleasure. The boys loved having you out and... so did I."

His voice was low, intense. Shivers rippled down her spine and she couldn't resist meeting his gaze. All those glittery feelings of earlier seemed to ignite all over again, as if someone had just stirred a hearth full of embers inside her and sent a crackling shower of sparks flaring through her.

They gazed at each other for a long moment and then he uttered a long, heartfelt oath before he lowered his mouth to hers.

Chapter Nine

As his mouth descended and his arms enfolded her against him, Ella caught her breath at the heat and strength of him surrounding her. For a moment, she couldn't think straight and stood frozen in his arms while his mouth brushed over hers once, then twice.

As she blinked in shock, her brain trying to catch up to what was going on, the amazing reality of it seeped in.

She was kissing Beck McKinley—and it was so much better than she ever could have imagined. Still not quite believing this was real, she returned the kiss with all the hunger she had been fighting down for so very long.

She forgot about the boys inside, about the snow spiraling down around them, the cold metal of her SUV seeping through the back of her wool coat.

The only thing she could focus on was Beck—his delicious mouth on hers, the strength of his muscles under her exploring hands, the heat and wonder and sheer thrill of kissing him at last.

She wasn't sure how long he kissed her there in the cold

December night—long enough, anyway, that when he pulled away, she felt disoriented, breathless, aware that her entire body pulsed with a low, delicious ache.

"I told myself I wasn't going to do that."

"I… Why?" His words jerked her out of that happy daze.

"Because I was afraid as soon as I kissed you once, I would only want to do it again and again. I was right."

"I wouldn't mind." Some part of her warned her that she probably shouldn't admit that, but the words spilled out before she could stop them.

He gazed down at her, his eyes flashing in the moonlight. He was so gorgeous, rough and masculine. How could any woman resist him?

"I like you, Ella. More than I should."

A thrill shot through her at his words, even though it was tempered by the reluctant way he said them. He liked her, but was obviously not crazy about that fact.

"I like you, too," she admitted. She didn't add that the more time she spent with him, the more she liked him.

Something bright flashed in his gaze and he kissed her again, this time with a fierce intensity that completely took her breath away.

After another moment, he sighed and pulled away, his forehead pressed to hers. "I have to stop, while I still can."

"You don't *have* to."

"It's freezing out here. That snow is going to start in about ten minutes and the temperature will drop more. I have a feeling it might be pretty traumatic for my boys to find us here after the spring thaw, still locked together."

With clear reluctance, he eased away. "That shouldn't have happened, Ella. You get that, right? I can't…start something with you."

Maybe he should have thought of that little fact before he kissed her until she forgot her own name, she thought tartly.

After the heated embrace they had just shared, something had already started between them, like it or not.

Oh, this was going to get awkward quickly. She couldn't just ignore the man. They lived in the same community, were neighbors, for heaven's sake. He was at her father's ranch nearly every day for some reason or other.

How was she supposed to be able to look at him in the grocery store or the library or parent-teacher conferences without remembering this moment—the heat of his mouth on hers, the taste of him, minty and delicious.

"You should probably go. Your father will be home soon, if he isn't already."

"Right." Shaky and off balance, she managed to make her limbs cooperate long enough to climb into her driver's seat.

He stood for a moment, looking as if he wanted to say something else, but ultimately he only gave a little wave, closed the door, then stood back so she could drive away.

Her SUV had a key remote that started with a push button. She fumbled with it for several seconds, aware her hands shook and her thoughts were scattered. After an uncomfortably long moment, she somehow remembered she needed to press the brake at the same time she pushed the button before it could start. Finally she managed to combine all the steps and the engine roared to life.

As she drove away, she forced herself not to check the rearview mirror to see if he was still standing there. Her head spun with a jumble of emotions—shock, regret and, most of all, an aching hunger.

He was right. They shouldn't have done that. How on earth was she supposed to go back to treating him with polite distance, when all she would be able to remember was how magical it had felt to be in his arms?

Beck couldn't force himself to move for several moments, even after the taillights of Ella's SUV disappeared down the drive.

What the hell just happened? He felt as if a hurricane had just blown through his world, tossing everything comfortable and familiar into weird, convoluted positions.

Ella Baker.

What was he *thinking*, to kiss her like that?

He had been contemplating the idea of reentering the dating waters for the last year, had even dipped his toe in a bit and asked out a neighbor, Faith Nichols Dustin. That hadn't turned out so well—for him, anyway. Faith was now married to another rancher and friend, Chase Brannon.

He was happy for them. His heart had never really been involved, but he liked Faith and thought they had many things in common. They had both lost their spouses, were raising their children alone, ran successful ranch operations.

On paper, they would have made a good fit. It wasn't to be, though. Faith and Chase were obviously in love, and Beck was happy they'd been able to find joy together after all these years.

He envied them, really. The truth was, he was lonely, pure and simple. His life wasn't empty. Far from it. He had the boys and the ranch, his brother and his uncle, but he missed having a woman in his life. He missed soft skin and sweet smiles, the seductive scent of a woman's warm neck, the protective feeling of sleeping with someone he wanted to watch over in his arms.

He sighed. In the end, it didn't matter how lonely he was. He couldn't make another mistake like Stephanie. He had the boys to worry about now. If he ever became seriously involved with a woman again, he would have to pick someone he absolutely knew would stick—a woman who loved it here as much as he did, who could not only be *content* with the ranching life, but could also embrace it, hardships and all.

Too bad the one woman he had been drawn to in longer than he could remember was someone so completely inappropriate.

Ella Baker was delicate and lovely, yes. He could look at her all day long and never grow tired of it. She made him want to tuck her inside his coat and protect her from the cold, the wind and anything else that might want to hurt her.

She wasn't for him.

He needed a woman from this world, someone tough and hardy and resilient. Someone who wouldn't mind the wind or weather, the relentlessly long hours a rancher had to put in during calving and haying seasons, the self-reliance that was a vital, necessary part of this life.

He couldn't put his boys through losing someone else they loved, simply because he was drawn to sweet, pretty, delicate types like Ella Baker.

He pressed a hand to his chest, to the sudden ache there. Just a little heartburn, he told himself. It certainly couldn't be something as useless and unwanted as yearning.

His boys were up to something, but damned if Beck could figure out what.

Despite his best and most subtle efforts to probe in the week following that Sunday dinner with Ella, they were being uncharacteristically closemouthed about things.

Still, it was obvious they had secrets. Seemed like they spent half their free time whispering to each other, then going suspiciously quiet whenever he happened to walk in.

He tried to give them a little latitude. It was Christmastime, when everybody seemed to turn into covert operatives, with secrets and hidden stashes of treasure. He had his own secrets right now.

He didn't like that Dan and Jax seemed to be in on the whole thing. More than once, he had seen the boys talking to them, only to shut things off again if Beck walked in.

Knowing something had been stirring at the Broken Arrow all week, he should have been prepared on Friday morning when the boys ganged up and ambushed him at breakfast.

"Dad, can we have Miss Ella over again tomorrow to ride Creampuff?" Trevor asked.

His skin seemed to catch fire just at the mention of her name. The ache in his chest that had been there since their kiss Sunday night seemed to intensify.

He had dreamed about her every single night, but hadn't seen her since then.

"She only rode here two times," Colter reminded him. "That's not enough."

"We promised we would teach her how to ride. If we're gonna do that, it has to be more than two times."

What sort of arrangement had they made with their music teacher? He still couldn't shake the suspicion that there was something fishy about the whole thing from the outset. He thought they were doing a nice thing to invite her out to ride, but he was beginning to wonder if there was something more to it, something he was missing.

What weren't they telling him?

"We thought maybe she could bring us home after practice tomorrow morning and then we can ride in the arena for a while, and then she could go see the new puppies with us," Colter said in what seemed like a deceptively casual tone.

Yes. They were definitely cooking up something.

"And maybe she could stay for dinner again," Trevor suggested blithely. Beck didn't miss the way Colter poked him with his elbow and gave him a shut-up sort of look.

"I don't know about dinner," he said slowly, "but she can certainly come out and ride again, if she wants to. You can invite her at practice. She might be busy, though. It wouldn't surprise me. Everyone seems to be, this time of year."

"We'll ask her," Trevor said. He cast a sidelong look at his brother, who nodded, another of their unspoken twin-talk kind of communications.

"You'll be here tomorrow, won't you?"

"I don't know. Like I said, it's a busy time of year. I'll have to see how my schedule plays out. I have to run into Idaho Falls at some point this weekend to pick up a few things for Sal and the puppies." And for two certain little caballeros for Christmas, but he didn't tell them that.

"I can always run to Idaho Falls for you." Jax looked up from his coffee and his iPad long enough to make the offer.

"Yeah." Colter seized on that. "Maybe Uncle Jax can go to Idaho Falls for you. It would be better if you could be here when Miss Ella comes over."

"Why's that?" he asked with a frown.

The twins exchanged looks that were not at all subtle. He had seen that look before, too many times to count—usually just moments before they did something dangerous or destructive, like jump from the barn loft or try to take out ornaments on the Christmas tree with their little peashooters.

"Because you're, you know, a really good teacher and good with horses and stuff."

Colter's ready response didn't ease Beck's suspicions any.

"Uncle Jax is a good teacher, too, and he's even better than I am with horses." That wasn't always easy for him to admit, but it was true. His younger brother had an uncanny way with them. "Miss Baker will be okay."

Jax had been watching this exchange with unusual interest. Usually his brother kept to himself until at least his second cup of coffee. "Sure," he answered. "For the record, I'm happy to teach Ella Baker anything she would like to know."

Beck knew he had no right to the giant green tide of jealousy that washed over him at the thought of the sweet Ella in his brother's well-practiced hands.

"We're talking about horses, right?"

Jax gave him an innocent look that didn't fool Beck any more than the boys' had. His brother had the same uncanny way with women that he did with animals.

"Sure. That's what I was talking about. What else would be on my mind?"

Beck could only imagine. His brother was a notorious flirt whose favorite pastime, when he wasn't following the rodeo circuit or training his own horses, was hanging out with buckle bunnies who liked to admire his...trophies.

Come to think of it, he wasn't sure he wanted Jax within half a mile of Ella Baker.

"Maybe she can't even come over," Trevor said. "But we can ask her, right?"

He didn't miss the little thread of yearning in his son's voice. It made him wary and sad at the same time. Since Judy retired, they seemed a little more clingy than usual, probably hungry for a woman's softer arms and gentle ways.

"All you can do is ask. Find out if she's available and then we'll figure out the rest."

"Okay. Thanks, Dad."

"Finish your breakfast and load your dishes. You'd better hustle or you're going to miss the bus."

They shoveled in their eggs, then raced to brush teeth, grab homework and don coats and backpacks. Through it all, they continued to whisper, but he sent them on their way without making any progress at figuring out what secrets they were keeping from him.

Ella did her best to put the memory of that kiss behind her. It should have been easy. She was insanely busy as the calendar ticked inexorably toward Christmas.

In addition to the daily practices for the show at The Christmas Ranch, each of the grades at the elementary school was preparing a small performance for their parents—with plenty of music needed—and her middle school choir presented their annual holiday concert.

She also volunteered at the local senior citizen center in Pine Gulch and had agreed to lead carols for their holiday luncheon.

It was chaotic and hectic and...wonderful. She loved being part of the Pine Gulch community. She loved going to the grocery store and being stopped by at least two or three people who wanted to talk. She loved the way everyone waved as she drove past and gave genuine smiles, as if they were happy to see her.

Though she had good neighbors and friends in Boston, she had never known the same sense of community as she did here in Idaho.

Her life had changed drastically since she came to live with her father the previous year.

Occasionally, she missed her job there, her friends, the active social network and many cultural opportunities she found in Boston. She even missed her mother and stepfather and their lovely home in the Back Bay neighborhood.

She wouldn't go back. Her life here was rich and full and rewarding—even when she found her schedule packed with activities.

She hadn't seen Beck all week, but even her busy routine hadn't kept her from spending entirely too much time thinking about him and about that amazing kiss.

She wasn't sleeping well. Each night she fell into bed, completely exhausted, but her stupid brain seemed to want to replay every moment of that kiss, from the first brush of his mouth on hers to the strength of his muscles against her to the cold air swirling around them.

By the time Friday rolled around, she was completely drained. The show at The Christmas Ranch would be the following Tuesday, which meant only three more rehearsals—that afternoon, Saturday morning and Monday after school. With everything else going on, this would be her last chance to practice with Colter and Trevor for their special number.

Now, as they rehearsed one more time in her classroom, her fingers strummed the last chord of the song and she beamed at the boys.

"That time was perfect!" she exclaimed. "I can't believe how well you've picked up the harmony and you've memorized the words and everything. Your dad is going to love this so much. Everyone else will, too."

She wasn't exaggerating or giving false praise. Colter and Trevor actually sounded so good together, she would have loved to record it.

All her instincts told her that if she ever uploaded it to social media, the song would go viral instantly. Their voices blended perfectly and the twins had a natural harmony that brought out all the emotional punch of the song, the angst of a cowboy who has to spend the holiday alone in the cold elements instead of by a warm fire, surrounded by loved ones.

Beyond that, there was something utterly charming about these two redheaded little boys who looked like the trouble-makers many thought they were, but when they opened their mouths, they sang like little cowboy angels.

On the night of the performance, she would have to make sure it was recorded. More than one parent had offered to film the entire show. She would have to be sure Beck could obtain a copy, especially since he wouldn't be prepared to record it himself, considering the whole thing would be a total surprise.

"Thanks a lot for helping us," Trevor said.

"You're very welcome. I've enjoyed it. And you boys have been so good during the rehearsals. You've more than repaid me."

"No, we haven't," Colter argued. "We still need to take you horseback riding again. You only went two times and we practiced our song almost every day."

"Our dad said we could invite you to come over again tomorrow after practice, if you have time," his brother said.

"Yeah! You've got to come and see the puppies. They're growing *fast*."

"Their eyes are open now and they're not always sleeping every minute. They're so cute. You have to see them," Trevor said. "We got to hold one yesterday. Sal didn't like it much but Dad just petted her and talked to her so she didn't get too mad at us."

"I'm glad to hear that," Ella said, charmed despite herself by the image of Beck giving his boys a chance to hold the puppy.

Only a few weeks ago, she had thought him cold, emotionless. How had she managed to get things so very wrong?

He certainly didn't kiss like he was cold and emotionless. The memory made her ache.

"So do you want to come over after practice tomorrow afternoon?"

With everything on her docket, that was really her only free chunk of time all week to finish her own Christmas preparations, but this appeared to be a matter of honor to the boys. It was clear Trevor and Colter wanted to be sure they repaid her accordingly, after all her work helping them prepare the song.

Beyond that, she felt a little rush of anticipation at the prospect of riding again. She had begun recapturing something she thought had been lost forever and couldn't help being eager to continue on that journey.

"I have a busy day tomorrow, but I think I could make that work. I would love to visit Creampuff again and see Sal and her puppies."

"Yay!" Colter said.

"I'll plan on taking riding clothes again and we can practice after I take you home from rehearsal tomorrow."

"Maybe we can show you how to rope a calf," Colter said.

"I think I'll stick with trying to stay in the saddle," she said with a smile. "Are you sure this is okay with your father?"

Trevor's features fell a little. "He said we could ask you, but he might not be there."

"Yeah. He said he had some stuff to do tomorrow, so our uncle Jax said he could teach you anything you want to know."

"Dad didn't like that very much, though. He was kind of mad at Uncle Jax. He got a big, mean face, but Uncle Jax only laughed."

"Is that right?" she said faintly.

Jax McKinley was a flirt of the highest order. From the moment she moved to town, friends had warned her not to take him too seriously.

"Yeah. Uncle Jax is really good with horses. He even rides broncs in the rodeo and stuff."

"But our dad is even better," Colt assured her. "He's the best cowboy ever."

"And he's nice, too."

"Plus, he can cook good. He makes really good popcorn."

Don't forget that he can kiss like he was born knowing his way around a woman's mouth.

"I'll be grateful to anyone who might be there tomorrow to give me a lesson," she assured them. "Now, we'd better hurry or we'll be late to rehearsal."

As the boys grabbed backpacks and coats and she gathered her own things, she couldn't stop thinking about Beck. Big surprise. What would he think of the boys' special musical number? He would have to possess a heart of lead not to be touched by their effort on his behalf.

They were adorable kids. She would always be grateful she had been able to get to know them a little better these past few weeks.

She had completely changed her perspective about them, too. Somehow they had worked their charming little way into her heart when she wasn't looking.

The trick after the holidays would be figuring out how to extricate them all.

"I thought you were planning to be in Idaho Falls all day."

Beck fought the urge to rearrange that smirk on Jax's too-handsome face. His brother always seemed to know instinctively which buttons to push. Apparently Beck was more transparent than he thought.

"I took care of everything I had to do in town," he said. "It took less time than I expected. I knew what I wanted and where to get it, so there was no sense dawdling, was there?"

"Words to live by, brother." Jax grinned, obviously taking his words to mean something entirely different from what Beck intended. "Too bad for me, I guess that means you can take over the riding lesson with our pretty little neighbor this afternoon. But I imagine you already knew that."

Beck frowned at his brother's teasing. "I don't know what you're talking about," he lied.

Jax only chuckled. "I guess since you're here, you can do the honors of saddling up all the horses for the lesson. I suddenly find myself with an afternoon free. Maybe I should run into town, do a little Christmas shopping."

"Sounds good." He wouldn't mind if his brother decided to stay away all afternoon.

He checked his watch. Practice was supposed to have ended about fifteen minutes ago, which meant Ella and the boys should be here shortly.

As unwelcome anticipation churned through him, Beckett tried to keep himself busy in the horse barn, readying the horses and the arena for their visitor. He was mostly unsuccessful, with little focus or direction, and was almost relieved when he finally heard a vehicle approach.

He set down the leather tack he had been organizing and walked out to greet them, his heart pounding in his chest.

How had he forgotten how pretty she was? As she climbed out of her vehicle, winter sunlight glinted on her hair and her cheeks were rosy and sweet. She wore jeans, boots and a ranch coat open to reveal another Christmas sweater. Instantly, he remembered that moment in his room the week before, when she had appeared there like something out of a dream he hadn't dared remember.

"Hey, Dad," Trevor said, his features lighting up at the sight of them. "I thought you weren't gonna be here!"

"I took care of my business in Idaho Falls faster than I expected," he answered. They didn't need to know that he had practically bought out the entire toy aisle at the big-box store in his rush to get out of there quickly, before the Saturday rush.

"Great!" Colter said. "This way you can give this Ella her lesson."

The two exchanged delighted grins and an uncomfortable suspicion began to take root.

Something was up, all right, and he had a feeling he was beginning to know what that might be. The little troublemakers had romance on their minds. Somehow they must have got it in their heads that he and their music teacher might make a match of it.

Was Jax in on it? What about Dan? Was that the reason Jax was conveniently taking off and that Dan had made a point of saying he had plans today and couldn't help?

Were they all trying to throw him and Ella together?

His cheeks suddenly felt hot as he wondered if that was the whole reason the boys had come up with the idea for these riding lessons.

This wouldn't do. The idea was impossible. Completely out of the question. He didn't have the first idea how to break it to them.

They were children. They only saw a pretty woman who was kind to them, not all the many reasons why a relationship between Ella and Beck could never work.

He suddenly wished he'd stayed in Idaho Falls, so he could head off this crazy idea before it had any more time to blossom.

Was it too late to drag Jax back to handle the lessons? He still didn't like the idea of his brother here with his flirty smiles and his admiring gaze. Beck would just have to tough it out.

Things would be easier, though, if they didn't stick around here in the intimate confines of the riding arena.

"What do you say we take a quick trail ride up above the house? You can only learn so much while you're riding around in a circle."

"Outside?" Her gaze shifted to the mountains then back to him, her big blue eyes widening.

She had been injured in those mountains, he remembered. He couldn't blame her for being nervous, yet he knew it was a fear she had to overcome if she would ever be able to truly rediscover the joy of riding horses again.

"You'll be okay. We'll keep you safe," he promised. "Do you have warm enough clothing for that?"

"Is anything ever warm enough for the winters around here?"

He had to smile. "Good point. There's no cold like trying to pull a stubborn calf at two in the morning when it's below zero, with a windchill that makes it even colder."

"Brrr."

He looked over her winter gear. "We should have some warmer gloves that will fit you and a snug hat. I would hate to be responsible for you coming down with frostbite."

"You make this whole outing sound so appealing."

Despite her dry tone, he could see the hint of panic in her eyes and in the slight trembling in her hands.

"Don't worry. We won't go far. I've got a fairly well-groomed trail that winds around above the house a little. We can be back in less than an hour. It will be fun, you'll see."

She still didn't look convinced.

"Trust me," he said. "You're never going to love riding a horse again until you let one take you somewhere worth going."

That seemed to resonate with her. She gazed at him, then at the mountains, then finally nodded.

Even if she wasn't for him, the woman had grit. He wanted to tell her so, right there. He wanted to kiss her smack on the lips and tell her she had more gumption than just about anybody he'd ever met.

He couldn't, of course, without giving the boys encouragement that their devious plan was working, so he only smiled and walked back to the barn to bring out the horses.

Chapter Ten

Ella refused to give in to the tendrils of panic coiling through her.

As the boys led out Creampuff and their two horses, saddled and ready to go, she drew in a deep, cleansing breath.

Beck was right. Riding around in an indoor space had been a great introduction for her, but it wasn't much different from a child atop a pony, going around in circles at the county fair. If she truly wanted to get past her fear, she had to take bigger steps, like riding outside, no matter how stressful.

Beck came out leading his own big horse and for a moment, she let herself enjoy the picture of a gorgeous cowboy and his horse in the clear December air.

"Need a boost?" Beck asked as he approached.

She wanted to tell him no, but the placid and friendly Creampuff suddenly loomed huge and terrifying. "Yes. Thank you," she said.

He helped her into the saddle and gave her thigh a reassuring squeeze that filled her with a complex mix of gratitude and awareness.

"You've got this, El. We'll be with you the whole time."

"Thanks," she mumbled through lips that felt thick and unwieldy.

Beckett mounted his own horse. Ella was again distracted long enough from her worries to wish she didn't have to hold the reins in a death grip so she could pull out her phone and snap his photograph. Her friends back in Boston should have visual proof that she was actually friends with someone who should be featured in men's cologne advertisements.

The Great American Cowboy, at one with his horse and his surroundings.

"Trev, you go in front, then Colt, then Miss Baker," Beck ordered. "I'll bring up the rear. We're just heading up to the springs. You know the way, right, boys? Not too fast, okay? Just an easy walk this time."

"Okay, Dad," Trevor said.

The boys turned their horses and urged them around the ranch house. Creampuff followed the other horses without much direction necessary from Ella as they made their way around the ranch house and toward a narrow trail she could see leading into the foothills.

At first, she was too focused on remaining in the saddle to notice anything else. Gradually, she could feel her muscles begin to relax into the rhythm of the horse. Creampuff really was a gentle animal. She wasn't placid, but she didn't seem at all inclined to any sudden movements or abrupt starts. She responded almost instantly to any commands.

Ella drew in a deep breath scented with pine, snow, leather and horse. It truly was beautiful here. From their vantage point, she could see Beck's ranch, orderly and neat, joining her father's land. Beyond spread the town of Pine Gulch, with the silvery ribbon of the Cold Creek winding through the mountains.

In summer, this would be beautiful, she knew, covered in wildflowers and sagebrush. Now it was a vast, peaceful blanket of snow in every direction.

This was obviously a well-traveled trail and it appeared to have been groomed, as well.

Had he done that for her, so she would be able to take this ride?

Warmth seeped through her at the possibility and she hardly noticed the winter temperature.

Colter turned around in his saddle. "You're doing great," the boy said. "Isn't this fun?"

"Yes," she answered. "It's lovely up here."

Everything seemed more intense—the cold air against her skin, the musical jangle of the tack, the magnificent blue Idaho sky.

After about fifteen or twenty minutes, they reached a clearing where the trail ended at a large round black water tank.

Trevor's horse went straight to the water and the others followed suit.

"This looks like a well-used watering spot."

"Our cattle like to come up here, but if you stuck around long enough, you could also see elk and deer and the occasional mountain lion," Beck said.

"A mountain lion. Oh, my!"

"They're not real scary," Colter assured her. "They leave you alone if you leave them alone."

"We even saw a wolf up here once," Trevor claimed.

"A coyote, anyway," Beck amended.

"I still think it was a wolf, just like the ones we saw in Yellowstone."

"Want to stretch your legs a little before we ride home? We can show you the springs, if you want. There's a little waterfall there that's pretty this time of year, half-frozen."

"Sure."

This time she dismounted on her own and the boys tied the horses' reins to a post there. Beck waded through the snow to blaze a trail about twenty yards past the water tank to a small fenced-off area in the hillside that must be protecting the source of a natural springs from animal contamination. The springs rippled through the snow to a series of small waterfalls that sparkled in the sunlight.

"This is lovely," she murmured. "Do you come up here often?"

"I maintain it year-round. The springs provides most of our water supply on the ranch. We pipe it down from the source but leave some free-flowing. In the winter, this is as far as we can go without cross-country skis or snowshoes. The rest of the year, there's a beautiful backcountry trail that will take you to Cold Creek Canyon. It's really a stunning hike or ride."

"Last year, we rode our horses over to see our friend Thomas."

"That sounds lovely."

What an idyllic place for these boys to grow up. Though they had lost their mother so young, they didn't seem to suffer for love and affection. She didn't envy them precisely—how could she, when they didn't have a mother? Still, she wished she could have grown up on the Baker's Dozen with her parents together, instead of having been constantly yanked in opposite directions.

They seemed so comfortable here, confident and happy and loved.

"You should see the wildflowers that grow up here," Beck said as they headed back to the horses. "There's something about the microclimate, I guess, but in the summer this whole hillside is spectacular, with flowers of every color. Lupine and columbine, evening primrose and firewheel. It's beautiful."

"Oh, I would love to see that." She could picture it vividly.

"You're welcome back, anytime," he said. "June is the best time for flowers."

"I'll keep that in mind."

It always amazed her when she went into the backcountry around Pine Gulch that all this beauty was just a few moments away. It only took a little effort and exploration to find it.

"Can we go back now?" Colter asked. "I'm kind of cold."

"Yeah. Me, too," his brother said, with a furtive look at the two of them. "You don't have to come with us. You two can stay up here as long as you want. We're okay by ourselves."

Before their father could answer, the boys hopped back on their horses and headed down in the direction they'd come up.

She glanced at Beck, who was watching his sons with a look of consternation.

"Those two little rascals." He shook his head with an expression that suggested he was both embarrassed and annoyed.

"What was that all about?"

"It's more than a little embarrassing," he admitted. "I think they're up to something. They've been acting oddly all week."

Oh, dear. She hoped the boys didn't reveal their surprise musical number before the performance in a few days.

"I'm sure it's nothing," she said. "Probably just, you know, typical Christmas secrets."

"That's what I thought at first, but not anymore. Today proved it." He was silent for a moment. "I think they're matchmaking."

She stared. "Matchmaking? Us?"

She felt hot suddenly, then cold. Did the boys know she was developing feelings for their father? Had she let something slip?

"I know, it's crazy. I don't have any definite proof, just a vibe I've picked up a time or two. I'm sorry about that."

Was he sorry because he was embarrassed or sorry that his boys might actually be crazy enough to think Ella and he could ever be a match?

"I... It's fine."

"If this keeps up, I'll talk to them. Make sure they know they're way off base."

"It's fine," she said again, though she felt a sharp pang in her heart at his words. "They are right about one thing, though. It is getting cold up here."

"Yeah. Guess we better head down."

"Thank you for showing me the waterfall, for making me ride up here, when I was afraid to try it. It is beautiful."

"You're welcome. Here. Let me help you mount up again."

She wanted to try herself, but her bad leg was aching from the ride and she wasn't sure she could manage it.

He gave her a boost up. This time, though, because of the stiffness in her leg, she faltered a little and his hands ended up on her rear instead of her waist.

Both of them seemed to freeze for just a moment and then he gave a nudge and she was in the saddle.

He cleared his throat. "I swear, I didn't mean to do that."

"I believe you. Don't worry. I guess it's a good thing the boys weren't here to see, right? They might get the wrong idea."

"True enough."

He looked as if he wanted to say something else but finally mounted his own horse. "You go first. I'll be right behind you. Creampuff knows the way."

She drew in a deep breath and headed down the mountainside.

A wise woman would have jumped back in her car and driven away from Beck McKinley and his cute twins the moment she rode back to the barn. Ella was discovering she wasn't very wise, at least not when it came to the McKinley men.

As soon as they arrived back at the horse barn, the twins came out, two adorable little cowboys. "We can put up Creampuff and Ace for you," Colter offered.

Beck looked surprised, then pleased. "That's very responsible of you, boys."

They beamed at the two of them. "While we do that," Trevor said, "you can take Miss Ella to see the puppies again."

"She has to see how much they've grown," his brother agreed.

"We'll wait until you're done with the horses, then we can all go see the puppies together."

"We've already seen them this morning, when we had to feed them," Colter reminded him. "And you said it's better if

Sal doesn't have that many visitors at once. It stresses her. You said so."

"That's right. I did say that." Above their heads, Beck raised his eyebrows at Ella in a told-you-so kind of look.

"Go on, Dad. We promised Miss Baker she could see them."

"I guess I have my orders," he murmured to Ella. "Shall we?"

She didn't see a graceful way out of the situation, so she shrugged and followed him toward the older barn.

"What did I tell you?" Beck said as they headed inside from the cold December afternoon to the warm, cozy building.

"You might be right," she said.

"I'm sorry. I don't know what's come over them."

"You don't need to apologize. I think it's rather sweet. I'm flattered, if you want the truth, that they think I'm good enough for you."

You *obviously don't, but it's nice that your sons do.*

He gazed at her for a moment, before shaking his head. "They're rascals. I'll have a talk with them."

Though she fought the urge to tell him not to do that, at least until after Christmas, she knew he had to set them straight. Nothing would ever happen between her and Beck. He had made that abundantly clear.

They stood just inside the door of the barn. It was warm here and strangely intimate and she had to fight the urge to step forward and kiss away that rather embarrassed expression.

He was gazing at her mouth, she realized, and she saw awareness flickering there in his eyes.

He wanted to kiss her and she ached to let him.

No. That wouldn't do, especially if they wanted to convince the boys there was nothing between them.

She curled her hands into fists instead. "We'd better take a look at the puppies, since that's the reason we came in here."

After an awkward moment, he shrugged. "You're right. Absolutely right."

He turned and headed farther into the barn and she followed him to the stall that housed Sal and her new little brood.

Holding on to her suddenly grim mood was tough in the presence of the eight adorable little black-and-white puppies, who were now beginning to toddle around the stall. They appeared less rodentlike and more like cute puppies, furry and adorable, with paws and ears that seemed too big for their little bodies.

"The boys were right!" she exclaimed. "They've grown so much since I saw them last."

"You can hold one, if you'd like. Sal can be a bit territorial so I'll have to grab one and bring it out to you."

"I'm all right. I'll just watch this time."

"Come back in a few weeks and they'll be climbing all over. She'll be glad to let someone else entertain them for a moment."

"They're really beautiful, Beck."

He gazed down at her with a slight smile and she was aware of the heat of him and the breadth of his shoulders. She felt a long, slow tug in her chest, as if invisible cords were pulling her closer to him.

"Thank you for sharing them with me—and for the rest of today. I'm glad you made me go on that trail, even though it scared me to death."

"I could tell."

She made a face. "Was I that obvious? I thought I was doing so well at concealing my panic attacks"

"There was nothing overt, just a few signs I picked up." He paused. "I hope you realize there's nothing wrong with being afraid, especially after your experience in childhood. Anyone would be. But not everyone would have the courage to try to overcome it."

"I don't think it's *wrong*, necessarily. Only *frustrating*. I don't want to be afraid."

"But you did it anyway. That's the important thing. You've got grit, El. Pure grit."

His words slid around and through her, warming her as

clearly as if he'd bundled her in a soft, sweet-smelling quilt just off the clothesline. "I do believe that's the sweetest thing you've ever said to me."

He scratched his cheek, looking sheepish. "It must be the puppies. They bring out my gooey side."

"I like it," she confessed.

As he looked down at her, she again felt that tug in her chest, as if everything inside her wanted to pull her toward him. He must have felt it, too. She watched his expression shift, saw the heat spark to life there. His gaze slid to her mouth then back to meet her gaze and he swallowed hard.

Sunlight slanted in through a high window, making his gorgeous features glow, as if the universe was somehow telling her this was right. She had never been so aware of a man. He could carry her over his shoulders to one of the straw-covered stalls and she wouldn't utter a peep of protest.

The air around them seemed to hiss and snap with a sweet, fine-edged tension, and when he sighed and finally kissed her, it seemed as inevitable as a brilliant summer sunset.

Kissing him felt as familiar and *right* as being on a horse had earlier that afternoon. His mouth fit hers perfectly and he wrapped his arms around her as if he had been waiting for just this moment.

She returned his kiss eagerly, with all the pent-up longing of the previous week, when she had been tormented by heated memories.

Through the thrill and wonder of the kiss, as his mouth explored hers and his hands somehow found their way beneath her sweater to the bare skin of her lower back, she was aware of a tiny, ominous thread weaving through the moment.

It took several more long, delicious kisses before she could manage to identify the source of that little niggling worry, the grim truth she had been trying to ignore.

This was more than simple attraction.

She was falling in love with Beckett McKinley.

The realization seemed to knock the air right out of her lungs and she was suddenly more afraid than she'd been the first time she faced his horses.

He would hurt her. Badly. Oh, he wouldn't mean to—Beck was a good man, a kind one, as she had figured out over the last little while. But he had no real use for her beyond a few kisses. He had made that perfectly clear—as far as Beck was concerned, she didn't belong here. She was no different from his late wife or her own mother.

Like her father, he couldn't see the truth of her, the part that loved afternoon thundershowers over the mountains or the sight of new crops breaking through the ground or a vast hillside covered in wildflowers.

One of the puppies made a little mewling whimper that perfectly echoed how she felt inside. Somehow it gave Ella the strength to slide her mouth away from his.

She caught her breath and tried to make light of the kiss, purely in self-defense. "Good thing your sons didn't come in just now. If they had seen us wrapped together there, they might have made the mistake of thinking we're both falling in exactly with their plans."

"Good thing," he murmured, looking dazed and aroused and gorgeous.

She had to get out of here, before she did something stupid, like yank him against her again and lose her heart the rest of the way. She drew a deep gulp of air into her lungs and forced a casual smile that she was fairly sure didn't fool him for a moment.

"I should, um, go. I've got a Christmas party tonight with some friends and still have to bake a dozen cookies for the exchange."

He said nothing for a long moment, then sighed. "Should we talk about that?"

She opted to deliberately misunderstand. "The cookies? I'm making my favorite white-chocolate cranberry recipe. There's really nothing to it. The secret is using a high-quality shortening and a little more flour, especially in this altitude."

"I'm sure you know I didn't mean we should talk about the cookies—though those sound delicious. I meant the kiss."

He shoved his hands into the pockets of his coat, as if he was afraid if he didn't, he would reach for her again.

Or maybe his fingers were simply cold.

"There's nothing to say," she said with that fake smile that made her cheek muscles hurt. "The boys can play matchmaker all they like, but we both know it won't go anywhere. I'll just make a point not to visit any cute puppies alone with you again."

While she was at it, she would have to add walking together to her car to that list of no-no's, as well as helping her onto a horse and washing dishes side by side.

Come to think of it, maybe it would be better if they kept a nice, safe, ten-foot perimeter between them at all times.

"I really do have to go," she lied.

"I guess I'll see you next week at the Christmas show."

She nodded and hurried out before she did something else stupid.

Beck followed her out to be sure she made it safely to her vehicle. There were a few icy spots that worried him, but she hurried across the yard to her SUV and climbed inside without faltering or looking back, as if one of his cow dogs was nipping at her heels to drive her on.

He had screwed up. Plain and simple.

For nearly a week, he'd been telling himself all the reasons he couldn't kiss her again. What did he do the first moment they were really alone together? Yep. He kissed her. He hadn't been able to help himself. She had been so soft and sweet and lovely and all he could think about was tasting her mouth one more time.

The trouble was, he was not only fiercely attracted to her, but he also genuinely liked her.

He meant what he said to her. She had more grit than just about anybody he knew.

If she had the kind of raw courage necessary to ride again after an accident that nearly killed her, why was he so certain she didn't belong out there, that she would turn tail and run at the first sign of trouble?

She wasn't like Stephanie. That was clear enough. Yes, they had both been raised back east in big cities. They both came from wealthy, cultured backgrounds that seemed worlds away from this small Idaho town.

But Stephanie had been...*damaged*. He should have seen that from the start. She had managed to hide it fairly well at first, but when he looked back, he could clearly see all the warning signs he should have discerned much earlier. He hadn't *wanted* to see them. He had been busy growing the ranch, getting ready for the arrival of his sons, coping with a moody, temperamental wife.

If he had been more aware, maybe he could have found help for her earlier and headed off the debilitating depression that came later.

The truth was, he didn't trust himself these days. Things had gone so horribly wrong with Stephanie, and his sons had been the ones to suffer. He couldn't afford to mess up again.

If he didn't have the boys to consider—only himself—he might take the chance to see if these tender young feelings un-curling inside him for Ella Baker could grow into something sturdy and beautiful.

How could he take that risk, though?

If he pursued things between them and she ended up leaving, too, like their mother—and like her own, for that matter—the boys would be shattered.

He couldn't do that to them.

He turned around and headed back to the barn, aware as he walked that Ella had the strength to confront her fears while he was letting his own completely chase him down and wear him out like one of the Yellowstone wolves on a wounded calf.

Chapter Eleven

If he could have avoided it, Beck would have stayed far away from the Baker ranch until he could manage to figure out a way to purge Ella out of his system.

He had a feeling he faced a long battle on that particular front.

Meanwhile, he couldn't avoid the place, especially not while he and Curt were still the copresidents of the local cattle growers association.

They had end-of-year paperwork to finish for the association. It had been on his desk for a week, but he had been putting it off. Finally, the day of the Christmas show the boys had been working so hard on, he knew he couldn't put it off any longer.

It was no coincidence that he tried to time his visit around noon, as he was certain Ella would be busy teaching music at the school and not here to torment him with visions of what could never be.

If that made him a yellow-bellied chicken, he would just have to live with it.

"Thanks for bringing this by," Curt said, gesturing to the folder of papers he needed to sign.

"No problem. I was out anyway," Beck assured him. "I'm heading over to Driggs to pick up the last thing for the boys' Christmas. I commissioned new saddles for each of them, since they're growing so fast and are too big for the ones they've been using."

"Watch those two. They'll be taller than you before you know it."

Since he was six-two and the boys were only seven years old, Beckett was pretty sure he was safe for a few more years on that front, unless they had an explosive growth spur.

"Need anything while I'm out?"

Curt shook his head and Beck couldn't help thinking his friend looked more frail every time he saw him.

"I can't think of anything," he said. "I did most of my shopping online this year, since it's hard for me to get around the crowded stores."

"Got it."

Curt gazed out the window, where a light snow had begun to fall in the last hour. "It's not coming down too much, but you'd still better hurry back from town. We've got a big storm heading this way."

"That's what I heard."

The weather forecast was predicting the storm might break records.

"It's not supposed to hit until tonight, but you never know. Better safe than sorry. I know you would hate to miss the show tonight at The Christmas Ranch."

"I'll be back in plenty of time. I'm only making one stop to the saddle maker's place."

"Good. Good." Curt reached for the big water bottle on the table beside him but his hands were trembling so badly today that it took him three tries to find the straw.

"How are you doing?" Beck asked. "Really doing?"

It seemed as if they always talked *around* Curt's condition and the challenge it presented, instead of talking *about* it. The older man frowned. For once, he didn't give his stock answer.

"I can't do a damn thing anymore," he said, frustration vying with self-pity in his voice and expression.

"I'm sorry," Beck said, though the words were hardly adequate.

"Parkinson's is the worst. I can barely sign my damn name on those papers. You saw me. If I could climb up on a horse right now, I would borrow one from you. He and I would ride up into the backcountry to die and you'd never see me again."

Man, it was hard to see such an independent, strong man laid low by this debilitating disease.

"That would be a waste of a good horse. Not to mention a good friend," he said quietly.

Curt sipped at his water again, then set it down on the desk in his ranch office. "Have you thought more about buying me out?"

There it was. The other thing he didn't know what to do about.

"Sure I've thought about it. I've run the numbers dozens of times. It's an amazing offer, Curt. I would love the chance to combine our two ranches and build the Baker-McKinley brand into one of the strongest in the world."

"You sound hesitant, though. Is it the asking price? We can negotiate a little."

He could handle the hefty price tag Curt was asking. It would mean leveraging his capital, but he'd had some great years and had money in the bank. What better use for it than taking advantage of the chance to double his usable acreage and water supply, not to mention keeping the Baker's Dozen land out of the hands of developers?

Like everywhere else in the West, this part of Idaho was experiencing a population boom, with people wanting to relocate here for the beautiful views, serenity and slower pace.

As developers built houses and newcomers moved in, they tended to crowd any agricultural operations farther and farther to the outskirts. It was the eternal paradox. People moved to an area because they loved the quiet way of life and what it represented, then immediately set out to change it.

"It's not the price," he said.

"Then what?" Curt persisted. "I'd like to seal this deal as soon as we can."

"What about Ella?" he asked, finally voicing the one concern that seemed to override all the others.

"What about her?"

"How does she feel about you selling the ranch to me?"

Curt flicked off the question with a dismissive gesture. It was obvious from his expression that he didn't consider that an obstacle at all. "She'll be fine with it. It's not like I'm *giving* it to you out of the goodness of my heart, right?"

True enough. He would pay a hefty sum, even slightly above market value.

"Ella stands to inherit my entire estate," Curt went on. "She's all I've got, so the whole kit and caboodle goes to her. Believe me, she's not stupid. She'll be better off having cold hard cash in the bank than being saddled with a cattle ranch she doesn't know the first thing to do with."

The words were barely out of the other man's mouth when Beck heard a gasp from the hallway outside the office.

With a sinking heart, he shifted his gaze and found Ella standing there, holding a tray that looked like it contained a bowl of soup and a sandwich for her father.

The tray wobbled in her hands and he thought for a moment she would drop it, but she righted it at the last moment. She didn't come inside, simply stood there looking devastated.

"Dad," she whispered.

Curt had the grace to look embarrassed. "How long have you been home?"

She ignored the question. "You're selling the ranch? To *Beck*?"

She said his name like it was a vile curse word and he

flinched a little. None of this was his idea but he still felt guilty he had even discussed it with Curt.

"I offered it to him. We're still working out terms, but it makes the most sense for everyone."

She aimed a wounded look at Beck, which made him feel sandwiched between father and daughter. "You never said a word to me," she said to him.

He should have mentioned it. Now he wished he had, especially after the first time they kissed.

"Why didn't you tell me?"

Guilt pinched at him, harsh and mean. On its heels, though, was defensiveness. *He* had nothing to feel guilty about, other than not telling her Curt had approached him with an offer to sell. It hadn't been his idea or anything he had deliberately sought out. He had assumed her father had already told her about it.

Anyway, Curt was right. She would inherit the proceeds from the ranch and could live comfortably the rest of her life.

"It makes the most sense for everyone—" he began.

"Not for me! I love this ranch. I'd like to try running it, if my stubborn father would ever let me. I'm trying to learn everything I can. Why do you think I wanted the boys to teach me how to ride?"

"Ride what? I hope you're not talking about horses," Curt interjected, color suffusing his features.

"I am," Ella declared as she finally moved into the room and set down the lunch tray on the desk. "I've been to the Broken Arrow several times to go riding with Trevor and Colter."

"I can't believe you went horseback riding without telling me!"

"Really?" she snapped. "That's what you're taking out of this discussion? Considering you've all but sold my legacy out from under me without bothering to mention it, I don't think you've got much room to be angry about me riding a horse a few times."

"It's not your legacy until I'm gone," her father snapped back.

"Until then, I've got every right to do what I want with *my* ranch."

The color that had started to rise on her features leached away and she seemed to sway. Beck half rose to catch her but earned only a scathing glare for his efforts.

"You certainly would never consider trusting me with it, would you?"

"You have no idea how hard this life is."

"Because you've shielded me from it my entire life!"

"For your own good!"

Now she was trembling, he saw, just as much as she had when facing down her fears and riding a horse.

"I'm twenty-seven years old, Dad. I'm not a broken little girl in a hospital bed. I'm not some fragile flower, either. I'm tough enough to handle running the Baker's Dozen. Why can't you see that?"

Curt's jaw clenched. "You have other talents, honey. You don't need to wear yourself out on this ranch."

"What if I want to? I love it here. You know I do."

"You love it *now*. Who's to say that won't change in a week or month or year from now? You have lived on the Baker's Dozen maybe a total of two years your entire life. I just don't want you to be saddled with more than you can handle."

"That's my decision to make, isn't it?"

"No," he said bluntly. "Beckett can take what I've built over my whole life—and what my father's built and his father—and make it even better. Can you say the same?"

She said nothing, only pressed her lips together. Her eyes looked haunted now, hollow with shadows.

Curt appeared oblivious to her reaction. He shrugged. "I wouldn't sell the ranch to Beck just to hurt you, honey. You know that, right?"

"But it *would* hurt me," she answered. "What hurts me more is that you will never even give me the chance to try."

She took a deep breath, as if fighting for control, then turned toward the door. "I can't do this right now. Not today. We can talk about it later. Right now, I have to go back to take my afternoon classes then focus on the children's Christmas show. I'll take the things I need for the show tonight. Don't expect me home between school and the performance."

She left without looking again at either of them, leaving behind an awkward, heavy silence.

Curt winced and picked up his water bottle again in hands that seemed to be shaking more than they had earlier. "I didn't want her finding out about our deal like that."

Beck frowned. "We don't have a deal. Not yet."

He was angry suddenly that Curt had dragged him into the middle of things and felt terrible for his part in hurting her. "If Ella wants to try running the ranch, Curt, I don't think I can stand in the way of that."

"She might think she wants it but she has no idea what it takes to keep this place going. She's never had to pull a calf when it's thirty below zero outside, or be up for forty-eight hours straight, trying to bring the hay in on time."

"So she can hire people to help her. You're not doing it on your own, either. Your foreman has stepped up to take on more and more of the load over the last few years. Why can't he do the same for her?"

"It's not the same. I know what I'm doing! I'm still involved in the day-to-day operations. What does Ella know about cattle? She can play four instruments and sings like a dream but she's not a rancher!"

"Not if you don't let her learn, Curt. Why are you trying so hard to protect her?"

"This ranch almost killed her once. I can't let it finish the job."

Curt blurted out the words, then looked as if he wished he could call them back.

Beck sat back, understanding dawning. He had suspected something like that after Ella told him about her accident.

"Your daughter inherited more from you than your eye color, Curtis Baker. She's tougher than you give her credit. You should have seen the grit she used to get back in the saddle, when it was obvious it scared her to death."

"I can't lose her," the man said, his voice low. "She's all I have."

"If you keep treating her like she's incompetent, you might not have much choice," he answered firmly. "You'll lose her anyway."

Ella sat in her SUV at the end of the driveway, trying to control the tears that burned her eyes.

No good deed goes unpunished, right? She thought it would be a nice thing to surprise her dad for lunch by bringing home a sandwich and some of his favorite takeout tomato bisque from the diner in town.

She never expected she would find Beck in her father's office, or walk in on the two of them negotiating away her future.

Her father had no faith in her.

She had suspected as much, but there was something heartbreaking and final about hearing it spoken so bluntly.

She'll be better off having cold hard cash in the bank than being saddled with a cattle ranch she doesn't know the first thing to do with.

Since coming to live here, she had done her best to learn the ropes. When she wasn't teaching music, she had helped with the roundup, she had driven the tractor, she had gone out with Manny to fix fences.

It wasn't enough. It would never be enough. Curtis Baker could never see her as anything more than a weak, frightened girl.

Did she know everything about running a ranch? No. But she was willing to learn. Why wouldn't her father let her try?

She brushed away a tear that fell, despite her best efforts.

She was stuck here. Her father needed her help. She couldn't just abandon him. But how could she face living here day after day with the knowledge that the ranch she loved—the ranch that felt like a huge part of her—would someday belong to someone else?

To Beck?

The pain intensified, bringing along the bitter taste of betrayal. Damn him. Why hadn't he bothered to mention that Curt had approached him about buying the ranch?

That hurt almost as much as her father's disregard for her feelings.

She let out a breath and swiped at another tear. Just as she dropped her hand, a knock on the window of her vehicle made her jump halfway out of her seat.

She turned to find Beck, big and rugged and gorgeous, standing out in the gently falling snow.

She thought about putting her SUV in gear and spraying him with mud as she peeled out, but that would be childish.

Wouldn't it?

He gestured for her to roll down her window. After a moment, she did but only about three inches. Cold air rushed in, heavy with the impending storm.

"I don't have time to talk to you," she snapped. "I have a class in twenty minutes."

"The school is only a ten-minute drive from here. That means we still have ten minutes."

She set her jaw. Did he think she could just run into her classroom and miraculously be in a mental space to take on thirty-three fourth graders who had been dreaming of sugarplums for weeks?

"What do you want?" she said. Even as she spoke, she was aware she sounded like one of those fourth graders having a verbal altercation with a schoolmate.

"I'm sorry I didn't tell you your father had offered to sell me the ranch. I guess I assumed you and Curt had already talked about it. I thought maybe that was the reason you're sometimes a little…cool to me."

Had she been cool to him? She was remembering a few specific encounters when the temperature had been the exact opposite of cool.

"He never said a word to me. But why would he? As he made it abundantly clear in there, he doesn't need to tell me anything."

Beck sighed. "He should have. Told you, I mean. That's what I just said to him. More than that, I think he should give you a chance to run the Baker's Dozen along with him for a few years, then both of you can decide if you want to sell."

"That's a lovely idea. He would never consider it."

"Have you talked to him about it?"

"Of course! Dozens of times. My father sees what he wants to see. Like I said in there, to him, I'll always be that broken girl in a hospital bed."

"He loves you and worries about you. Speaking as a father, it would be hell to see your child hurt and spend all these years afraid it was your fault."

Curt had sold all his horses after her accident, though he had always loved to ride.

She sighed. "I can't worry about this today," she said. "In a few hours, I'm in charge of a show that involves dozens of children, twenty songs and an audience of three hundred people. I don't have time to stress about my stubborn father right now."

Tomorrow she would. Tomorrow her heart would probably break in jagged little pieces. She would compartmentalize that for now and worry about it after the show. The children had worked too hard for their music director to fall apart because her father had no faith in her.

"I'm sorry," he said again.

"I'm sure you are. Not sorry enough that you would refuse to buy the ranch, though, are you?"

A muscle worked in his jaw but he didn't answer. His silence told her everything she needed to know.

"That's what I thought. I have to go. Goodbye, Beckett."

She put her SUV in gear and pulled out into the driveway, her heart aching with regret and sadness and the tantalizing dream of what might have been.

Chapter Twelve

"Okay, kids. This is it. Our audience is starting to arrive. You've practiced so hard, each one of you. I hope you know how proud of you I am. Each number sounds wonderful and I know you've all put in so much effort to memorize your parts and the words to the music. This show is going to be amazing! Let's make some people happy!"

The children cheered with nervous energy and she smiled reassuringly at them all, though she could feel emotion building in her throat.

This was her second year directing the Christmas show and it might just be her last. If her father sold the ranch to Beckett, she wasn't sure she could stay in Pine Gulch, as much as she loved it here. It would be too difficult to watch.

She snared her thoughts before they could wander further down that path. Tonight wasn't about sadness and regret, but about the joy and wonder and magic of Christmas. For the children's sake, she needed to focus on the show right now. She would have time to process the pain and disappointment of the day later, when this program was behind her.

"Our guests are arriving now but they will need to eat dinner first. That gives us about thirty minutes before our show. Everyone follow the older girls into the office. We have a special treat in store for you. Celeste Delaney is going to read to you from the newest, still-unpublished Sparkle the Reindeer book!"

An electric buzz crackled through the crowd at that announcement. She knew the children would be excited about the prospect of a new Sparkle book, as everyone adored the charming stories.

When she was certain the children were settled comfortably, Ella returned to the large reception room in the lodge to check on the rapidly filling tables. She greeted a few friends and made small talk as she assessed the crowd.

"We crammed in three more tables, so fifty more people can squeeze in." Hope Santiago came to stand beside her and watch people jostling for space. "I hated to turn people away last year. I hope we've got enough room this year."

It still might be tight, judging by the crowds still coming in.

"How's the weather?" she asked. It wasn't a casual question.

Hope shrugged. "It's snowing a bit but it's not too bad, yet. I still enlisted everybody with four-wheel drive to pick up some of the senior citizens who don't like to drive in the snow. I was hoping we wouldn't have to do that again this year but Mother Nature didn't cooperate. Thanks for signing up Beck, by the way. He's out there now, bringing in his last shuttle group."

So much for trying not to think about the man. She couldn't seem to escape him.

"The show is amazing, El," Hope said, her expression earnest. "You've outdone yourself this year. Every number is perfect. Honestly, I don't know what we would do without you."

She wasn't yet ready to tell her friend The Christmas Ranch might have to do just that next year.

Instead, she forced a smile and prepared to go back and check on the children. To her shock, she came face-to-face with her father, who was just coming in from outside.

What was he doing there? Curtis hadn't said a word to her earlier about attending the show.

An instant later, Beck came in behind him, helping a woman whose name she didn't know navigate the crowd with a walker.

Beck must have given her father a ride. Big surprise. The two of them were no doubt plotting their ranching world domination.

That wasn't really fair, she acknowledged, a little ashamed of herself. Her father and Beck had been friends and neighbors a long time.

Beck looked up from helping the woman and caught sight of her. Something flashed in his gaze, something intense and unreadable.

She let out a breath. Despite her hurt over that scene in her father's office that afternoon, she couldn't help a little shiver of anticipation.

He was going to love the special number his twins had prepared for him out of sheer love. She had no doubt it would touch everyone at the performance—especially Beck.

In a small way, she felt as if the gift was coming from her, as well.

She turned away just as Hope hurried over to her. "We've got a little problem. Somehow two of the angels showed up without their wings. There's no time for someone to fetch them. I know we had extras. Do you remember where we put them?"

"Absolutely. I can picture the box in the storage room perfectly. I'll grab them." She hurried away, forcing herself again to focus on the show and not on her impending heartbreak.

"Oh, Ella. This show has been nothing short of magnificent this year," Celeste whispered backstage as a trio of girls, including her stepdaughter, Olivia, bowed to thunderous applause out on stage. "We could stop there and it would be absolutely perfect. Well done!"

She smiled at her friend. She had to agree. So far the show had gone off without a hitch.

"Is it time for us to go out for 'Silent Night'?" one of the older girls asked.

"In a moment. We have one more special number."

None of the other volunteers or the children in the program had heard Colter and Trevor's song yet, as she and the twins had practiced in secret. Only Hope knew about it, since Ella had to work out the lighting and sound with her and Rafe.

"After we're done, I need you girls to lead the younger children out, then we'll sing the final number. Boys, are you ready?"

Trevor and Colter both nodded, though their features were pale in the dim light backstage. She had a feeling they would look nervous under any light conditions, as if only now realizing the magnitude of what they had signed up for that long-ago day when they had approached her about singing in the show.

She picked up her guitar from the stand and walked out ahead of the boys, who looked absolutely adorable in matching white shirts with bolo ties and Christmas-patterned vests that Hope had sewn for them. They wore matching cowboy hats and boots and giant belt buckles that were just about as big as their faces.

Oh, she hoped Rafe was videoing this.

Ella sat on a stool as the boys took to the microphone. The crowd quieted, all the restless stirring and rustling fading away.

She had performed enough times to know when she had an audience's attention. With the spotlights on her, it was tough to see Beckett's reaction, but she thought she saw his eyes widen. He would no doubt be completely shocked to see his sons up here onstage, since he had no idea they were performing a duet.

Ella didn't want this number to be about her, but she felt compelled to take the microphone before the boys began.

"It is my great pleasure to introduce to you Colter and Trevor McKinley. They're seven years old. And yes, you guessed it, they're twins."

This earned a ripple of laughter, since that was more than obvious to anyone without cataracts.

Ella waited for the reaction to fade away before she went

on. "A few weeks ago, Trevor and Colter approached me with a rather unusual request. They wanted to perform a special song at this Christmas show as a gift to someone they love very much. They asked me to help them prepare, so it would be perfect. Since then, they have been practicing several times a week with me after school, trying to learn the harmony, the pitch, the dynamics."

She smiled at the boys. "They have worked very hard, which I see as a testament to the value of this gift, which is intended for one person—their father, Beckett."

Though she was a little afraid to look at him, her gaze seemed to unerringly go in his direction. In the brief instant their gazes met, she saw complete shock on his features as people around him smiled and patted him on the back.

"This is his favorite Christmas song, apparently," she went on, "and I have it on good authority he sings it to himself when no one is around."

She didn't look at him now, but she was quite certain he would be embarrassed at that snippet of information. Too bad for him.

"While Trevor and Colter prepared this song especially for their father," she continued, "this is one of those rare and wonderful gifts that benefits more than its recipient. We all are lucky enough to be able to enjoy it. Boys."

She leaned back and softly strummed the opening chords on her guitar. For just a moment, the boys stood frozen in the spotlight, missing their cue by about a half second, but Trevor nudged his brother and a moment later, their sweet young voices blended perfectly as they sang the slow, pensive opening bars.

The crowd seemed hypnotized while the boys sang about spending Christmas Eve in the saddle, about feeling alone and unloved, about finding the true meaning of Christmas while helping the animals.

They had never sung the song so beautifully or with such stirring emotion. When they finished, even Ella—who had heard them sing it dozens upon dozens of times—had to wipe away a tear.

After the last note faded, the crowd erupted into thunderous applause.

"You did great," she murmured over the noise of the crowd. The boys beamed and hugged her, which made more tears slip out.

"Thank you for playing your guitar and teaching us the song," Trevor said solemnly over the noise of the crowd.

Oh, she would miss these sweet boys. She wasn't sure how her heart would bear it.

"You're very welcome," she said. "Now, go find your places for the final song."

The boys rushed to their designated spots as the other children surged onto the stage—angels and shepherds, candy canes and cowboys and ballet dancers in tutus. It was a strange mishmash of costumes, but somehow it all worked perfectly together.

Olivia, who had a pure, magical voice and performed professionally, took the guitar from Ella as they had arranged, and stepped forward to strum a chord. She sang the first line of the song, then the other children joined her to sing "Silent Night" with a soft harmony that rose to fill the St. Nicholas Lodge with sweet, melodious notes.

On the last verse, the senior citizens were encouraged to sing along, which they did with stirring joy.

When the last note died away and the audience again erupted in applause, Hope went to the microphone, wiping away a few of her own tears.

"If you're all not overflowing with Christmas spirit now, I'm afraid there's no hope for you," she declared stoutly, which earned appreciative laughter.

"Wasn't that a spectacular show?" Hope asked.

She had to wait for the audience to quiet before she could speak again. "So many people had a hand in bringing this to you. The fabulous caterer, Jenna McRaven, the high school students who volunteered to serve the meal to you, those who provided the transportation."

She paused and smiled at Ella. "I would especially like to thank the one person without whom none of this would have happened tonight. Our director, organizer, producer and general talent-wrangler, Miss Ella Baker."

The crowd applauded her and she managed a smile. These were her friends and neighbors. They had embraced her, welcomed her in their midst. How would she be able to say goodbye to them?

"Now, I do have a rather grave announcement," Hope went on. Her tone was serious enough that the crowd quieted again and fixed attention on her. "While we were here enjoying this fantastic dinner and truly memorable entertainment, Mother Nature decided to let loose on our little corner of paradise outside with a vengeance. I guess she was mad she wasn't invited to the show so decided to put on her own. As much as I know we all love to visit with each other, I'm afraid that's not a good idea tonight. There will be other chances. We're going to cut things short now and encourage you all to head for home as soon as you can, before conditions get even worse—though if all else fails, we can hitch up the reindeer and sleigh to carry you home. Safe travels to you all, friends. Good night and merry Christmas."

The audience applauded one last time and gave the children a standing ovation, then people began to gather up their coats and bags and stream toward the door.

For the next several moments, Ella tried to hug as many of the children as she could and thank them for their hard work. Through it all, she noticed The Christmas Ranch staff quietly ushering people out.

"I'm sensing urgency here," she said when her path intersected with Hope's through the crowd. "Is it really that bad?"

Hope's eyes were shadowed. "I've never seen a storm come on so quickly," she admitted. "We've already got a foot of new snow and the wind out there is howling like crazy. If the crowd wasn't so noisy in here, you would hear it rattling the windows. I want people to hurry home, but I don't want to incite a panic. It's going to take some time to get everyone out of here."

"I can take more than one group." Somehow, Beckett had appeared at her side without warning and she jumped. She told herself it was only surprise, but she suspected it was more nerves. She was dying to ask how he enjoyed the song, but the urgency of the storm evacuation took precedence.

"Thanks, Beckett. I knew there was a reason I adored you." Hope smiled at him so widely that Ella might have felt a twinge of jealousy if she didn't know Hope adored her husband, Rafe.

"I'll have to factor in taking the boys, too. I'll drop them off in the first batch, then come back for a second trip."

"I can take my father home, so you don't have to do that," Ella said, though she was still so angry with her father, she didn't know if she could be in the same vehicle with him. "If you want, I can also drop the boys off at the Broken Arrow, as it's on our way home. That should free up a couple more spots in your truck for people who need rides home."

He looked torn. "That's true, but I would feel better if you could head straight home, instead of having to detour to our place."

"We'll be fine," she said. She couldn't believe the storm was really that bad. "I have four-wheel drive and new snow tires. I'm not worried."

One of The Christmas Ranch workers came up to ask Hope a question and she walked away to deal with the situation. When they were gone, Beck turned to her, his expression solemn.

"El, I… Thank you for helping the boys with that song. I've never been so touched. It means more than I can ever say."

Warmth seeped through her at the intensity in his voice. "They did all the hard work. I only guided them a little," she said. "Anyway, we made a fair trade. They agreed to give me riding lessons if I would help them learn the song."

Surprise flickered in his eyes. "That's the reason you've been coming out to ride?"

"The opportunity was too good to pass up. I wanted to ride again for a long time. They wanted to learn the song. This seemed the perfect arrangement."

It *had* been perfect, until she made the mistake of falling hard for the boys—and for their father.

"Well, thank you. Every time I hear that song now, I'll remember them…and you."

Before she could answer, Rafe Santiago came over looking harried. "It's crazy out there. Several people have decided to leave their vehicles here and come back for them when the storm passes, so we've got even more to take home. Do you think you could take home Martha Valentine and Ann and Max Watts? They all live on the same street near the park."

"Absolutely." He turned to her. "Are you sure you don't mind taking the boys home? That would help."

"No problem. I'll get them home safely," she promised.

"Thanks."

He gave her one more smile then turned to take care of his responsibilities.

That was just the kind of guy he was. When something needed doing, he would just tip his hat back and go to work.

It was one of the many reasons she loved him.

She couldn't stand here mooning over him when she had her own responsibilities, people who needed her. After one last look at him helping the frail Martha Valentine into her coat with a gentleness that brought tears to her eyes, she turned away to gather up her own charges.

The storm was worse than she had imagined.

The moment they stepped out of the St. Nicholas Lodge, snow blew at them from every direction and the wind nearly toppled them over. Everyone was huddling inside their winter coats as they made their way through the deepening drifts to the parking lot.

"Boys, grab hold of me and my father so you don't blow away." She had to raise her voice to be heard over the whining wind. She wasn't really worried about that, but needed their help more to support her father—something she couldn't tell him.

Fortunately, her vehicle was parked close to the entry and it only took them a few moments.

She opened the driver's side first so she could start the engine to warm up the heater and defrost, then hurried around to help her father inside. Her SUV passenger seat was just a little too high for him and Curt didn't have enough strength to pull himself into it alone.

"Thanks," he muttered when she gave him a boost, clearly embarrassed about needing help.

By the time he was settled and the twins were buckled into the back seat, Ella was frozen through from that icy wind—and she still had to brush the snow from the windows so she could see to drive.

Finally, they were on their way. She took off at a ponderous pace, her shoulders taut and her hands gripping the steering wheel. She could hardly see through the blinding snow that blew across the windshield much faster than her wipers could handle.

Her father looked out the window at the relentless snow while the boys, oblivious to the storm outside or the tension inside, chattered to each other about the show and the approaching holidays.

"We had about ten people tell us our song was the best one," Trevor said proudly.

"You did a great job," she said, tightening her fingers on the wheel as a particularly strong gust of wind shook the vehicle and sent snow flying into the windshield.

Usually she didn't mind driving in a storm, but this was coming down so fast. Coupled with the wind and blowing snow, it made visibility basically zero.

"Can we listen to the radio?" Colter asked.

"I need to concentrate right now. Can you just hum to yourselves?"

"We can sing our song again," the boys offered.

"I'd like that," Curt said, to her surprise.

While her eyes were glued to the road, she was vaguely aware from her peripheral vision that he had half turned in his seat to face the twins. "I always loved that song. You boys *were* the best thing on the show," he told them.

She couldn't spare a look in the rearview mirror right now. If she did, she was sure the twins would be grinning.

"We'll have to do it without the guitar," Trevor warned.

"That's okay. You can sing without it." Her father turned to her and spoke with a guarded tone. "That won't be too stressful for you while you're driving, will it?"

She shook her head and the boys started singing the song she had heard them practice so many times before. There was something special about this time, in the warm shelter of her vehicle while the storm raged outside.

"That was wonderful," her father said when they finished, his voice gruff. "I'm sure your dad loved it."

"He did," Trevor said. "He came and found us after and gave us big hugs and said he was so proud of us and had never been so touched."

"He said it was the best gift anybody ever gave him," Colter added. "He said it made him cry and that there's nothing wrong with a guy crying when something makes him too happy to hold it in! Can you believe that?"

She didn't answer as she felt emotion bubble up in her chest.

"It's a good song," her father said gruffly.

"Want us to sing another one? We can do 'Jingle Bells' or 'Rudolph' or 'Away in a Manger.'"

"Sure. We'll have our own private Christmas show," Curt said.

The boys launched into song and she was grateful to her father for distracting them so she could focus on driving.

She could usually make it between The Christmas Ranch and the Broken Arrow in about ten minutes, but she was creeping along at a snail's pace because of the weather conditions.

"Almost there," she finally said after about a half hour. "Your turnoff should be just ahead."

At least she was fairly certain. It was hard to be sure with the poor visibility and the heavy snow making everything look alien and *wrong* somehow.

She turned her signal on, though she couldn't see any lights in either direction, when suddenly her own headlights caught something big and dark on the middle of the road just ahead of them.

It was an animal of some kind. A cow or horse or moose. She couldn't be sure and it really wouldn't matter when two thousand pounds of animal came through the windshield.

Reflexively, she slammed the brakes. She wasn't going fast at all but the road was slick, coated in a thick layer of ice, and the tires couldn't seem to catch. The vehicle fishtailed dangerously and she fought to regain control.

She tried to turn the wheel frantically, with no success. It was a terrible feeling, to be behind the wheel of a vehicle she had absolutely no control over.

"Hang on," she called.

The boys screamed and her father swore as the vehicle went down a small embankment and into a snowbank about ten feet down.

Her heartbeat raced like she had just finished an Olympic sprint and her stomach twirled in an awful imitation of her wheels spinning out of control.

"Is everybody okay?" she asked.

"Yeah," her dad said gruffly. "Gave me a hell of a start."

"We're okay," Trevor said.

She turned around to reassure herself but all she could see in the darkness were their wide eyes.

"Are we stuck?" Colter asked.

She tightened her shaking fingers on the steering wheel. "I don't know. I haven't tried to get us out yet. You're sure you're both all right?"

"Yeah. It was like the Tilt-A-Whirl at the county fair."

Now she remembered why she had always hated that ride.

"Well, that was fun. Let's get everybody home."

Ella put the vehicle in Reverse and accelerated but the wheels just spun. The snow was too deep here for them to find purchase. She pulled forward a little, then tried to reverse again. She thought she made a little progress but, again, the SUV couldn't pass a certain point.

She went through the same process several times until her father finally stopped her. "You're only making things worse," he said. "Face it. With that incline, this thing doesn't have the horsepower, at least not in Reverse. We're going to need somebody to pull us out."

The boys had fallen silent in the back and she could tell they were beginning to grasp the seriousness of the situation.

It could be hours before someone came by. As the snow piled up, their tracks would quickly be wiped away.

She could still call for help. She could tell Beck how to find them. She reached for her purse and fumbled for her cell phone, scrolling through until she found his number.

She tried to connect but the call didn't go through that time, or the second time she tried.

"What's wrong?" her father asked.

"Why don't I have any service?" she wailed.

"Must be in one of the dead zones around here."

Naturally. It was just her luck to get stuck in one of the few places where she couldn't call for help. "What about yours, Dad?"

"I didn't bring it."

"Why on earth not?"

He didn't answer for a long moment, then shrugged. "What's the point? You know I can't work that damn thing very well."

He could barely hold it in his trembling hands. Hitting the numbers was even harder. She had tried to coach him through speech-to-text methods but he couldn't quite master it.

It wouldn't make much difference. They had the same carrier. If she didn't have service, he likely wouldn't, either.

That gave her very few options.

"In that case, I don't see a choice," she said after a moment of considering them. "I better head to the Broken Arrow for help. Jax and Dan are there. Somebody should be able to pull us out with the one of the ranch tractors."

"You can't wander around in that storm. Just wait here. Beck will be home soon."

"Yes, but all the people he was taking home live south of here, which means he'll likely be coming to the ranch from the other direction. He won't even pass this way."

"When he sees the boys haven't made it home, don't you think he'll come looking for us?"

"Probably." That did make sense and provided some comfort to the worry and grave sense of responsibility she was feeling for the others in her vehicle. "The problem is, he might be shuttling multiple groups of people home. I have no idea how long he'll be at it, and to be honest, I don't feel good about waiting here, Dad. The snow keeps piling up and the temperature is dropping. I need to get you and the twins home where it's safe. The fastest way to do that is to walk to the ranch house. It can't be far. I can be there and back with help in no time."

"I don't like it."

What else was new? She could write a book about the things her father didn't like about her, apparently.

"I'm sorry, but right now I have bigger things to worry about than your opinion of me," she said, more sharply than she intended.

Curt opened his mouth, then closed it again. Good. She didn't have time to argue with him.

"I need you to stay here with the boys and watch over them. I have a full tank of gas. I'll make sure there's no snow obstructing the exhaust, so no worries about carbon monoxide building up inside. You should be fine to keep the engine running and the heater on."

"We can come with you," Colter said.

She had no doubt that the boys would be able to keep up with her. Her father, on the other hand, would not, and she didn't want to leave him here alone.

Torn, she gazed at all three of them. She didn't want to go out into that storm but she didn't dare take her chances of Beck miraculously just stumbling onto them. From the road above, they would be impossible to spot once the snow obscured their tracks, especially with that blowing wind and poor visibility.

This was serious, she realized. This country could be unforgiving and harsh and she would have to draw on all her reserves of strength to help them get through this.

"I need you boys to stay here where it's warm. Do what my dad says, okay? I'll be back shortly."

"Here. Take my coat. It's heavier than yours," Curt said gruffly.

"Mine is plenty warm. You might need yours. I will take the flashlight in the glove box, though."

She reached across him to get it out, grateful she had changed the batteries to fresh ones a few weeks earlier.

"In the back, there's a bag filled with bottled water, some granola bars and a couple of emergency blankets. You're probably not going to need them, but you should know about them, just in case."

"You're prepared," her father said, surprise in his voice.

"I have a father who taught me well about the harshness of Idaho winters."

She wanted to tell him she could learn all sorts of things, if only he were willing to teach her, but this wasn't the time to rehash that argument.

"Sounds like a smart man," he said after a moment.

"About some things, anyway," she said tartly.

Focused on the job at hand, she wrapped her scarf around her face and buttoned up her coat. "I'm going to give you my phone. You don't have cell service here but if I'm not back in a timely manner, you can try climbing up the incline and see if you have better service up there. Give me half an hour to get help first, though. I would rather you didn't leave the vehicle."

After a tense moment, her father finally nodded. "Be careful. I've only got the one daughter, and I'm fairly fond of her."

His words made tears thicken in her throat. Why did he have to be so stubborn?

"I'll be careful. You, too. See you in a little bit." She paused. "I love you, Dad."

She climbed out of the vehicle and whatever he said in response was snatched away by the howling wind that bit through her clothing and stung her face like a thousand knives.

She slipped several times as she tried to make it up the slight hill. Her boots were lined and warm but they weren't meant for heavy-duty hiking, more for walking through the snowy streets of Boston.

By the time she made it back to the road, she was already out of breath and perspiring inside her coat. She stood for a moment to catch her bearings. Everything was disorienting. White upon white upon white.

Fear was heavy on her shoulders. This was serious, she thought again. She had heard horror stories of people being lost in blizzards, their frozen corpses only found months later. Perhaps she would have been better off staying in the car.

But even now, knowing it was just below her, she could hardly see her SUV. Someone with no idea what had happened to them would never find it.

She headed off in the direction of the ranch house, tucking her chin in against the wind, praying she didn't miss his driveway and struggling step by step through the deepening snow.

It was much harder going than she had imagined, but she

remained solely focused on doing what she had to, to save her father and the twins.

Shouldn't she have found the ranch road by now?

Panic began to flutter through her. She had to be close, but where was it? She couldn't even see the roadway anymore. She was almost certain she was still on it, but what if she wasn't? What if she had somehow taken a wrong turn and was somehow heading in the wrong direction? She would die out here—and her father and the twins would eventually run out of gas and would freeze to death, too.

What had she done? She should never have trusted her instincts. She should have stayed in the SUV with Curt and the twins. Had she doomed them all?

The panic ratcheted up and she tried frantically to see if she could find a light, a landmark, anything. All she could see was white.

Dear God, she prayed. *Please help me.*

The only answer was the constant whine of the wind churning the snow around her.

She had to keep moving. This had to be the way. There. Was that a light? She peered through the darkness to a spot set back from the road about the correct distance to be the Broken Arrow ranch house.

Was that the log arch over his driveway? She thought so but couldn't quite be sure. Instinct had her moving in that direction, when suddenly a dark shape again loomed out of the darkness.

Ella's instinctive scream tangled in her throat as the dark shape trotted closer. In her flashlight's glow, she suddenly recognized the calm, familiar features of an old friend.

She had never been so very grateful to see another living soul.

"Creampuff! What are you doing out here?" Ella exclaimed. At her voice, the horse ambled closer.

She must have somehow gotten out. She remembered the

boys telling her the horse could be an escape artist. Why on earth would she have chosen this particular moment to get out?

Was Creampuff the thing she had almost hit on the road, the shape that had frightened her into hitting the brakes and sliding off the road?

Ella didn't like the consequences, but she was very grateful she hadn't hit the horse.

"You shouldn't be out here," she said to the horse. "It's dangerous."

Creampuff whickered and nudged at her. She seemed happy to see Ella, too.

She suddenly had an idea. It was completely impractical, but if it worked, it might be the answer to her current dilemma.

The storm was so disorienting, she was worried that she would end up miles from her destination. What were the chances that the horse could get her to Beckett's ranch house?

It was worth a try. Better than wandering aimlessly out here on her own. The only trick would be mounting up without a saddle, stirrups or reins—especially when she could barely manage it when she had all those necessary items.

The horse would lead her back to the barn on the Broken Arrow. Somehow she knew it.

If she wanted to save her father and the twins, she had to try.

Chapter Thirteen

"What the hell do you mean, they're not here? They left forty-five minutes before I did!"

Beckett stared at his brother, fear settling like jagged shards of ice in his gut.

"I don't know what to tell you. Nobody is here but Dan and me. We haven't seen a soul. Maybe she took them to her ranch house instead."

Wouldn't she have called him if her plans had changed? He couldn't believe she would simply abscond with his children with no word.

Those ice shards twisted. "Something's wrong."

"You don't know that," Jax said, his tone placating.

"I do. Something's wrong. They should have been here half an hour ago. They're in trouble."

Jax started to look concerned. "Before you run off, why don't you try to call them?"

Good idea. "You call the Baker's Dozen. I'll try their cell phones."

He dialed Curt's first and it went immediately to voice mail.

He left a short message, telling the man to call him when he heard the message, then tried Ella's. It rang twice and he thought it would be connected but it shortly went to voice mail, too.

"No answer at the ranch," Jax said. He was beginning to look concerned, as well.

Beck had just spent an hour driving through these terrible conditions. He knew how bad it was out there—just as he knew Ella and her father had left with the boys well before he could load his first group of senior citizens into his vehicle to take them home.

Something was wrong. He knew it in his bones.

He hung up the phone after leaving her a terse message, as well, then faced his brother.

"I'm going to look for them. Call me if they show up."

Jax was smart enough to know when to not argue. He nodded. "What do you need me to do?"

"Stay in touch. For now, that's all."

He rushed out the door, doing his best to ignore the panic. He knew what could happen under these conditions. A few years ago, a rancher up north of them had gotten lost in a blizzard like this and ended up freezing to death just a few feet from his own back door.

The storm hadn't abated a whit in the few minutes he'd been inside. It whistled down through the mountains like a wild banshee. This was going to be one hell of a white Christmas. No doubt about it. He wouldn't be surprised if they ended up with at least two or three feet out of one storm, with much deeper drifts in spots from that wind.

He headed down the long, winding driveway, his heart in his throat and a prayer on his lips.

He had just started down the driveway when his headlights flashed on something dark and massive heading straight for him. If he had been going any faster, he would have inevitably hit it. As it was, he had to tap his brakes, even in four-wheel-drive low, to come to a stop.

It was a horse, he realized as he muscled the truck to a stop and his eyes adjusted to the shifting light conditions.

A horse carrying a rider!

What in the world? Who would be crazy enough to go riding on a night like tonight?

He yanked open his door and stepped out of his truck, boots crunching in calf-high snow, even though Jax had already cleared the driveway once that night.

"Beck! Oh, Beck. I'm so happy to see you!"

"Ella!" he exclaimed.

She jumped off of the horse and slipped to the ground and an instant later, she was in his arms. He didn't know if he had surged forward or if she had rushed to him, but he held her tightly as she trembled violently in the cold.

"What's happened?" he demanded. "Where are the boys?"

Her voice trembled. "I—I slid into a ditch back on the r-road. I don't know how far b-back. I thought it was closer b-but it seemed like f-forever that I w-walked."

"Why were you walking in the first place? Why didn't you call me to come find you?"

"I t-tried. I didn't have cell service. We're off the road, out of sight. E-even if someone t-tried to find us, they wouldn't be able to. I—I knew I had to f-find help, but I think I must have been lost or missed the road or something. I was panicking but I—I prayed and suddenly Creampuff appeared."

She shivered out a sob that made his arms tighten around her. For just a moment, she rested her cheek against him and he wanted to stay keep her safe and warm in his arms forever.

"It f-felt like some kind of m-miracle."

She was a miracle. She was amazing. If she hadn't faced her fear of horses, she might be wandering out there still. Somehow she had found the strength to climb on a horse without tack or saddle and made her way here, to him.

What would he have done if Creampuff hadn't found her, if she was still wandering around out there, lost in the storm?

He couldn't bear to think about it. If anything had happened to her, it would shatter him. His arms tightened as the feelings he had been fighting for weeks burst to the surface.

He shoved them back down, knowing this wasn't the time or the place to deal with them.

"You're frozen. Let's get you up to the house."

"No! I—I have to show you where to find my dad and the boys. You'll never see my car from the road."

She was so certain of that, he had to accept she was right. "At least hop inside the truck while I put Creampuff in the barn. Jax can take care of her. She deserves extra oats after tonight."

He helped her inside his cab—something he should have done the moment she hopped off that horse, he realized with self-disgust. The heater was blasting and he found the emergency blanket behind the seat and tucked it around her.

"We have to hurry."

"We will. This will only take a moment, I promise."

He closed the door and called his brother as he led the heroic Creampuff toward the barn, thirty yards away.

"Need my help?"

"Maybe. Not yet. Take care of Creampuff for me and give her all the crab apples she wants right now. I'll stay in touch."

He hurried back out to his truck through the storm, trying not to think about how very close they had come to a tragedy he couldn't bear to think about.

Ella had never been so cold, despite the blanket and the blessed warmth pouring full-blast from the heater of Beck's pickup. Occasional shivers still racked her body and Beck continued casting worried looks her way.

"How much farther?" he asked.

She peered out the window at the landscape that seemed familiar but not familiar. Everything was white, blurred by blowing snow.

She recognized that fence line there, and the curve ahead, and knew they had to be close but she could see no sign of her SUV.

"There!" she suddenly exclaimed. "Down there, just ahead. See the glow of my taillights?"

He tapped his brakes and brought the truck to a stop. "Wow. You were right. There are no tracks left on the road and it's well out of view from up here. If you hadn't pointed it out, I would have missed it."

"The engine is still running. I had a full tank of gas so they should have had enough for a few more hours."

He opened his door and frowned when she opened hers, too. "Ella, stay here. You're still half-frozen. I'll get them."

She shook her head. "Dad's going to need help getting up that little slope. It might take both of us."

Her father had grown so frail this past year that she suspected Beck could carry the other man up the slope over his shoulder in a fireman's carry without even having to catch his breath, but after a moment he nodded.

"I'm sorry you'll have to go out in the cold again."

"Only temporarily. I'll be okay."

She opened her door before he could argue further and climbed out, then headed down the slight slope to her snow-covered SUV.

The door opened before she could reach it and her father stuck his head out.

"Ella? Is that you?" he called, peering into the snowy darkness.

"Yes."

"Oh, thank heavens. I've been worried sick," he exclaimed.

With good reason, she acknowledged. She could have died out there—and there was a very good chance her father and the boys might have, too, before help could arrive.

"I brought Beck."

"I knew you could do it."

"How are the boys?" she asked as she reached the vehicle, with Beck right behind her.

"See for yourself," her father said. "They're sound asleep."

Sure enough, the boys were cuddled together under one of her emergency blankets.

Colter was the first one to open his eyes. He blinked at her sleepily, then his gaze caught his father, just behind her.

"Hey, Dad!" Colter smiled. "I think I fell asleep."

"Looks like it. We'll get you to the truck and then home in no time."

"Okay." He yawned, then shook his brother awake. Trevor looked just as happy to see both of them. Neither boy seemed the worse for wear after their ordeal.

"Boys, let's get you back to the truck. It's probably better if I carry you, since your cowboy boots aren't the best for snow. Ella, why don't you stay here where it's warm for a few moments?"

She wanted to offer to take one of the boys and then come back down to help her father, but she wasn't sure she would have the strength to make that trip twice more.

"Me first," Trevor said.

Beck scooped him up onto his back and Ella slid into his warm spot as they headed up the slope. In seconds, the still-blowing snow obscured their shapes from view.

"You guys did okay?" she asked Colter.

He nodded. "You were gone a long time."

"I know. I'm sorry. I had some complications."

"We sang just about every song we knew, then Mr. Baker told us stories about Christmas when he was a kid."

He started reciting a few of the stories, one she remembered her father telling her and another that seemed new. Maybe Curt had told it to her once, but it had been lost along with everything else the summer she was eight.

It seemed like forever but had probably been only two or

three minutes when Beck opened the door. "Okay, kid. You're next."

He repeated the process with Colter, leaving her alone with her father.

"You sure you're okay?" Curt said, his voice gruff.

"I got lost. You were right. I probably should have stayed with you until the help arrived."

"That's funny. I was about to say *you* were right. Nobody would have found us until morning, when it would have been too late."

She was spared from having to imagine all the grim possibilities when Beck opened the door.

"Turn off your engine and bring along the key."

"What about my SUV?"

"Jax and I can come down and pull it out after I get you home."

She nodded and did as he said, hoping he would be able to find it again without the gleam of the taillights to light the way.

"I wish I could give you a piggyback ride, too," Beck said to her father.

"I'll be fine. I just need a little support."

In the end, Beck all but carried her father, anyway. She was deeply grateful for his solid strength but also for the gentle way he tried to spare her father's pride as he helped him into the truck's passenger seat. Once he was settled, Ella slipped into the back seat of the crew cab pickup with the boys and Beck headed for the Baker's Dozen, driving with slow care.

Just before he reached their turnoff, she heard her phone's ringtone distantly. It took her a moment to remember it was in her father's pocket. He fumbled with it but finally managed to pull it out. Before he could hand it over, Curt checked out the display with the caller ID.

"It's Manny. Wonder why he's calling you?"

"Maybe because you usually leave your cell phone at home," she replied, reaching over the seat for her phone.

"Do you know where your padre is?" the foreman asked as soon as she answered. "Is he with you?"

"Yes. We've had a rough evening but should be home soon. Beck is bringing us."

"He can't. Turn around."

"Turn around? Why?"

"You can't get through. One of the big pines along the driveway blew over in the wind and there's no way around it. It's a good thing nobody was driving under it when it fell."

"What's going on?" Beck asked, coming to a slow stop just before the turn.

"The driveway is blocked. We won't be able to get through."

Could this evening get any worse? First she ran off the road, now they were stranded away from home.

"Okay. No problem," Beck answered. "You can just come back to the Broken Arrow with us. I'll feel better about that, anyway."

"Will you be okay for tonight?" Manny asked.

"I suppose," she answered, though she dreaded the prospect. "What about you?" she asked the foreman. "You're stuck on the ranch."

"We're fine. We have plenty of food and so far the electricity is still on. I can take care of everything up here, as long as I know the two of you are safe and have a place to sleep."

"Thanks, Manny. Be safe."

"Same to you."

She hung up. "I guess we're spending the night at the Broken Arrow, if that's okay with you."

"Just fine."

He turned the pickup around slowly and began inching back to his own ranch.

"Dad, what about your prescriptions?" Ella asked, as the thought suddenly occurred to her.

"I took my evening pills before I went to the show, since I wasn't sure what time we'd be back. I'll be fine."

"You're staying at our house?" Trevor asked, excitement in his voice.

"You can have our beds," Colter offered. "Only someone will have to sleep on the top bunk."

"We have plenty of space," Beckett assured them. "We don't have to kick anybody out of bed. We've got a couple spare bedrooms and a comfortable sofa in the family room. You're more than welcome, and in the morning we can head over with chainsaws and clear a path."

"Thank you," she murmured. She really didn't want to spend the night at his house, but unless she wanted to take another merciless trudge through that storm, she didn't see that they had any choice.

"Are you sure you're okay, Dad? Is there anything else I can get you?"

An hour later, she stood in a comfortable guest room with a leather recliner, a wide bed and a flat-screen TV. Her father was already stretched out on the bed with a remote and a glass of water. He wore his own shirt and a pair of pajama bottoms borrowed from Beck's uncle.

She wore another pair, but they were about six sizes too big, baggy and long.

"I don't think so. I haven't been this tired in a long time. I'm probably going to crash the minute the news is over."

If not before. Curt had become good at dozing off while the television still played.

"All right. Good night." She leaned in to kiss his stubbly cheek. As she turned to go, she was surprised when Curt reached his trembling fingers out to touch her arm.

"I didn't say this earlier, but… I was proud of you tonight."

Her father's unexpected words sent a soft warmth seeping through her. "Thank you. I'm happy you enjoyed the program, but it was the children who did all the work."

"I'm not talking about the show, though that was excellent,

too. I meant later. When you went to find help. You risked your life for me and those twins of Beckett's. I was never more proud to call you my daughter."

He gave her arm a squeeze and she looked down, wanting to wrap his liver-spotted, trembling fingers in hers and tuck them against her cheek.

"I can do all sorts of things, if you only give me the chance," she said softly.

His hand stiffened and he pulled it away. "You're talking about running the ranch again."

Stupid. She wanted to kick herself. Why bring up a point of contention and ruin what had been a rare, lovely, peaceful moment between them?

"Yes. I am talking about running the ranch. I want to. Why won't you even give me the chance?"

To her chagrin, her voice wobbled on the last word. Exhaustion, she told herself. Still, she couldn't seem to hold back the torrent of emotions. "No matter what I do, you can't see me as anything but the silly girl who fell off a horse."

"You were in a coma for weeks. You nearly died."

"But I didn't! I survived."

"More than that," he said gruffly. "You thrived, especially after your mother took you away from here."

She stared, speechless at his words. "Is that what you think?" she asked, when she could trust her voice. "That I only thrived because Mom took me back to Boston? I grieved every day I was away. I love it here, Dad. I came back, didn't I?"

"To care for a feeble old man. Not because you belong here."

"The ranch is part of me, no matter what you say."

"So is Boston! You have a life there. I can't ask you to give up everything that's important to you. You love music—the opera, the symphony. Not J. D. Wyatt and his Warbling Wranglers. You belong to a different world."

"Yes, I love those things you mentioned. But I also love J.D. and George Jones and Emmylou Harris. The music you and I listened to together. Why can't I have both? Why do I have to choose?"

He appeared struck by this, his brow furrowed as he considered her words. She didn't know what might be different this time, when they had had similar arguments before, but something she said seemed to be trickling through his stubbornness.

"Honey, you don't know anything about running the ranch." She might have been imagining it, but his voice sounded a little less certain.

"You can teach me, Dad. I've been telling you that for months. There's no better time than now. I want to learn from you, while you're still here to teach me. This is my heritage, half of what makes me who I am. I don't understand why you can't see that."

He appeared struck by her words and she decided to quit while she was ahead. Perhaps she had given him something to think about—but why should this time make the difference when all those other times hadn't?

"I don't want to fight with you, Dad. It's been a long day. Can we agree to focus on the holidays and talk about this again after Christmas?"

"That sounds like a good idea." Her father paused. "I love you, you know. No matter what else you think. I love you and I've always been proud of you."

Tears welled up in her throat at this hard, stubborn man she had considered her hero all of her life. "I love you, too, Dad. Get some rest."

Beck slipped into his own room across the hall as he heard her last words and realized she would be coming out at any moment. He didn't want her to leave her father's guest room and find him standing outside the door.

He hadn't meant to eavesdrop, had only been there to check on his guests and see if they needed anything. The slightly raised voices had drawn his attention and he stopped, not wanting to walk in on an argument between Ella and her father.

This is my heritage, half of what makes me who I am. I don't understand why you can't see that.

Her words seemed to howl through his mind like that wind, resonating with truth.

He couldn't buy the ranch out from under her.

Beck leaned against his bedpost as the assurance settled deep in his chest. On paper, purchasing the Baker's Dozen was the smart play. He needed to expand his own operations and grow the Broken Arrow and it made perfect sense to merge the two ranches.

A month ago, he would have jumped at the chance without a second thought, assuming Ella had no interest in ranching and would be happy to take the money and run back to Boston.

He knew better now. He knew her hopes and her dreams and her yearnings. He had seen her face when they went on that ride into the backcountry as she looked at her family's land from the foothills. He had watched her tackle her own fear of horses in order to prove her own mettle. He had seen the courage she showed during a blizzard, her willingness to put her own comfort and safety at risk to help those she loved.

Her heart would break if Curt sold the ranch out from under her.

Beck couldn't do that to her.

He loved her too much.

The truth seemed to blow through him with all the impact of that storm rattling the windows of his room, crashing over him as if he were standing directly under the big pine that had fallen on the Baker's Dozen.

He loved Ella Baker.

He loved her sweetness, her grace, the gentle care she took with his sons. He loved her sense of humor and her grit and the soft, sexy noises she made when he kissed her.

He loved her.

What in heaven's name was he supposed to do about that now?

He assumed the normal course of action in this sort of situation would be to tell the woman in question about his feelings and see if she might share them—or at least see if she didn't reject them outright.

This wasn't a typical situation.

He thought of the precious gift she had helped his boys give him that day, the song that always touched him about a cowboy being alone on Christmas. He didn't want to be alone, like that cowboy. He wanted sweetness and warmth and a woman's smile, just for him.

He wanted Ella.

Did he have the courage to try again? His marriage had left him uncertain about his own instincts, completely aware of all the ways he had screwed up.

He couldn't afford to make a disastrous mistake like that again, but something told him with sweet certainty that allowing himself to love Ella could never be anything but perfect.

She filled his life with joy and wonder, reminded him of everything good and right in his world.

His boys loved her, too. They had thrived under her loving care, in a way he hadn't seen them do with anyone else. Somehow, she had managed to reach them, to sand away a few of their rough edges.

They needed that in their lives. *He* did, too.

Could he find the strength and courage to overlook all the ugliness of his past to build a brighter future with Ella?

As he stood in his bedroom with the storm raging outside, he wasn't sure he knew the answer to that.

He still hadn't figured it out an hour later as he finally settled the boys for the night and closed the door to their room, confident they were finally asleep.

The combined excitement of their stellar performance at the Christmas show, being trapped in a snowbank during the blizzard and then having their favorite teacher staying in their house seemed to have made sleep elusive, but exhaustion at last had claimed them.

It was late, past midnight, but they could sleep in the next day. He had already received an alert that school would be canceled tomorrow because of the storm, still raging throughout the region. It hadn't surprised him. Nobody would be able to get through on the roads out there until at least noon or later.

He needed to sleep, too. The next day was bound to be a busy one and would start early.

Like his sons, though, he felt too wired to sleep. He had a feeling that if he tried to climb into bed now, he would only toss and turn.

His thoughts were in tumult and he still didn't know what to do about Ella and his feelings for her. Meantime, he decided to grab a drink of water and maybe one of those cookies a neighbor brought over earlier, then head into his ranch office to catch up on paperwork.

He was heading through the great room toward the kitchen when he spotted someone sitting in the darkness, just out of reach of the glow emanating from the Christmas tree and the dying embers of the fire burning in the hearth.

His gaze sharpened when he realized it was Ella. He had almost missed her.

Had she fallen asleep out here? Her day had been more strenuous than anyone's, between orchestrating that amazing performance earlier, then rescuing her father and the boys.

What was she doing out here? Was she all right?"

Her face was in shadows but he thought he glimpsed the streak of tears on her cheeks, reflecting the colored Christmas lights. As he moved closer, she must have sensed his presence. She looked up then quickly away but not before he was able to confirm his suspicion.

She was crying.

"Oh. You startled me." She swiped her cheeks and kept her face averted, obviously trying to hide them from him. He was torn between wanting to respect her obvious desire for privacy and being unable to bear the thought of her hurting.

Finally he sat beside her on the sofa. "El. What is it? What's wrong?"

"Nothing. I'm fine. It's just…been a long day."

"You need to be in bed. Why are you sitting out here by yourself?" *Crying*, he added silently.

She sighed. "Do you ever have those times when it feels like your mind is spinning so fast you can't keep up with it?"

"All the time. If it's not the ranch I'm worrying about, it's the boys or Jax or Uncle Dan."

Or her father, he wanted to add, but didn't want to upset her more. Most likely, that conversation with Curt was the reason for these tears.

He couldn't bear them, especially when he had the ability to dry them right here, right now.

"Ella, I don't—"

"Beck, I have to—"

They started to speak at the same time, then both faltered. After an awkward little moment, she gestured to him. "It's your house. You first."

He wanted to argue, but couldn't see any point. Better to tell her what was on his mind as quickly as he could.

"You should know, I've decided to tell your father I won't be purchasing the Baker's Dozen."

Her eyes looked huge in the multicolored light from the tree as she stared at him. "You *what*?"

"It was early days in the discussions between us. Whatever you heard today when he and I were talking, nothing has been signed. There's no breach of contract or anything. So I'm officially backing out. I won't buy it."

"But... I don't understand. I thought you needed the watering rights and the pasture land to expand your operations."

"I do. I will, someday, but I'll figure something out when the need is more critical."

"Why?"

He needed to expand the Broken Arrow, but he couldn't do it in good conscience by buying her father's land out from under her.

"You should be running your family's ranch, Ella."

She made a disbelieving sound and though he feared it might be a mistake, he reached for her hand. "You are perfectly capable. You've got exactly all the traits it takes to make a go of things out here. You're tough, spunky and bold. You're willing to learn and you're not afraid to ask for help when you need it. You've shown all those things, again and again. Your father knows it, too—it's just taking him longer than it should to admit it."

Her fingers trembled in his as if she were still cold, and he wanted to wrap her in his arms until her shivering ceased.

"I don't understand," she finally said.

"What's to understand? I'm withdrawing my tentative agreement to purchase the property. It's yours. Curt can show you how to run it, just like he helped me figure things out here after my father died. If he doesn't, *I* will show you the ropes and find other local ranchers to do the same. Wade Dalton. Chase and Faith Brannon. Justin Hartford. You have good neighbors who will want nothing more than to see you succeed."

In the light of the Christmas tree, he saw something bright and joyful flash across her expression—hope and an eagerness to prove herself. For one beautiful instant, she looked exactly what she was, strong and capable of anything.

That's why he was doubly shocked after a moment when she pulled her hand away from his and rose as if to put space between them.

"I don't think I can do that."

"Why not? There's not a single doubt in my mind you'll make a go of it, with or without your father's help."

She gave him one quick look, her lips pressed together and her chin quivering, then she shook her head.

"I...can't. I'm not staying here. I've made up my mind to return to Boston right after Christmas."

Shock tangled his thoughts and his words. Had he misheard her? Not an hour ago, she had pleaded with her father to give her a chance at running the Baker's Dozen and now she was turning tail and taking off? What in Hades had happened?

"Why would you do that? I just told you that I won't be making an offer on the ranch—and I'll make sure nobody else around here does, either. There won't be much I can do about things if Curt decides to sell to an outsider, but I don't think that's what your dad wants, anyway."

As he watched, another tear dripped down her cheek, iridescent in the Christmas tree lights.

"I can't do it," she whispered.

"Are you kidding me? You can do any damn thing you put your mind to. You tamed the twin terrors, didn't you?"

He meant his words as a joke. It seemed to fall flat and she hitched in a breath that sounded more like a sob.

"That's why I...can't stay. Because of the boys and—and you."

Another tear dripped. He couldn't bear this. What had he done to offend her so grievously that she couldn't even stand to stay in the same county with him? He would fix it, whatever it was.

He rose. "I'm sorry. You're going to have to forgive me for being a big, dumb cowboy, but I don't know what the heck you're talking about."

She didn't answer him for several moments, the only sound the relentless wind and the click of branches from the red-twigged dogwoods outside the window.

Finally she swallowed. "I have come to...care deeply for—

for Trevor and Colter. I don't see how I could continue to live here, always stuck on the edges of your, er, *their* lives. Just the nice neighbor who once taught them how to sing a song for their dad. I don't want that. I—I want more."

He couldn't catch his breath, suddenly. She was talking about the boys, right? Or did she mean something else? "Ella."

She didn't meet his gaze. "I'm sorry. Forget I said anything. I shouldn't have. It's late and I'm tired and not thinking straight. I'll go to bed now."

She tried to slip past him but he couldn't let her. Not yet. He blocked her path, never more grateful for his size than he was in that moment. "Stop. What are you saying?"

"It doesn't matter."

He tipped up her chin, until she had no choice but to look at him, his strong, amazing Ella. "I think it matters more than anything else in my world right now."

Her mouth wobbled a little again, then tightened with belligerence. "Do you want me to completely humiliate myself? Why not? I've already made a complete fool of myself. Fine. I'll say it. I'm in love with you. Are you happy now?"

She hadn't finished the words before he kissed her fiercely, pouring out all the emotions he had been fighting for weeks. Months, he realized. He had fallen for her when she first came back to Pine Gulch to stay with her father, he just hadn't been able to admit it to himself until now.

He kissed her until they were both breathing hard and the room was beginning to spin and he wasn't sure he would ever be able to bring himself to move from this spot.

"Does that answer your question?" he finally asked against her mouth. Joy continued to pulse through him, bright and shining and as beautiful as any Christmas tree. "*Happy* doesn't begin to cover how I feel to know the woman I love with all my heart shares a little of my feelings."

She stared at him, shock warring with the arousal in her eyes. "You love me? That's impossible."

"Need another demonstration?" He kissed her again, this time with a sweet, aching tenderness he felt from the depths of his soul. He lowered them to the sofa and held her on his lap, teasing and touching and tasting.

"I guess that wasn't really an answer, was it?" he murmured, after another long moment. "Kisses are wonderful, don't get me wrong, but any guy who's attracted to you—which would have to be every sane guy with a pulse—could give you those."

She swallowed, her hands tangled in his hair and her lips swollen from his mouth. "That's right." Her voice sounded thready, low, and made him ache all over again. "You'll have to be more persuasive than that if you expect me to believe you want me and not my father's ranch."

He tightened his arms around her, loving this playful side of her. As he gazed at her eyes reflecting the lights of the Christmas tree, he thought that he had never loved the holidays so very much as he did right now, with his own Christmas miracle in his arms.

"I stand by what I said before. I don't want the Baker's Dozen, and I'll be sure to tell Curt that as soon as I get the chance. We can go wake him up, if you want."

"You really think I would be stupid enough to want to wake my father up right now? I'm a little busy here," she said, pressing her mouth to his jawline in a way that made his breath catch and everything inside him want to slide over her to show her just what her teasing did to him.

He gazed into her eyes, hoping she could see he meant his words. "Curt will come to his senses. I'll make sure of it. As far as I'm concerned, that ranch is yours, to do with as you see fit. If you want to sell all the cattle and start raising alpacas, that's your business."

Beck decided he wouldn't mind spending the rest of his life trying to make that soft, sweet smile appear again.

"I do love alpacas," she murmured. "They're so much cuter

than cattle—and think of all the adorable Christmas sweaters I could make out of their wool."

"I can picture it now. And to show you what a great guy I am, I would even let you take those sweaters off in my bedroom, if you wanted."

She laughed. "Wow. That's very generous of you."

This was what he had missed—what he had never really known. This laughter and tenderness, this binding of his heart to hers. It seemed perfect and easy and absolutely right.

He kissed her once more, wishing they could stay here all night wrapped together by the fire and the Christmas tree while the storm raged outside.

"I meant what I said earlier," she said a long time later. "I love you and I love the boys. I wasn't expecting it, but you McKinley men are pretty hard to resist."

"We do our best," he drawled.

His sons would be over the moon to know their not-so-subtle matchmaking had paid off. He hoped that didn't set a dangerous precedent. Maybe he should warn Jax he had better watch out, or they might turn their attention to him next.

On second thought, Jax was a big boy. He could fend for himself.

He gazed down at her, unable to believe she was really here in his arms. He would never need another Christmas gift as long as he lived. This moment, this night, this woman were beyond his wildest dreams.

He turned serious, compelled to tell her a small portion of what was in his heart. "I love you, Ella. I hope you know that. I wasn't expecting it, either, but nothing has ever felt so right. I love your strength and your courage. I love how sweet you are with my sons. I love that you sacrificed to come back to Pine Gulch and take care of your father, though he's given you nothing but grief in return."

He kissed her again, his heart overflowing with joy and wonder and gratitude. "Most of all, I love that whenever you're near me, I could swear I hear music."

She gave that slow, tender smile he was quickly coming to crave, wrapped her arms around him and let the song carry both of them away.

Epilogue

"I don't know how you did it, but somehow that show was even bigger and better than last year's," Ella's father said as Beck drove away from The Christmas Ranch after her third successful Christmas show in a row.

"You'd better dial it back a bit, babe," her husband said, with that teasing smile she adored. "Everybody's got such high expectations now, you're going to find yourself having to throw a Broadway-quality production in order to meet them."

"I still think last year's show was better," Trevor said from the back seat. "This year Colt and me didn't even get to sing a duet together."

"No, but you played your guitar while all your friends sang 'We Three Kings,'" she answered. "You guys brought down the house, kiddo."

"We were awesome, weren't we?" he said, with that complete lack of humility that always made her smile.

"Hey, Grandpa Curt, what was your favorite part this year?" Colt asked.

Ella knew it always tickled her dad when the boys called him

Grandpa Curt, as they had taken to doing since her and Beck's wedding over the summer.

They still usually called her Ella, but had recently asked if she would mind if they called her Mom once in a while. She still teared up every time they did.

As she listened to the twins chatter away to her father, Ella leaned back in the seat and closed her eyes, a wave of fatigue washing over her. The adrenaline rush of finishing a performance was always exhausting, but this seemed to be hitting her harder than usual.

She knew why. After two weeks of achy breasts, mild nausea in the mornings and this unusual fatigue, she'd taken a drugstore test that morning that confirmed her suspicions.

She still hadn't told Beck yet. She was trying to figure out exactly how. Maybe she would wait until Christmas Eve and tell him during their own private celebrations after everyone was in bed and the house was quiet.

Or maybe she would do it tonight. She didn't know how to contain this joy that bubbled through her.

However she told him, she knew Beck would be as happy as she was about adding to their family.

As he drove them toward home, he reached for her hand and brought it to his mouth. He was a big, tough rancher, but every once in a while he did these sweet, spontaneous gestures that completely swept her off her feet.

"You've had quite a day."

She smiled, eyes still closed. "Quite a year, actually."

"It has been amazing, hasn't it?"

Amazing was an understatement. A year ago, she never would have believed her life could be filled with this much joy.

Somehow they were making it work. Shortly after the New Year, her father had finally come to his senses—persuaded in large part by Beck, she knew—and started giving her more and more responsibility at the Baker's Dozen. As of now, she and Curt were comanaging the ranch. She envisioned a day when she and Beck would merge the two operations, as her father intended, but for now the system worked.

She still taught at the elementary school but had surrendered her middle school choir to another teacher.

She even had a small but growing herd of alpacas. The first breeding pair had been Beck's surprise wedding gift to her and she had added three more since then, plus the new offspring of the first pair. She adored them all and had become obsessed with learning all she could about alpaca husbandry.

"Hey, remember last year, when we had that big storm?" Colter said.

"Yeah, and we slid into the ditch and had to wait while you went for help?" Trevor added.

Her journey through the storm had become something of a family legend. Creampuff had earned crab apples for life because of her heroic rescue. Ella still rode her often, as well as the younger, more energetic mare she and Beck had picked out.

"There's the spot, right there," Curt said.

Though it had been a harrowing experience, Ella always smiled when she passed this spot. It had been such a pivotal moment in her life, she would have liked to put a little commemorative plaque on a nearby tree.

A short time later, they pulled up to the ranch house of the Baker's Dozen.

"Can we go see the cria while we're here?" Colter asked.

Cria was the official word for an alpaca baby and her new one was the most adorable thing in the world.

Her father complained the animals were a waste of space, but she couldn't count the number of times she'd caught him sitting by their paddock, just watching them play.

"Sure. Check their water for me while you're there, okay?"

The boys raced off through the cold night to the barn, where the alpaca sheltered in cold weather.

"Let's get you inside," Beck said to her father.

As he helped her father out of the truck, her heart seemed to sigh inside her chest. Every time she saw him offer this kind of patient, gentle care for her father, she fell in love all over again.

Curt's health issues had been the one gray cloud in what had otherwise been a year overflowing with happiness. He was trying a new medicine, though, and so far it seemed to be slowing the progression of his Parkinson's and even reducing some of his trembling.

She knew it was a temporary improvement, but she would take whatever bright spot she could.

The lights were on in the house, which meant Manny and Alina had made it home before them. The ranch foreman and his wife had moved into the big house shortly after Ella's marriage, along with Alina's older brother, Frank. Between the three of them, they took amazing care of Curt and he seemed to enjoy their company.

At some point, she anticipated that her father would end up moving into the Broken Arrow ranch house with them. He spent much of his time there, anyway, and having him closer would make it easier for her to keep an eye on him. For now, he treasured whatever small portion of independence he still had, and she tried to facilitate that as much as she could.

Now, she saw the Christmas lights were on inside and the Baker's Dozen ranch house was warm and welcoming.

"I'd better go make sure the boys don't try to ruin their good shoes," Beck said after he helped Curt inside.

"I can help you into your room, Dad," she said.

For the next few moments, she was busy easing his swollen feet out of the boots he insisted on wearing and taking off his coat.

"Manny or Frank can help me with the rest," he said.

"All right. I'm glad you came with us, Dad."

"So am I. It really was a great show."

She smiled. "Thanks. I'll be by first thing in the morning to meet with the vet."

Her father tilted his head and gave her a considering look.

"You know you're not going to be able to juggle everything when you have that grandbaby of mine, don't you?"

She stared. "How did you know?"

His eyes widened for just a moment, then his expression shifted to a smirk. "You make a poor poker player, honey. That was just a lucky guess—or maybe wishful thinking on my part—but you just confirmed it."

"Don't say anything to Beck," she pleaded. "I haven't told him yet."

"I won't say a word," he promised, then paused. "You picked a good man, Ella."

She smiled. "You don't have to tell me that, Dad. I'll see you in the morning. And don't forget, we have the McRavens' annual party tomorrow night, remember?"

"You ask me, this town has too many damn parties," her father grumbled, though she knew he enjoyed every one of them.

"Good night. Love you."

When she returned to the living room, Beck and the boys had all come back inside and sat in the glow of the Christmas tree they had all decorated here a few Sundays ago. The twins were telling him a story about one of their friends and he nodded solemnly, his gorgeous, masculine features intense as he listened.

As she watched the three of them, her heart couldn't contain all the joy.

Her life was everything she might have wished for and so much more. She had a husband she adored and two stepsons who filled her world with laughter and Legos and tight hugs. She had music and horses, her father, her friends and now this new little life growing inside her.

This was the season of miracles and she would always be grateful for her own—and it had all started with a song.

* * * * *

A Cold Creek Christmas Story

Dear Reader,

I am sometimes asked what I would like to do if I hadn't become an author. That's a tough question to answer—I really can't imagine doing anything else! But if I did have to pick another vocation at some point in my life, I think I would like to be either a teacher or a librarian.

In *A Cold Creek Christmas Story*, children's librarian Celeste Nichols has the best of both worlds. She's an author and a librarian! In fifty books, I've never written a character who is a writer before and while Celeste is not at all autobiographical, it was still fun to write about the writing journey through my heroine's eyes.

I wish you and your loved ones the merriest of holidays.

All my very best,

RaeAnne

Chapter One

If she didn't have thirty children showing up in the next half hour, Celeste Nichols would have been tempted to climb into her little SUV, pull out of the Pine Gulch library parking lot and just keep on driving.

She shifted the blasted endlessly ringing cell phone to the crook of her shoulder while she sorted through the books scattered across her cubicle in the offices of the library to find what she would be reading for story hour.

"I told you earlier in the week, I'm not ready to make a decision about this yet."

Joan Manning, her and Hope's long-suffering literary agent, gave a low, frustrated sound of disapproval. "We can't hold them off much longer. We've already stalled for two weeks. They want to start production right after the holidays, and they can't do that without signatures from you and Hope."

Celeste gazed down at a copy of Dr. Seuss's perennial holiday favorite, *How the Grinch Stole Christmas*. She had a feeling she was the one being the Grinch here. Hope was completely on board with the extraordinary offer one of the leading animation companies had made for movie rights to their book, *Sparkle and the Magic Snowball.*

Celeste was the one who couldn't quite be comfortable with the idea of someone else taking control of her words, her creation, and turning *Sparkle* into an animated movie, complete with the attendant merchandising and sublicensing. A fast-food chain was already talking about making a toy for its kids' meals, for crying out loud.

The whole journey of the past twelve months seemed like a bizarre, surreal, completely unbelievable dream.

A year ago she had known exactly who she was—an unassuming children's librarian in the small town of Pine Gulch, Idaho, in the western shadow of the Teton Mountain Range.

Now, to her immense shock, she was a celebrated author about to see the release of her second children's book with several more scheduled in the next few years. Along with that had come things she had never imagined when she'd been writing little stories for her niece and nephew—she had a website, a publicist, a literary agent.

Her quiet, safe world seemed to be spinning out of her control, and this movie deal was the prime example.

"A few more days, Celeste," Joan pushed. "You can't keep stalling. You have to make a decision. Hollywood has a short attention span and an even shorter supply of patience. Do you want your story made into a movie or not?"

She liked Joan very much, as brash and abrupt as the woman could be, but everything with her was an emergency and had to be decided *right now.* Pressure pains stabbed with little forks behind her eyes and her shoulders felt as if someone had jammed them in a vice and was cranking down hard.

"I know. I just need to be sure this is the right choice for Sparkle."

"Sparkle is a fictional character. You need to be sure it's the right choice for *you* and for your sister. We've been going over this for weeks. I don't know what else I can say to convince you this is the best deal you're going to get."

"I know that. You've done a great job with the negotiations. I just need…a little more time."

"A few days," Joan said, her voice clipped with frustration. "That's all, then I have to give them some kind of an answer."

"I know. Thank you. I'll get back with you tomorrow or the day after."

"Just remember, most people would see this as a dream come true."

Apparently, she wasn't *most people*. After they said their goodbyes, Celeste set her cell phone back on the desk, again fighting the urge to climb into her SUV and keep on driving.

That was her sister Hope's way, to wander from place to place as they had done in their itinerant childhood. Celeste was different. She liked security, consistency.

Normalcy.

In the past twelve months her life had been anything *but* normal. She had gone from writing only for herself and her niece and nephew to writing for a vast audience she never could have imagined.

It had all started when her sister Hope had come home the previous Christmas for what was supposed to be a brief stay between overseas teaching jobs. Hope had overheard her reading one of her stories to Louisa and Barrett and had put her considerable artistic skills to work illustrating the story to sell in the gift store of their family's holiday-themed attraction, The Christmas Ranch.

The result had been a sweet, charming Christmas story about a brave little reindeer named Sparkle. Neither Hope nor Celeste had ever imagined the book would be touted by a presenter on one of the national morning news program—or that the resulting sales would explode internationally and end up saving the floundering Christmas Ranch *and* the family's cattle operation, the Star N Ranch.

She was beyond gratified that so many people liked her writing and the story—and especially Hope's delightful illustrations—but some part of her wanted to go back to that peaceful time when her biggest decisions revolved around what to read for her weekly story hour at the Pine Gulch Public Library.

With a sigh, she turned back to the job at hand. She was still sorting through the final choices when the head librarian poked her head into the cubicle.

"Looks as if we're going to have a nice crowd." Frankie Vittori, the head librarian, looked positively gleeful. "I hope we have room for everybody."

"Oh, that's terrific!" she exclaimed, mentally shelving her worries about the movie deal for now.

She meant the words. She loved nothing more than introducing children to the wonder and magic to be found inside the pages of a good book.

Books had saved her. During the chaos of her childhood, they had offered solace and safety and *hope* amid fear. She had no idea how she would have survived without friends such as Anne of Green Gables, Bilbo Baggins, Matilda, Harry Potter and Hermione and Ron Weasley.

"I only hope we've got enough of our craft project to go around. It seems as if the crowd increases every month."

Frankie grinned. "That's because everybody in town wants to come hear our local celebrity author read in hopes of catching a sneak peek at the new Sparkle story coming down the pike."

She managed to conceal her instinctive wince. She really didn't like being a celebrity.

On one level, it was immensely gratifying. Who would have ever dreamed that she—quiet, awkward, introverted Celeste Nichols—would be in this position, having people actually *care* what she had to say?

On another, it was terrifying. At some point the naked emperor was always exposed. She feared the day when somebody would finally ask why all the fuss about her simple little tales.

For now, Frankie was simply thrilled to have a crowd at the library for any kind of reason. Celeste's boss and friend vibrated with energy, as she always did, her toe tapping to unheard music and her fingers fidgeting on the edge of the desk. Frankie was as skinny as a flagpole, probably because she never stopped moving.

Her husband, Lou, on the other hand, was the exact opposite—a deep reservoir of calm serenity.

They made the perfect pair and had two adorable kids who fell somewhere in the middle.

"I know it's more work for you," Frankie went on. "But I have to say, it's a brilliant idea to have two story times, one for the younger kids in the morning and one for early and middle readers after school."

Celeste smiled. "If you do say so yourself?"

Frankie beamed. "What can I say? I'm brilliant sometimes."

"That you are." Since Frankie had come to the library from upstate New York two years earlier, patron usage was way up and support had never been higher.

Frankie was bold and impassioned about the need for libraries, especially in the digital age. Celeste was more than a little envious of her overwhelming confidence, which helped the director fight for every penny of funding from the city council and the community in general.

Celeste would never be as outgoing and vivacious as Frankie, even though she was every bit as passionate about her job as the children's librarian. She liked being behind the scenes—except for the weekly story times, her favorite part of the job.

She checked her watch and quickly stood up. "I guess I'd better get out there."

She picked up the box of craft supplies they would use for the activity she had planned and headed for the large meeting room they had found worked best for story times.

"Oh, I almost forgot," Frankie said with a sly grin. "Make sure you check out the major hottie dad out there at ten o'clock."

Despite her amazing husband, Frankie was always locating hot guys, whether at their weekly lunches at one of the restaurants in town or on the few trips they'd taken into Jackson Hole or Idaho Falls. She always said she was only scouting possible dates for Celeste, which made Celeste roll her eyes. Her last date had been months ago.

"Is he anybody I know?"

"*I've* never seen him before. He's either new in town or a tourist. You can't miss him. He's wearing a Patek Philippe watch and a brown leather jacket that probably costs as much as our annual nonfiction budget. He's definitely not your average Cold Creek cowboy with horse pucky on his boots."

Okay, intriguing. She hadn't heard of anybody new moving into the small town, especially not someone who could afford the kind of attire Frankie was talking about. Sometimes well-to-do people bought second or third homes in the area, looking for a mountain getaway. They built beautiful homes in lovely alpine settings and then proceeded to visit them once or twice a year.

"I'll be sure to check him out while I'm trying to keep the kids entertained."

Frankie was right about one thing—the place was packed. Probably thirty children ranging in age from about six to eleven sat on the floor while roughly that same number of parents sat in chairs around the room.

For just an instant she felt a burst of stage fright at the idea of all those people staring at her. She quickly pushed it down. Normally she didn't like being in front of a crowd, but this was her job and she loved it. How could she be nervous about reading stories to children? She would just pretend their parents weren't there, like she usually did.

When she walked in, she was heartened by the spontaneous round of applause and the anticipation humming in the air.

She spotted a few people she recognized, friends and neighbors. Joey Santiago, nephew to her brother-in-law Rafe, sat beside his father, waving wildly at her.

She grinned and waved back at him. She would have thought Rafe was the hot dad—all that former navy SEAL mojo he had going on—but Frankie knew him well and he wasn't wearing a leather jacket or an expensive watch anyway.

She loved Rafe dearly, for many reasons—most important because he adored her sister Hope—but also because she wasn't sure she would be standing here, ready to entertain a group of thirty children with the magic of literature if not for his role in their lives so many years ago.

She saw a few other hot dads in the crowd—Justin Hartford, who used to be a well-known movie star but who seemed to fit in better now that he had been a rancher in Cold Creek Canyon for years. Ben Caldwell, the local veterinarian, was definitely hot. Then there was the fire chief, Taft Bowman, and his stepchildren. Taft always looked as though he could be the December cover model on a calendar of yummy firefighters.

All of them were locals of long-standing, though, and Frankie knew them well. They couldn't be the man she was talking about.

Ah, well. She would try to figure out the mystery later, maybe while the children were making the snowman ornaments she had planned for them.

"Thank you so much for coming, everybody. We're going to start off with one of my favorite Christmas stories."

"Is it *Sparkle and the Magic Snowball*?" Alex Bowman, Taft's stepson, asked hopefully.

She blushed a little as everyone laughed. "Not today. Today we're focusing on stories about Christmas, snow and snowmen."

Ben's son raised his hand. "Is Sparkle going to be here today, Ms. Nichols?"

Was that why so many people had turned out? Were they all hoping she'd brought along the *actual* Sparkle, who was the celebrity in residence at The Christmas Ranch?

Last year, Hope had talked her into having their family's beloved reindeer—and the inspiration for her eponymously named series of stories—make a quick appearance in the parking lot of the library.

"I'm afraid not. He's pretty busy at The Christmas Ranch right now."

She tried to ignore the small sounds of disappointment from the children and a few of their parents. "I've got tons of other things in store for you, though. To start out, here's one of everyone's favorite holiday stories, *How the Grinch Stole Christmas.*"

She started reading and, as usual, it only took a few pages before a hush fell over the room. The children were completely enthralled—not by her, she was only the vehicle, but by the power of story.

She became lost, too, savoring every word. When she neared the climax, she looked up for dramatic effect and found the children all watching her with eager expressions, ready for more. Her gaze lifted to the parents and she spotted someone she hadn't seen before, a man sitting on the back row of parents with a young girl beside him.

He had brown hair shot through with lighter streaks, a firm jaw and deep blue eyes.

This had to be the hot dad Frankie had meant.

Her heart began to pound fiercely, so loud in her ears she wondered if the children could hear it over the microphone clipped to her collar.

She knew this man, though she hadn't seen him for years.

Flynn Delaney.

She would recognize him *anywhere*. After all, he had been the subject of her daydreams all through her adolescence.

She hadn't heard he was back in Pine Gulch. Why was he here? Was he staying at his grandmother's house just down the road from the Star N? It made sense. His grandmother, Charlotte, had died several months earlier and her house had been empty ever since.

She suddenly remembered everything else that had happened

to this man in the past few months and her gaze shifted to the young girl beside him, blonde and ethereal like a Christmas angel herself.

Celeste's heart seemed to melt.

This must be her. His daughter. Oh, the poor, poor dear.

The girl was gazing back at Celeste with her eyes wide and her hands clasped together at her chest as if she couldn't wait another instant to hear the rest of the story.

Everyone was gazing at her with expectation, and Celeste realized she had stopped in the middle of the story to stare at Flynn and his daughter.

Appalled at herself, she felt heat soak her cheeks. She cleared her throat and forced her attention back to the story, reading the last few pages with rather more heartiness than she had started with.

This was her job, she reminded herself as she closed the book, helping children discover all the delights to be found in good stories.

She wasn't here to ogle Flynn Delaney, for heaven's sake, even when there was plenty about him any woman would consider ogle-worthy.

Flynn didn't think he had ever felt quite so conspicuously out of place—and that included the times he had walked the red carpet with Elise at some Hollywood premiere or other, when he had invariably wanted to fade into the background.

They all seemed to know each other and he felt like the odd man out. Was everybody staring? He didn't want to think so, but he seemed to feel each curious sidelong glance as the residents of Pine Gulch tried to figure out who he was.

At least one person knew. He was pretty sure he hadn't imagined that flicker of recognition in Celeste Nichols's eyes when she'd spotted him. It surprised him, he had to admit. They had only met a few times, all those years ago.

He only remembered her because she had crashed her bike in front of his grandmother's house during one of his visits. Charlotte hadn't been home, so Flynn had been left to tend her scrapes and bruises and help her get back to the Star N up the road.

Things like that stuck in a guy's memory bank. Otherwise he probably never would have made the connection between the author of his daughter's favorite book, *Sparkle and the Magic Snowball*, and the shy girl with long hair and glasses he had once known in another lifetime.

He wouldn't be here at the library if not for Celeste, actually. He had so much work to do clearing out his grandmother's house and really didn't have time to listen to Dr. Seuss, as great as the story might be, but what other choice did he have? Since leaving the hospital, Olivia had been a pale, frightened shadow of the girl she used to be. Once she had faced the world head-on, daring and curious and funny. Now she was afraid of so many things. Loud noises. Strangers. Crowds.

From the moment she'd found out that the author of her favorite book lived here in Pine Gulch where they were staying for a few weeks—and was the children's librarian, who also hosted a weekly story hour—Olivia had been obsessed with coming. She had written the date of the next event on the calendar and had talked of nothing else.

She was finally going to meet the Sparkle lady, and she couldn't have been more excited about it if Celeste Nichols had been Mrs. Santa Claus in the flesh.

For the first time in weeks she showed enthusiasm for something, and he had jumped at the chance to nurture that.

He glanced down at his daughter. She hadn't shifted her gaze away from Celeste, watching the librarian with clear hero worship on her features. She seemed utterly enchanted by the librarian.

The woman was lovely, he would give her that much, though

in a quiet, understated way. She had big green eyes behind her glasses and glossy dark hair that fell in waves around a heart-shaped face.

She was probably about four years younger than his own thirty-two. That didn't seem like much now, but when she had crashed her bike, she had seemed like a little kid, thirteen or so to his seventeen.

As he listened to her read now, he remembered that time, wondering why it seemed so clear to him, especially with everything that had happened to him since.

He'd been out mowing the lawn when she'd fallen and had seen her go down out of the corner of his gaze. Flynn had hurried to help her and found her valiantly trying not to cry even though she had a wide gash in her knee that would definitely need stitches and pebbles imbedded in her palm.

He had helped her into his grandmother's house and called her aunt Mary. While they'd waited for help, he had found first-aid supplies—bandages, ointment, cleansing wipes—and told her lousy jokes to distract her from the pain.

After Mary had taken her to the ER for stitches in her knee and he had finished mowing for his grandmother, he had gone to work fixing her banged-up bike with skills he had picked up from his mother's chauffeur.

Later that day, he had dropped off the bike at the Star N, and she had been almost speechless with gratitude. Or maybe she just had been shy with older guys; he didn't know.

He had stayed with his grandmother for just a few more weeks that summer, but whenever he had seen Celeste in town at the grocery store or the library, she had always blushed fiercely and offered him a shy but sweet smile.

Now he found himself watching her intently, hoping for a sight of that same sweet smile, but she seemed to be focusing with laser-like intensity on the books in front of her.

She read several more holiday stories to the children, then

led them all to one side of the large room, where tables had been set up.

"I need all the children to take a seat," she said in a prim voice he found incongruously sexy. "We're going to make snowman ornaments for you to hang on your tree. When you're finished, they'll look like this."

She held up a stuffed white sock with buttons glued on to it for eyes and a mouth, and a piece of felt tied around the neck for a scarf.

"Oh," Olivia breathed. "That's so cute! Can I make one, Dad?"

Again, how could he refuse? "Sure, if there are enough to go around."

She limped to a seat and he propped up the wall along with a few other parents so the children each could have a spot at a table. Celeste and another woman with a library name badge passed out supplies and began issuing instructions.

Olivia looked a little helpless at first and then set to work. She seemed to forget for the moment that she rarely used her left hand. Right now she was holding the sock with that hand while she shoved in pillow fluff stuffing with the other.

While the children were busy crafting, Celeste made her way around the tables, talking softly to each one of them.

Finally she came to them.

"Nice job," she said to his daughter. Ah, there it was. She gave Olivia that sweet, unguarded smile that seemed to bloom across her face like the first violets of springtime.

That smile turned her from a lovely if average-looking woman into a breathtaking creature with luminous skin and vivid green eyes.

He couldn't seem to stop staring at her, though he told himself he was being ridiculous.

"You're the Sparkle lady, aren't you?" Olivia breathed.

Color rose instantly in her cheeks and she gave a surprised laugh. "I suppose that's one way to put it."

"I love that story. It's my favorite book *ever*."

"I'm so happy to hear that." She smiled again, though he thought she looked a little uncomfortable. "Sparkle is pretty close to my heart, too."

"My dad bought a brand-new copy for me when I was in the hospital, even though I had one at home."

She said the words in a matter-of-fact tone as if the stay had been nothing more than a minor inconvenience. He knew better. She had spent two weeks clinging to life in intensive care after an infection had ravaged her system, where he had measured his life by each breath the machines took for her.

Most of the time he did a pretty good job of containing his impotent fury at the senseless violence that had touched his baby girl, but every once in a while the rage swept over him like a brush fire on dry tinder. He let out a breath as he felt a muscle flex in his jaw.

"Is that right?" Celeste said with a quick look at him.

"It's my very favorite book," Olivia said again, just in case Celeste didn't hear. "Whenever I had to do something I didn't want to, like have my blood tested or go to physical therapy, I would look at the picture of Sparkle on the last page with all his friends and it would make me feel better."

At Olivia's words, Celeste's big eyes filled with tears and she rocked back on her heels a little. "Oh. That's...lovely. Thank you so much for letting me know. I can't tell you how much that means to me."

"You're welcome," Olivia said with a solemn smile. "My favorite part is when Sparkle helps the animals with their Christmas celebration. The hedgehog is my favorite."

"He's cute, isn't he?"

The two of them gazed at each other in perfect charity for a moment longer before a boy with blond hair and a prominent widow's peak tried to draw Celeste's attention.

"Ms. Nichols. Hey, Ms. Nichols. How do we glue on the hat?"

"I'll show you. Just a minute." She turned back to Olivia. "It was very nice to meet you. You're doing a great job with your snowman. Thanks for letting me know you enjoy the book."

"You're welcome."

When she left, Olivia turned back to her project with renewed effort. She was busy gluing on the button eyes when the woman beside Flynn finally spoke to him.

"You're new in town. I don't think we've met." She was blonde and pretty in a classic sort of way, with a baby on her hip. "I'm Caroline Dalton. This is my daughter, Lindy. Over there is my son, Cole."

He knew the Daltons. They owned much of the upper portion of Cold Creek Canyon. Which brother was she married to?

"Hello. I'm Flynn Delaney, and this is my daughter, Olivia. We're not really new in town. That is, we're not staying anyway. We're here just for a few weeks, and then we're going back to California."

"I hope you feel welcome here. This is a lovely place to spend the holidays."

"I'm sure it is, but we're not really tourists, either. I'm cleaning out my grandmother's home so I can put it up for sale."

He could have hired someone to come and clean out the house. There were companies that handled exactly that sort of thing, but as he and Olivia were Charlotte's only surviving descendants, he'd felt obligated to go through the house himself.

"Delaney. Oh, Charlotte! She must have been your grandmother."

"That's right."

Her features turned soft and a little sad. "Oh, everyone adored your grandmother. What a firecracker she was! Pine Gulch just doesn't feel the same without her."

His *life* didn't feel the same, either. He hadn't seen her often the past few years, just quick semiannual visits, but she had been a steady source of affection and warmth in his chaotic life.

He had barely had the chance to grieve her passing. That bothered him more than anything else. He hadn't even been able to attend the memorial service members of her church congregation had held for her here. He had been too busy in the ICU, praying for his daughter's life.

"I miss her, too," he said quietly.

She looked at him with kindness and warmth. "I'm sure you do. She was an amazing person and I feel blessed to have known her. If you need help sorting through things, please let me know. I'm sure we could find people to give you a hand."

With only a little more than a week to go before Christmas? He doubted that. People were probably too busy to help.

He didn't bother to express his cynicism to Caroline Dalton. "Thanks," he said instead.

"Despite your difficult task, I hope you're able to find a little holiday spirit while you're here."

Yeah, he wasn't a huge Christmas fan for a whole slew of reasons, but he saw no reason to share that with a woman he'd just met.

"Daddy, I can't tie the scarf. Can you help me?" Olivia asked.

She *could* use her left arm and hand. He'd seen her do it at therapy or when she lost herself in an activity, but most of the time she let it hang down uselessly. He didn't know how to force her into using it.

"Try again," he said.

"I can't. It's too hard," she answered plaintively. He sighed, not wanting to push her unnecessarily and ruin her tentative enjoyment of the afternoon.

He leaned down to help her tie the felt scarf just as Celeste made her way back around the table to them.

"I love that snowman!" she exclaimed with a smile. "He looks very friendly."

Olivia's answering smile seemed spontaneous and genuine. Right then Flynn wanted to hug Celeste Nichols on the spot, even though he hadn't talked to her for nearly two decades.

His little girl hadn't had much to smile about over the past few months. He had to hope this was a turning point, a real chance for her to return to his sweet and happy daughter.

At this point, he was willing to bring Olivia to the library every single day if Celeste could help his daughter begin to heal her battered heart.

Chapter Two

She was late.

By the time she helped the last little boy finish his snowman, ushered them all out of the meeting room and then cleaned up the mess of leftover pillow stuffing and fleece remnants, it was forty minutes past the time she had told her sisters to expect her.

They would understand, she was sure. Hope might tease her a little, but Faith probably wouldn't say anything. Their eldest sister saved her energy for the important things like running the cattle ranch and taking care of her children.

She stopped first at the foreman's little cottage, just down the driveway from the main house. It felt strange to be living on her own again after the past year of being back in her own bedroom there. She had moved back after her brother-in-law Travis died the previous summer so she could help Faith—and Aunt Mary, of course—with the children and the housekeeping.

Hope had lived briefly in the foreman's house until she and Rafe married this fall. After she'd moved into the house they purchased together, Faith and Mary had taken Celeste aside and informed her firmly that she needed her own space to create. She was a bestselling author now. While Faith loved and appreciated her dearly, she didn't want Celeste to think she had to live at the ranch house for the rest of her life.

Rather reluctantly, she had moved to the foreman's cottage, a nice compromise. She did like her own space and the quiet she found necessary to write, but she was close enough to pop into the ranch house several times a day.

As she walked inside, her little Yorkie, Linus, rolled over with glee at the sight of her.

She had to smile, despite her exhaustion from a long day, the lingering stress from the phone call with Joan and the complete shock of seeing Flynn Delaney once more.

"How was your day?" she asked the little dog, taking just a moment to sink onto the sofa and give him a little love. "Mine was *crazy*. Thanks for asking. The weirdest I've had in a long time—and that's saying something, since the entire past year has been surreal."

She hugged him for a moment. As she might have predicted, a sleek black cat peeked her head around the corner to see what all the fuss was about.

Lucy, who had been with her since college, strutted in with a haughty air that only lasted long enough for her to leap onto the sofa and bat her head against Celeste's arm for a little of the same attention.

The two pets were the best of friends, which helped her feel less guilty about leaving them alone during the day. They seemed to have no problem keeping each other company most of the time, but that didn't stop them from exhibiting classic signs of sibling rivalry at random moments.

She felt her tension trickle away as she sat in her quiet living room with her creatures while the Christmas tree lights that came on automatically gleamed in the gathering darkness. Why couldn't she stay here all evening? There were worse ways to spend a December night.

Linus yipped a little, something he didn't do often, but it reminded her of why she had stopped at the house.

"I know. I'm late. I just have to grab Aunt Mary's present. Give me a second."

She found the gift in her bedroom closet, the door firmly shut to keep Lucy from pulling apart the tissue paper inside the gift bag.

"Okay. I'm ready. Let's go."

Linus's tail wagged with excitement, but Lucy curled up on the sofa, making abundantly clear her intent to stay put and not venture out into the cold night.

"Fine. Be that way," she said, opening the door for the dog. The two of them made their way through lightly falling snow to the ranch house, a sprawling log structure with a steep roof and three gables along the front. Linus scampered ahead of her to the front door. When she opened it, the delicious scents of home greeted her—roast beef, potatoes and what smelled very much like cinnamon apple pie.

As she expected, her entire family was there, all the people she loved best in the world. Aunt Mary, the guest of honor, was busy at the stove stirring something that smelled like her heavenly brown gravy. She stepped aside to let Faith pull a pan of rolls out of the oven as Hope helped the children set the table, where her husband, Rafe, sat talking with their neighbor Chase Brannon.

The children spotted Linus first. They all adored each other—in fact, the children helped her out by letting him out when they got home from school and playing with him for a little bit.

"There you are," Faith exclaimed. "I was beginning to worry."

"Sorry. I sent you a text."

Faith made a face. "My phone ran out of juice sometime this afternoon, but I didn't realize it until just now. Is everything okay?"

Not really, though she wasn't sure what bothered her more—

the movie decision she would have to make in the next few days or the reappearance of Flynn Delaney in her world. She couldn't seem to shake the weird feeling that her safe, comfortable world was about to change.

"Fine," she said evasively. "I hope you didn't hold dinner for me."

"Not really. I was tied up going over some ranch accounts with Chase this afternoon, and we lost track of time."

"Fine. Blame me. I can take it," Chase said, overhearing.

"We always do," Hope said with a teasing grin.

Chase had been invaluable to their family since Faith's husband died, and Celeste was deeply grateful to him for all his help during the subsequent dark and difficult months.

"I'm happy to blame you, as long as that means I wasn't the cause of any delay in Aunt Mary's birthday celebration," Celeste said with a smile as she headed for her great-aunt.

She kissed the woman's lined cheek as the familiar scent of Mary's favorite White Shoulders perfume washed over her. "Happy birthday, my dear. You are still just as stunning as ever."

Mary's grin lit up her nut-brown eyes. "Ha. Double sevens. That's got to be lucky, right?"

"Absolutely."

"I don't need luck. I've got my family around me, don't I?"

She smiled at them all and Celeste hugged her again, deeply grateful for her great-aunt and her great-uncle Claude, who had opened their hearts to three grieving, traumatized girls and gave them a warm haven and all the love they could need.

"We're the lucky ones," she murmured with another hug before she stepped away.

For all intents and purposes, Mary had been her mother since Celeste turned eleven. She had been a wonderful one. Celeste was all too aware that things could have been much different after their parents died if not for Mary and Claude. She and her sisters probably would have been thrown into the foster care system, likely separated, certainly not nurtured and cared for with such love.

She had a sudden, unexpected wish that their mother could be here, just for a moment, to see how her daughters had turned out—to meet her grandchildren, to see Hope so happily settled with Rafe, to see the completely unexpected success of their Sparkle book.

December always left her a little maudlin. She supposed that wasn't unexpected, considering it had been the month that had changed everything, when she, her sisters and their parents had been hostages of a rebel group in Colombia. Her father had been killed in the rescue effort by a team of US Navy SEALs that had included Rafe Santiago, who was now her brother-in-law.

She wouldn't think about that now. This was a time of celebration, a time to focus on the joy of being with her family, not the past.

She grabbed a black olive out of a bowl on the counter and popped it in her mouth as she carried the bowl to the table.

"I talked to Joan this afternoon," she told Hope.

"I know. She called me, too. I reminded her that any decision about making a movie had to be made jointly between us, and each of us had veto power. Don't worry, CeCe. I told her firmly that I wouldn't pressure you. You created the Sparkle character. He belongs to you."

That wasn't completely true and both of them knew it. She might have written the words, but it was Hope's illustrations that had brought him to life.

"I don't know what to do," she admitted as Faith and Mary joined them at the table carrying bowls and trays of food.

"Your problem has always been that you analyze everything to death," Mary pointed out. "You know someone is going to make a Sparkle movie at some point. It's as inevitable as Christmas coming every year. People love the story and the characters too much. If you like this production company and think they'll do a good job with it based on their reputation, I don't know why you're dragging your feet."

Mary was right, she realized. She was overthinking, probably because she was so concerned with making the right decision.

She hated being afraid all the time. She knew it was a by-product of the trauma she and her sisters had endured at a young age, but neither Hope nor Faith seemed as impacted as she had been.

Hope seemed absolutely fearless, spending years wandering around underdeveloped countries with the Peace Corps, and then on her own teaching English. Faith had plowed all her energy and attention into her family—her marriage, her children, the ranch.

Celeste's life had become her job at the library and the stories she created.

In some ways, she supposed she was still a hostage of Juan Pablo and his crazy group of militants, afraid to take a move and embrace her life.

"Everything's ready and I'm starving," Mary said cheerfully. "What are we waiting for? Let's eat."

Dinner was noisy and chaotic, with several different conversations going at once.

"How did story time go?" Faith asked when there was a lull in the conversation.

She instantly remembered the shock of looking up from Dr. Seuss to see Flynn and his daughter.

"Good." She paused. "Charlotte Delaney's grandson, Flynn, and his daughter were there. I guess he's in town to clean out Charlotte's house."

"Flynn Delaney." Hope made a sound low in her throat. "I used to love it whenever he came to stay with Charlotte. Remember how he used to mow the lawn with his shirt off?"

Celeste dropped her fork with a loud clatter, earning her a curious look from Hope.

"Really?" Rafe said, eyebrow raised. "So all this time I should have been taking my shirt off to mow the lawn?"

Hope grinned at him. "You don't *need* to take your shirt off. You're gorgeous enough even when you're wearing a parka. Anyway, I was a teenage girl. Now that I'm older and wiser I prefer to use my imagination."

He shook his head with an amused look, but Celeste was certain his ears turned a little red.

"You said Flynn came into the library with his daughter," Faith said, her voice filled with compassion. "That poor girl. How is she?"

Considering Flynn's connection to Charlotte, whom they all had loved, everyone in Pine Gulch had followed the news reports. Celeste thought of Olivia's big, haunted eyes, the sad, nervous air about her.

"Hard to say. She limped a little and didn't use her left arm while we were doing the craft project, but other than that she seemed okay."

"Who is Flynn Delaney and what happened to his daughter?" Rafe asked.

"It was all over the news three or four months ago," Chase said. "Around the time Charlotte died, actually."

"You remember," Hope insisted. "We talked about it. He was married to Elise Chandler."

Understanding spread over Rafe's handsome features. "Elise Chandler. The actress." He paused. "Oh. That poor kid."

"Right?" Hope frowned. "What a tragedy. I saw on some tabloid in the supermarket that Flynn never left her side through the whole recovery."

Somehow that didn't seem so surprising, especially considering his devotion to his daughter during story time.

"What happened to her?" Louisa asked. At eleven, she was intensely interested in the world around her.

Her mother was the one who answered. "Elise Chandler was a famous actress," Faith said. "She was in that superhero movie you loved so much and a bunch of other films. Anyway, she was involved with someone who turned out to be a pretty messed-up guy. A few months ago after a big fight, he shot Elise and her daughter before shooting and killing himself. Even though she was injured, Olivia managed to crawl to her mother's phone and call 911."

Celeste had heard that 911 call, which had been made public shortly after the shooting, and the sound of that weak, panic-stricken voice calling for help had broken her heart.

"She seems to be doing well now. She didn't smile much, but she did tell me she loves the Sparkle book and that her dad used to read it to her over and over again in the hospital."

"Oh, how lovely!" Hope exclaimed. "You should take her one of the original Sparkle toys I sewed. I've still got a few left."

"That's a lovely idea," Mary exclaimed. "We definitely should do something for that poor, poor girl. It would have broken Charlotte's heart if she'd still been alive to see Flynn's little girl have to go through such a thing."

"You *have* to take it over there," Hope insisted. "And how about a signed copy of the book and the new one that hasn't come out yet?"

Her heart pounded at just the *idea* of seeing the man again. She couldn't imagine knocking on his door out of the blue. "Why don't *you* take it over? You're the illustrator! And you made the stuffed Sparkle, too."

"I don't even know him or his daughter."

"As if that's ever stopped you before," she muttered.

"It would be a really nice thing to do," Faith said.

"I baked an extra pie," Aunt Mary said. "Why don't you take that, too?"

All day long people had been pushing her to do things she didn't want to. She thought longingly of jumping in her SUV again and taking off somewhere, maybe Southern California where she could find a little sunshine. As tempting as the idea might be sometimes, she knew she couldn't just leave her family. She loved them to bits, even when they did pressure her.

She wanted to tell them all no, but then she thought of Olivia and her sad eyes. This was a small expenditure of effort on her part and would probably thrill the girl. "That's a very good idea," she finally said. "I'll go after dinner. Linus can probably use the walk."

"Perfect." Hope beamed at her as if she had just won the Newbery Medal for children's literature. "I'll look for the stuffed Sparkle. I think there's a handful of them left in a box in my old room."

What would Flynn think when she showed up at his house with a stuffed animal and an armful of books? she wondered as she chewed potatoes that suddenly tasted like chalk.

It didn't matter, she told herself. She was doing this for his daughter, a girl who had been through a terrible ordeal—and who reminded her entirely too much of herself.

Chapter Three

"Are you sure you don't want to help? This tinsel isn't going to jump on the tree by itself."

Flynn held a sparkly handful out to his daughter, who sat in the window seat, alternating between watching him and looking out into the darkness at the falling snowflakes.

She shook her head. "I can't," she said in a matter-of-fact tone. "My arm hurts too much."

He tried to conceal his frustrated sigh behind a cough. The physical therapist he had been taking her to since her injury had given him homework during this break while they were in Idaho. His assignment was to find creative activities that would force her to use her arm more.

He had tried a wide variety of things, like having Olivia push the grocery cart and help him pick out items in the store, and asking her help in the kitchen with slicing vegetables. The inconsistency of it made him crazy. Sometimes she was fine; other times she refused to use her arm at all.

After their trip to the library, he'd realized his grandmother's house was severely lacking in holiday cheer. She had made a snowman ornament and they had nowhere to hang it.

Any hope he might have harbored that she would show a little enthusiasm for the idea of decking their temporary halls was quickly dashed. She showed the same listless apathy toward Christmas decorations as she had for just about everything else except Celeste Nichols and her little reindeer story.

Other than hanging her own snowman ornament, she wasn't interested in helping him hang anything else on the small artificial tree he had unearthed in the basement. As a result, he had done most of the work while she sat and watched, not budging from her claim of being in too much pain.

He knew using her arm caused discomfort. He hadn't yet figured out how to convince an almost-seven-year-old she needed to work through the pain if she ever wanted to regain full mobility in her arm.

"Come on. Just take a handful and help me. It will be fun."

She shook her head and continued staring out at the falling snow.

Since the shooting, these moods had come over her out of nowhere. She would seem to be handling things fine and then a few moments later would become fearful, withdrawn and just want him to leave her alone.

The counselor she had seen regularly assured him it was a natural result of the trauma Olivia had endured. He hated that each step in her recovery—physical and emotional—had become such a struggle for her.

After hanging a few more strands, he finally gave up. What was the point when she didn't seem inclined to help him, especially since he'd never much liked tinsel on trees anyway?

His father hadn't, either, he remembered. He had a stray memory of one of his parents' epic fights over it one year. Diane had loved tinsel, naturally. Anything with glitz had been right down her alley. Her favorite nights of the year had been red carpet events, either for her own movie premieres or those of her friends.

His father, on the other hand, had thought tinsel was stupid and only made a mess.

One night when he was about seven or eight, a few years before they'd finally divorced, his mother had spent hours hanging pink tinsel on their tree over his father's objections, carefully arranging each piece over a bough.

When they'd woken up, the tinsel had been mysteriously gone. As it turned out, Tom had arisen hours before anyone else and had pulled off every last shiny strand.

After a dramatic screaming fight—all on his mother's side— she had stormed out of their Bel Air house and hadn't been back for several days, as he recalled.

Ah, memories.

He pushed away the bitterness of his past and turned back to his daughter. "If you don't want to hang any more tinsel, I guess we're done. Do you want to do the honors and turn out the lights so we can take a look at it?"

She didn't answer him, her gaze suddenly focused on something through the window.

"Someone's coming," Olivia announced, her voice tight. She jumped up from the window seat. "I'm going to my room."

He was never sure which she disliked more: large, unruly crowds or unexpected visitors showing up at the door. Nor was he certain she would ever be able to move past either fear.

With effort he forced his voice to be calm and comforting. "There's no reason to go to your room. Everything is fine. I'm right here. You're okay."

She darted longing little glances down the hall to the relative safety of her bedroom, but to her credit she sat down again in the window seat. When the doorbell rang through the house, Flynn didn't miss her instinctive flinch or the tense set of her shoulders.

He hoped whoever it was had a darn good excuse for showing up out of the blue like this and frightening his little girl half to death.

To his shock, the pretty librarian and author stood on the porch with a bag in her hand and a black-and-brown dog at the end of a leash. In the glow from the porch light he could see her nose and cheeks were pink from the cold, and those long, luscious dark curls were tucked under a beanie. She also wasn't wearing her glasses. Without the thick dark frames, her eyes were a lovely green.

"Hello." She gave him a fleeting, tentative smile that appeared and disappeared as quickly as a little bird hunting for berries on a winter-bare shrub.

"Celeste. Ms. Nichols. Hello."

She gave him another of those brief smiles, then tried to look behind him to where Olivia had approached. At least his daughter now looked more surprised and delighted than fearful.

"And hello, Miss Olivia," the librarian said. "How are you tonight?"

Her voice was soft, calm, with a gentleness he couldn't help but appreciate.

"Hi. I'm fine, thank you," she said shyly. "Is that your dog?"

Celeste smiled as the dog sniffed at Olivia's feet. "This is Linus. He's a Yorkshire terrier and his best friend is a black cat named Lucy."

"Like in *Charlie Brown's Christmas*!" She looked delighted at making the connection.

"Just like that, except Linus and Lucy are brother and sister. My Linus and Lucy are just friends."

Olivia slanted her head to look closer at the little dog. "Will he bite?"

Celeste smiled. "He's a very sweet dog and loves everybody, but especially blonde girls with pretty red sweaters."

Olivia giggled at this, and after another moment during which she gathered her courage, she held out her hand. The little furball licked it three times in quick succession, which earned another giggle from his daughter.

"Hi, Linus," she said in a soft voice. "Hi. I'm Olivia."

The dog wagged his tail but didn't bark, which Flynn had to appreciate given how skittish Olivia had been all evening.

She knelt down and started petting the dog—using her injured left arm, he saw with great surprise.

"He likes me!" Olivia exclaimed after a moment, her features alight with a pleasure and excitement he hadn't seen in a long time.

"Of course he does." Celeste smiled down at her with a soft light in her eyes that touched something deep inside him.

"I'm sorry to just drop in like this, but I couldn't help thinking tonight about what you told me earlier, how the Sparkle book helped you in the hospital."

"It's my favorite book. I still read it all the time."

"I'm so happy to hear that. I told my sister, who drew all the pictures, and she was happy, too. We wanted to give you something."

"Is it for my birthday in three days? I'm going to be seven years old."

"I had no idea it was your birthday in three days!" Celeste exclaimed. "We can certainly consider this an early birthday present. That would be perfect!"

She reached into the bag and pulled out a small stuffed animal.

"That's Sparkle from the book!" Olivia rose to see it more closely.

"That's right. My sister made this while she was drawing the pictures for the first Sparkle book last Christmas. We have just a few of them left over from the original hundred or so she made, and I wondered if you might like one."

Olivia's eyes went huge. "Really? I can *keep* it?"

"If you want to."

"Oh, I do!" Almost warily, she reached for the stuffed animal Celeste held out. When it was in her hands, she hugged it to her chest as if afraid someone would yank it away.

For just a moment she looked like any other young girl, thrilled to be receiving a present. The sheer normalcy made his throat suddenly ache with emotions.

"He's *sooo* cute. I love it! Thank you!"

Olivia threw her arms around Celeste in a quick hug. Flynn wasn't sure if he was more shocked at her use of her injured arm or at the impulsive gesture. Like a puppy that had been kicked one too many times, Olivia shied away from physical touch right now from anyone but him.

Her therapist said it was one more reaction to the trauma she had endured and that eventually she would be able to relax around others and return to the sweet, warm little girl she once had been. He wondered if Dr. Ross ever would have guessed a stuffed reindeer might help speed that process.

Celeste probably had no idea what a rare gift she had just been given as she hugged Olivia back. Still, she looked delighted. "You're very welcome," she said. "You will have to come up to The Christmas Ranch sometime. That's where the real Sparkle lives."

Olivia stepped away, eyes wide. "The real Sparkle lives near here?"

"Just up the road." Celeste gestured vaguely in the direction of her family's place. "We've got a herd of about a dozen reindeer. Sparkle happens to be a favorite of my niece and nephew—of all of us, really. That's where I got the inspiration for the stories."

"Can we go see them, Dad? Can we?"

He shrugged. That was the thing about kids. They dragged you to all kinds of places you didn't necessarily want to go. "Don't know why not. We can probably swing that before the holidays."

Christmas was just around the corner and he was completely unprepared for it. He didn't like celebrating the holidays in the first place. He didn't really feel like hanging out at some cheesy Christmas moneymaking venture aimed at pouring holiday spirit down his throat like cheap bourbon.

But he loved his daughter, and if she wanted to go to the moon right now, he would figure out a way to take her.

"I like your tree," Celeste said, gazing around his grandmother's cluttered living room. "I especially like the tinsel. Did you help your dad put it up?"

A small spasm of guilt crossed her features. "Not really," she admitted. "My dad did most of it. I have a bad arm."

She lifted her shoulder and the arm in question dangled a little as if it were an overcooked lasagna noodle.

To her credit, Celeste didn't question how she could use that same arm to pet the dog or hold a stuffed reindeer.

"Too bad," she only said. "You're probably really good at hanging tinsel."

"Pretty good. I can't reach the high parts of the tree, though."

"Your dad helps you get those, right?"

"I guess."

Celeste picked up the bag of tinsel where Flynn had left it on the console table. "Can I help you put the rest of it up on the side you didn't get to yet? I'm kind of a tinsel expert. Growing up on The Christmas Ranch, I had to be."

Olivia looked at the tree, then her father, then back at Celeste holding the tinsel. "Okay," she said with that same wariness.

"It will be fun. You'll see. Sparkle can help. He's good at tinsel, too."

How she possibly could have guessed from a half-tinseled tree that he had been trying to enlist his daughter's help with decorating, he had no idea. But he wasn't about to argue with her insight, especially when Olivia obediently followed her new heroine to the tree and reached for a handful of tinsel.

"Can I take your coat?" he asked.

"Oh. Yes. Thanks." She gave a nervous little laugh as she handed him her coat. At the library, she had been wearing a big, loose sweater that had made him wonder what was beneath it. She had taken that layer off apparently, and now she wore a cheerful red turtleneck that accentuated her luscious curves and made his mouth water.

He had an inkling that she was the sort of woman who had no idea the kind of impact she had on a man. As he went to hang her coat by the front door, he forced himself to set aside the reaction as completely inappropriate under the circumstances, especially when she was only trying to help his kid.

When he returned to the living room, he found her and Olivia standing side by side hanging tinsel around the patches of the tree he had left bare.

Her cute little dog had finished sniffing the corners of the room and planted himself on his haunches in the middle of the floor, where he could watch the proceedings.

Flynn leaned against the doorjamb to do the same thing.

How odd, that Olivia would respond to a quiet children's librarian and author more than she had her counselor, her physical therapist, the caregivers at the hospital. She seemed to bloom in this woman's company, copying her actions on the lower branches she could reach. While she still seemed to be favoring her injured arm, occasionally she seemed to forget it hurt and used it without thinking.

All in all, it wasn't a terrible way to spend a December evening while a gas fire flickered in Grandma Charlotte's fireplace and snowflakes fluttered down outside the window.

After several moments, the two of them used the last of the tinsel and Celeste stepped away to take in the bigger picture.

"That looks perfect!" she exclaimed. "Excellent job."

Olivia's smile was almost back to her normal one. She held up the stuffed animal. "Sparkle helped."

"I told you he would be very good at hanging tinsel."

Whatever worked, he figured. "Let me hit the lights for you," he said. "We can't appreciate the full effects with the lights on."

He turned them off, pitching the room into darkness except

for the gleaming tree. The tinsel really did reflect the lights. His mom had been right about that, even if she had gotten so many other things wrong.

"Oh. I love it. It's the prettiest tree *ever*," Olivia declared.

"I have to agree," Flynn said. "Good job, both of you."

"And you," Olivia pointed out. "You did most of it earlier. We only filled in the gaps."

"So I did. We're all apparently excellent at decorating Christmas trees."

Celeste met his gaze and smiled. He gazed back, struck again by how lovely she was with those big green eyes that contrasted so strikingly with her dark hair.

He was staring, he realized, and jerked his gaze away, but not before he thought he saw color climb her high cheekbones. He told himself it must have been a trick of the Christmas lights.

"Oh, I nearly forget," she exclaimed suddenly. "I have another birthday present for you. Two, actually."

"You do?" Olivia lit up.

"Well, it's not actually your birthday yet, so I completely understand if you want to wait. I can just give them to your dad to hold until the big day."

As he might have predicted, Olivia didn't look all that thrilled at the suggestion. "I should open them now while you're here."

"I guess I should have asked your dad first."

He shrugged, figuring it was too late to stop the cart now. "Go ahead."

With a rueful, apologetic smile, she handed the bag to Olivia. "It's not wrapped, since I didn't know it was your birthday when I came over. I'm sorry."

His daughter apparently didn't care. She reached into the bag and pulled out a book with colorful illustrations on the cover.

"Ohhh," she breathed. "It's another *Sparkle and the Magic Snowball* book!"

"This one is signed by both me and my sister, who did the

illustrations. I figured since it's your favorite book, you ought to have a signed copy."

"I love it. Thank you!"

"There's something else," Celeste said when his daughter looked as if she were going to settle in right on the spot to re-read the story for the hundredth time.

Olivia reached into the bag and pulled out a second book. While it was obvious the artist had been the same, this had different, more muted colors than the original Sparkle book and hearts instead of Christmas ornaments.

"I haven't seen this one! *Sparkle and the Valentine Surprise.*"

"That's because it's brand-new. It's not even in stores yet. It's coming out in a few weeks."

"Dad, look!"

She hurried over to him, barely limping, and held out the book.

"Very nice. We can read it tonight at bedtime."

"I can't wait that long! Can I read it now?"

"Sure. First, do you have something to say to Ms. Nichols?"

Olivia gazed at the woman with absolute adoration. "Thank you *so much*! I just love these books and the stuffed Sparkle." Again, she surprised him by hugging Celeste tightly, then hurried to the window seat that she had claimed as her own when they'd first arrived at Charlotte's house.

He gazed after her for a moment, then turned back to Celeste.

"How did you just do that?" he asked, his voice low so that Olivia couldn't hear.

She blinked, confusion on her features. "Do what?"

"That's the first time I've seen her hug anyone but me in months."

"Oh." Her voice was small, sad, telling him without words that she knew what had happened to Elise and Olivia and about Brandon Lowell.

"I guess you probably know my daughter was shot three months ago and her mother was killed."

Her lovely features tightened and her eyes filled with sorrow. "I do. I followed the case, not because I wanted to read about something so terribly tragic, but because I…knew you, once upon a time."

Color rose on her cheeks again, but he had no idea why.

"She's been very withdrawn because of the post-traumatic stress. I haven't seen her warm up to anyone this quickly since it happened."

"Oh." She gazed at Olivia with a soft look in her eyes. "It's not me," she assured him. "Sparkle is a magic little reindeer. He has a comforting way about him."

He was quite certain Celeste was the one with the comforting way, especially as she had created the fictional version of the reindeer, but he didn't say so.

"Whatever the reason, I appreciate it. I had hoped bringing her here to Idaho where we can be away from the spotlight for a few weeks might help her finally begin to heal. It's good to know I might have been right."

The concern and love in his voice came through loud and clear. Flynn obviously was a devoted father trying his best to help his daughter heal.

Celeste's throat felt tight and achy. This poor little girl had watched her mother's life slip away. "She's been through a horrible ordeal. It might be years before the nightmares fade."

"You sound as if you know a little something about nightmares." He studied her closely.

She didn't want to tell him she *still* had nightmares from those terrible weeks in captivity and then their miraculous rescue with its tragic consequences. She had cried herself to sleep just about every night for weeks. In a second rapid-fire blow, just as the overwhelming pain of losing their father had begun to ease a little, their mother had lost her short but intense battle with cancer and they had come here to stay with Uncle Claude and Aunt Mary.

She couldn't tell him that. She barely knew the man, and he had demons of his own to fight. He didn't need to share hers.

"Everybody has nightmares," she answered. "To paraphrase John Irving, you don't get to pick them. They pick you."

"True enough."

Her dog made a little whiny sound and started looking anxious, which meant he probably needed to go out.

"I need to take Linus home. Sorry again to drop in on you like this out of the blue."

He smiled a little. "Are you kidding? This has been the best thing to happen to us in a long time. She's completely thrilled. And thanks for helping with the Christmas tree. It looks great."

"You're welcome. If you need anything while you're here, my family is just a short walk away. Oh. I nearly forgot. This is for you."

She reached into the bag and pulled out the pie Aunt Mary had boxed up for easier transport.

"What is it?"

"My aunt makes amazing berry pies. She had an extra and wanted you to have it."

He looked stunned at the gesture. "That's very kind. Please give her my thanks."

"I'll do that." She reached for her coat but he beat her to it, tugging it from the rack so he could help her into it.

She was aware of him behind her again, the heat and strength of him, and her insides jumped and twirled like Linus when he was especially happy.

She was being ridiculous, she told herself. She wasn't a thirteen-year-old girl with a crush anymore.

She quickly shoved her arms through the sleeves and stepped away to tie her scarf.

"Are you sure you're okay walking home?" he asked. "Looks as if it's snowing harder. Let me grab my keys and we'll drive you home."

She shook her head, even as she felt a warm little glow at

his concern. "Not necessary. It's not far. I like to walk, even in the snow, and Linus still has a little energy to burn off. Thank you, though."

He still looked uncertain, but she didn't give him a chance to press the matter. She returned to the living room doorway and waved at his daughter.

"Goodbye, Olivia. I hope you enjoy the book."

She looked up with that distracted, lost-in-the-story sort of look Celeste knew she wore frequently herself. "I'm already almost done. It's super good."

It was one thing in the abstract to know people enjoyed her work. It was something else entirely to watch someone reading it—surreal and gratifying and a bit uncomfortable at the same time.

"I'm glad you think so."

Olivia finally seemed to register that she had on her coat. "Do you really have to go?"

"I'm afraid so. I have to take Linus home or Lucy will be lonely."

To her surprise, Olivia set aside the book, climbed down from the window seat and approached to give her one last hug.

"Thank you again for the books and for the stuffed animal," she said. "It was the best birthday ever—and I haven't even had it yet!"

"I'm so glad."

"Goodbye, Linus," Olivia said. She knelt down to scratch the Yorkie again and Linus obliged by licking her face, which made her giggle.

When Celeste turned to go, she found Flynn shaking his head with astonishment clear on his handsome features. She remembered what he had said about Olivia not warming to many people since her mother's death, and she was deeply grateful she had made the small effort to come visit the girl.

"I hope we see you again," he said.

Oh, how she wished he meant for *his* sake and not for his

daughter's. "I'm sure you will. Pine Gulch is a small place. Good night."

She walked out into the snowy December night. Only when she was halfway back to the Star N did she realize she didn't feel the cold at all.

Chapter Four

Over the weekend she tried not to think about Flynn and his
sweet, fragile daughter. It wasn't easy, despite how busy she
was working an extra shift at the library and helping out in the
gift shop of The Christmas Ranch.

Even the multiple calls she and Hope took from Joan about
the movie development deal couldn't completely distract her
random thoughts of the two of them that intruded at the oddest times.

She knew the basics of what had happened to Elise Chandler and her daughter at the hands of the actress's boyfriend,
but she was compelled to do a few internet searches to read
more about the case. The details left her in tears for everyone
involved, even the perpetrator and his family.

Brandon Lowell obviously had been mentally ill. He had been
under treatment for bipolar disease and, according to evidence
after the shooting, had stopped taking his medication a month
before, claiming it interfered with his acting abilities and the
regular television role he was playing.

He never should have had access to a firearm given his mental health but had stolen one from Elise's bodyguard a few days before the shooting.

She found it a tragic irony that the woman used a bodyguard when she went out in public but had been killed by someone close to her using the very tool intended to protect her.

The whole thing made her so very sad, though she was touched again to read numerous reports about Olivia's dedicated father, how Flynn had put his thriving contracting business in the hands of trusted employees so he could dedicate his time to staying with his daughter every moment through her recovery.

None of that information helped distract her from thinking about him. By Monday afternoon, she had *almost* worked the obsession out of her system—or at least forced herself to focus on work as much as possible, until Frankie came in after a morning of online seminars.

"I figured out who he is!" her friend exclaimed before she even said hello.

"Who?"

"You know! The hot dad who came to story time last week. I spent all weekend trying to figure out why he looked so familiar and then this morning it came to me. I was washing my hair and remembered that shower scene in *Forbidden* when the hero washes the heroine's hair and it came to me. Elise Chandler! Sexy dad is her ex-husband. It has to be! That cute little girl must be the one who was all over the news."

Flynn must hate having his daughter be a household name, even though her mother certainly had been.

"Yes. Flynn Delaney. Charlotte Delaney, his grandmother, lived close to The Christmas Ranch and he used to come spend summers with her."

"You knew all this time and you didn't say anything?"

It wasn't her place to spread gossip about the man. Even now, just talking to her dear friend, she felt extremely protective of him and Olivia.

"I'm sure they would appreciate a little privacy and discretion," she said. "Olivia has been through a terrible ordeal and is still trying to heal from her injuries. I don't think they need everybody in town making a fuss over them."

"Oh, of course. That makes sense. That poor kid."

"I know."

"How is she doing?"

She thought of Olivia's excitement the other day when she had taken the books to her and that spontaneous, sweet embrace. "She's still got a long road but she's improving."

"I'm so glad."

"Olivia is apparently a big Sparkle fan, and that was the reason they came to the story time."

She had been touched several times to remember the girl telling her how much her book had helped during her recovery. Who would have guessed when she had been writing little stories for her niece and nephew that an emotionally and physically damaged girl would one day find such comfort in them?

To her relief, Frankie dropped the subject. Celeste tried once more to return to her work, vowing to put this ridiculous obsession out of her head. An hour later her hopes were dashed when Frankie bustled back to the children's section, her eyes as wide as if she'd just caught somebody trying to deface a book.

"He's here again!"

She looked up from the books she was shelving. "Who's here?"

"Hottie Dad and his cute little girl! Elise Chandler's poor daughter. They just walked in."

"Are you sure?"

"He's a hard man to miss," Frankie said.

Celeste's heartbeat kicked up several notches and her stomach seemed tangled with nerves. She told herself that was ridiculous. He wasn't there to see her anyway. Maybe he wouldn't even come back to the children's section.

"I wonder what they're doing here," Frankie said, her dark eyes huge.

It wasn't to see her, Celeste reminded herself sternly. She was a dowdy, shy librarian, and he couldn't possibly have any interest in her beyond her status as his daughter's favorite author.

"Here's a wild guess," she said, her tone dry. "Maybe they're looking for books."

Frankie made a face. "He doesn't have a library card, does he?"

"Probably not," she acknowledged. "They're only here for a few weeks, then they'll be returning to California."

The thought was more depressing than it should have been.

"Well, ask him if he wants a temporary one while he's here."

Why did *she* have to ask him anything? She wanted to hide here in the children's section and not even have to face him. But a moment later Olivia limped in, Sparkle the stuffed reindeer in her hand along with the new book.

"Hi, Ms. Nichols! Hi!"

Celeste smiled at both of them. "Hello. It's lovely to see you today. Happy birthday!" She suddenly remembered.

"Thank you," Olivia said. "I begged and begged my dad to bring me to the library today."

"Did you?"

She held up Sparkle. "I had to tell you how much I liked the new book, just as much as the first one. Sparkle is *so funny*. I've read it about ten times already."

"Wow. That's terrific. Thanks for letting me know."

"And my dad read it to me twice and he laughed both times. He hardly *ever* laughs."

"Not true," he protested. "Okay, it's true that I laughed at the book. It's hilarious. But it's not true that I hardly ever laugh. I don't know where you came up with that. I laugh all the time. I'm a freaking hyena."

Celeste laughed out loud, which earned her a surprised look from Frankie.

"You're so lucky that you had the chance to read the new book," Frankie informed her. "Half the children in town would willingly forgo all their presents under the tree if they could lay their hands on the next Sparkle book."

Even though she was grossly exaggerating, the library director had the perfect tone with Olivia—friendly and polite, but not overly solicitous. She had a feeling Flynn would hate the latter.

"It's really, really good," Olivia said solemnly. "I still like the first one best, but the second one is almost my favorite."

Frankie smiled, but before she could answer, one of the other library volunteers came over with a question about checking out DVDs, and she reluctantly excused herself to deal with the crisis.

"Is there something I can help you with?" Celeste asked after her friend walked away. "Would you like a temporary card so you can check out materials? I'm sure that wouldn't be a problem, considering I know where to find you."

"No. Actually, we have another reason for being here."

If she wasn't mistaken, Flynn looked a little uncomfortable, which made her even more curious.

"Oh? What is it?"

He didn't answer and Olivia didn't say anything, either. Finally Flynn nudged her. "Go ahead."

"It's my birthday," the girl began.

"I know. I think it's great that you decided the library is the perfect place to celebrate a birthday. I completely agree!"

Olivia giggled a little. "No, we're not celebrating my birthday here. I told my dad the only thing I want for my birthday is to have pizza."

"Ooh, pizza. My favorite," she said, though she was still mystified about why they might be at the library and why Flynn still looked uncomfortable. "Are you looking for a book on how to make pizza?"

The girl shook her head. "We're going to the pizza restaurant down the street."

"I can highly recommend it. It's one of my favorite places."

Olivia gave her a shy look. "That's good. Because I want to have pizza with *you* on my birthday."

She blinked, taken by surprise. "With…me?"

"Yes. That would be the best birthday ever. My favorite thing to eat and my new friend and the lady who writes such good Sparkle books." She beamed as if the matter was settled.

"Don't feel obligated," Flynn said quickly. "If you already have plans, we completely understand. Isn't that right, Olivia?"

"Yes," the girl said.

Dinner. With Olivia and Flynn. She thought of a hundred reasons why she should say no. How could she possibly eat with these nervous butterflies racing around in her stomach? And she probably wouldn't be able to think of anything to say and would look even more stupid than she felt.

All those reasons paled into insignificance. Olivia wanted to have pizza with her for her birthday, and Celeste couldn't let her own social awkwardness stand in the way of making that particular wish come true.

"I would be honored to come help you celebrate your birthday. Thank you for inviting me."

Olivia's smile was sweetly thrilled. "She said yes, Dad!"

The sight of this tough-looking man gazing down at his daughter with such love just about broke Celeste's heart. "So I heard. That's great." He turned to her. "What time are you finished with work?"

"Five-thirty."

"Would seven work for pizza? We can pick you up."

"I can meet you at the restaurant."

"We don't mind. Do you still live at the Star N?"

She knew he probably didn't mean for that to sound pitiful, but she still had to wince. That wasn't exactly true. She had gone off to Boise for her undergraduate work, then Seattle for her master's degree. She wasn't *completely* a homebody, even if she had jumped at the chance to return to her hometown library to work.

If she was living on her family's ranch, it wasn't because of any failure to launch, only because of the tragic circumstances of Travis's death.

"I live on the ranch but not in the main house," she told him. "I'm at the foreman's place, the small log house closest to the entrance."

"Perfect. Plan on us at seven."

She was going out to dinner with Flynn Delaney and his daughter. This certainly wasn't the way to get the man out of her head, but she didn't see how she could refuse.

The truth was she didn't want to anyway. She was both touched and flattered that sweet Olivia wanted to spend time with her for her birthday.

"Sounds good. Meanwhile, are you sure you don't want to check out some books on a temporary library card? We still have a great selection of holiday books available. It's the section there against the wall."

"Can we?" Olivia asked her father.

"Just a few," he said with a reluctant nod. "It might be tough to keep track of more than that while we're clearing out Grandma Charlotte's house."

Olivia headed immediately toward the Christmas storybooks, leaving Flynn alone with Celeste—or at least as alone as they could be in a public library.

A few moms she knew were browsing through the children's section with their toddlers, and she was pretty sure she caught more than one appreciative glance in his direction. As Frankie said, he was a hard man to overlook.

"Thanks for agreeing to come with us," Flynn said. "It probably wasn't fair to spring that on you out of the blue. I would have called first, but I didn't have a phone number. I guess I could have found the number for the library, but I didn't think about it until we pulled up."

"It's fine."

"Seriously, you made her day. She has been asking me all

afternoon if you could come to her birthday celebration. I didn't want to disappoint her. It's still pretty tough for me to deny her anything these days."

She couldn't imagine almost losing a child. The fear must have been overwhelming.

"I'm touched, if you want the truth. I don't believe I've ever been anyone's birthday wish before."

A strange glint appeared in his gaze, an expression she couldn't quite identify. After a moment he smiled. "Face it. You sealed your fate the other day when you showed up in person with a new book *and* a cute stuffed toy. You're now officially the coolest person in town."

She had to laugh at that ridiculous statement. "If that's the case, you both need to get out and meet more people in Pine Gulch."

Amusement crinkled the corners of his eyes. "We won't be here long enough to move in social circles around here. Anyway, I think Olivia and I are both quite happy with those we have already met in Pine Gulch."

Her heartbeat seemed to accelerate all over again at the teasing note in his voice. Her gaze met his and he was smiling at her with a warm look in his eyes that sucked away any ability she might have had to offer a semi-intelligent response.

To her relief, one of the moms came over to ask her a question about the puppet-book packages they lent out—probably more to get a closer look at Flynn, she suspected, than out of any genuine quest for information.

He moved away to join his daughter while she picked a few other books and the moment was gone.

He had to finish taking care of things at his grandmother's house and get out of Pine Gulch.

As Flynn drove the short distance from Charlotte's house to the Star N Ranch, he was aware of a low, insistent unease. This town was growing on him, sucking him in.

He had always enjoyed coming here as a kid to spend time with his grandmother. The setting was beautiful, nestled against the Tetons, with pine forests and crystal clear streams.

The pace here seemed so very different from his childhood home in Southern California, quieter, gentler somehow. Almost like a foreign country, without convertibles and palm trees and self-absorbed celebrities.

He always felt a sense of peace settle over him the moment he passed through the city limits into town.

He thought he loved it here because of Charlotte, because she was such a steady source of love and support despite the chaos of the rest of his world. When he came to Pine Gulch, there were no raging fights that could go on for days, no slamming doors, no screaming voices. Only his calm, funny, laughing grandmother, with her colorful aprons and her bright smile and her small, tidy house beside the Cold Creek.

She was gone now, but he was aware of that same peace seeping through him, so very welcome after the terrible past few months.

It didn't make sense, he knew. He was only here to finish taking care of Charlotte's house, not to find some kind of peace.

That was part of the reason he was so drawn to Celeste Nichols, he acknowledged as he neared her family's ranch. She had a calming way about her that drew him to her.

He couldn't imagine any two people more different than Celeste and Elise—the sweet children's librarian and author and the passionate, flamboyant, ambitious actress.

His marriage had been a mistake from the beginning. After growing up with a mother in the entertainment business—and a father who had hated it—and seeing the neuroses and the superficiality of that way of life, he had wanted no part of it.

After high school and college, he had set his business degree aside and obtained a contractor's license instead. After only a few years his construction company had established a reputation for quality and dependability. Then at one of his mother's frequent parties, he had met a stunning—and hungry—young actress.

She had pursued him aggressively, and he—like probably most guys in their early twenties—had been too flattered to use his brain. In his lust-addled state, it had taken him several weeks to realize she was more interested in his connection to his mother and her powerful Hollywood circle than in him.

But by then Elise had become pregnant, despite the precautions they had taken. He had done what he thought was right and married her, but it had been the ultimate exercise in futility. Both of them had known from the beginning it would never last. The two years before she had filed for divorce had been among the toughest of his life, sweetened only by his complete adoration for his baby girl.

Everything he did, then and now, was for Olivia. That was the only reason he was driving to pick up Celeste Nichols right now, not because of this powerful attraction he hadn't been able to shake since that first day in the library.

What was it about her? Yes, she was pretty in a calm, buttoned-down kind of way with those lovely dark-fringed green eyes and dark curls. She had an understated loveliness she seemed to be doing her best to hide from the world.

His entire life he had been surrounded by beautiful women who were empty shells once a guy broke through the surface to the person inside. Despite their short acquaintance, he was certain Celeste wasn't like that.

Her kindness to Olivia touched him. He tried to tell himself that was the reason for this strange reaction to her. It was gratitude; that was all.

Somehow he wasn't buying it as he passed the entrance to The Christmas Ranch on his way to the Star N.

"What is that place?" Olivia asked, gazing out the window at the colorful holiday display they could see from the road.

"It's a place where people pay money to help find the Christmas spirit," he explained. "They have different activities here like sledding, sleigh rides, that kind of thing."

"Look, Dad! That sign says Home of the Real Sparkle," she read. "That must be where he lives! Can we pay the money and see him and maybe do some of the other stuff? The sledding and stuff?"

Her request took him by surprise, especially considering how apathetic she had been about decorating their house for Christmas. She hadn't summoned much energy at all for celebrating this year. He couldn't blame her after what she had endured, but it was one more thing that broke his heart, especially considering how excited she had been about the holiday season in years past.

Maybe Celeste Nichols and her reindeer book were rubbing off on Olivia.

"We'll have to see. I thought you weren't very interested in Christmas this year."

"I guess we could do a *few* Christmas things," she said slowly. "Whether we do them or not, Christmas is coming anyway."

"True enough." For a girl who had just turned seven, she could be remarkably wise sometimes. She was tough and courageous, he told himself. Even if she was struggling now, she would make it through this eventually.

"Is this where Celeste lives?" Olivia asked when he pulled up in front of the little house not far from the bigger Star N ranch house.

"That's what she said. The foreman's house."

"Look. She has a Christmas tree, too."

Since her family ran The Christmas Ranch, he would have been more shocked if she *didn't* have one.

"I wonder if I can see her cute little dog, Linus."

"I wouldn't be a bit surprised," he told her.

Olivia opened the passenger door almost before he had the SUV in Park, and she raced up the driveway without him, only limping a little. While he was still unbuckling his seat belt, she was already at the doorbell, and by the time he reached the door, Celeste had opened it and was greeting his daughter.

"Of course," she was saying. "You can absolutely come in and meet Lucy the cat. She loves new friends."

Apparently his daughter had invited herself inside. He rolled his eyes but followed her when Celeste held open the door for both of them.

The house wasn't large, perhaps only eight or nine hundred square feet. The living room was decorated in a casual, comfortable style, heavy on bright colors, with lots of plump pillows and books. The Christmas tree was about the only holiday decoration, he was surprised to see.

"Nice place," he said.

"Thanks. I just moved over a few months ago from the main house, but so far I've been enjoying it. I'm close enough to help out with my niece and nephew when my sister Faith needs me. At the same time, I'm far enough away from the chaos that I can write. I've even got my own writing space in the second bedroom."

"It's comfortable."

She smiled. "I like it."

Her furry-faced little dog scampered in from the kitchen, followed by an elegant-looking black cat, who watched them carefully from the doorway as if trying to determine whether they were friends or foes.

"Hi, Linus." Olivia sank to the floor to pet the dog. After a moment, the cat sidled over.

"That's Lucy," Celeste said. "She can be a little snooty at first, but once she warms up, she'll be your best friend. Just give her a moment."

Sure enough, while Olivia mostly paid attention to the small dog, the cat moved closer and closer until she rubbed her head against Olivia's leg.

"I think she likes me," she whispered.

"I'm sure of it," Celeste said with a smile.

"Looks as if you need to pick up a pet or two," she said to Flynn in an undertone.

"Don't give her any ideas," he said in the same low voice. Their gaze met and he felt a strange jolt in his gut at the impact of those green eyes behind the glasses.

"You don't want a little dog?"

He shrugged. When he was a kid, the only pets had been his mother's annoying, yippy little purse pooches. He had never really thought seriously about it before, too busy with work and his shared custody of Olivia.

When things settled down for her a little, maybe he would think about it. She did seem to be enjoying Celeste's pets.

Both he and Celeste seemed content to watch her petting the two pets, and he was aware of that elusive sense of peace seeping in again.

"How's the house cleaning going?" she asked him.

He thought of the work still ahead. "I don't think I realized what an undertaking it was to clear out eighty-five years of living. After about three days of work, we got one of the rooms cleared out today."

"Good work." She paused. "If you need help, I'm available most evenings."

She looked embarrassed after she spoke, though he wasn't quite sure why, when he took the offer as nothing but generous and kind, especially in the hustle-bustle of the holidays.

"Thank you," he said sincerely.

She gazed at him for a moment, then shifted her attention back to Olivia, but not before he saw a hint of color climb her cheeks.

"What are you doing with your business in California while you're here?"

"I'm doing as much as I can long-distance, but it hasn't been easy. Since the shooting, I've basically had to trust my second-in-command to take much of the load at the sites. I've been handling the administrative things after Olivia goes to bed. Everyone who works for me has been great. I couldn't ask for better people in my company, but I think we're all ready for things to start getting back to normal after the holidays."

She looked between him and his daughter, her expression soft. "You're a good father, Flynn. Olivia is lucky to have you."

"I don't know about that," he muttered. "A good father would have known what was going on at her mother's house. I should have seen it. It wasn't a stable situation for a young girl. Elise had boyfriend after boyfriend traipsing in and out of their lives, all tabloid fodder. Brandon Lowell at least had stuck around for longer than a few months. I was stupidly grateful for that, but if I had been paying more attention, I would have seen his downward spiral. Maybe I could have stepped in earlier."

"What would you have done?"

"I don't know. Found him the help he needed, at the very least. Maybe filed for an emergency custody order so we could have avoided all this trauma and pain." The nightmare of the shooting was as vivid and stark as if it had happened the day before. "Elise called me right before it all went south."

"She did?"

He checked to be sure Olivia wasn't paying attention to them but to the animals before he continued. "She told me Brandon had been drinking all day and was acting strangely. She was worried about him, but she didn't sound panicked or anything, was just calling to ask my advice. She'd done this before, called me for advice when he was drinking too much or having a manic episode, but something told me this time was different. I was on a job site fifty miles away, so I told her to grab Olivia and take her to my house, and I would deal with the situation when I got back."

He was quiet, regret a harsh companion. "I wish to hell she

had listened to me. She was always so stubborn, thinking she knew best. I was about five miles from her place when I got the call from the police. I'll never forget that instant when it felt as if the whole world changed."

Chapter Five

She couldn't imagine what he must have gone through, knowing his daughter had been hurt. She also could tell by the threads of guilt twining through his voice that he blamed himself for not being able to control the situation and keep his daughter safe.

"What happened wasn't your fault," she murmured.

"Wasn't it?" he asked, the words clipped.

Unable to resist the need to offer him comfort, she reached out her hand and rested it softly on his.

She completely understood where he was coming from. She knew all about that crushing weight of responsibility.

In that last panicked rush toward the helicopter and the navy SEALs, she had been terrified as usual. She had hesitated, frozen in fear. Her father had paused to go back for her and shoved her in front of him, pushing her forward with his usual words of encouragement as they had raced to safety.

He had thrust her into the helicopter ahead of him, but her split second of fear had had a terrible cost. Her father had been shot just before he would have been able to make it to safety.

If she hadn't been so afraid, if she had started to run when he had first told her to go, maybe her father would still be with them now.

"Wouldn't it be wonderful if we were all given one do-over in life?" she murmured. "One free pass to go back and change one action, one decision, one thoughtless word?"

He gave her a searching look, as if trying to figure out what moment she would alter. Finally he nodded. "One would be a start, I suppose, though I probably could use about a half dozen free passes."

"Instead, we have to do our best to live with the consequences of our choices."

"Not an easy task, is it?"

No. She had been trying for nearly twenty years.

He flexed his hand and she realized with great chagrin that she was still touching him. She pulled her fingers back quickly, her skin still tingling from the heat of him.

After an awkward moment, he turned to his daughter.

"Olivia, we should probably take off or someone else will eat our delicious pizza."

"We haven't ordered it yet," she said with a concerned frown. "Do you think they'll run out?"

"I was just teasing. But we really should go."

"Okay," she said reluctantly. She rubbed noses with Linus and petted Lucy one last time, then stood up.

She might have been mistaken, but Celeste thought she seemed to be moving better, even than a few days before.

Flynn drove a luxury SUV that smelled of expensive leather with hints of his woodsy, intoxicating aftershave. As he drove to the pizza place in town, she and Olivia talked about the books the girl had checked out of the library and about her schoolwork and her home in California.

He seemed content to listen, though once or twice she caught him giving her a sidelong glance, no doubt trying to figure out how he had gotten saddled spending the evening with the boring children's librarian.

Monday night was family night at the Rocky Mountain Pizza Company—The Rock, as they called it in town. From the outside it looked as though the place was hopping.

This was one of the more family-friendly hangouts in Pine Gulch. Though it had a pool table in the back room, it also featured foosball and air hockey tables, as well as a few vintage video games like Ms. PAC-MAN and pinball.

Celeste came here about once a month, either with her sister or with friends. Usually she enjoyed the delicious wood-fired pizza and the comfortable, familiar atmosphere. The scent alone—garlic and yeast and a fabulous red sauce—made her stomach rumble.

On the heels of that first sensory overload, though, Celeste became aware that people were looking with curiosity at her and her companions.

She saw the police chief, Trace Bowman, and his wife, Becca, at one table with their children. In the next booth were Nate Cavazos and his wife, Emery, one of her good friends. Emery and Becca both looked intrigued.

For a wild moment, she wished she had refused the invitation from Olivia—or that she had persuaded Flynn to take them all the way to Jackson Hole or even Idaho Falls, somewhere far away from Pine Gulch where people didn't know her.

Instead, she squared her shoulders, waved at her friends and did her best to ignore their speculative looks.

"Hi, Celeste," Natalie Dalton, the hostess chirped the greeting while looking at Flynn and Olivia with curiosity.

She used to babysit for Nat and her siblings. "Hi, Natalie. Great to see you. I miss seeing you at the library these days."

"I still come in, though mostly at night for study groups. I just don't have much reason to hit the children's section anymore unless I've got one of the little ones with me."

Her father and stepmother had two children together, in addition to the four Wade Dalton had had with his first wife, who had died tragically in childbirth.

Natalie turned her attention to Olivia and Flynn. "Hi, there. Welcome to The Rock. I don't think we've met. I'm Natalie."

Celeste felt as though she had the manners of a dried-up turnip right now. "Sorry. This is Flynn Delaney and his daughter, Olivia."

She smiled at them both. "Hi, Olivia. Hi, Flynn."

"We're here celebrating a certain young lady's seventh birthday today," Celeste said.

"Happy birthday!" Natalie exclaimed, beaming at her and holding her hand out for a fist bump.

"Thank you," Olivia said. She didn't meet her eye, and though she raised her hand halfheartedly to bump Nat's, she quickly lowered it again and looked at the floor.

What had happened to the animated birthday girl who had chattered in the car about her favorite Jan Brett Christmas book? Now she seemed nervous and uneasy, as if she wanted to be anywhere else in the world than the best pizza place in the entire region.

Celeste placed a comforting hand on her shoulder. When she'd first arrived in Pine Gulch after their Colombian ordeal, it had taken her a long time before she could completely relax in public places like this. She imagined Olivia was feeling the same way.

"I've got the perfect table for a birthday girl," Natalie said, her cheerfulness undeterred by Olivia's reticence. "Follow me, guys."

Indeed, she led them to an excellent table overlooking the Christmas lights on Main Street. From here, they even could see the fun display in the window of the local toy store.

"Thanks," Flynn murmured. Olivia slid into the booth first and Flynn went in after her. Celeste slid across from them.

"What's good here?" Flynn asked, scanning one of the menus Natalie left them.

"Everything," she answered honestly. "The pizza, the pasta, the sandwiches. You can't go wrong."

"I wanted pizza," Olivia said, her voice still small.

"Pizza it is," Flynn said. "Why don't we order three personal size? Then everybody can choose the toppings they like."

"The personal size is usually huge," she told him. "At least enough for two people."

"That's okay. Pizza leftovers are one of the true joys in life, right?"

When he smiled, she thought *he* should have been the movie star in the family instead of his mother and former wife. He would break hearts all over the world with those completely natural good looks.

Her stomach jumped all over the place again. Oh, this crush was *so embarrassing.* She would be lucky if she could eat any pizza at all.

At least she was able to talk casually when he asked her to help him choose between pizza selections. A few moments later the server, Lucy Boyer—Natalie's cousin—headed over to take their order.

She beamed when she spotted Celeste. "Hey, Ms. N. How are things?"

"Great, Lucy. How are you?"

"Can't complain. I'm working on my college essays and it's such a pain. You probably love that kind of thing, since you're a genius author and all. You might not know this, but for some people writing is *hard.*"

She didn't want to burst that particular fantasy by telling her the truth, that sometimes every single word was a struggle.

"Hey, what's this I hear about a Sparkle movie in the works?"

How on earth did rumors spread like that? She hadn't made her final decision yet, though she knew she couldn't wait much longer.

"A movie?" Olivia exclaimed. "Really?"

For some reason, Flynn's easy expression had tightened, and he was gazing at her with his brow furrowed.

"I don't know yet. Possibly." Probably.

She still wasn't sure she wanted to see her baby on the big screen, but at this point she didn't know how to stop that particular train.

"That's seriously cool. I'll be the first in line to buy tickets. That's such a great story."

"It's my favorite, too," Olivia said.

"Cool! I heard from a little squirrel that you've got a birthday today."

Olivia nodded. She looked as though she was torn between withdrawing into herself to hide from the attention and any kid's natural excitement about being the star of the day.

"We'll make sure your pizza is perfect, then. What kind do you want?"

Olivia ordered cheese, which Lucy assured them would come with a special birthday surprise. Celeste picked her favorite, margherita, which came with fresh basil and the hand-pulled mozzarella The Rock was famous for, and Flynn went for the meat lover's delight.

After she left, Flynn picked up the conversation.

"A movie?" he asked.

"We're in talks," she answered. "It's a terrifying proposition, to be honest."

"Will the real Sparkle be in the movie?" Olivia asked.

Celeste smiled. "It's going to be animated, so no."

She and the little girl started talking about their favorite holiday films—Olivia's was *Elf*, while Celeste still favored *It's A Wonderful Life*.

In no time, their pizza arrived. Olivia's surprise was that her pizza was shaped like a Christmas tree.

The pizza was every bit as good as usual, cooked just right in the wood-fired oven.

Flynn apparently agreed. "Wow," he said after the first bite. "That's a good pie. If I'd known how good, we would have been eating here every night since we came to town."

"Doug and Jacinda DeMarco, the owners, are big on the ar-

tisan pizza scene. They make their own mozzarella and bur-
rata and try to use locally sourced produce and meats wherever
they can. They have an extensive greenhouse where they grow
their own fresh herbs and vegetables year-round. It's quite an
operation."

"Who would have thought I could find such a good pizza in
the wilds of eastern Idaho?"

She smiled, proud of her little community. While it might be
primarily a ranching town, Pine Gulch was gaining a reputation
as a foodie destination and a magnet for artists.

"I understand they get customers from as far away as Jackson
Hole who read about the pizza online and want to try a slice."

She was finishing her second slice when she spotted her
friend Caidy Caldwell coming in with her husband, the local
veterinarian, and their children. Caidy had grown up in Cold
Creek Canyon and had been a friend for a long time. Celeste
loved seeing her so happy with Ben.

When she spotted Celeste, she waved, said something to Ben
and the kids, then headed in her direction.

"Hi, Celeste! I'm so glad I bumped into you. Great story time
last week. The kids really enjoyed it."

"Thanks. It was great to see you there."

"I don't know how you always manage to find such absolutely charming stories—old favorites and then so many that
no one has ever heard before."

"That's my job," she said with a smile. That was one of her
favorite parts about it, seeking out the new and unusual along
with the classics everybody expected and loved.

"You do it well," Caidy said. "Almost *too* well. We might
have to quit coming to the library. Every time you read a new
book the kids have to buy it."

"Because they're all so good." Her stepdaughter, Ava, had
joined her.

"Right. But now the shelves of our home library are bulging."

"You can never have too many books," Celeste answered.

"That's what I always say," Ava exclaimed. She turned to Olivia. "Hi. I'm Ava Caldwell."

"Sorry. This is Flynn Delaney and his daughter, Olivia. Flynn, this is my friend Caidy Caldwell and her daughter, Ava. Ava also has a brother about your age named Jack and a new baby brother who is the cutest thing around, Liam."

As her friend smiled at the two of them, Celeste didn't miss the flash of recognition or sympathy in her gaze before she smoothly masked her reaction. Caidy obviously had followed the news stories and knew what had happened to the girl.

"I'm happy to meet you both," her friend said with a smile. "Welcome to Pine Gulch. I hope you're staying around for a while."

He shook his head. "I'm afraid not. Only until after the holidays."

"Well, you picked one of the best times of the whole year to be here. You won't find many prettier winter wonderlands than this part of Idaho."

"It's lovely," he agreed.

"I didn't mean to interrupt your dinner. I just needed to ask you again what time practice is tomorrow. I know you've told me a half dozen times but I swear Christmas makes my brain leak out of my ears."

"Four thirty sharp at the St. Nicholas Lodge at the ranch. We should be done by six thirty."

"Perfect. My kids are so excited about it."

Celeste had no idea how Hope had persuaded her to take on one more thing, in this case organizing a small program to be performed at an inaugural Senior Citizens Christmas dinner a few days before the holiday.

Hope's particular skill was getting Celeste to do things she ordinarily never would attempt—like publish her books and then agree to allow one of those books to be made into a movie.

"Olivia, if you're going to be here through Christmas, you should think about being in the play," Ava suggested.

Flynn tensed up at the idea, his jaw taut. To Celeste's surprise, Olivia only looked intrigued.

"I was in a play in school once. It was fun."

"This isn't a huge production," Celeste assured Flynn. "We're just doing a simple Christmas program. Everybody who wants to participate gets a part. We're mostly singing songs everybody already knows."

"Can I do it, Dad?"

He frowned. "We'll have to talk about that. We're pretty busy cleaning out the house. I don't know if we'll have time to go to practices and things."

"There are only three practices," Celeste said. "Tomorrow, Thursday night and Saturday morning, and then the show is Tuesday, the day before Christmas Eve. She would be more than welcome to come. The rehearsals and the show are all at the St. Nicholas Lodge at The Christmas Ranch, just five minutes from your place."

A Christmas program. With an audience, applause. The whole bit. He wanted to tell them all absolutely not, to grab his daughter and drag her out of here.

He'd had enough of performers to last him a lifetime. His entire life, he had been forced to wait on the sidelines while the important females in his life sought fame and recognition. His mother had made it clear from the time he was old enough to understand that he could never be the most important thing in her life—not when her adoring public already held that honor.

Elise had pretended otherwise, but when it came down to it, he had been even less important to her, only a stepping-stone on her journey to success.

He didn't want Olivia anywhere near a stage or a movie set. So far she hadn't shown any inclination in that direction, much to his relief. He wanted to keep it that way.

He told himself he was being ridiculous. It was only a Christmas program, not a Broadway production. Still, he didn't want to offer her any opportunity to catch the performing bug.

She was still so fragile. While her physical wounds had mostly healed, emotionally and mentally she was still had a long journey.

Was he being too protective? Probably. Her therapist in California told him he needed to relax and let go a little. He didn't need to watch over her every single moment. Right now he had a tendency to want to keep her close, to tuck her up against him and make sure nothing terrifying or tragic ever touched her again.

That wasn't a healthy approach, either. He couldn't protect her from everything, even though he wanted to.

"Can I do it, Dad?" she asked again.

This was the same girl who freaked out in large crowds, who didn't like loud noises and who tended to panic if strangers tried to talk to her.

Did she seriously think she could handle being onstage in front of a bunch of strangers?

"We can talk about it later," he said.

"Absolutely," Caidy said with a cheerful smile, though he thought he saw soft compassion in her gaze.

Did she know about what had happened to Olivia? Probably. Most of the damn world knew. It had led media reports around the world for a week, had been on the cover of all the tabloids and celebrity rags.

When an Oscar-nominated actress is gunned down by her equally famous if mentally ill boyfriend—who then shoots her young child before killing himself—people tended to pay attention.

If he thought he could come to this remote corner of Idaho and escape notice, he was delusional. He doubted he could find anywhere on the planet where the news hadn't reached.

Maybe he could have taken Olivia on an African safari or

something, but even then he wouldn't have been surprised if people in the veld knew of Elise Chandler.

"It was nice to meet you," Ava said politely. "I hope we see you at rehearsal tomorrow."

His daughter needed friends, he thought again. They had always been important to her. Before everything happened, she always had been begging to have a friend over to use the pool or watch a movie.

Since her release from the hospital, she hadn't been interested in doing the normal things a seven-year-old girl would do. Ava Caldwell was older than his daughter, maybe eleven or twelve, but she seemed very kind. Maybe Celeste knew of some other likely candidates Olivia could hang out with while they were in town.

If it helped her interact with children around her age, would the Christmas program really be that bad?

Being a parent was a tough enough gig under the best of circumstances. Throw in the kind of trauma his daughter had endured and he felt as though he was foundering, trying to stay afloat in thirty-foot swells.

The Caldwells waved and headed for their table, and Flynn returned to his delicious pizza. The people at the Rocky Mountain Pizza Company knew what they were doing when it came to pie, he had to admit. Olivia, he saw, ate two pieces and even some of the family-style tossed salad, which seemed something of a record for her, given her poor appetite these days.

While they ate, they talked about Christmas and books and a couple of movies they had all seen. Three different times, people who came into the restaurant stopped at their booth to say hello to Celeste.

Olivia seemed to find that of great interest. "Do you know everybody who lives here?" she finally asked.

Celeste laughed, a light, musical sound. "Not even close, though it feels like it sometimes. When you live in a place for a long time you get to know lots of people. I've been in Pine

Gulch since I was eleven—except for the years I was away in Boise and Seattle for school."

"Where did you live before that?" he asked, suddenly intensely curious about her.

He was even more curious when her cheerful features seemed to go still and closed. She didn't say anything for several long seconds, so long that he wasn't sure she was going to answer him at all.

"It didn't seem like a tough question," he said mildly.

"For you, maybe," she retorted. "You grew up in California with your mother after your parents divorced, and spent your summers here with Charlotte, right?"

How did she know that? he wondered. He only remembered meeting her a few times back when he would come to visit and didn't remember ever sharing that information with her. Maybe Charlotte had told her.

He gave her a close look but she seemed lost in her own thoughts.

"That's right," he answered. "And you?"

"No one specific place," she finally answered. "I lived all over the globe, if you want the truth. I was born in a hut in Ghana, and before I was eleven, I lived in about two dozen countries. My parents were missionaries who started health clinics in underserved places of the world. Before I came to Pine Gulch, we were living in Colombia."

Some kind of vague, unsettling memory poked at him, a whisper he had once heard about Celeste and her sisters. Something to do with a kidnapping, with her parents.

He couldn't put his finger on the details. What was it? Was that the reason for those secrets in her eyes, for the pain he sensed there?

He opened his mouth to ask her, but before he could a loud clatter echoed through the place as a server busing the table next to them dropped the bin of dishes.

At the sudden, unexpected sound, Olivia gave one terrified gasp and slid from her seat under the table.

Damn, he hated these moments when her PTSD took over. They left him both furious and profoundly sad. He took a breath and leaned down to talk her through it, but Celeste beat him to it. She reached down and gave Olivia's shoulder a comforting squeeze beneath the table.

"It's okay. You're okay. It was only dishes. That's all. I know you were startled, but you're safe, sweetheart."

Olivia was making little whimpering noises that broke his heart all over again.

"I don't like loud noises," she said.

"Especially when you don't expect them and don't have time to prepare. Those are the *worst*, right?"

To his shock, Celeste spoke with a tone of experience. He gazed at her, trying to remember again what he knew about her and her sisters.

"They are," Olivia said. Though she still sounded upset, he could no longer hear the blind panic in her voice.

"Why don't you come up and finish your pizza? If you want, I can ask Lucy about fixing you one of their best desserts. It's a big gooey chocolate-chip cookie they bake in the wood-fired oven and top with hand-churned ice cream. I think you'll love it. I know it's my favorite thing to eat when I've been startled or upset about something."

After another moment, Olivia peeked her head out from under the booth. "They're not going to make that sound again, are they?"

"I don't think so. That was an accident."

"I hope they don't have another accident," she answered in a small voice.

"If they do, your dad and I are right here to make sure nothing hurts you."

That seemed enough to satisfy her. His daughter slid back onto the seat. She still had a wild look in her eyes, and he noticed she edged closer to him and constantly looked toward Celeste for reassurance while they finished their pizza.

He didn't miss the protective expression Celeste wore in return, an expression that turned *his* insides just as gooey as that chocolate-chip cookie she was talking about.

He couldn't let himself develop feelings for this woman, no matter how amazing she was with his child, he reminded himself.

He had to focus on his daughter right now. She was the only thing that mattered.

Chapter Six

"Is she asleep?" Celeste whispered an hour later, when they made the turn onto Cold Creek Road.

He glanced in the rearview mirror and could see Olivia curled into the corner, her eyes closed and her cheek resting on her hand.

"Looks like it." He pitched his voice low. "She's always been a kid who can sleep anywhere, especially when she's had a long day. Driving in the car has always knocked her right out. When she was going through the terrible twos and used to fight going to bed, I would strap her in her car seat and drive her around the block a few times. She always ran so hard that when she finally stopped, she would drop like a rock by the time we hit the first corner."

"Did she stay asleep?"

"Yeah. That was the amazing part. She never seemed to mind when I unstrapped her from her car seat and carried her into the house to her bed. I was kind of sorry when she outgrew that phase and started sleeping in her own bed without a fuss."

Beside him, he caught a flash of white in the darkness as Celeste smiled a little. "I imagine she was an adorable toddler."

"Oh, she was. Scary smart and curious about everything."

He felt a sharp pang in his heart when he thought again about how much she had changed, how she had become so fearful and hesitant. Would the old Olivia ever return, or was this their new version of normal?

"I wish you could have known her three months ago. Before."

Celeste reached out to touch his arm briefly, like a little bird landing on a branch for only a moment before fluttering away again.

"She's a wonderful girl, Flynn. A terrible thing happened to her, yes, but she's already demonstrated what a survivor she is. Trust me. She'll get through it in time. She may always have those dark memories—nothing can take them away completely—but eventually she'll learn how to replace them with happier thoughts."

He glanced over at her. "Is that how you coped?"

He could sense her sudden fine-edged tension. "I don't know what you mean."

"What happened to you? I vaguely remember my grandmother saying something about you and your sisters enduring a terrible ordeal, but I've been racking my brain and can't remember what. I should. I'm sorry."

She was silent for a long time and he didn't press, just continued driving through the quiet night through Cold Creek Canyon.

The creek here wound beside the road and through the trees, silvery in the moonlight. Tall pines and firs grew beside cottonwoods along the banks, at times almost forming a tunnel over the road. It was beautiful and mysterious at night with the snow fluttering gently against the windshield and the occasional house or ranchette decorated with Christmas lights.

She finally spoke when they were almost to the Star N. "It's a time of my life I don't like to think about," she murmured.

"Oh?"

She sighed. "I told you my parents moved us around the globe under sometimes difficult circumstances."

He nodded, wondering what her life must have been like without any kind of stable place to call home. Had she thrived there or had she always felt as if something were missing in her life?

She loved to read. Perhaps books had been her one constant friend through all the chaos and uncertainty.

"When I was eleven, we moved to Colombia to open a clinic in a small, undeveloped region. My parents were assured over and over that it was a safe area to bring their daughters."

"It wasn't?"

"The village where we lived might have been safe, but several in the region were not."

With reluctance he pulled up in front of her house, wishing he could keep driving. He shouldn't have worried. She didn't appear to notice where they were, that he had parked the vehicle and turned to face her. She hardly seemed aware he was there as she spoke, her features tight and her eyes focused on some spot through the windshield that he had a feeling wasn't anywhere close to eastern Idaho.

"We had been living in the village about six weeks when the clinic drew the attention of the local rebel leader in one of those unstable villages who happened to be in need of some extra cash to fund his soldiers. I guess Juan Pablo thought he could get a handsome sum in ransom if he kidnapped the crazy American do-gooders. The only trouble with that plan was that my parents weren't associated with any larger organization with deep pockets. They were free agents, I guess you could say. There was no money to pay a ransom and no one to pay it."

"What happened?"

"Juan Pablo didn't believe my parents when they insisted no one could pay a ransom. He thought if he held us long enough, the US government at least would step in, especially with the lives of three young girls at stake. We were held hostage for several weeks in a squalid prison camp."

What the hell had her parents been thinking, to drag three young girls all over the world into these unstable situations? He was all for helping others and admired those selfless people who only wanted to make a difference in the world, but not when it cost the well-being of their own children.

"Did someone eventually pay the ransom?"

She shook her head. "That was never one of the options. Juan Pablo was just too stupid or too blinded by greed to realize it. Instead, after we had been held for several weeks, a team of US Navy SEALs mounted an early-morning rescue."

She paused, her head bowed and her dark curls hiding her features. When she spoke, her voice was low, tight with remembered pain.

"The rescue wasn't a complete success. My father was... shot by Juan Pablo's rebels while we were trying to escape. He died instantly."

"Oh, Celeste. I'm so sorry."

"You can see why I feel great empathy for Olivia and what she's going through. Seeing a parent die violently is a trauma no child should have to endure."

"I completely agree," he said. "Again, I'm so sorry."

She lifted one shoulder. "It happened. I can't change it. For a long time, I struggled to deal with the injustice of it all. My parents were only trying to help others and my father paid the ultimate price for his benevolence. I can't say I've ever really found peace with that or ever will, but I've been able to move forward. For what it's worth, I freaked out at loud noises for a long time, too. Probably a good year or two after the accident."

"You seem to handle them fine now."

She gave a small laugh. "I wouldn't be a very good children's librarian if I couldn't handle a little noise, believe me. I would have run screaming into the night after the very first story time."

"So how did you come to live with your aunt and uncle?" he asked.

She shifted her gaze to his for only a moment before she looked out the windshield again, as if she couldn't quite bear to make eye contact while she told the rest of the story.

"In possibly the cruelest twist of all, our mother was diagnosed with cancer shortly after we were rescued from Colombia. She had been sick for a while but hadn't sought the necessary medical care. She'd apparently suspected something was wrong before we were taken and had made an appointment for tests in Bogota in the days right around our kidnapping—an appointment she couldn't make, for obvious reasons. It was…an aggressive and deadly form of cancer. Largely because she didn't get the treatment she needed in a timely manner, she died four months later, after we came back to the States."

Unable to resist, he reached for her hand and held it in his for a moment, wishing he had the words to tell her how much he admired her.

So many people he knew would have pulled inside themselves and let the tragedy and injustice of it turn them bitter and angry at the world. Instead, she had become a strong, compassionate woman who was helping children learn to love words and stories, while she wrote uplifting, heartwarming tales where good always triumphed.

She looked down at their joined hands, and her lips parted just a little before she closed them and swallowed. "After our mother died, Uncle Claude and Aunt Mary opened their home and their hearts to us, and we've been here ever since."

"And thus you entered the world of Christmas extravaganzas."

This time her laugh sounded more natural—a sweet, spontaneous sound that seemed to slide through his chest and tug at his heart. He liked the sound of her laughter. It made him want to sit in this warm car with her all night while soft Christmas music played on the stereo and snow fluttered against the windshield and his daughter slept soundly in the backseat.

"There was no Christmas Ranch before we came here. Uncle Claude had the idea a year later. My sisters and I share the theory that he did it only to distract us because he knew the holidays would be tough for us without our parents, especially that first anniversary."

"You were kidnapped at Christmastime?" That only seemed to add to the tragedy of it, that people could cruelly and viciously use an innocent family for financial gain during a time that was supposed to be about peace on earth and goodwill toward men.

"Yes." She leaned back against the seat and gazed out at the snowflakes dancing against the windshield. "My mother and father would try to keep up our spirits during our captivity by singing carols with us and encouraging us to make up Christmas stories."

"Ah. And you've carried on their storytelling tradition."

"In my feeble way, I guess you're right."

"Not feeble," he protested. "*Sparkle and the Magic Snowball* is a charming story that has captured the hearts of children and parents alike."

She looked embarrassed. "Mostly because of Hope and her beautiful illustrations."

"And because the story is sweet and hopeful at a time when people desperately need that."

She shifted in the seat, her cheeks slightly pink in the low light.

"I never expected any of this. I only wanted to tell stories to my niece and nephew. I don't know if I would ever have found the courage to submit it to a publisher. I didn't, actually. If not for Hope, all the Sparkle stories would still be in a box under my bed."

He released her fingers, not at all sure he liked this soft tenderness seeping through him. "Your parents would be so proud of you. Who would have guessed when you were sharing stories with your parents and sisters while you were all hostages during a dark Christmastime that one day you would be a famous author?"

"Not me, certainly."

"Does writing make you feel closer to your parents?"

She stared at him for a long moment, her eyes wide. "I... Yes. Yes, it does. I never realized that until right this moment when you said it. Sometimes when I'm writing, I feel as if they're with me again, whispering words of comfort to me in the darkness."

It would be easy to fall for her. Something about her combination of vulnerability and strength tugged at him, called to him in a way no other woman ever had.

He didn't have *time* for this, he reminded himself sternly. His daughter needed all his attention right now while she tried to heal. He couldn't dilute that attention by finding himself tangled up with a lovely librarian, no matter how much he might want to be.

"I had better go," she said after a moment. Did she also sense the growing attraction between them? Was that the reason for that sudden unease in her expression? "You should get a certain exhausted birthday girl home to her bed. Besides that, Linus and Lucy are probably wondering what in the world I'm doing out here for so long."

"Of course."

With far more reluctance than he knew he should feel, he opened his door and walked around the vehicle through the lightly falling snow to her door.

The December night smelled of pine and smoke from a fireplace somewhere close. The familiar mingle of scents struck deep into his memories, of the happy times he used to spend here with his grandmother. She had been his rock, the one constant support in the midst of his chaotic family life.

He breathed in deeply as he opened her car door. As they walked to her house, he realized with shock that this was the most peaceful he had felt in weeks, since that horrible day when he'd pulled up to Elise's house to find sirens and flashing lights and ambulances.

"You don't have to walk me to the door, Flynn. This isn't a date."

He suddenly *wished* it had been a date, that the two of them had gone to dinner somewhere and shared secrets and stories and long, delicious kisses.

If it had been a date, he possibly could give into this sudden hunger to kiss her at the doorstep, to finally taste that lush mouth that had been tantalizing him all evening.

"I want to make sure you don't slip," he said. It wasn't exactly a lie, just not the entire truth. "Ice can be dangerous."

She said nothing, though he thought her eyes might have narrowed slightly as if she sensed he had more on his mind than merely her safety.

They both made it up the steps without incident, and it only took her a moment to find a key in her purse.

"Good night," she said after she unlocked her door. "Thank you for including me in Olivia's birthday celebration. It was an honor, truly."

"We were the lucky ones that you agreed to come. It was a dream come true for her, sharing delicious pizza with her favorite author."

"I imagine her dreams will become a little more lofty as she gets older, but I'm happy I could help with this one." She gave him a sidelong look. "I hope I see her at the rehearsal tomorrow for the Christmas program. She really seemed to be interested in participating, and we would love to have her. Don't worry. She'll have fun."

Damn. He had almost forgotten about that. The peace he had been feeling seemed to evaporate like the puffs of air from their breaths.

"Don't plan on her," he warned.

"Why not?" she asked with a frown.

He raked a hand through his hair. "She's been through a brutal experience. Would you have been ready for something like this right after your own trauma?"

"I don't know," she admitted. "But if I expressed any interest at all, my aunt and uncle would have been right in the front row, cheering me on."

"I'm not your aunt and uncle," he said, with more bite in his voice than he intended.

She froze for just a moment, then nodded, her sweet, lovely features turning as wintry as the evening. "I'm sorry. You're right. I overstepped."

Her words and the tight tone made him feel like an ass. She was only trying to help his child.

"I'm sorry," he said. "I just can't see how getting up in front of a bunch of strangers and singing about peace on earth will help a young girl suffering from PTSD."

"I suppose you're right. I will say that my parents firmly believed a person could ease her own troubles while helping others—or at least trying to see them in a different light. Living here with Uncle Claude and Aunt Mary only reinforced that message. They started The Christmas Ranch so my sisters and I could find comfort in the midst of our own pain by bringing the joy of the holidays to others. It worked for us. I guess I was hoping it would do the same for Olivia, but you're her father. It's ultimately your decision."

Talk about backing a guy into a corner. What was he supposed to do?

Olivia *had* expressed a desire to participate, the first time anything had sparked her interest in weeks. He certainly had the right as her father to make decisions about what he thought was best for her, but what if he was wrong? What if she truly did need this? How could he be the one to say no to her?

"Fine," he said reluctantly. "I'll bring her tomorrow. If she enjoys herself, she can come back. But if I believe this is at all stressing her, I'll immediately put an end to it."

She smiled and he was struck again by how lovely she was. Behind her quiet prettiness was a woman of true beauty; she just seemed determined to hide it.

"Oh, that's wonderful. We'll be thrilled to have her. We'll see you tomorrow afternoon, in the main lodge at the ranch. Do you know where it is?"

"I'll figure it out."

"Excellent. I'll see you both tomorrow, then."

He knew that idea shouldn't leave him with this bubbly anticipation.

"Good night. Thanks again for having dinner with us."

"You're welcome. It was truly my pleasure."

He started to leave and then, prompted by the impulse that had been coursing through him all evening, he reached forward and kissed her softly on the cheek, the light sort of kiss people gave to even their casual acquaintances in California.

She smelled delicious—of laundry soap and almonds and some kind of springtime flowers. It took him a moment to place her scent. Violets—sweet and fresh and full of hope.

Instantly, he knew this was a mistake, that he would be dreaming of that scent all night.

Her eyes, wide and shocked behind her glasses, were impossibly green. It would be easy—so very easy—to shift his mouth just a few inches and truly kiss her. For an instant the temptation was overwhelming, but he drew on all his strength and forced himself to step away.

"Good night," he said again. To his dismay, his voice sounded ragged.

"Yes," she answered with a dazed sort of look that he told himself was only surprise.

He didn't give himself the chance to explore if that look in her eyes might have some other source—like a shared attraction, for instance. He just turned around and headed down the steps of her porch and toward his vehicle and his sleeping child.

* * *

When she was certain Flynn was in his car, driving back down the lane toward the main road, Celeste moved away from the window and sank into her favorite chair. Lucy—all sleek, sinuous grace—immediately pounced into her lap. She took a moment to pet the cat, her thoughts twirling.

For a moment there she had been almost positive Flynn Delaney had been about to *really* kiss her. That was impossible. Completely irrational. She must have been imagining things, right?

Why on earth would he want to kiss *her*? She was gawky and awkward and shy, more comfortable with books and her fictional characters than she was with men.

They were from completely different worlds, which was probably one of the reasons she'd had such a crush on him when she was a girl. He represented the unattainable. His mother was a famous movie star, and he was certainly gorgeous enough that *he* could have been one, too, if he'd been inclined in that direction.

He had been married to Elise Chandler, for Pete's sake, one of the most beautiful women on earth. How could he possibly be interested in a frumpy, introverted *children's librarian*?

The absurdity of it completely defied reason.

She must be mistaken. That moment when he'd kissed her cheek and their gazes had met—when she'd thought she'd seen that spark of *something* kindling in his gaze—must have been a trick of the low lighting in her entryway.

What would it have been like to kiss him? *Really* kiss him?

The question buzzed around inside her brain like a particularly determined mosquito. She had no doubt it would have been amazing.

She was destined never to know.

She sighed, gazing at the lights of her little Christmas tree sparkling cheerily in the small space. If she weren't careful, she could end up with a heart as shattered as one of the ornaments Lucy liked to bat off the branches.

It would be so frighteningly easy for her to fall for him. She was already fiercely attracted to him and had been since she was barely a teenager. More than that, she liked and admired him. His devotion to Olivia and his concern for her were even more attractive to Celeste than those vivid blue eyes, the broad shoulders, the rugged slant of his jaw.

If he were to kiss her—truly kiss her—her poor, untested heart wouldn't stand a chance.

After a moment she pushed away the unease. This entire mental side trip was ridiculous and unnecessary. He wasn't interested in her and he wouldn't kiss her, so why spend another moment fretting about it?

Still, she couldn't help wishing she never had encouraged him to allow Olivia to participate in the Christmas program at the ranch. He was only here for a few weeks. The likelihood that she would even *see* the man again would have been very slim if not for Olivia and the program, and then she could have let this hopeless attraction die a natural death.

No worries, she told herself. She would simply do her best to return things to a casual, friendly level for his remaining time in Cold Creek.

How hard could it be?

Chapter Seven

Dealing with thirty jacked-up children a week before Christmas was not exactly the best way to unwind after a busy day at work.

Celeste drew in a deep breath, let it out slowly and ordered herself to chill. The noise level inside the two-story St. Nicholas Lodge was at epic levels. In one corner, a group of third-grade boys tossed around a paper airplane one of them had folded. In another, two girls were singing "Let it Go" at the top of their lungs. Three of the younger boys were chasing each other around, coming dangerously close to the huge Christmas tree that was the focal point of the lodge.

All the children were so excited for Christmas they were putting off enough energy to power the entire holiday light displays of three counties.

How she was supposed to whip this frenzy into organized chaos she had no idea.

"Whose crazy idea was this again?" her sister said, taking in the scene.

She sent Hope an arch look. "Go ahead. Raise your hand."

Hope offered up a rueful smile. "Sorry. It seemed like a fun idea at the time, a way to keep the local kids engaged and involved and give their parents a little break for shopping and baking, with the payoff of a cute show for the senior citizens at the end. I suppose I didn't really think it through."

"How very unlike you," Faith said drily from Celeste's other side.

Faith's presence was far more of a shock to Celeste than the wild energy of the children. Their eldest sister was usually so busy working on the cattle-raising side of the business that she didn't participate in many activities at The Christmas Ranch.

Perhaps she had decided to stop by because Louisa and Barrett were participating. Whatever the reason, Celeste was glad to see her there. The past eighteen months had been so difficult for Faith, losing her childhood sweetheart unexpectedly. It was good to see her sister reaching outside her comfort zone a little.

"I guess I didn't expect them all to be so…jacked up." Hope couldn't seem to take her gaze away from the younger children, who were now hopping around the room like bunny rabbits.

"You obviously don't have children," Faith said.

"Or work in a children's library," Celeste added.

"All kids act as if they're on crack cocaine the whole week before Christmas," Faith continued. "How could you not know that?"

"Okay, okay. Lesson learned. Now we just have to do our best to whip them into shape. We can do this, right?"

At the note of desperation in Hope's voice, Celeste forced a confident smile. "Sure we can."

Though she had her own doubts, she wouldn't voice them to Hope. She was too grateful for her sister for bringing light and joy back to the ranch.

After Travis's death in a ranching accident, Celeste, Mary and Faith had decided to close The Christmas Ranch, which had been losing money steadily for years. It had seemed the logical course of action. The Star N had been all but bankrupt and the Christmas side of things had been steadily losing money for years.

The plan had been to focus on the cattle side of the Star N, until Hope came back from years of traveling. She put her considerable energy and enthusiasm to work and single-handedly brought back the holiday attraction.

Part of that success had come because of the Sparkle books, which still managed to astonish Celeste.

She would always be deeply grateful to Hope for reminding them all of the joy and wonder of the season. Helping her with this Christmas program was a small way to repay her for all her hard work on behalf of the family.

"We've got this," she said to her sisters with a firm smile that contained far more assurance than she really felt.

She stepped forward and started to clap her hands to gather the children around when the door opened and a couple of newcomers came in. She turned with a smile to welcome them and felt an actual physical jolt when she saw Flynn and Olivia.

Despite his agreement the night before, she had been certain Flynn would end up not bringing Olivia. She had seen the clear reluctance in his eyes and knew he worried the girl wasn't ready for this sort of public appearance.

She was thrilled for Olivia's sake that he had changed his mind, even if it meant she would have to do her best to ignore her own reaction to him—and even though she wouldn't have been nearly as exhausted today if not for him.

Her night had been restless. She couldn't seem to shake the memory of that moment when he had kissed her cheek—the warmth of his mouth, the brush of his evening shadow against her skin, the delicious, outdoorsy scent of him.

She shivered now in remembered reaction.

"Are you cold?" Faith asked in a low voice.

No. Exactly the opposite. "I'm fine." The lie rolled out far more easily than she would have expected. She had never been very good at stretching the truth.

"That must be Flynn," Hope said in an undertone, following her gaze to the newcomers. "Wow. He's really filled out since he was a teenager. Where's a nice lawn to be mowed when we need it?"

Faith laughed aloud, something she did very rarely these days. She had become so much more sober since Travis died.

"Good luck with that, finding a patch of bare lawn in Idaho in December," Faith said. "Too bad you can't talk him into shoveling snow without his shirt."

That was an image Celeste didn't need to add to the others in her head. She felt herself color, then immediately regretted the reaction when her sisters both looked between her and Flynn with renewed interest. Drat. They were both entirely too perceptive. The last thing she needed was for either Hope or Faith to get any matchmaking ideas where Flynn was concerned.

She quickly left her annoying sisters and moved forward to greet the newcomers.

Olivia looked nervous, half hiding behind her father. She visibly relaxed when Celeste approached.

"Hi, Celeste."

"It's my favorite just-turned-seven-year-old. Hi."

"It's noisy in here," Olivia informed her in an accusing sort of voice, as if it was *Celeste's* fault all the children were so wild.

"I know. Sorry about that. We're just about to get started. Once we focus everybody's attention, things will calm down. How are you today?"

Olivia smiled a little. "Okay, I guess. My dad didn't want to bring me, but I asked him and asked him until he finally said yes."

"I'm so glad," she said.

She shifted her gaze finally to Flynn and found him watching her with an unreadable look. She was suddenly aware that she must look tousled and harried. She had come straight from work, stopping at home only long enough to let Linus out and yank her hair up into a messy bun. She wore jeans and her favorite baggy sweater, and she was pretty sure her makeup had worn off hours ago.

For just a moment, she wished she could be beautiful and sophisticated instead of what she was—boring.

"Hi," she said to him. To her dismay, her voice sounded breathless and nervous. "I wasn't sure you would come."

"Apparently my daughter is relentless. Kind of like someone else I know."

She had to smile at the slightly disgruntled note in his voice.

"This will be fun. You'll see. We're going to practice until about six thirty. If you have shopping to do or want to go back to work on your grandmother's house, you're welcome to return for her then. Actually, I could even drop her off. It's not far."

He looked around at the chaos of the jacked-up children and then back at his nervous daughter.

"I believe I'll stay, if you don't mind."

What if she *did* mind? What if the idea of him watching her for the next two hours made her more nervous than a turkey at Thanksgiving?

She didn't know what else she could do but nod. "Sure. Of course. There are sofas over by the fireplace where you can make yourself comfortable. If you'd rather be closer to the action here, feel free to bring over a chair."

"Thanks."

He then proceeded to take neither of those suggestions. Instead, he leaned against the wall, crossed his arms over his chest and turned his full attention in her direction.

"Right." She swallowed and glanced at her watch. They should have started practicing five minutes ago.

She clapped her hands loudly and firmly three times to grab everyone's attention and said in her most firm librarian voice. "By the count of ten, I need everybody to gather around me and freeze in your best Christmas statue pose. Ready? One. Two. Three…"

By the time she hit four, all thirty children—thirty-one now, including Olivia—had made their way to her and adopted various positions. Destry Bowman, one of the older girls, was stretched out on the floor pretending to be asleep. Cute little Jolie Wheeler looked as if she was trying to do a figure eight on skates. Her niece, Louisa, appeared to be reaching on tiptoes for something, and it took Celeste a moment before she realized she was trying to put ornaments on an invisible Christmas tree.

Olivia looked uncertain, standing nervously with her hands clasped in front of her.

Celeste gave her a reassuring smile and then turned her attention to the other children.

"Perfect. Statues, you can all relax now and sit down."

The children complied instantly and she smiled. They might be a wild bunch but she loved them all. Each was someone whose name she knew, either from being neighbors and friends with their parents or from church or her work at the library.

"Thank you! This is going to be great fun, you'll see. The senior citizens and your families are going to *love* it, trust me, and you'll have fun, too. Are you all ready to put together a great show for your families?"

"Yes!" they shouted as one.

"Let's get to it, then."

He never would have predicted it when he walked into chaos, but somehow the ragtag collection of hyperactive children had calmed down considerably and were working hard together.

Celeste had organized the children into small groups of five or six and assigned one older child to teach them the song or dance they were to perform. She in turn moved between the groups offering words of advice or encouragement, working on a lyric here or a dance move there.

He found it charming to watch, especially seeing her lose her natural reserve with the children.

Was that why she had become a children's librarian, because she was more comfortable interacting with them? He was curious—but then he was curious about *everything* that had to do with Celeste Nichols.

Naturally, he kept a careful eye on his daughter, but she seemed to have relaxed considerably since they'd walked in. Just now she was talking and—yes!—even *laughing* with three children he'd heard call Celeste their aunt, a couple of boys about her age and a girl who appeared to be a few years older.

Had Celeste said something to them, somehow encouraged them to be especially welcoming to Olivia? He wouldn't have been surprised, but maybe they were as naturally compassionate and caring as their aunt. Whatever the reason, the children seemed to have gone out of their way to show kindness and help her feel more comfortable, which went a long way toward alleviating his own concerns.

He doubted anything could make him feel totally enthusiastic about Olivia performing in the little production, but it helped considerably to see her enjoying herself so much and interacting with her peers.

He wasn't sure he was ready to admit it, but Celeste might have been right. This little children's performance in a small community in Idaho might be exactly what Olivia needed to help her begin to heal from the horrors she had endured.

He finally relaxed enough to take a seat on one of the sofas by the fireplace and was reading through email messages from his office on his cell phone when one of the women Celeste had been talking with when he and Olivia arrived took a seat on the sofa across from him.

"Hi, Flynn. You probably don't remember me, but I'm Hope Santiago. Used to be Nichols. I'm Celeste's sister."

Ah. No wonder she had looked familiar, though she only shared green eyes in common with her sister. Instead of Celeste's silky brown hair and quiet, restful loveliness, Hope Santiago was pretty in a Bohemian sort of way, with long, wavy blond hair and a cluster of exotic-looking bracelets at her wrist.

He had met her before, he thought, back when he used to come here for the summers.

"Hello. Sure, I remember you. You're married now. Congratulations."

She gave a pleased-as-punch smile and gestured through the doorway to what looked like an office where a big, tough-looking dude with a couple of tats was speaking on a cell phone.

"That's my husband, Rafe. He and I run The Christmas Ranch together."

"The two of you must just be overflowing with Christmas spirit."

She chuckled. "We do our best. Thanks for letting your daughter participate in the show. It means a lot to Celeste."

He wasn't sure he had exactly "let" Olivia do anything. He'd been steamrollered into it, when all was said and done, but so far things seemed to be working out.

He shrugged. "It's for a good cause, right? Making some older people happy. That can only be a good thing, right?"

"Exactly." She beamed at him.

"You're the artist," he realized suddenly. "The one who took Celeste's Sparkle story and turned it into a book."

She nodded. "That's me," she answered.

"They're charming illustrations that go perfectly with the story," he told her. "I read the second book again to my daughter last night, for about the twentieth time in just a few days. It's every bit as sweet as the first one. The two of you make a great team."

She looked pleased at his words. "Thanks, but Celeste is the creative genius. I just took her fabulous story and drew little pictures to go with it. Any success the Sparkle book has seen is because of her story."

"That's funny. She said almost exactly the same thing about you and your illustrations."

"She would," she said with a laugh. "Don't make the mistake of thinking we're always adoring sisters, so sweet to each other we'll make your teeth hurt. We're not afraid to have it out. I think I've still got a little bald spot in the back of my head where she yanked out some hair during a fight when we were kids. She might look sweet and all, with that quiet librarian thing she has going, but she can fight dirty, even when you're bigger than she is."

He had to laugh. He glanced over at Celeste, who was holding an upset preschooler on her lap and trying to calm him, her face close to his. Flynn did his best to imagine her in a physical fight with one of her sisters. He couldn't quite make the image fit, but had to admit he enjoyed trying.

She must have felt his gaze. She looked up from the little boy and whatever she was saying to him. He saw her swallow and watched her features turn rosy, much to his secret enjoyment. After a moment, she turned back to the child and he shifted his gaze back to Hope, who was watching him with interest.

"Looks as if we're just about wrapping up here," she said casually. "If you haven't had dinner, why don't you and your daughter come up to the ranch house after practice? Aunt Mary is making lasagna and her famous crusty bread sticks. You can celebrate with us."

"What are you celebrating?"

"We just agreed to let a film studio begin work on an animated Sparkle movie. It's going into production immediately, with hopes that it will be out by next Christmas. And with the money we're getting for the film rights, we're paying off the second mortgage our uncle took on the Star N. We'd love to have you celebrate with us."

His stomach rumbled on cue while he was still trying to take in the surprising invitation. "That's very kind of you, but I don't want to intrude."

"Intrude on what?" Another woman who looked enough like Celeste and Hope to make him certain this was their other sister joined them by the fireplace.

"I invited Flynn and his daughter over for lasagna. Aunt Mary won't mind, will she?"

"Are you kidding? She'll be over the moon to have a few more people to fuss over, and you know she always makes enough to feed half the town."

His first inclination was to say no. He even opened his mouth to refuse the invitation, but then he caught sight of Olivia looking more relaxed and animated than he had seen her in a long time. Right next to her was Celeste, apparently done calming the upset little boy and now smiling at something Olivia had said.

He couldn't seem to look away.

"Sure," he answered before he had a chance to think it through. He had no plans for dinner beyond warming up the pizza they'd had the night before, and he had a feeling Olivia was getting a little tired of his meager culinary abilities. "Thank you for inviting us. Lasagna sounds delicious, and we would be honored to celebrate with you, especially since Olivia is your biggest fan."

"Excellent," Hope said, looking delighted.

"I'd better call Aunt Mary and let her know to set two more places at dinner," Faith said.

The two of them walked away, leaving him wondering what he had just done.

Chapter Eight

This was a mistake.

Flynn sat at the big scarred kitchen table at the Star N wondering what on earth he had been thinking to agree to this.

Since the moment he sat down he had been aware of an itch between his shoulders, a feeling that he didn't belong here.

He couldn't quite put his finger on why.

The food was delicious, he had to admit. The lasagna was perfectly cooked, cheesy and flavorful with a red sauce his late mother's Italian chef would definitely have endorsed. The bread sticks were crispy and flavorful, and even the tossed salad seemed fresh and festive.

He couldn't fault the company. It was more than pleasant. He enjoyed listening to Celeste's family—her aunt Mary, who turned out to be a jolly woman with warm eyes and an ample girth, her two sisters as well as Hope's husband, Rafe Santiago, and Chase Brannon, a neighboring rancher who seemed more like part of the family.

More important, Olivia seemed to be more relaxed and comfortable than he had seen her in a long time. She sat at one end of the table with Celeste's niece, Louisa, her nephew, Barrett, and the other boy he had seen them with at the rehearsal. It turned out the boy was Rafe's nephew. From what Flynn could tell, the boy lived with Rafe and Hope, though Flynn didn't completely understand why.

The children were deep in conversation, and every once in a while he heard laughter coming from that end of the table. Olivia even joined in a few times—a total shocker.

So why did he feel so uneasy? He didn't want to admit that it might have been because he was enjoying himself *too* much. He didn't need to find more things that drew him to Celeste, when he already couldn't seem to get the woman out of his head.

"So what do you do in California?" Chase asked.

The man treated all the Nichols sisters as if he were an older brother. He seemed especially protective of Faith, though she hardly seemed to notice.

"Construction. I've got a fairly good-size operation, with offices in San Diego, Los Angeles and Sacramento."

"Delaney Construction. Is that you?" Rafe piped up.

He nodded, intensely proud of what he had built out of nothing. The company had become a powerhouse over the past decade, even in the midst of a rough economy.

"You do good work," Rafe said. "A buddy of mine is one of your carpentry subs. Kevin O'Brian. I flew out for a few weeks last spring to help him on a job, a new hospital in Fullerton."

"Right. He's a good man."

"That's what he said about you."

"Wow. Small world," Hope said.

He and the men spent a few moments talking about some of the unique challenges of working in the construction industry in Southern California.

"Have you ever thought about moving your operations out to this neck of the woods?" Chase asked. "We don't have a lot of hospitals and the like going up, but there are always construction projects around here, especially in the Jackson area."

The question took him by surprise. Three months ago he would have given an emphatic no to that question. He had a business in Southern California, contacts and subcontractors and jobs he had fought hard to win.

He glanced at Olivia. He had other things to concern himself with now, like what might be best for his daughter.

Small-town life seemed to agree with her, he had to admit. Maybe she would be able to heal better if she were away for longer than just a few weeks from the life they had both known in California.

A change of scenery appeared to have helped the Nichols sisters move beyond the trauma in their past.

"I haven't," he answered truthfully. "It's definitely something to think about."

He glanced across the table to see Celeste listening in, though she was pretending not to.

What would she think if he stuck around town a little longer than a few weeks?

Probably nothing, he told himself. They meant nothing to each other.

"What are you doing with that property of your grandmother's?" Mary asked.

"I'm hoping to put it up for sale in the next few weeks."

"You're not planning to subdivide it, are you?" she asked, her gaze narrowed.

He could probably make more money if he did that, but somehow he didn't think his grandparents would approve.

"That's a nice piece of land there by the Cold Creek," Brannon said. "Somebody could build a beautiful house on it if they were so inclined."

If he were going to stay here—which he most definitely *wasn't*, based on a simple dinner conversation—he probably would take the bones of the house and add on to it, opening up a wall here or there and rebuilding the kitchen and bathrooms.

It was a nice, comfortable house, perfectly situated with

a gorgeous view of the mountains, but it was too small and cramped for comfort, with tiny rooms and an odd flow.

All this was theoretical. He planned to sell the property as-is, not take on another project. He had enough to do right now while he was helping his daughter recover the shattered bits of her life and learn to go on without the mother she had adored.

The conversation drifted during the dinner from topic to topic. The Nicholses seemed an eclectic group, with wide-ranging interests and opinions. Even the children joined in the discussion, discussing their projects at school, the upcoming show, the movie deal they were celebrating.

He was astonished to discover he enjoyed every moment of it. This was exactly what a family should be, he thought, noisy and chaotic and wonderful.

He had never known this growing up as an only child whose parents had stayed together much longer than they should have. He had learned to live without a family over the years, but it made his chest ache that his daughter would never have it, either.

Her sisters were matchmaking.

Celeste could tell by the surreptitious glances Faith and Hope sent between her and Flynn, the leading little questions they asked him, the way they not-so-subtly discussed the upcoming movie deal, careful to focus on Celeste's literary success, as if they were trying to sell a prize pig at the market.

It was humiliating, and she could only hope he hadn't noticed.

How could they possibly think Flynn might be interested in her in the first place? If they had bothered to ask her, she would have explained how ludicrous she found the very idea.

They didn't ask her, of course. They'd simply gone ahead and invited the poor man to dinner. Why he agreed to come, she had no idea. By the time dessert rolled around, she still hadn't figured it out—nor did she understand how he and Olivia seemed to fit in so effortlessly with her family.

Hope and Faith and Aunt Mary all liked him, she could tell, and Chase and Rafe treated him with courtesy and respect.

As for her, she liked having the two of them here entirely too much.

She tried to reel herself back, to force herself to remember this was only temporary. They were only at the ranch for the evening. Her sisters' matchmaking intentions were destined to failure. Not only *wasn't* he interested in her, but he had made it abundantly clear he was going back to California as soon as he could.

"Practice went well, don't you think?" Hope asked, distracting her from that depressing thought. "The kids seemed to be into it, and what I heard was wonderful."

"It won't win any Tony Awards, but it should be fun," she answered.

"With all you have going on around here, I still can't figure out why you decided to throw a show for local senior citizens," Flynn said.

Hope took the chance to answer him. "We've always had so much community support over the years here at The Christmas Ranch, from the very moment Uncle Claude opened the doors. The people of Pine Gulch have been great to us, and we wanted to give back a little. I guess we picked senior citizens because so many of them feel alone during the holiday season."

"Many of these people have been friends with me and my late husband for years," Mary added. "This seemed a good chance to offer them a little holiday spirit."

"I think it's nice," Louisa declared. "So do my friends. That's why they agreed to do it."

Celeste smiled at her niece, who had a very tender heart despite the tragedy of losing her father.

"I do, too," she answered.

"Is Sparkle going to show up at the party?" Barrett asked.

"I think we're going to have to see about that next week,"

Faith answered her son. "He's been acting a little down the past few days."

Celeste frowned at her sister. "What's wrong with him?" she asked, alarmed.

"Oh, I'm sure it's nothing," she answered. "He's just off his feed a bit. I ended up bringing him up here to his stall at the main barn to see if being back with the horses for a day or two would cheer him up."

Sparkle had a particularly soft spot for Mistletoe, an old mare who used to be Uncle Claude's. "I'm sure that's it," Celeste said.

"Maybe he just misses *you*, CeCe," Hope suggested. "You haven't been down to see him in a while."

Celeste rolled her eyes. "Right. I'm sure he's pining away."

It was true that she and Sparkle were old friends. The reindeer was warm and affectionate, far more than most of their small herd.

"You ought to go down to the barn to say hello while you're here," Faith suggested.

"Can I go meet Sparkle?" Olivia asked, her eyes huge as she followed the conversation. "I would *love* to."

She *had* told the girl she would take her to meet the inspiration for the books she loved so much. "He enjoys company. I'm sure he would love to meet you."

"Can we go now?" the girl pressed.

She looked at the table laden with delicious dishes she had done nothing to help prepare. Yes, she could claim a good excuse—being busy directing the show and all—but Uncle Claude and Aunt Mary had always been clear. If you didn't help cook a meal, you were obligated to help clean it up.

"I need to help clear these dishes first," she said.

"Oh, don't worry about this," Faith said.

"Right. We can take care of things," Hope insisted.

"Yes, dear," Aunt Mary added. "We've got this completely covered. It won't take a moment to clean this up. Meantime, why don't you take our guests down to the barn to meet Sparkle?"

Who were these women and what had they done with her family members? She frowned, fighting the urge to roll her eyes at all of them for their transparent attempts to push her together with Flynn. For heaven's sake, what did they think would possibly happen between the two of them with his daughter along?

"I don't know," Flynn said, checking his watch. "It's getting late."

"It's not even eight o'clock yet!" Olivia protested. "Since I don't have to get up for school, I haven't been going to bed until nine thirty."

"I suppose that's true."

"So we can go?"

He hesitated, then shrugged. "If Celeste doesn't mind taking us. But we can't stay long. She's already had a long day."

"Oh, yay!" Olivia jumped up instantly from the table and headed for her coat.

"Does anyone else want to go down to the barn with us?" Celeste asked.

She didn't miss the way Barrett practically jumped out of his chair with eagerness but subsided again with a dejected look when his mother shook her head firmly.

Oh, she hoped Flynn hadn't noticed her crazy, delusional, interfering sisters.

He rose. "We'll probably need to head out after we stop at the barn. It's late and I have to get this young lady home to bed, whatever she says."

"Understandable," Aunt Mary said with a warm, affectionate smile for both of them.

With a sweet, surprising charm, he leaned in and kissed her aunt's plump cheek. "Thank you for the delicious meal. We both truly enjoyed it."

She heard a definite ring of truth to his words, even as he looked a little surprised by them. She had the feeling he hadn't expected to enjoy the meal—which again made her wonder why he had agreed to come.

"You are most welcome," Aunt Mary said. "I hope both of you will come again before you return to California. Your grandmother was a dear, dear friend, and I miss her terribly. Having you and your daughter here helps ease that ache a little."

He looked touched. "I miss her, too. I only wish I could have visited her more the past few years."

Mary patted his hand. "She told me you called her every Sunday night without fail, and sometimes during the week, too. She was very proud of that fact, especially as so many young people these days get so busy with their lives that they forget that their parents and grandparents might be a touch lonely without them."

"A phone call was nothing. I can't tell you how much I appreciate all of her friends here in Pine Gulch who helped keep her busy and involved."

Celeste liked to consider herself one of that number. Charlotte had volunteered at the library almost up to the end of her life, never letting her physical ailments or the frailties of age prevent her from smiling and trying to lift someone else.

"She was always so proud of you," Mary went on. "Especially because of what you came from."

He gave a snort at that. "What I came from? Beverly Hills? Yeah. I overcame so much in life. I don't know why nobody has come out with a made-for-television movie about my sad life."

Mary made a face. "Charlotte was proud of many things about you, but perhaps most of all that despite every advantage you had, you always stayed grounded and didn't let your head get turned by your mother's fame or fortune. Now that I've met you, I understand what she meant. You're a good boy, Flynn Delaney."

She smiled and patted his hand again. Flynn looked a bit taken aback at anyone calling him a boy, but he only had time to give Aunt Mary a bemused sort of look before Olivia cut off anything he might have said in response.

"Are you ready, Daddy? I can't wait to see Sparkle. I can't *wait*."

"Yes. I'm ready. We can grab our coats on the way out. Thank you all again."

"You're so welcome," Faith and Hope said at the same time, almost as if they had rehearsed it. Chase and Rafe both nodded in the odd way men had of speaking volumes with just a simple head movement.

"Bye, Olivia. We'll see you at the next practice," Louisa said cheerfully.

They put on their coats quickly and headed out into the December evening.

The snow had increased in intensity, still light but more steady now. The air was still, though, with no wind to hurl flakes against them.

The night seemed magical somehow, hushed and beautiful with the full moon trying to push through the cloud cover.

Celeste was fiercely aware of him as they made their way to the barn. He was so very...male, from the jut of his jaw to his wide shoulders to the large footsteps his boots made in the snow beside her much smaller ones. He made her feel small and feminine in comparison.

To her relief, she didn't have to make conversation. Olivia kept up a steady stream of conversation about the ranch. She couldn't help noticing the girl had talked more that day than she had in all their previous encounters combined. Either she was more comfortable with Celeste now, or she was beginning to return to the girl she had been before the shooting.

If she wasn't mistaken, the girl had hardly limped that afternoon or evening. That had to be a good sign, she supposed.

"Here we are," she said when they reached the barn. The smell of hay and animals and old wood greeted them, not at all unappealing in its way.

She flipped on the lights and heard Mistletoe's distinctive whinny of greeting. She took time as they passed the old horse to give Misty a few strokes and an apple she pulled from her pocket before she led them to Sparkle's stall next door.

"Olivia, this is Sparkle. Sparkle, meet my good friend Olivia."

After a moment of coyness, the reindeer headed to the railing of the stall.

"I've never seen a real reindeer before. He's small!"

"Reindeer are generally much smaller than people think they should be." She petted him, much the way she had Mistletoe. He lipped at her, trying to find a treat.

"Would you like to feed him an apple?"

"Can I?"

She glanced down at the girl and decided not to miss this opportunity. "I don't know. You'll have to use your left arm. He prefers it when people feed him from that side."

That was an out-and-out lie. Sparkle would eat with great delight any apple that came his way, but she decided Olivia didn't need to know that.

Flynn made a low sound of amusement beside her that seemed to ripple down her spine. She barely managed to hold back her instinctive shiver as she handed the apple to Olivia.

The girl narrowed her gaze at Celeste, obviously trying to figure out if this was some kind of a trick. In the end, the appeal and novelty of feeding a reindeer outweighed her suspicions.

She took the apple with her injured left hand and, with effort, held it out to the reindeer, who nibbled it out of her hand. Olivia giggled. "Can I pet him?"

"Sure. He won't hurt you."

She rubbed his head for a moment. "What about his antlers?"

"Go ahead. Just be gentle."

She reached out and tentatively touched an antler. "It's hard and soft at the same time. Weird!"

Sparkle visited with her for a moment, and it was plain he was happy to find a new friend. Any malaise the reindeer might have been feeling was nowhere in evidence. Maybe he really *had* been pining for her, but she doubted it. Maybe, like the rest of them, he just needed a little break from the hectic pace of the holiday season.

"What's special about this particular reindeer?" Flynn asked.

She considered how to answer. "Well, he was the first reindeer Uncle Claude ever obtained, so he's been here the longest. And he's always been so much more affectionate than the others—not that they're mean or anything, just…standoffish. Not Sparkle. He's always been as friendly as can be. It rubs off on everyone."

They watched the reindeer a few moments longer. When she heard a little sound from the stall at the end of the barn, she suddenly remembered what other treasure the barn contained. Clearly, she didn't spend enough time here.

"I nearly forgot," she said. "There's something else here you might like to see."

"What?" Olivia asked eagerly. The girl loved animals; that much was obvious. Perhaps she and Flynn ought to look into getting a dog when they returned to California.

She didn't want to think about that now, not when the night seemed hushed and sweet here in the quiet barn.

"Come and see," she answered. She led the way and pulled open the stall gate. Olivia peered in a little warily but her nervousness gave way to excitement.

"Puppies! Dad, look!"

"I see them, honey."

The half dozen black-and-white pudgy things belonged to Georgie, one of the ranch border collies.

"Can I pet them?"

"Sure. I'll warn you, they're probably not super clean. You're going to want to wash your hands when you're done."

"I will. I promise."

She knelt down and was immediately bombarded with wriggling puppies.

Celeste felt her throat tighten as she watched this girl who had been through so much find simple joy in the moment. Flynn had almost lost her. It seemed a miracle that they were here in this barn on a snowy night watching her giggle as a puppy licked her hand.

"She did all right today at the rehearsal," she said in a low voice to Flynn as they watched together. "I know you were concerned about the noise and confusion, but she handled it well. Wouldn't you agree?"

They were standing close enough together that she could feel his sigh. "I suppose."

"Does that mean you'll bring her to the next rehearsal, then?"

He gave a small sound that was almost a laugh. "Anybody ever tell you that you're relentless?"

"A few times, maybe," she said ruefully. *More than a few* was closer to the truth.

Needing a little distance, she eased down onto the bench next to the stall. To her surprise, he followed and sat beside her.

"Fine," he answered. "You win. I'll bring her to the next one. That doesn't mean I have to like it."

She glanced at his daughter playing with the puppies a dozen feet away, then turned back to Flynn. "Why do you have a problem with her performing?" she asked, her voice low. "Especially when it seems to be something she enjoys?"

"I don't *want* her to enjoy it," he answered in an equally low tone. "If I had my way, I would have her stay far away from any kind of stage or screen."

She frowned at the intensity of his words. "Because of your mother or because of Elise?"

"Either. Both. Take your pick." He watched as a puppy started nibbling on Olivia's ponytail, which only made her giggle again as she tried to extricate it from the little mouth.

After a moment he spoke with fierce resolve. "I want my daughter to find happiness in life based on her own decisions and accomplishments, not because of how many pictures of her holding a latte from Starbucks showed up in the tabloids this week. There's an artificiality to that world that crumbles to nothing in a heartbeat. Take it from someone who grew up on the edge of that spotlight."

She thought of what Aunt Mary had said about his grandmother's pride in him for staying grounded. Unlike his mother or his wife, he hadn't sought that spotlight. He had gone into a career outside Hollywood and had built a successful business on his own merits. She had to admire that.

"That must have been tough for you," she said.

He shrugged. "How can I complain, really? It sounds stupid, even to me. I grew up with the sort of privileges most people only dream about. A-list celebrities hanging out in my swimming pool, a BMW in the driveway on my sixteenth birthday, vacations in Cannes and Park City and Venice."

By worldly standards, her family had been very poor. Her parents had given everything they had to helping others, to the point that she remembered a period in their lives when she and her sisters each had had only two or three outfits that they swapped back and forth.

She hadn't necessarily enjoyed moving from country to country, never feeling as if she had a stable home. In truth, she still carried lingering resentment about it, but she had always known she was deeply loved.

She had a feeling that for all his outward privilege, Flynn had missed out on that assurance, at least from his parents. She was grateful he had known the unwavering love and devotion of his grandmother.

"We don't get to choose the circumstances of our birth families, do we?" she said softly. "The only thing we have control of is the life we make for ourselves out of those circumstances."

His gaze met hers and the intensity of his expression left her suddenly breathless. Something shimmered between them, something bright and fierce. She couldn't seem to look away, and she again had the oddest feeling he wanted to kiss her.

Now? Here? With his daughter just a few feet away? She must have been imagining things. Still, the idea of him leaning forward slightly, of his mouth sliding across hers, made nerves jump in her stomach and her knees feel suddenly weak.

She felt as if she stood on the brink of something, arms stretched wide, trying to find the courage to jump into the empty space beyond.

She could lose her heart so easily to this man.

The thought whispered into her mind and she swallowed hard. With the slightest of nudges, she would leap into that empty space and doubtless crash hard back to earth.

Careful, she warned herself, and looked away from him, pretending to focus on his daughter and the cute, wriggling puppies.

After a long pause, he finally spoke. "Despite everything you and your sisters have been through, you've made a good life for yourself here in Pine Gulch."

"I'd like to think so." Okay, maybe she was a little lonely. Maybe there were nights she lay in bed and stared at the ceiling, wondering if she was destined to spend the rest of her nights alone.

"I guess you know a little about being in the spotlight now, don't you?" Flynn said.

She forced a little laugh. "Not really. My particular spotlight is more like a flashlight beam. A very tiny, focused flashlight. That's the nice thing about being only a name on a book cover."

"That will change when the Sparkle movie hits the big screen," he predicted.

Oh, she didn't want to think about that. Just the idea made her feel clammy and slightly queasy. "I hope not," she said fervently. "I like being under the radar."

He frowned. "Why agree to let someone make the movie, then? You had to know that's only going to increase your celebrity status. You won't be able to stay under the radar for long."

In her heart, she knew he was right. What had she gotten herself into?

She hadn't had a choice, she reminded herself. Not really.

"I love my family," she said. "They're everything to me."

"It only took me a few minutes at dinner tonight to figure that out. You have a great family. But what does that have to do with signing a movie deal you don't appear to want?"

For someone who loved the magic and power in words, sometimes in conversation she felt as if she never could manage to find the right ones.

"Things haven't been...easy around here the past few years, even before my brother-in-law's accident. My uncle was a wonderful man but not the best businessman around, and the ranch hasn't exactly been thriving financially."

"I'm sorry to hear that."

"The, um, increased interest in The Christmas Ranch after the first Sparkle book came out last season helped a great deal but didn't completely solve the cash flow woes." She felt her face heat a little, as it always did when she talked about the astonishing success of the book. "With the deal Hope and I will be signing for the movie rights, we can pay off the rest of the ranch's debts and push the operation firmly into the black, which will lift considerable pressure from Faith. How could I turn down something that will benefit my family so much?"

He studied her for a moment, that funny intensity in his expression again. "So it's not necessarily what you really want, but you're willing to go through with it anyway for your family."

"Something like that," she muttered.

"If having a movie made out of your book doesn't sit well with you, couldn't you have found an alternative revenue stream?"

She shrugged. "Hope and I talked at length about this. Our agent and publisher were clear. *Someone* was going to make a Sparkle movie—which, believe me, is an amazing position to find ourselves in. The terms of this particular deal were very favorable for Hope and for me, and we were both impressed by the other projects this particular production company has engineered. The moment seemed right."

"I'm *glad* they're making a Sparkle movie," Olivia said suddenly. Celeste had been so busy explaining herself, she hadn't realized the girl had left the puppies on the floor of the stall and rejoined them. "I can't wait to see it."

Flynn smiled at his daughter with that sweet tenderness that tugged at her heart. "We'll probably be back in California, and you can tell everyone else at the movie theater that you actually had the chance to meet the real Sparkle and the women who created the fictional version."

"I guess." Olivia didn't look as excited about that prospect as Celeste might have expected. In fact, she appeared downright glum.

Why? she wondered. Was the girl enjoying her time in Pine Gulch so much that she didn't like thinking about their eventual return to California?

"Maybe we could come back and see the movie here," Olivia suggested.

"Maybe."

Celeste felt a sharp little kick to her heart at the noncommittal word. They wouldn't be back. She was suddenly certain of it. After Flynn sold his grandmother's house, he would have no more ties here in Pine Gulch. She likely would never see him or his daughter again.

This was why she needed to be careful to guard her heart better. She already hurt just thinking about them leaving. How much worse would it be if she let herself take that leap and fell in love with him?

He stood up and wiped the straw from the back of Olivia's coat where she had been sitting on the floor of the stall.

"We should probably take off," he said. "You need to tell Celeste thank-you for bringing you out here to meet Sparkle and to play with the puppies."

"Do we have to go?" she complained.

"Yes. It's late and Celeste probably has to work at the library tomorrow."

She nodded and was suddenly overwhelmed by a wave of fatigue. The day had been long and exhausting, and right now she wanted nothing more than to be in her comfy clothes, cuddled up with her animals and watching something brainless on TV.

"Okay," Olivia said in a dejected voice. "Thank you for bringing me down here to meet Sparkle and play with the puppies."

"You are very welcome," Celeste said. "Anytime you want to come back, we would love to have you. Sparkle would, too."

Olivia seemed heartened by that as she headed for the reindeer's stall one last time.

"Bye, Sparkle. Bye!"

The reindeer nodded his head two or three times as if he was bowing, which made the girl giggle.

Celeste led the way out of the barn. Another inch of snow had fallen during the short time they had been inside, and they walked in silence to where his SUV was parked in front of the house.

She wrapped her coat around her while Flynn helped his daughter into the backseat. Once she was settled, he closed the door and turned to her.

"Please tell your family thank you for inviting me to dinner. I enjoyed it very much."

"I will. Good night."

With a wave, he hopped into his SUV and backed out of the driveway.

She watched them for just a moment, snow settling on her hair and her cheeks while she tried to ignore that little ache in her heart.

She could do this. She was tougher than she sometimes gave herself credit for being. Yes, she might already care about Olivia and be right on the brink of falling hard for her father. That didn't mean she had to lean forward and leave solid ground.

She would simply have to keep herself centered, focused on her family and her friends, her work and her writing and the holidays. She would do her best to keep him at arm's length. It was the only smart choice if she wanted to emerge unscathed after this holiday season.

Soon they would be gone and her life would return to the comfortable routine she had created for herself.

As she walked into the house, she tried not to think about how unappealing she suddenly found that idea.

Chapter Nine

She didn't have a chance to test her resolve, simply because she didn't see Flynn again for longer than a moment or two over the next few days.

At the Thursday rehearsal, he merely dropped Olivia off and left after making sure to give Hope—not Celeste—a card with his cell phone number on it.

She supposed she should take that as some sort of progress. From what she gathered, he hadn't let Olivia out of his sight since the accident. She had to feel good that he felt comfortable enough with her and her family to leave the girl at The Christmas Ranch without him.

On the other hand, she had to wonder if maybe he was just trying to avoid her.

That really made no logical sense. Why would he feel any sort of need to avoid her? *He* wasn't the one who was developing feelings that could never go anywhere.

Still, she had to wonder, especially when he did the same thing Saturday morning for their final practice before the per-

formance, just dropping Olivia off as most of the other parents
had done.

She should be grateful he'd brought the girl at all, especially
when he obviously wasn't thrilled about the whole thing.

It was too bad, really, because Olivia was a natural in front
of an audience. She seemed far more comfortable onstage than
the other children.

The performance was nothing elaborate, a rather hodgepodge
collection of short Christmas skits mixed with songs and poems,
but considering the few practices they'd had, the show came
together marvelously.

When they finished the second run-through Saturday morning, Celeste clapped her hands.

"That was amazing!" she exclaimed. "I'm so proud of each
one of you for all your hard work. You are going to make some
people very, very happy next week."

Jolie Wheeler raised her hand. "Can we take the costumes
home to show our moms and dads?"

None of the costumes was anything fancy, just bits and pieces
she and Hope had thrown together with a little help from Faith
and a few of the parents. "We need to keep them here so we can
make sure everyone has all the pieces—the belts and halos and
crowns—they need for the performance. When you take them
off, put your costume on the hanger and everything else in the
bag with your name on it in the dressing room. Remember, you
will all have to be here at five thirty sharp so we can get into
costume and be ready for the show. We'll have the performance
first, and then you are all welcome with your families to stay
for dinner with our guests, if you'd like. There should be plenty
of food for everyone."

"Then can we take the costumes home?" Jolie asked.

She smiled at the adorable girl. "We need to keep them here
just in case we decide to do another show at The Christmas
Ranch next year."

"Rats," Jolie complained and a few others joined her in grumbling. What they wanted to do with a few hokey costumes, Celeste had no idea, but she had to smile at their disappointment.

"You'll all just have to be in the show next year so you can wear them again," she said.

Not that she intended to be part of it, even if Hope begged her. Writing the little show had taken her almost as long as a full-fledged children's book.

"Thank you all again for your hard work, and I'll see you Tuesday evening at five thirty if you need help with your hair and makeup."

The children dispersed to the boys' and girls' dressing rooms—really just separate storage spaces that had been temporarily converted for the show. She cleaned up the rehearsal space and supervised the pickup of the children.

Finally, only Louisa, Barrett, Joey and Olivia were left. They didn't seem to mind. Indeed, they had gone to the game drawer Hope kept in her office to keep the children occupied when they were hanging out at the lodge and were playing a spirited game of Go Fish with a Christmas-themed deck of cards.

Though she had a hundred things to—including finishing the paint job on the backdrop for the little stage they had rigged up—she sat down at the table near the refreshment booth where they were playing.

"You did so well today. All of you."

"Thanks," Louisa said. "It's really fun. I hope we do it again next year."

Not unless Hope found some other sucker to be in charge, she thought again.

"I've had lots of fun, too," Olivia said. "Thanks for inviting me to do it."

"You're very welcome. How are things going at your great-grandmother's house?"

As soon as she asked the question, she wished she hadn't. It sounded entirely too much as if she was snooping. She might as well have come out and asked when they were leaving.

"Good, I guess. We have two more rooms to do. My dad said we'll probably go back to California between Christmas and New Year's."

She tried to ignore the sharp pang in her chest. "I'm sure you'll be glad to be back in your own house."

"You're lucky! You can go swimming in the ocean," Louisa said.

"Sometimes. Mostly, it's too cold, except in summer."

"And you can go to Disneyland whenever you want," Joey added.

"No, I can't," she protested. "I have to go to school and stuff."

They talked more about the differences between their respective homes. Olivia was quite envious that they could ride horses and go sledding all winter long while the other children thought California was only palm trees and beaches.

While the seasonal staff of The Christmas Ranch started arriving and getting ready for the busiest day of their season, the children continued their game, and Celeste sat at the table next to them working on a drawing for a complicated part of the stage she was hoping Rafe could help her finish later that day.

Finally, about forty-five minutes after practice ended, Flynn burst through the front doors looking harried. "Sorry I'm late. I was taking a load of things to the county landfill and it took longer than I expected."

"Don't even worry about it. The kids have been enjoying themselves. Haven't you?"

"Yep," Barrett said. "'Cause I won Go Fish three times and Joey and Olivia both won once. Louisa didn't win any."

"Next time, watch out," his sister declared.

Flynn smiled at the girl, that full-fledged charming smile Celeste remembered from when he was a teenager. She had to swallow hard and force herself to look away, wondering why it suddenly felt so warm in the lodge.

"How was practice?" he asked.

"Good," she answered. "Great, actually. Everyone worked so hard."

"I can't wait for you to see the show, Dad," Olivia declared. "It's going to be *so* good. Celeste says all the ladies will cry."

He looked vaguely alarmed. "Is that right? Will I cry, too? I'd better bring a big hankie, just in case."

She giggled hard, then in the funny way kids have, she looked at Barrett and Louisa and something in their expressions made her laugh even harder, until all three were busting up. Their laughter was infectious and Celeste couldn't help smiling.

Flynn gazed at the three children, certain he was witnessing a miracle.

This was really his daughter, looking bright and animated and...happy.

This was the daughter he remembered, this girl who found humor in the silliest things, who was curious about the world around her and loved talking with people. He'd feared she was gone forever, stolen by a troubled man who had taken so much else from her.

Seeing her sitting at a table in the St. Nicholas Lodge, laughing with Celeste and her niece and nephew, he wanted to hug all three of the children. Even more, he wanted to kiss Celeste right on that delicious-looking mouth of hers that had haunted his dreams for days.

Her smiling gaze met his and a wave of tenderness washed over him. She had done this. He didn't know how. She had seen a sad, wounded girl and had worked some kind of Sparkle magic on her to coax out the sweet and loving girl Olivia used to be.

Her smile slid away and he realized he was staring. He drew in a deep breath and forced himself to look away.

His gaze landed on a piece of paper with what looked like a complicated drawing. "I didn't know you were an artist."

She looked embarrassed. "I'm *so* not an artist, Hope is. I'm just trying to work up a sketch I can show Rafe. I'm trying to figure out how to build wings on the side of the stage so the children have somewhere to wait offstage. There's no time to sew curtains. I just need some sort of screen to hide them from view.

He studied her sketch, then took the paper from her and made a few quick changes. "That shouldn't be hard," he said. "You just have to build a frame out of two-by-fours and then use something lightweight like particle board for your screen. If it's hinged and connected there, it should be solid and also portable enough that you can store it somewhere when you're not using it."

She studied the drawing. "Wow. That's genius! You know, I think that just might work. Can you just write down what supplies you think it might need? Rafe will be back from Jackson Hole shortly, and I can put him to work on it if he has time."

He glanced at the stage, then at his daughter, still smiling as she played cards with the other two children. Though he knew he would probably regret it—and he certainly had plenty of things still to take care of at Charlotte's house—he spoke quickly before he could change his mind.

"If you've got some tools I can use and the two-by-fours, I can probably get the frame for it done in no time."

She stared at him, green eyes wide behind those sexy glasses she wore. "Seriously?"

He shrugged. "I started out in carpentry. It's kind of what I do. This shouldn't be hard at all—as long as Olivia doesn't mind hanging around a little longer."

"Yay!" Louisa exclaimed. "She can come to the house and decorate the sugar cookies we made last night with Aunt Celeste while our mom was Christmas shopping."

Olivia looked suitably intrigued. "I've never decorated sugar cookies."

"Never?" Celeste exclaimed. She looked surprised enough that Flynn felt a pinch of guilt. Apparently this was another area where he had failed his daughter.

Olivia shook her head. "Is it hard?"

"No way," Louisa answered. "It's easy and super, super fun. You can decorate the cookies any way you want. There's no right or wrong. You can use sparkly sugar or M&M's or frosting or whatever you want."

"The best part is, when you mess it up, you get to eat your mistakes," Barrett added. "Nobody even cares. I mess up a *lot*."

Olivia snickered and Flynn had a feeling *she* would be messing up plenty, too. What was it with all these Christmas traditions that filled kids with more sugar when they least needed another reason to be excited?

He had struck out miserably when it came to Christmas traditions this year. At least they had the little Christmas tree at his grandmother's house for decoration, but that was about it.

Olivia had insisted she hoped Santa Claus wouldn't come that year, but he had disregarded her wishes and bought several things online for her. A few other presents would be waiting back in California, sort of a delayed holiday, simply because the new bike her physical therapist suggested was too big for the journey here in his SUV.

Next year would be different, he told himself. By this time next year they would be established in a routine back in California. They could hang stockings and put up a tree of their own and decorate all the sugar cookies she wanted, even if he had to order ready-made plain cookies from his favorite bakery.

The idea of returning to a routine after the stress of the past few months should have been appealing. Instead, it left him remarkably unenthused.

"May I go, Dad? I really, really, *really* want to decorate cookies."

He was torn between his desire to keep her close and his deep relief that she was so obviously enjoying the company of other children. She would enjoy the cookie decorating far more than she would enjoy sitting around and watching him work a band saw.

"Are you sure your aunt won't mind one more?" he asked Celeste.

"Are you kidding? Mary loves a crowd. The more the merrier, as far as she's concerned." She smiled a little. "And look at it this way. You'll probably come out of the whole thing with cookies to take home."

"Well, in that case, how can I say no? A guy always needs a few more cookies."

"Yay! I can go," Olivia told the other children as if they hadn't been right there to hear her father's decision.

"Put the cards away first and then get your coats on. Then you can walk up to the house."

"You're not coming?" Olivia asked.

"I'll be up later," she answered with a smile. "But first I have to finish painting some of the scenery."

The children cleaned up the cards and returned them to a little tin box, then put on their coats, hats and mittens. As soon as they were on their way, Celeste turned to him with a grateful smile. She looked so fresh and lovely that for a crazy moment, he wished they were alone in the lodge with that big crackling fire.

Instead, an older woman was setting out prepackaged snacks in what looked like a concessions area and another one was arranging things on a shelf in a gift store. Outside the windows, he could see families beginning to queue up to buy tickets.

"Is there somewhere I can get going on this? A workshop or something?"

"Oh." She looked flustered suddenly and he wondered if something in his expression revealed the fierce attraction simmering through him. "Yes. There's a building behind back where Rafe keeps his tools. That's where I've been painting the scenery, too. I'll show you."

She led the way through the lodge to a back door. They walked through the pale winter sunshine to a modern-looking barn a short distance away.

In a pasture adjacent to the barn, he saw several more reindeer as well as some draft horses.

"This is where we keep the reindeer at night during the holiday season," she explained. "There's Sparkle. Do you see him?"

As far as he could tell all the reindeer looked the same, but he would take her word for it. "Is he feeling better?"

"Much. Apparently he only wanted a few days off."

"Olivia will be happy to hear that."

"He'll need his strength. This afternoon and evening will be crazy busy."

"For the reindeer, too?" he asked, fascinated by the whole idea of an entire operation devoted only to celebrating the holidays.

"Yes. Hope will probably hook them up to the sleigh for photo ops and short rides. The draft horses, of course, will be taking people on sleigh rides around the ranch, which is a highlight of the season. You should take Olivia. She would love it. It's really fun riding through the cold, starry night all bundled up in blankets."

It did sound appealing—especially if he and Celeste were alone under those blankets...

He jerked his brain back to the business at hand. He really needed to stop this.

"We're only open a few more nights," she said. "But if you want to take her, let me know and I'll arrange it."

As much as he thought Olivia would enjoy the sleigh ride, he wasn't at all certain that spending more time at The Christmas Ranch with Celeste and her appealing family would be good for either of them.

"We'll see," he said, unwilling to commit to anything. "Shall we get to it?"

"Right. Of course."

She led him into a well-lit, modern building with stalls along one wall. The rest seemed to be taken up with storage and work space.

She led him to an open area set up with a band saw, a recip-rocating saw, a router and various other power tools, as well as a stack of two-by-fours and sheets of plywood.

"You might not need to have Rafe run to the lumber yard. You might have everything here."

"Great."

She pointed to another area of the barn where other large pieces of plywood had been painted with snowflakes. "I need to finish just a few things on the scenery, so I'll be on hand if you need help with anything."

The best help she could offer would be to stay out of his way. She was entirely too tempting to his peace of mind, but he couldn't figure out a way to say that without sounding like an idiot, so he just decided to focus on the job at hand.

"Do you mind if I turn on some music?" she asked.

"That's fine," he answered. Her place, her music.

It wasn't Christmas music, he was happy to hear. Instead, she found some classic-rock station and soon The Eagles were harmonizing through the barn from a speaker system in the work area.

She returned to her side of the area and started opening paint cans and gathering brushes, humming along to the music. Though he knew he needed to get started, he couldn't seem to look away.

He liked watching her. She seemed to throw herself into everything she did, whether that was directing a ragtag group of children in a Christmas show, telling stories to a bunch of energetic school kids or writing a charming story about a brave reindeer.

He was fascinated with everything about her.

He had to get over it, he told himself sternly. He needed to help build her set, finish clearing out his grandmother's house and then go back to his normal life in California.

He turned his attention to the pile of lumber and found the boards he would need. Then he spent a moment familiarizing himself with another man's work space and the tools available to him. Rafe Santiago kept a clean, well-organized shop. He would give him that.

The moment he cut the first board, he felt more centered than he had in a long time. He was very good at building things. It gave him great satisfaction to take raw materials and turn them into something useful, whether that was a piece of furniture or a children's hospital.

For nearly an hour, they worked together in a comfortable silence broken only by the sounds of tools and the music. He made good progress by doing his best to pretend she wasn't there, that this growing attraction simmering through him would burn itself out when it no longer had the fuel of her presence to sustain it.

The barn was warmer than he would have expected, especially with the air compressor going to power the tools, and soon he was down to his T-shirt. Before she started painting, she had taken off the sweater she wore, but it wasn't until he took a break and looked up from connecting two boards that he saw the message on it: Wake up Smarter. Sleep With a Librarian.

For an instant his mind went completely blank as all the blood left his head at the image. Unfortunately, his finger twitched on the trigger of the unfamiliar nail gun, which was far more reactive than any of the guns he was used to.

He felt a sharp biting pain as the nail impaled the webbing between the forefinger and thumb of his left hand to the board. He swore and ripped out the nail, mortified at his stupidity.

It wasn't the first time he'd had an accident with a nail gun or a power tool—in his line of work, nobody made it through without nicks and bruises and a few stitches here or there, especially starting out—but it was completely embarrassing. He hadn't made that kind of rookie mistake in years. Apparently, she wasn't very good for his concentration.

"What happened?" she asked.

"Nothing. It's fine." It was, really. The nail hadn't gone through anything but skin.

"You're bleeding. Let me see."

"It's just a poke. Hazard of the job."

"I think Rafe keeps a first-aid kit somewhere in here." She started rifling through cabinets until she found one.

"I don't need anything. It's almost stopped bleeding."

It still burned like hell, but he wasn't about to tell her that.

"I'll feel better if you let me at least clean it up."

"Really, not necessary."

She ignored him and stepped closer, bringing that delicious springtime scent with her that made him think of sunlit mornings and new life.

"Hold out your hand."

Since he was pretty certain she wouldn't let up until he cooperated, he knew he had no choice but to comply. Feeling stupid, he thrust out his arm. She took his injured hand in both of hers and dabbed at it with a wipe she'd found inside the kit.

"It's not bad," she murmured. "I don't think you're going to need stitches."

He did his best to keep his gaze fiercely away from that soft T-shirt that had caused the trouble in the first place—and the curves beneath it.

The gentle touch of her fingers on his skin made him want to close his eyes and lean into her. It had been so long since he'd known that kind of aching sweetness.

She smiled a little. "Do you remember that time I fell on my bike in front of your grandmother's house?"

"Yes." His voice sounded a little ragged around the edges, but he had to hope she didn't notice.

"You were so sweet to me," she said with soft expression as she applied antiseptic cream to the tiny puncture wound. "I couldn't even manage to string two words together around you, but you just kept up a steady stream of conversation to make me feel more comfortable until my aunt Mary could come pick me up. I was so mortified, but you made it feel less horrible."

He swallowed. He'd done that? He didn't have much memory of it, only of a quiet girl with big eyes and long dark hair.

"Why would you be mortified? It was an accident."

She snorted a little. "Right. I ran into your grandmother's mailbox because I wasn't paying attention to where I was going. It was all your fault for mowing the lawn without your shirt on."

He stared down at her. "*That's* why you crashed?"

She looked up and he saw shadows of remembered embarrassment there. "In my defense, I was thirteen years old, you were a much older boy and I already had a huge crush on you. It's a wonder I could say a word."

"Is that right?" he asked softly. Her fingers felt so good on his skin, her luscious mouth was *right there* and he wanted nothing but to find a soft spot of hay somewhere for the two of them to collapse into.

"Yes," she murmured, and he saw answering awareness in her eyes. "And then you made it so much worse by being so kind, cleaning me up, calling my aunt, then fixing my bike for me. What shy, awkward bookworm alive could have resisted that, when the cutest boy she'd ever met in real life was so sweet to her?"

He didn't want to be sweet right now. At her words, hunger growled to life inside him, and he knew he would have to appease it somehow.

Just a kiss, he told himself. A simple taste and then they both could move on.

He lowered his mouth and felt her hands tremble when his lips brushed hers.

She tasted just as delicious as he would have imagined, sweet and warm and luscious, like nibbling at a perfectly ripe strawberry.

She froze for just a moment, long enough for him to wonder if he'd made a terrible error in judgment, and then her mouth softened and she kissed him back with a breathy sigh, as if she had been waiting for this since that day half a lifetime ago.

Her hands fluttered against his chest for just a moment, then wrapped around his neck, and he pulled her closer, delighting in her soft curves and the aching tenderness of the kiss.

Chapter Ten

Life could take the strangest turns sometimes.

If someone had told her a week ago that she would be standing in The Christmas Ranch barn on a Saturday afternoon kissing Flynn Delaney, she would have advised them to see somebody about their delusions.

Here they were, though, with her hands tangled in his hair and his arms wrapped around her and his mouth doing intoxicating things to her.

She wanted the moment to go on forever, this sultry, honeyed magic.

Nothing in her limited experience compared to this. She'd had a couple of boyfriends in college, nothing serious and nothing that had lasted more than a month or two—and absolutely nothing that prepared her for the sheer sensual assault of kissing Flynn.

She made a little sound in her throat and he deepened the kiss, his tongue sliding along hers as his arms tightened around her. Sensation rippled through her, and she could only be grateful when he pushed her against the nearest cabinet, his mouth hot and demanding.

She couldn't seem to think about anything other than kissing him, touching him, finding some way to be closer to him. She wrapped her arms more tightly around his neck, wanting this moment to go on forever.

They kissed for a long time there with the scents of sawdust and hay swirling around them. Even as she lost herself in the kiss, some tiny corner of her brain was trying to catalog every emotion and sensation, storing it up so she could relive it after he was gone. The taste of him, of coffee and mint and sexy male, the silky softness of his hair, the delicious rasp of his whiskers against her skin, his big, warm hands slipping beneath the back of her T-shirt to slide against her bare skin…

"Celeste? Are you in here?"

She heard her brother-in-law's voice and felt as if he had just thrown her into the snow. Rafe and Hope must have returned earlier than they'd planned.

She froze and scrambled away from Flynn, yanking her T-shirt back down and trying frantically to catch her breath.

He was having the same trouble, she realized, as he quickly stepped behind one of the power tools to hide the evidence of his arousal.

Had *she* done that to him? She couldn't quite believe it.

"Celeste?" she heard again.

"In…" The words caught in her throat and she had to clear them away before she spoke again. "In here."

An instant later Rafe walked into the work space. He stopped and gazed between the two of them and she saw his mouth tighten, a sudden watchful glint in his eyes.

Rafe was a tough man, extremely protective of each Nichols sister—probably because he had once saved all their lives. His sharp gaze took in the scene and she doubted he could miss her heightened color, her swollen lips, their heavy breathing.

She was sure of it when he aimed a hard, narrow-eyed look at Flynn.

She could feel herself flush more and then told herself she was being ridiculous, feeling like a teenager caught necking on the front porch by her older brother. She was a grown woman, twenty-eight years old, and she could kiss half the men in town if she wanted.

She'd just never wanted to before.

"Hope said you might need some help building a few things for the set."

"Flynn has been helping me."

"So I see," Rafe drawled.

"Thanks for letting me use your shop," Flynn said. "I tried to be careful with the tools, but your nail gun got away from me." He held up the hand she had bandaged.

"It's got a fast trigger. Sorry about that. Anything I can do to help you wrap things up so you can get out of here?"

"Another pair of hands never hurts," Flynn answered.

Celeste finally felt as if her brain cells were beginning to function again.

"I'm about done painting. I...think I'll just clean my brushes and leave you to it. I should probably head up to the house to help Aunt Mary with the cookie decorating."

She couldn't meet either of their gazes as she walked past the men, feeling like an idiot.

"Nice shirt," Rafe murmured in a low voice as she passed him.

Baffled, she glanced down and then could have died from mortification. It was the Sleep with a Librarian shirt that Hope and Faith had given her one Christmas as a joke. She never wore it, of course—it wasn't her style *at all*—but she'd thrown it on that morning under her sweater, knowing she was going to be painting the scenery later and it would be perfect for the job.

She gathered her brushes quickly and headed for the sink in the small bathroom of the barn.

While she cleaned the brushes, she glanced into the mirror and saw it was worse than she had thought. Her hair had come half out of the messy bun, her lips were definitely swollen and her cheeks were rosier than St. Nicholas's in "'Twas the Night Before Christmas."

Oh, she wanted to *die*. Rafe knew she had just been making out with Flynn, which meant he would definitely tell Hope. Her sisters would never let her hear the end of it.

That was the least of her problems, she realized.

Now that she had kissed the man and knew how amazing it was, how would she ever be able to endure not being able to do it again?

What just happened here?

Even after Celeste left to clean her brushes, Flynn could feel his heart hammering, his pulse racing.

Get a grip, he told himself. It was just a kiss. But for reasons he didn't completely understand, it somehow struck him as being so much more.

He couldn't seem to shake the feeling that something momentous had occurred in that kiss, something terrifying and mysterious and tender.

Why had he kissed her?

The whole time they'd shared the work space, he had been telling himself all the reasons why he needed to stay away from her. At the first opportunity and excuse, he had ignored all his common sense and swooped right in.

What shy, awkward bookworm alive could have resisted that, when the cutest boy she'd ever met in real life was so sweet to her?

She'd once had a crush on him. He didn't know why that made him feel so tender toward the quiet girl she had been.

That kiss had rocked him to the core and left him feeling off balance, as if he'd just slipped on the sawdust and landed hard on his ass. For a moment, he closed his eyes, remembering those lush curves against him, her enthusiastic response, the soft, sexy little sounds she made.

"What are you doing here?" For one horrible moment he thought Rafe was calling him out for kissing Celeste, until he realized the other man was gazing down at the set piece he was building.

Focus, he told himself. Get the job done, as he'd promised.

"She wants some kind of wings on the side of the stage for the children to wait behind until it's their turn to go on," he explained. He went into detail about his plan and listened while Rafe made a few excellent suggestions to improve the design.

"This shouldn't take us long to finish up," the other man said. "In fact, I probably could handle it on my own, if you want to get out of here."

That sounded a little more strongly worded than just a suggestion. "I'm good," he answered, a little defiantly. "I like to finish what I start."

He was aware as they went to work of her cleaning up her brushes, closing up the paint cans, putting her sweater back on to hide that unexpectedly enticing T-shirt.

He was also aware that she hadn't looked at him once since she'd jerked out of his arms when her brother-in-law had come in.

Was she regretting that they had kissed? He couldn't tell. She *should* regret it, since they both had to know it was a mistake, but somehow it still bothered him that she might.

Did he owe her some kind of apology for kissing her out of the blue like that? Something else he didn't know.

He had been faithful to his vows, as misguided as they had been, and his relationships since then had been with women who wanted the same thing he did: uncomplicated, no-strings affairs.

Celeste was very different from those women—sweet and kind and warm—which might explain why that kiss and her enthusiastic response had left him so discombobulated.

A few minutes later she finished at the sink and set the brushes to dry.

"I guess that's it," she said, still not looking at Flynn. "The brushes are all clean and ready for Hope when she has time to come down and finish. I'm just going to head up to the house to check on the cookie decorating. Thanks again for doing this, you guys."

She gave a vague, general sort of smile, then hurried out of the barn.

He and Rafe worked in silence for a few more moments, a heavy, thick tension in the air.

The other man was the first to speak.

"Do you know what happened to Celeste and her sisters when they were kids?"

Rafe's tone was casual, but the hard edge hadn't left his expression since he had walked into the work space earlier.

"In Colombia? Yeah. She told me. I can't imagine what they must have gone through."

Rafe's hard expression didn't lighten. "None of them talks about it very much. Frankly, I'm surprised she told you at all."

He didn't know why she had, but he was touched that she would confide that very significant part of her life to him.

He also didn't know why Rafe would bring it up now. It didn't seem the sort of topic to casually mention in general conversation. Something told him Rafe wasn't a man who did things without purpose.

"She was the youngest," the man went on. "Barely older than Louisa, only about twelve. Just a little kid, really."

His chest ached, trying to imagine that sweet vulnerability forced into such a traumatic situation. It was the same ache he had whenever he thought about Olivia watching her mother's murder.

"They went through hell while they were prisoners," Rafe went on. "The leader of the rebels was a psycho idiot bastard. He didn't give them enough to eat that entire month they were there, they were squished into squalid quarters, they were provided no medical care or decent protections from the elements, they underwent psychological torture. It's a wonder they made it through."

His hand tightened on the board he held, and he wanted to swing it at something, hard. He didn't need to hear about this. It only seemed to heighten these strange, tender feelings in his chest.

"It affected all of them in various ways," Rafe went on. "But I think it was hardest on Celeste. She was so young and so very softhearted, from what Hope tells me. She's always been a dreamer, her head filled with stories and music. The conditions they were forced into must have been particularly harsh on an innocent young girl who couldn't really comprehend what was happening to her family."

The ache in his chest expanded. He hated that she had gone through it and wished, more than anything, that he could make it right for her.

"Why are you telling me this?"

Rafe gave him a steady look, as if weighing how to respond. He could see in his eyes that her brother-in-law knew exactly what they had been doing just before he walked in. Flynn fought the urge to tell the man to back off, that it was none of Rafe's damn business.

"I was there," Rafe finally said. "Did she tell you that?"

Flynn stared. "Where?"

"In Colombia. I was part of the SEAL team that rescued the Nichols family. It was my very first mission. A guy doesn't forget something like that."

Rafe was big and tough enough that somehow Flynn wasn't surprised he'd been a SEAL. He supposed the only remarkable thing about the situation was that the man seemed content now to live in a small town in Idaho, running a holiday attraction.

"So you saw their father get shot."

Rafe's jaw tightened. "Yeah. I saw it. And I saw Celeste weep and weep during the entire helicopter flight when she realized what had happened. I thought she would jump right out after her father."

Flynn swallowed at the image. After the past three months he hadn't thought he had much of his heart left to break, but he was most definitely wrong.

"I also shot two revolutionaries who were trying to keep us from leaving with them," Rafe went on. "You might, in fact, say I've had CeCe's back since she was eleven years old."

Yeah. The man definitely knew he had walked in on them kissing.

"She's very important to me," the other man said. "The whole Nichols family is mine now."

He met Flynn's gaze and held it as if he wanted to be perfectly clear. "And make no mistake. I protect what's mine."

He could choose to be offended, he supposed. He hadn't been called out for kissing a woman in...*ever.* Somehow he couldn't drum up anything but respect for Rafe. He was actually touched in an odd way, grateful that she had someone looking out for her.

"Warning duly noted." He made his own voice firm. "But anything between Celeste and me is just that. Between the two of us."

Rafe seemed to accept that. "I just don't want to see her hurt. Despite everything she's been through, CeCe somehow has still managed to retain a sweetness and a generosity you won't find in many people on this planet. If you mess with that, I won't be the only member of this family who won't be happy about it. Trust me. You do *not* want to tangle with the Nichols women."

This, more than anything else the man had said, resonated with truth. She had become a friend, someone he liked and respected. He didn't want to hurt her, either, but he couldn't see any other outcome. He had a business, a life in LA. Beyond that he wasn't in any position right now to start a new relationship with anyone, not when Olivia was still so needy.

He had made a mistake, kissing her. A mistake that couldn't happen again.

He gave the other man a steady look. "I got it. Thanks. Now can we just finish this job so I can grab my daughter and go home?"

After a moment, Rafe nodded and turned back to work, much to Flynn's relief.

The walk from the lodge to the main house helped a great deal to cool her flaming cheeks, but it didn't do much for the tumult inside her.

Oh, that kiss. How was she supposed to act around him now when she was afraid that every second she was near him she would be reliving those wild, hot moments in his arms? His hands on her skin, his mouth on hers, all those muscles pressing her against the cabinet.

She shivered in remembered reaction. How was she supposed to pretend her world just hadn't been rocked?

It had happened. She couldn't scrub those moments from her memory bank—indeed, she had a feeling they would haunt her for a long time—but surely she was mature enough to be able to interact with him in a polite, casual way. What other choice did she have?

When she reached the house, she drew in a deep breath, hoping all trace of those heated moments was gone from her features in case either of her eagle-eyed sisters was inside, then she pushed open the door.

The scents of cinnamon and pine and sugar cookies greeted her and the warmth of the house wrapped around her like one of Aunt Mary's hand-knitted scarves. As she stood in the entry, she had a sudden, familiar moment of deep gratitude for her aunt and uncle who had taken in three lost and grieving girls and given them safe shelter from the hard realities of life.

This was home. Her center.

Some of the storm inside her seemed to calm a bit. This was

how she made it through, by focusing on what was important to her. Her family, her stories, the ranch. That was what mattered, not these fragile feelings growing inside her for Flynn and Olivia.

Before she could even hang up her coat, she heard the click of little paws on the floor. A moment later Linus burst into the room and greeted her merrily. She had nearly forgotten she'd brought him up to the house during the rehearsal to hang out with Mary, since Lucy had been in one of her snooty moods where she just wanted to be left alone.

"Hi, there. There's my darling boy." She scooped him up in her arms, and he licked her face and wriggled in her arms as if they had been away from each other for years instead of only a few hours.

"Have you been good?" she asked. He licked her cheek in answer, then wiggled to be let down again. She followed him and the sound of laughter to the kitchen, where she found her niece and nephews decorating cookies with Aunt Mary and Olivia.

"Look at all our cookies!" Barrett said. "The old people are going to *love* them."

He was such an adorable child, with a huge reservoir of compassion and love inside him for others.

This was a prime example—though she decided at some point she probably would have to gently inform him that the senior citizens coming to the show next week might not appreciate being called "old people."

"What a great job."

"Look at this one, Aunt CeCe. See how I made the stars sparkle with the yellow sugar things?" Joey, joined at the hip with Barrett, thrust his cookies at her.

"Fabulous."

"And look at my Christmas trees," Barrett said.

"I see. Good work, kid. And, Lou, I love how you swirled the icing on the candy canes. Very creative."

She turned to Olivia. "What about you? Have you decorated any?"

"A few." She pointed to a tray where a dozen angel cookies lay wing to wing. They all had hair of yellow frosting, just like the blonde and lovely Elise Chandler. Celeste had a feeling that wasn't a coincidence.

"I love them. They're beautiful, every one."

"Decorating cookies is *hard*," Joey declared. "You have to be careful you don't break them while you're putting on the frosting."

"But then you get to eat them when they break," Barrett pointed out.

"They've all been very good not to eat too many broken cookies," Aunt Mary said from the stove, where she was stirring something that smelled like her delicious ham-and-potato soup.

"Can you help us?" Louisa asked.

She had a million things to do before the show—not to mention a pile of unwrapped gifts in the corner of her office at home—but this suddenly seemed to take precedence over everything else.

"Of course," she answered her niece with a smile. "I can't imagine anything I would enjoy more."

Mary replaced the lid on the stockpot on the stove and turned down the burner. "Since you're here to supervise now, I think I'll go lie down and put my feet up. If you don't mind anyway. These swollen ankles are killing me today."

"Go ahead, my dear. You've done more than enough."

"I've got soup on the stove. The children had some earlier, but there's more than enough for anyone who pops in or out."

Celeste left the children busy at the table and headed over to hug her aunt before she reached in the cupboard for a bowl. "I know Hope and Rafe are back. I bumped into Rafe." She felt herself blush when she said it and hoped Aunt Mary wouldn't notice. "What about Faith? Is she around?"

"No. She ran into Idaho Falls for some last-minute *g-i-f-t-s*,"

Aunt Mary spelled, as if the children were tiny instead of excellent readers. Fortunately none of the children seemed to be paying attention to them.

"Poor girl," her aunt went on. "She's been too busy around the ranch to give Christmas much thought, and now here it is just a few days away."

The reminder instantly made Celeste feel small. She was fretting about a kiss while her sister had lost a husband and was raising two children by herself—albeit with plenty of help from Aunt Mary, Rafe, Hope and Celeste.

She was so grateful for her loving, supportive family—though she experienced a pang of regret for Flynn, who had no one.

She sat down at the table with her soup and listened to the children's chatter while she ate each delicious spoonful. When she finished, she set her bowl aside and turned to the serious business of cookie decorating.

"All right. Help me out, kids. What kind of cookie should I decorate first?"

"The angels are really hard," Olivia said.

Well, she'd already faced down a bunch of holiday-excited children and been kissed until she couldn't think straight. What was one more challenge today? "Bring on an angel, then."

Aunt Mary always had Christmas music playing in the house and the children seemed to enjoy singing along. Olivia didn't join them, she noticed. The girl seemed a little withdrawn, and Celeste worried maybe the day had been too much for her.

After she had decorated her third cookie, the song "Angels We Have Heard on High" came over the stereo.

"Ooh, I love this one," Louisa said. Her niece started singing along to the Glorias with a gusto that made Celeste smile.

"My mom is an angel now," Olivia said in a matter-of-fact sort of tone that made emotions clog Celeste's throat.

"I know, sweetheart," she said softly. "I'm so sorry."

"Our dad is an angel, too," Barrett informed her.

"Mom says he's probably riding the prettiest horses in heaven right now," Louisa said.

"My mom is in jail," Joey offered. That made her just as sad for him.

"Aren't you lucky to have Uncle Rafe and Aunt Hope, though?"

"Yep," he answered.

Barrett nodded. "And we still have our mom. And you have your dad," he reminded Olivia.

"Your mom *and* your dad are angels, aren't they?" Louisa said to Celeste. "I asked my mom once why Barrett and me don't have a grandma and a grandpa, and she told me."

The pain of losing them still hurt, but more like an old ache than the constant, raw pain she remembered.

"They both died," she agreed. "It's been a long time, but I still feel them near me."

At some moments she felt them closer than others. She was quite certain she had heard her father's voice loud and clear one wintry, stormy night when she was driving home from college for the holidays. As clear as if he had been sitting beside her, she'd heard him tell her to slow down. She had complied instantly and a moment later rounded a corner to find a car had spun out from the opposite lane into hers. She was able to stop in time to keep from hitting it, but if she hadn't reduced her speed earlier, the head-on collision probably would have killed her and the other driver.

"Do you ever *see* your mom and dad angels?" Olivia asked, studying Celeste intently.

Oh, the poor, poor dear. She shook her head. "I don't see them as they were, but whenever I see the angel decorations at Christmastime, it helps me think about them and remember they're always alive in my heart."

"I really need to ask my mom something," Olivia said, her little features distressed. "Only I don't know how."

Celeste reached for the girl's hand and squeezed it. Oh, how she recalled all those unspoken words she had wanted to tell her parents, especially her father, who had died so abruptly. With her mother, she'd had a little more time, though that didn't ease the difficulty of losing her.

She chose her answer carefully, trying to find the right words of comfort.

"When you see an angel decoration you really like, perhaps you could whisper to the angel what you need to say to your mom. I believe she'll hear you," she said softly, hoping she was saying the right things to ease the girl's grief and not just offering a useless panacea.

Olivia considered that for a long moment, her brow furrowed. Finally she nodded solemnly. "That's a good idea. I think I'll do that."

She smiled and gave the girl a little hug, hoping she had averted that particular crisis. "Excellent. Now, why don't we see how many more cookies we can decorate before your father comes in?"

"Okay."

They went to work, singing along to the Christmas music for another half hour before the doorbell rang.

"I'll get it!" Joey announced eagerly. He raced for the door and a moment later returned with Flynn.

She had known it would be him at the door, but somehow she still wasn't prepared for the sheer masculine force of him. Suddenly she couldn't seem to catch her breath and felt as if the vast kitchen had shrunk to the size of one of Louisa's dollhouse rooms.

The memory of that kiss shivered between them, and she could feel heat soak her cheeks and nerves flutter in her stomach.

She shoved aside the reaction and forced a smile instead. "That was faster than I expected. Are you finished?" she asked.

He shrugged. "Your brother-in-law is a handy dude. With both of us working together, it didn't take us long."

"Wonderful. I can't tell you how much I appreciate it, especially with everything else you have going on. Thank you."

He met her gaze finally, and she thought she saw an instant of heat and hunger before he blinked it away. "You're very welcome."

His gaze took in the table scattered with frosting bowls, sugar sprinkles and candy nonpareils. "This looks fun," he said, though his tone implied exactly the opposite.

"Oh, it is, Daddy," Olivia declared. "Look at all the cookies I decorated! About a hundred angels!"

More like fifteen or sixteen, but Celeste supposed it had felt like much more than that to a seven-year-old girl.

She handed over one of the paper plates they had been using to set the decorated cookies on when they were finished. "Here, fill this with several cookies so you and your dad can take some home to enjoy."

"They're for the old people, though, aren't they?"

"I think it would be just fine for you to take five or six. We'll have plenty. Don't worry," she answered, declining again to give a lecture on politically correct terminology.

"Are you sure?"

"Yes. Go ahead. Pick some of your favorites."

Olivia pondered her options and finally selected five cookies—all blonde angels, Celeste noted—and laid them on the paper plate while Celeste found some aluminum foil to cover them.

"Here you go," she said, holding them out to Flynn.

"Thanks," he murmured and took the plate from her. Their hands brushed and she gave an involuntary shiver that she seriously hoped he hadn't noticed.

His gaze met hers for just an instant, then slid away again, but not before she saw a glittery, hungry look there that made her feel breathless all over again.

"Find your coat," he told his daughter.

"Can we stay a little bit longer?" Olivia begged. "Louisa and

Barrett and Joey said they're going to have sleigh rides later. I've never been on a sleigh ride."

"We have a lot to do today, bug. We've already hung around here longer than we probably should have."

If he and his daughter had left earlier, the kiss never would have happened. Judging by the edgy tension that seethed between them now—and despite the flash of hunger she thought she had glimpsed—Celeste had a feeling that was what he would have preferred.

"Please, Daddy. I would *love* it."

As he gazed at his daughter a helpless look came into his eyes. She remembered him saying he hated refusing Olivia anything after what she had been through.

"How long do these sleigh rides take?" he asked Celeste.

"Less than an hour, probably."

"They're super fun at night," her niece suggested helpfully. "You could go home and do your work and then come back later. Then you can see all the lights and stuff. There's even caroling."

"Ooh. Caroling!" Olivia looked delighted at the idea, while her father looked vaguely horrified.

"I must agree. It is really fun," Celeste said.

He sighed. "Would that work for you, Liv? We can go home and try to finish another room at the house, and then come back later."

"Will you all be there?" she asked her new friends.

"Sure! We love to take the sleigh rides."

Olivia looked enchanted by the idea.

"Our last sleigh ride for regular visitors of The Christmas Ranch is back at the St. Nicholas Lodge about 8:00 p.m. Why don't you meet us at the lodge a little before that, and we can take one that's not as crowded?"

"Oh, yay! I can't wait!" Olivia exclaimed. She spontaneously hugged Celeste, and she looked so adorably sweet with her eyes bright and pink frosting on her cheek that Celeste couldn't help it, she kissed the top of the girl's head.

When she lifted her head, she found Flynn gazing at her with a strange look on his features that he quickly wiped away.

"I guess we'll see you all later tonight, then," he said.

He didn't sound nearly as thrilled as his daughter about the idea.

Chapter Eleven

All afternoon Celeste did her best not to dwell on that stunning kiss.

Knowing she would see him again that evening didn't help. The whole busy December day seemed filled with sparkly anticipation, even though she tried over and over again to tell herself she was being ridiculous.

It didn't help matters that her sisters both attempted to back out of the sleigh ride and send her alone with the children. She couldn't blame them, since it had been completely her idea, but she still wanted them there. Though she knew the children would provide enough of a buffer, she didn't want to be alone with Flynn.

Finally she had threatened Hope that if she didn't go on the sleigh ride with them, Hope would have to direct the show Tuesday night by herself.

As she expected, Rafe had obviously told Hope what he had almost walked in on earlier in the barn. Her sisters hadn't come out and said anything specific about it, but after the third or fourth speculative look from Hope—and the same from Faith—she knew the word was out in the Nichols family.

If not for her beloved niece and nephews, she sincerely would have given some thought to wishing she had been an only child.

"You owe me this after dragging me into the whole Christmas show thing," Celeste said fiercely to Hope at dinner, when her sister once more tried to wriggle out of the sleigh ride.

Hope didn't necessarily look convinced, but she obviously could see that Celeste meant what she said. "Oh, all right," she muttered. "If I'm going out in the cold that means you have to come, too, Fae."

Faith groaned. "After an afternoon of tackling the stores on the busiest shopping day of the year, I just want to put my feet up and watch something brainless on TV."

Barrett added his voice. "You *have* to come, Mom. It won't be as fun without you. You've got the *best* caroling voice."

"Yeah, and you're the only one who knows all the words," Louisa added.

Faith gave her children an exasperated look but finally capitulated. "Fine. I guess somebody has to help you all carry a tune."

After dinner they all bundled up in their warmest clothing and traipsed down to the St. Nicholas Lodge. Even Rafe came along, which she supposed she was grateful for, though he kept shooting her curious little looks all evening.

They arrived at the lodge just as Flynn and Olivia walked in from the parking lot. Olivia wore her pink-and-purple coat with a white beanie and scarf. She looked adorable, especially when she lit up at the sight of them.

"Hi, everybody! Hi!" she said. "We're here. Dad didn't want to come, but I told him we promised, so here we are."

Celeste had to laugh at that, especially when Flynn's color rose. "It's good to see you both," she said.

It wasn't a lie. The December night suddenly seemed magical and bright, filled with stars and snow and the wonder of the season.

Olivia skipped over to her, hardly even limping in her excitement for the evening. "Guess what, Celeste?"

"What, sweetheart?"

"Today when we were cleaning we found boxes and boxes and *boxes* of yarn and scrapbook paper and craft supplies. Would you like to have them for your story times at the library? Dad said he thought you might."

"Seriously?" She stared, overwhelmed and touched that he would think of it.

"You don't have to take them," he said quickly. "I just didn't want to send everything to Goodwill if you could find a use for it."

"Are you kidding?" she exclaimed. "Absolutely! I can definitely use craft supplies. Thank you so much!"

"Good, because they're all in the back of the SUV. I took a chance that you would want them and figured if you didn't, I could drop them in the box at the thrift store in town after we were done here."

"Smart." She considered their options. "My car is still here in the parking lot from this morning. I can just pull next to you, and we can transfer them from your SUV to mine."

"Do you want to do it now or after the sleigh ride?"

"Go ahead and do it now while you're thinking about it," Hope suggested. Celeste narrowed her gaze at her sister, wondering if this was some sneaky way to get the two of them alone together, but Hope merely gave her a bland look in response.

"Sure," she said finally. "That way we won't forget later."

They walked out into the cold air, and she tried not to think about the last time they had been together—the strength of his muscles beneath her hands, the delicious taste of him, all those shivery feelings he evoked.

"I'm parked over there," he said, pointing to his vehicle.

"I parked at the back of the lot this morning to leave room for paying guests. Just give me a minute to move my car next to yours."

"I could just carry the boxes over to where you are."

"It will only take me a minute to move." She took off before he could argue further and hurried to her very cold vehicle, which had a thin layer of soft snow that needed to be brushed away before she could see out the windshield. Once that was done, she started it and drove the few rows to an open spot next to his vehicle, then popped open the hatch of her small SUV.

By the time she opened her door and walked around to the back, he was already transferring boxes and she could see at least half dozen more in the back of his vehicle.

She stared at the unexpected bounty. "This is amazing! Are you sure Olivia wouldn't like to keep some of this stuff?"

He shook his head. "She went through and picked out a few pairs of decorative scissors and some paper she really liked, but the rest of it was destined for either Goodwill or the landfill."

"Thank you. It was really kind of you to think of the library."

"Consider it a legacy from Charlotte to the library."

"I'll do that. Thank you."

He carried the last of the boxes and shoved it into her cargo area, then closed the hatch.

"There you go."

"Thanks again."

She expected him to head directly back to the lodge. Instead, he leaned against her vehicle and gave her a solemn look. The parking lot was mostly empty except for a family a few rows away loading into a minivan, probably after seeing Santa Claus inside.

"Do I owe you an apology?" he asked.

She fidgeted, shoving her mittened hands into her pockets. "An apology for what?"

He sighed. "We both know I shouldn't have kissed you, Celeste. It was a mistake. I didn't want to leave you with the... wrong impression."

Oh, this was humiliating. Was she so pathetic that he thought because she had told him she'd once had a crush on him, she now thought they were *dating* or something, because of one stupid kiss?

Okay, one *amazing*, heart-pounding, knee-tingling kiss. But that was beside the point.

"You don't owe me anything," she said.

He gazed up at the stars while the jingle of the sleigh returning to the lodge and the sound of shrieking children over on the sledding hill rang out in the distance.

"Here's the thing. Right now, my whole attention has to be focused on helping my daughter. I'm not…looking for anything else. I can't."

She leaned against the cold vehicle next to him and tried to pretend she was sophisticated and experienced, that this sort of moment happened to her all the time—a casual conversation with a man who had kissed her deeply just a few hours ago and was now explaining why he couldn't do it again.

"It was a kiss, Flynn. I get it. I've barely given it a thought since it happened."

He wasn't stupid. She didn't doubt he could tell that was a blatant lie, but he said nothing. He simply gave her a careful look, which she returned with what she hoped was a bland one of her own.

"Good. That's good," he said. "I just wanted to clear the air between us. The last thing I want to do is hurt you or, I don't know, give you the wrong idea. You've been nothing but kind to Olivia and to me."

"Do you really think I'm so fragile that I could be hurt by a single kiss?"

The question seemed to hang between them, bald and un-adorned, like a bare Christmas tree after the holidays.

He had a fierce wish that he'd never started this conversation, but the implications of that kiss had bothered him all afternoon as he'd carried box after box out of Charlotte's house.

He meant what he said. She had been very sweet to him and

Olivia. His daughter was finally beginning to heal from the trauma she had endured, and he knew a big part of the progress she'd made the past week was because of all the many kindnesses Celeste and her family had shown them.

It seemed a poor repayment for him to take advantage of that because he couldn't control his base impulses around her.

He also couldn't seem to shake the guilt that had dogged him since that conversation with Rafe. The other man hadn't come out and blatantly told him to leave her alone, but Flynn hadn't missed the subtle undercurrents.

"Your brother-in-law and I had quite a talk this afternoon while we were finishing the screens for you."

"Is that right?"

Her cheeks looked pink in the moonlight, but he supposed that could have been from the cold night air.

"He's very protective of you and wanted to be clear I knew you had people watching out for you."

She made a low noise in the back of her throat. "My family sometimes drives me absolutely crazy."

Despite the awkwardness of the conversation, he had to smile. "They're wonderful, all of them. It's obvious they love you very much."

"A little too much, sometimes," she muttered. "They apparently don't think I can be trusted to take care of myself. Sometimes it really sucks to be the youngest sibling."

He couldn't imagine having any siblings. While he was lucky to have very tight friends, he knew it wasn't the same.

"I think it's nice," he answered. "Having your sisters close must have been a great comfort after you lost your parents."

Her lovely features softened in the moonlight. "It was," she murmured. "They may drive me crazy, but I would be lost without them. Don't tell them I said that, though."

He smiled a little. "I wish I had that same kind of support network for Olivia, but I'm all she has right now. I can't forget that."

"I understand. You're doing a great job with her. Don't worry.

Children are resilient. She's working her way over to the other side in her own time."

His sigh puffed out condensation between them. "Thanks."

"And you can put your mind at ease," she said briskly. "You're not going to break my heart. Trust me, I don't have some crazy idea that you're going to propose to me simply because we shared one little kiss."

"It wasn't a little kiss. That's the problem," he muttered.

As soon as he said the words, he knew he shouldn't have, but it was the truth. That kiss had been earthshaking. Cataclysmic. He would venture to call it epic, which was the entire problem here. He knew he wouldn't forget those moments for a long, long time.

He wasn't sure how he expected her to respond but, as usual, she managed to surprise him. She flashed him a sideways look.

"What can I say? I'm a good kisser."

The unexpectedness of her response surprised a laugh out of him that echoed through the night. She seemed like such a sweet, quiet woman, but then she had these moments of sly humor that he couldn't seem to get enough of.

It made him wonder if she had this whole secret internal side of herself—contained and bundled away for protection—that she rarely showed the rest of the world.

She intrigued him on so many levels, probably because she was a study in contradictions. She could be tart and sweet at the same time, firm yet gentle, deeply vulnerable yet tough as nails.

Most of all, she seemed *real*. For a guy who had grown up surrounded by the artificial illusion of Hollywood, that was intensely appealing.

"It looks as if the other sleigh ride is done," she finally said. "The kids are probably anxious to get going."

"Right. Guess I'd better get my carol on."

She laughed, as he had hoped. At least the tension between them since the afternoon had been somewhat diffused.

As they walked, he was aware of a jumble of feelings in his chest. Regret, longing and a strange, aching tenderness.

For just a moment, he had a crazy wish that things could be different, that he had the right to wrap his hand around hers and walk up to the sleigh ride with her, then sit beneath a blanket cuddled up with her while they rode in a horse-drawn sleigh and enjoyed the moonlit wonder of the night together.

He could handle the regret and the longing. He was a big boy and had known plenty of disappointments in his life.

But he didn't have any idea what to do with the tenderness.

Celeste decided a sleigh ride through the mountains on a December evening was a good metaphor for being in love.

She was bumped and jostled, her face cold but the rest of her warm from the blankets. It was exhilarating and exhausting, noisy and fun and a little bit terrifying when they went along a narrow pass above the ranch that was only two feet wider on each side than the sleigh.

She'd been on the sleigh ride dozens of times before. This was the first time she'd taken one while also being in love, with these tangled, chaotic feelings growing inside her.

She was quickly reaching the point where she couldn't deny that she was falling hard for Flynn. What else could explain this jumbled, chaotic mess of emotions inside her?

"Oh. Look at all those stars," a voice breathed beside her, and she looked down to where Olivia had her face lifted to the sky.

She wasn't only falling for Flynn. This courageous, wounded girl had sneaked her way into Celeste's heart.

She would be devastated when they left.

When they'd climbed into the sleigh, Olivia had asked if she could sit beside Celeste. The two of them were sharing a warm blanket. Every once in a while the girl rested her cheek against her shoulder, and Celeste felt as if her heart would burst with tenderness.

"I never knew there were so many stars," Olivia said, her voice awestruck.

"It's magical, isn't it?" she answered. "Do you know what I find amazing? That all those stars are there every single night, wherever you are in the world. They're just hidden by all the other lights around that distract us away from them."

The whole evening truly *was* magical—the whispering jingle of the bells on the draft horses' harnesses, the creak of the old sleigh, the sweet scent of the snow-covered pines they rode through.

Except for Mary—who had stayed behind in the warm house—Celeste was surrounded by everyone she loved.

"I wish we could just go and go and never stop," Olivia said.

Unfortunately, the magic of sleigh rides never lasted forever. She had a feeling that, at least in her case, the magic of being in love wouldn't last, either. The *in love* part would, but eventually the heartache would steal away any joy.

"We'll have to stop at some point," the ever-practical Faith said. "The horses are tired. They've been working all night and are probably ready to have a rest."

"Besides that," Joey added, "what would we eat if we were stuck on a sleigh our whole lives?"

"Good point, kid," Rafe said. "We can't live on hot chocolate forever."

Olivia giggled at them and seemed to concede their point.

"I thought we were supposed to be caroling. We haven't sung *anything*," Louisa complained.

"You start us off," her mother suggested.

Celeste was aware that while both her sisters seemed to be dividing careful looks between her and Flynn, they did it at subtle moments. If she were very lucky, he wouldn't notice.

Louisa started, predictably enough, with "Jingle Bells." The children joined in with enthusiasm and soon even the adults joined them. Flynn, on the other side of Olivia, had a strong baritone. Under other circumstances, she might have been entranced by it, but Celeste's attention was fixed on his daughter as she sang.

Why hadn't she noticed during their rehearsals and the songs they had prepared that Olivia had such a stunning voice, pure and clear, like a mountain stream? It was perfectly on pitch, too, astonishing in a child.

She wasn't the only one who noticed it, she saw. Hope and Faith both seemed startled and even Rafe gave her a second look.

Flynn didn't seem to notice anything, and she thought of those stars again, vivid and bright but obscured by everything else in the way.

"What next?" Joey asked. "Can we sing the one about Jolly Old St. Nick?"

"Sure," Faith said. Of the three sisters, she had the most musical ability, so she led the children as the sleigh bells jingled through the night. With each song, Olivia's natural musical talent became increasingly apparent to everyone on the sleigh, but both she and Flynn seemed oblivious.

"What's that place with all the lights?" Olivia asked after they finished "Silent Night."

"That's the Christmas village," Barrett answered her. "It's awesome. Can we stop and walk through it?"

"You've seen it, like, a million times," his sister chided.

"Yeah, but Olivia hasn't. It's way more fun to see it with somebody else who has never been there. It's like seeing it for the first time all over again."

"You are so right, kiddo," Hope said, beaming at the boy. "Bob, do you mind dropping us off here so we can take a little detour through the village?"

"Not at all. Not at all."

The driver pulled the team to a stop, and everybody clambered out of the sleigh and headed toward the collection of eight small structures a short distance from the main lodge.

This was one of her favorite parts of the entire Christmas Ranch. With the lights strung overhead, it really did feel magical.

Each structure contained a Christmas scene peopled with animatronic figures—elves hammering toys, Mrs. Claus baking cookies, children decorating a Christmas tree, a family opening presents.

"This is quite a place," Flynn murmured beside her.

"The Christmas village is really what started the whole Christmas Ranch. You probably don't know this, but my family's name of origin was Nicholas. As in St. Nicholas."

"The big man himself."

"Right. Because of that, my aunt and uncle have always been a little crazy about Christmas. Before we came to live with them, my uncle Claude built the little chapel Nativity over there with the cow who nods his head at the baby Jesus and the two little church mice running back and forth. It became a hobby with him, and after that he came up with a new one every year."

With a pang, she dearly missed her uncle, a big, gruff man of such kindness and love. He had taught her and her sisters that the best way to heal a broken heart was to forget your troubles and go to work helping other people.

"He decided he wanted to share the village with the whole community, so he opened the ranch up for people to come and visit. The reindeer herd came after, and then he built the whole St. Nicholas Lodge for Santa Claus, and the gift shop and everything."

"This is really great. I have no idea how he did it. It's a fascinating exercise in engineering and physics."

She frowned up at the star above the chapel, just a dark outline against the mountains. "Usually the star up there lights up. I'm not sure what's wrong with it. I'll have to mention it to Rafe. He has learned the ins and outs of all the structures in the village. I don't know how everything works. I just love the magic of it."

Olivia appeared to agree. The girl seemed enthralled with the entire village, particularly the little white chapel with its Nativity scene—the calm Madonna cradling her infant son, and Joseph watching over them both with such care while a beautiful angel with sparkly white wings watched overhead.

"You guys are welcome to hang out, but we're going to head back to the house," Faith said after about fifteen minutes. "It's cold and I know my two are about ready for bed."

"We need to go, too," Hope said, pointing to a sleepy-looking Joey.

"Thank you all for taking us on one more ride," Flynn said. "I appreciate it very much. Olivia loved it."

"You're very welcome," Hope said. "It was our pleasure."

The rest of her family headed back up to the ranch house while Celeste and Flynn walked with Olivia to the lodge's parking lot.

"I'm glad you both came," Celeste said when they reached their vehicles.

"This is definitely a memory we'll have forever, isn't it, Liv?" Flynn said as he opened the backseat door for his daughter. "When we're back in California enjoying Christmas by the ocean, we'll always remember the year we went caroling through the mountains on a two-horse open sleigh."

She had to smile, even though his words seemed to cut through her like an icy wind whipping down the mountain.

"We'll see you Tuesday for the performance."

He nodded, though he didn't look thrilled.

"We'll be there. Thanks again."

She nodded and climbed into her own vehicle, trying not to notice how empty and cold it felt after the magic of being with them on the sleigh ride.

Chapter Twelve

"Are you sure we're not too early?" Flynn asked his daughter as they pulled up in front of the St. Nicholas Lodge on the night of the show. "It doesn't start for quite a while."

She huffed out her frustrated-at-Dad sigh. "I'm sure. She told me five thirty. This is when I'm supposed to be here, Celeste said, so they can help me get ready with my hair and makeup and stuff. I get to wear makeup onstage so my face isn't blurry."

Yeah, he was terrible with hair and didn't have the first idea what to do about makeup. Here was a whole new stress about having a daughter. Soon enough she was going to want to know about that stuff. Good thing he had friends in LA with wives who could help a poor single dad out in that department.

She opened the passenger door the moment he pulled into a parking space. "Okay. Thanks, Dad. I'll see you at the show."

When he turned off the engine and opened his own door, she gave him a look of surprise. "You don't have to come in yet."

He shrugged. "I'm here. I might as well see if they need help with something—setting up chairs or whatever."

"Okay," she said, then raced for the door without waiting to see if he followed. Clearly, he was far more nervous about this whole performance thing than she was.

She had made amazing progress in a short time. In a matter of days she already seemed much more at ease with herself and the world around her than she had been when he brought her to Pine Gulch. She used her arm almost without thinking about it now, and she hardly limped anymore.

He wasn't foolish to think all the pain and grief were behind them. She would be dealing with the trauma for a long time to come, but he was beginning to hope that they had turned a corner.

Children are resilient. She's working her way over to the other side in her own time.

He gave no small amount of credit to the Nichols family, for their warmth and acceptance of her. She had made friends with the children and she also completely adored Celeste.

Would he be able to keep that forward momentum when they returned to California? He had no idea, but he would sure as hell try—even if that meant figuring out the whole hair-and-makeup thing on his own sometime down the line.

He pushed open the front doors after her and walked into the lodge, only to discover the place had been transformed into an upscale-looking dining room.

What had been an open space was now filled with round eight-top tables wearing silky red tablecloths and evergreen and candle centerpieces. The huge Christmas tree in the corner blazed with color and light, joined by merry fires flickering in the river-rock fireplaces at both ends of the vast room. Glittery white lights stretched across the room and gleamed a welcome.

The air smelled delicious—ham and yeasty rolls and, if he wasn't mistaken, apple pie.

Like iron shavings to a magnet, his gaze instantly found Celeste. She was right in the middle of everything, directing a crew of caterers while they laid out table settings.

His stomach muscles tightened. She looked beautiful, with

her hair up in a dark, elegant sweep and wearing a simple tailored white blouse and green skirt. Again, the alluring contradictions. She looked prim and sexy at the same time.

"Hi, Celeste," Olivia chirped, heading straight to her for a hug, which was readily accepted and returned.

He didn't understand the bond between the two of them, but he couldn't deny the strength of it.

"Looks as if you've been busy," he said, gesturing to the tables.

"Hope and Rafe did all this while I was working at the library today. It looks great, doesn't it?"

"Wonderful," he agreed. "I was going to see if there was anything I could do to help, but you seem to have everything under control."

"I don't know if I'd go that far," she answered with a rather frazzled-sounding laugh. "I don't know what I was thinking to agree to this. If Hope ever tries to rope me into one of her harebrained ideas again, please remind me of this moment and my solemn vow that I will never be so gullible again."

He smiled even as he was aware of a sharp ache in his chest. He wouldn't be around to remind her of anything. Some other guy would be the one to do that—a realization that he suddenly hated.

"Thanks for bringing Olivia early. She wanted her hair fixed the same as Louisa's."

"She said it was going to be a big bun on her head," Olivia said. "That's what I want."

Celeste smiled at her. "Find your costume first, and then Louisa's mom is on hair-and-makeup duty in the office, and she'll help you out."

"Okay," she said eagerly, then trotted away.

Without the buffer of his daughter, he suddenly couldn't escape the memory of that earthshaking kiss a few days earlier. When she smiled like that, her eyes huge behind her glasses, he wanted to reach out, tug her against him and taste her one more time.

"How are you?" she asked.

He didn't know how to answer. That strange, irresistible tenderness seemed to twist and curl through him like an unruly vine. As he had no idea what to do with it, he said the first thing he could think of in a futile effort to put distance between them.

"Good. It's been a busy few days. We've made a lot of progress with Charlotte's house. We're now down to one room and a few cupboards here and there."

She didn't answer for about three beats, and he thought he saw her hand tighten. Would she miss them when they left? Olivia, no doubt. What about him?

"That's a huge job," she finally said. "I imagine you must be relieved to be nearing the finish line."

Relieved? No. Not really. It had been a strange, disquieting experience sorting through the pieces of his grandparents' lives, all the treasures and papers and worthless junk they had left behind. It made a man wonder what would remain of his own life once he was gone. Right now he didn't feel as though he had all that much to show for his years on the planet.

"I thought it would take me until at least New Year's, but we're ahead of schedule."

"That's great," she said. Was that cheerful note in her voice genuine or forced?

"At this point, I'm thinking we'll probably take off the day after Christmas. Maybe we'll drive to San Diego for a few days before we head back up the coast to LA."

"Oh. So soon? I… That will be nice for you, to be back in the warmth and sunshine after all this snow we've had."

Logically, he knew it *should* be what he wanted, to go home and begin cobbling together the rest of their lives, but he still couldn't manage to drum up much enthusiasm for it.

"If I don't get the chance to talk to you again, I wanted to be sure to give you my thanks for all you've done to help Olivia."

Surprise flickered in those lovely eyes. "I didn't do anything," she protested.

"You know that's not true," he said. "You have been nothing but kind to her from the first moment we met you at the library that day. You gave her an unforgettable birthday celebration and have helped her feel the Christmas spirit when I would have thought that impossible this year. She's beginning to return to her old self, and I give a great deal of the credit for that to you and your family."

Her smile was soft and sweet and lit up her face like a thousand twinkly lights. He was struck again by how truly lovely she was, one of those rare women who became more beautiful the more times a man saw her.

"She's a remarkable girl, Flynn. I feel honored to have had the chance to know her. I'll miss her. I'll miss both of you."

Before he could come up with a reply to that—before he could do something stupid like tell her how very much he would miss her, too—one of the catering crew came up to her to ask a question about the dessert trays. After an awkward little pause, she excused herself to help solve the problem.

I'll miss her. I'll miss both of you.

The words seemed to echo through the vast lodge. While his daughter's life had been changed for the better because of their stay here in Pine Gulch, he wasn't sure he could say the same thing for his own.

He would miss Celeste, too. Rather desperately, he realized suddenly. As he stood in her family's holiday lodge surrounded by the trappings of the season, he realized how very much she had impacted his world, too.

"Got a minute?"

He had been so lost in thought he hadn't notice Rafe come in. Though there was still a certain wariness between the two of them, Rafe seemed to have become much more accepting of him after their time together working in the barn the other day.

He liked and respected the other man. In fact, Flynn suspected that if he and Olivia *were* to stick around Pine Gulch, he and Rafe would become friends.

"I have more than a minute," he answered. "I'm just the chauffeur right now, apparently, delivering Olivia to get her hair fixed."

"Perfect. While you've got your chauffeur hat on, I've got about twenty older ladies in need of rides. None of them likes to drive after dark, apparently, and especially not when it's snowing. Naturally, Hope promised them all she would find a way to get them here without thinking of the impossible logistics of the thing. Chase was supposed to help me shuttle them all, but he got tied up with something at his ranch and won't be free until right before the show starts. Everybody else is busy right now with the kids, so I'm in a pinch."

He was honored to be asked, even though he wasn't part of the community. "Sure. I'm happy to help, but I don't know where anybody lives. You'll have to tell me where to go."

"I've got a list right here with addresses and names. I figure if we split it up, we'll have time to get everybody here before the show, but it's going to be tight. You sure you don't mind?"

He didn't. It felt good to be part of something, to feel as though he was giving back a little for all that had been done for him and Olivia.

"Not at all. Let's do it."

"Where's my dad?" Olivia asked. "I thought he was going to be here to watch."

She looked absolutely beautiful in the little angel costume she wore for the show—and for the special part they had just practiced at the last minute.

The costume set off her delicate features and lovely blond hair to perfection.

Celeste's gaze drifted from her to the other children in their costumes. They all looked completely adorable. Somehow, by a Christmas miracle, they were really going to pull this off.

"Do you see my dad?" Olivia asked.

She frowned and looked around the beautiful screens Rafe and Flynn had built to serve as the wings to their small stage. She saw many familiar, beloved neighbors and friends, but no sign of a certain gorgeous man.

"I can't see him, but I'm sure he'll be here."

"Who are you looking for?" Hope asked, looking up from adjusting Joey's crooked crown.

"Flynn."

"I don't think he's back yet from picking up the last group of ladies."

Celeste stared at her sister. "What ladies?"

"Oh, didn't you know? Rafe asked him to help shuttle some of the ladies who wanted to come to the dinner and show, but didn't want to be stuck driving after dark."

She gaped at her sister. "Seriously? Flynn?"

"Yeah. He's already dropped off one carload earlier, and then I think Rafe sent him out again."

She pictured him driving through the snow to pick up a bunch of older ladies he didn't even know, and her throat seemed suddenly tight and achy. What a darling he was, to step up where he was needed.

How was she supposed to be able to resist a man like that?

She was in love with him.

She drew in a shaky breath as the reality of it crashed over her as if the entire plywood set had just tumbled onto her head. It was quite possible that she had been in love with him since that summer afternoon so many years ago when he had picked her up from her bike, dried her tears and cleaned up her scratches and scrapes.

Was that the reason she had never really become serious about any of the other men she dated in college? She'd always told herself she wasn't ready, that she didn't feel comfortable with any of them, that she was too socially awkward. That all might have been true, but perhaps the underlying reason was because she had already given her heart to the larger-than-life boy he had been.

In the past few weeks she truly had come to know him as more than just a kind teenager, her secret fantasy of what a hero should be. She had come to admire so many other things about him. His strength, his goodness, the love he poured out to his daughter.

How could she *not* love such a wonderful man? She loved him and she loved Olivia, too. Her heart was going to shatter into a million tiny pieces when they left.

"What if he doesn't make it back?" Olivia fretted now. "He'll miss my big surprise."

Celeste drew in a breath and forced herself to focus on the show. There would be time for heartbreak later.

"He'll make it back. Don't worry. He wouldn't miss seeing you."

Actually, Flynn missing Olivia's big surprise might not be such a bad thing. She wasn't quite sure he would like it, but it was too late for regrets now.

Olivia still seemed edgy as the music started. Her uneven gait was more pronounced than usual as she followed the other children onstage for their opening number.

Just as the last child filed on, she saw him leading three older women: Agnes Sheffield, her sister and their friend Dolores Martinez.

She watched around the wings as he took their coats, then helped them find empty seats. Agnes touched his arm in a rather coquettish way. As he gave the octogenarian an amused smile, Celeste fell a little in love with him all over again.

Darn man. Why did he have to be so wonderful?

At last, when everyone was settled and the children were standing on the risers, Destry Bowman, one of the older girls, took the microphone.

"We welcome you all to the first ever holiday extravaganza

at The Christmas Ranch. Consider this our Christmas gift to each of you."

The children immediately launched into the show, which was mostly a collection of familiar songs with a few vignette skits performed by the older children. After only a few moments, she could tell it was going to be considered an unqualified success.

She saw people laughing in all the right parts, catching their breath in expectation, even growing teary eyed at times, just as she'd predicted to the children. Most of all, she hoped they had a little taste of the joy and magic of the season, which seemed so much more real when experienced through the eyes of a child.

This was different from writing a book. Here she could see the immediate impact of what she had created and helped produce.

Seeing that reaction in real time made her rethink her objections to the upcoming Sparkle movie. Maybe it wouldn't be such a bad thing. The story was about finding the joy and wonder of Christmas through helping others, as Uncle Claude and Aunt Mary had taught them. If Sparkle could help spread that message, she didn't see how she could stand in the way.

Finally, it was time for the last number, which they had changed slightly at the last minute.

"Are you ready, sweetheart?" she whispered to Olivia.

The girl nodded, the tinsel halo of her angel costume waving eagerly.

As all the children were onstage, she stepped out to the audience so she could watch. From this vantage point, she had a clear view of Flynn. His brow furrowed in confusion at first to see Olivia at the microphone, then when the piano player gave her a note for pitch and she started singing the first verse to "Silent Night" by herself a cappella, his features went tight and cold.

Her voice was pure and beautiful, as it had been the other night while they were caroling, and she sang the familiar song with clarity and sweetness. She saw a few people whispering and pointing and thought she saw Agnes Sheffield mouth the words *Elise Chandler* to Dolores.

When Olivia finished, the piano started and all the children sang the second verse with her, then Destry Bowman signaled the audience to join in on the third.

What they might have lacked in musical training or even natural ability, the children made up for in enthusiasm and bright smiles.

Beside her, Hope sniffled. "They're wonderful, CeCe. The whole show is so good."

She smiled, even though emotions clogged her own throat.

They finished to thunderous applause, which thrilled the children. She saw delight on each face, especially the proud parents.

A moment later, Hope took the stage to wrap up things. "Let's give these amazing kids another round of applause," she said.

The audience readily complied, which made the children beam even more. The show had been a smashing success—which probably meant Hope would want to make it a tradition.

"I have to give props to one more person," she went on. To Celeste's shock, Hope looked straight at her. "My amazing sister Celeste. Once again, she has taken one of my harebrained ideas and turned it into a beautiful reality. Celeste."

Her sister held out her hand for her to come onstage. She had never wanted to do some serious hair pulling more than she did at right that moment.

She thought about being obstinate and remaining right where she was, but that would only be even *more* awkward. With no choice in the matter, she walked onstage to combined applause from the performers and the audience.

Face blazing, she hurried back down the stairs and off stage as quickly as possible, in time to hear Hope's last words to the audience.

"Now, Jenna McRaven and her crew have come up with an amazing meal for you all, so sit back and enjoy. Parents, your kids are going to change out of their costumes and they'll be right out to join you for dinner. As a special treat for you, the wonderful Natalie Dalton and Lucy Boyer are going to entertain you during dinner with a duet for piano and violin."

The two cousins by marriage came out and started the low-key dinner music Hope had arranged while the caterers began serving the meal.

"You all did wonderfully," Celeste told the cast when they gathered offstage. "Thank you so much for your hard work. I'm so proud of you! Now hurry and change then come out and find your family so you can enjoy all this yummy food."

With much laughing and talking, the children rushed to the two dressing rooms they had set aside. She was picking up someone's discarded shepherd's crook when her sister Faith came around the screen.

"Great work, CeCe. It was truly wonderful." She gave one of her rare smiles, and in that moment, all the frenetic work seemed worth it.

"I'm glad it's over. Next year it's your turn."

"Great idea." Hope joined them and turned a speculative look in Faith's direction.

"Ha. That will be the day," Faith said. "Unlike Celeste, I know how to say no to you. I've been doing it longer."

Celeste laughed and hugged her sisters, loving them both dearly, then she hurried back into the hallway to help return costumes to hangers and hurry the children along.

Just before she reached the dressing room, Flynn caught up with her, his face tight with an emotion she couldn't quite identify.

Still caught up in the exhilaration of a job well done, she impulsively hugged him. "Oh, Flynn. Wasn't Olivia wonderful? She didn't have an ounce of stage fright. She's amazing."

He didn't hug her back and it took a moment for her to realize that emotion on his face wasn't enthusiasm. He was furious.

"Why didn't you tell me she was going to sing a solo?"

She didn't know how to answer. The truth was, she *had* worried about his reaction but had ignored the little niggling unease. For his own reasons, Flynn objected to his daughter performing at all, let alone by herself. But the girl's voice was so lovely, Celeste had wanted her to share it.

Her heart sank, and she realized she had no good defense. "I should have told you," she admitted. "It was a last-minute thing. After we went caroling and I heard what a lovely voice she had, I decided to change the program slightly. I didn't have a lot of time to fill you in on the details since we decided to make the change just tonight, but I should have tried harder."

"You couldn't leave well enough alone. I told you I didn't want her doing the show in the first place, but my feelings didn't seem to matter. You pushed and pushed until I agreed, and then you threw her onto center stage, even though I made my feelings on it clear."

"She loved it!" she protested. "She wasn't nervous at all. A week ago, she was freaking out in a restaurant over a bin of dropped dishes, and today she was standing in front of a hundred people singing her heart out without flinching. I think that's amazing progress!"

"Her progress or lack of progress is none of your business. You understand? She's my daughter. I get to make those choices for her, not some small-town librarian who barely knows either of us."

She inhaled sharply as his words sliced and gouged at her like carving knives.

Her face suddenly felt numb, as frozen as her brain. That was all she was to him. A small-town librarian who didn't even know him or his daughter. It was as if all the closeness they had shared these past few days, the tender moments, didn't matter.

As if her *love* didn't matter.

She drew in another breath. She would get through this. She had endured much worse in her life than a little heartbreak.

Okay, right now it didn't exactly seem *little*. Still, she would survive.

"Of course," she said stiffly. "I'm sorry. I should have talked to you first. Believe it or not, I had her best interests at heart. Not only do I think she has an amazing voice, but I wanted her to know that even though something terrible has happened to her, her life doesn't have to stop. She doesn't have to cower in a room somewhere, afraid to live, to take any chances. I wanted to show her that she can still use her gift to bring light and music to the world. To bring joy to other people."

The moment she said the words, realization pounded over her like an avalanche rushing down the mountain.

This was what the Sparkle books did for people. It was what *she* did for people. All this time she had felt so uncomfortable with her unexpected success, afraid to relish it, unable to shake the feeling that she didn't deserve it.

She had a gift for storytelling. Her mother and father had nurtured that gift her entire life, but especially when their family had been held captive in Colombia.

Tell us a story, CeCe, her father would say in that endlessly calm voice that seemed to hold back all the chaos. He would start her off and the two of them would spin a new tale of triumph and hope to distract the others from their hunger and fear. She told stories about dragons, about a brave little mouse, about a girl and a boy on an adventure in the mountains.

Tears welled up as she remembered how proud and delighted her parents had been with each story. Maybe that was another reason she'd struggled to accept her Sparkle success, because they weren't here to relish it with her.

Yes, it would have been wonderful. She would have loved to see in the pride in their eyes, but in the end, it didn't matter. Not really. Her sisters were here. They were infinitely thrilled for her, and that was enough.

More important, *she* was here. She had a gift and it was long past time she embraced it instead of feeling embarrassed and unworthy anytime someone stopped her to tell her how much her words meant to them.

"Excuse me," she mumbled to him, needing to get away. Just as she turned to escape, her niece, Louisa, came out of the dressing room holding a book.

"Aunt CeCe, do you know where Olivia went? We were talking about *The Best Christmas Pageant Ever.* She'd never read it, and I told her I got an extra copy at school and she could have it. I want to make sure I don't forget to give it to her."

She turned away from Flynn, hoping none of the glittery tears she could feel threatening showed in her eyes.

"She's probably in the dressing room."

"I don't think so. I just came from there and I didn't see her."

"Are you looking for Olivia?" Barrett asked, joining them from the boy's dressing room. "She left."

She frowned at her nephew even as she felt Flynn tense beside her. "Left? What do you mean, she left?"

He shrugged. "She said she wanted to go see something. I saw her go out the back door. I thought it was kind of weird because she didn't even have a coat on, just her angel costume."

Celeste stared down at the boy, her heart suddenly racing with alarm. The angel costume was thin and not at all suitable for the wintry conditions in the Idaho mountains. Even a few minutes of weather exposure could be dangerous.

"How long ago was this?" Flynn demanded.

"I don't know. Right after we were done singing. Maybe ten minutes."

"She can't have gone far," Celeste said.

"You don't know that," Flynn bit out.

He was right. Even in ten minutes, the girl *might* have wandered into the forest of pine and fir around the ranch and become lost, or she could have fallen in the creek or wandered into the road. In that white costume, she would blend with the snow, and vehicles likely wouldn't be able to see her until it was too late.

Her leg still wasn't completely stable. She could have slipped somewhere and be lying in the snow, cold and hurt and scared...

Icy fingers of fear clutched at her, wrapping around her heart, her lungs, her brain.

"We can't panic," she said, more to herself than to him. "I'll look through the lodge to find her first, and then I'll get Rafe and everyone out there searching the entire ranch. We'll find her, Flynn. I promise."

Chapter Thirteen

He heard her words as if from a long distance away, as if she were trying to catch his attention with a whisper across a crowded room.

This couldn't be real. Any moment Olivia would come around the corner wearing that big smile he was beginning to see more frequently. He held his breath, but she didn't magically appear simply because he wished it.

Cold fear settled in his gut, achingly familiar. He couldn't lose her. Not after working so hard to get her back these past few months.

"We'll find her, Flynn," Celeste said again, the panic in her voice a clear match to his own emotions.

She cared about his daughter, and he had been so very mean to her about it. He knew he had hurt her. He had seen a little light blink out in her eyes at his cruel words.

Her progress or lack of progress is none of your business. She's my daughter. I get to make those choices for her, not some small-town librarian who barely knows either of us.

He would have given anything at that moment to take them back.

He didn't even know why he had gotten so upset seeing

Olivia up onstage—probably because he still wanted to do anything he could to protect her, to keep her close and the rest of the world away.

He didn't want her to become like her mother or his, obsessed with recognition and adulation. At the same time, he had been so very proud of her courage for standing in front of strangers and singing her little heart out.

None of that mattered right now. She was missing and he had to find her.

He hurried to find his coat, aware of a bustle of activity behind him as Rafe jumped up, followed by Hope and Faith.

The instant support comforted him like a tiny flickering candle glowing against the dark night in a window somewhere. Yeah, they might be temporary visitors in Pine Gulch, but he and Olivia had become part of a community, like it or not.

Celeste's brother-in-law stopped for an instant to rest a hand on Flynn's shoulder on his way to grabbing his own coat off the rack. "Don't worry, man. We'll find her. She'll be okay."

He wanted desperately to believe Rafe.

He couldn't lose her again.

They would find her.

A frantic five-minute search of the lodge revealed no sign of one little girl. She wasn't in any of the bathrooms, the kitchen area, the closed gift shop or sitting beside any of the senior citizens as they enjoyed their meal, oblivious to the drama playing out nearby.

Rafe texted Celeste that he had searched through the barn with no sign of her. Faith and Hope had gone up to the house to see if they could find her there. Rafe told her he wanted to take a look around the reindeer enclosure for a little blonde angel next and then head for some of the other outbuildings scattered about the ranch.

As soon as she read the word *angel*, something seemed to click in her brain. Angel. She suddenly remembered Olivia's fascination the other night with the angel above the little chapel in the Christmas village.

Excitement bubbled through her, and she suddenly knew with unshakable certainty that was where she would find the girl.

She grabbed her coat off the rack—not for her, but for Olivia when she found her—and raced outside without bothering to take time throwing it on.

Though Hope and Rafe had elected to close the rest of the ranch activities early that night—the sleigh rides, the sledding hill, the reindeer photography opportunities—because all hands were needed for the dinner and show, they had chosen to keep on the lights at the Christmas village for anyone who might want to stop and walk through it.

She nodded to a few families she knew who were enjoying the village, the children wide-eyed with excitement, but didn't take time to talk. She would have to explain away her rudeness to them later, but right now her priority was finding Olivia.

When she reached the chapel, she nearly collapsed with relief. A little angel in a white robe and silver tinsel halo stood in front of it, hands clasped together as she gazed up at the Madonna, the baby and especially the angel presiding over the scene.

Before she greeted the girl, Celeste took a precious twenty seconds to send a group text to Flynn, her sisters and Rafe to call off the search, explaining briefly that she had found Olivia safe and sound at the Christmas village.

With that done, she stepped forward just in time to hear what the girl was saying.

"Please tell my mom I don't want to be sad or scared all the time anymore. Do you think that's okay? I don't want her to think I don't love her or miss her. I do. I really do. I just want to be happy again. I think my daddy needs me to be."

Oh, Celeste so remembered being in that place after her parents had died—feeling so guilty when she found things to smile about again, wondering if it was some sort of betrayal to enjoy things like birthday cakes and trick-or-treating and the smell of fresh-cut Christmas trees.

She swallowed down her emotions and stepped forward to wrap her coat around Olivia. As she did, she noticed something that made her break out in goose bumps.

"If it means anything," she murmured, "I think your mom heard you."

The girl looked up. Surprise flickered in her eyes at seeing Celeste, but she gave her a tremulous smile and took the hand Celeste held out. "Why do you think so?"

"Look at the star."

Sure enough, the star above the chapel that had been out the other night flickered a few times and then stayed on.

Celeste knew the real explanation probably had to do with old wiring or a loose bulb being jostled in and out of the socket by the wind. Or maybe it was a tiny miracle, a sort of tender mercy for a grieving child who needed comfort in that moment.

"It *is* working," Olivia breathed. "Do you think my mom turned it on?"

"Maybe."

The star's light reflected on her features. "Do you…do you think she'll be mad at me for being happy it's Christmas?"

"Oh, honey, no." Heedless of the snow, Celeste knelt beside the girl so she could embrace her. "Christmas is all about finding the joy. It's about helping others and being kind to those in need and holding on to the people we love, like your dad. I heard what you said to the angel, and you're right. It hurts his heart to see you sad. Dads like to fix things—especially *your* dad—and he doesn't know how to fix this."

"When I cry, he sometimes looks as if he wants to cry, too," she said.

Celeste screwed her eyes shut, her heart aching with love for both of them. She didn't know the right words to say. They were all a jumble inside her, and she couldn't seem to sort through to find the right combination.

When she looked up, the peaceful scene in the little church seemed to calm her and she hugged the girl close to her. "It's natural to miss your mom and to wish she was still with you. But she wouldn't want you to give up things like sleigh rides and Christmas carols and playing with your friends. If that angel could talk, I think that's exactly what she would tell you your mom wanted you to hear."

Olivia seemed to absorb that. After a moment she exhaled heavily as if she had just set down a huge load and could finally breathe freely. She turned to Celeste, still kneeling beside her, and threw her arms around her neck.

That ache in her chest tightened as she returned the embrace, wondering if this would be her last one from this courageous girl she had come to love as much as she loved her father.

"Thanks for letting me be in the show," Olivia said. "It made me really happy. That's why I wanted to come out here, to see if the angel could ask my mom if it was okay with her."

Celeste hadn't known Elise Chandler, but from what little she did know, she had a feeling the woman would love knowing her daughter enjoyed entertaining people.

"I'm glad you had fun," she answered. "Really glad. But you scared everybody by coming out here without telling anyone. In fact, we should probably find your dad, just to make absolutely sure he got the message that you're safe."

"I'm here."

At the deep voice from behind them, she turned around and found Flynn watching them with an intense, unreadable look in his eyes.

Her heartbeat kicked up a notch. How much had he heard? And why was he looking at her like that?

Olivia extricated herself from Celeste, who rose as the girl ran to her father.

Flynn scooped her into his arms and held her tight, his features raw with relief.

"I'm sorry I didn't tell you where I was, Daddy."

"You know that's the rule, kiddo. Next time, you need to make sure you tell me where you're going so I know where to find you."

"I will," she promised.

As he set her back to the ground, her halo slipped a little and he fixed it for her before adjusting Celeste's baggy coat around the girl's shoulders. "I've been worried about you, Livie."

He didn't mean just the past fifteen minutes of not knowing where she was, Celeste realized. He was talking about all the fear and uncertainty of the past three months.

Her love for him seemed to beam in her chest brighter than a hundred stars. How was she going to get through all the days and months and years ahead of her without him?

"I don't want to be sad anymore," Olivia said. "I still might be sometimes, but Celeste said the angel would tell me Mom wouldn't want me to be sad *all* the time."

His gaze met hers and she suddenly couldn't catch her breath at the intense, glittering expression there. "Celeste and the angel are both very wise," he answered. He hugged her again. "You'll always miss your mom. That's normal when you lose someone you love. But it doesn't mean you can't still find things that make you happy."

"Like singing. I love to sing."

He nodded, even though he did it with a pained look. "Like singing, if that's what you enjoy."

The two of them were a unit, and she didn't really have a place in it.

She thought of his words to her. *She's my daughter. I get to make those choices for her, not some small-town librarian who barely knows either of us.*

They stung all over again, but he was right. For a brief time she had been part of their lives, but the time had come to say goodbye.

"Since you're safe and sound now, I really should go," she said with bright, completely fake cheer. "Why don't you hurry back to the lodge and change out of your angel costume, then you can grab some dinner?"

"I *am* hungry," Olivia said.

She smiled at the girl, though it took all her concentration not to burst into tears. A vast, hollow ache seemed to have opened up inside her.

"I'm sure Jenna McRaven can find both of you a plate. It all looked delicious."

"Good idea."

"I'll see you both later, then," she answered.

Even though they would be heading in the same direction, she didn't think she could walk sedately beside him and make polite conversation when this ache threatened to knock her to her knees.

Without waiting for them, she hurried back toward the lodge. As she reached it, the lights gleamed through the December night. Through the windows, she saw the dinner still in full swing. Suddenly, she couldn't face all that laughter and happiness and holiday spirit.

She figured she had done her part for the people of Pine Gulch. Let her sisters handle the rest. She needed to go home, change into her most comfortable pajamas, open a pint of Ben & Jerry's and try to figure out how she could possibly face a bleak, endless future that didn't contain a certain darling girl and her wonderful father.

By another Christmas miracle, she somehow managed to hold herself together while she hurried through the cold night to her SUV, started the engine and drove back to the foreman's cottage.

The moment she walked into the warmth of her house, the tears she had been shoving back burst through like a dam break and she rushed into her bedroom, sank onto her bed and indulged herself longer than she should have in a good bout of weeping.

She was vaguely aware that Linus and Lucy had followed

her inside and were watching her with concern and curiosity, but even that didn't ease the pain.

While some part of her wanted to wish Flynn had never returned to Pine Gulch so that she might have avoided this raw despair, she couldn't be so very selfish. Olivia had begun her journey toward healing here. She had made great progress in a very short amount of time and had begun regaining all she had lost in an act of senseless violence.

If the price of her healing was Celeste's own heartache, she would willingly pay it, even though it hurt more than she could ever have imagined.

After several long moments, her sobs subsided and she grew aware that Lucy was rubbing against her arm in concern while Linus whined from the floor in sympathy. She picked up both animals and held them close, deeply grateful for these two little creatures who gave her unconditional love.

"I'm okay," she told them. "Just feeling sorry for myself right now."

Linus wriggled up to lick at her salty tears, and she managed a watery smile at him. "Thanks, bud, but I think a tissue would be a better choice."

She set the animals back down while she reached for the box on the table beside her bed.

She would get through this, she thought as she wiped away her tears. The pain would be intense for a while, she didn't doubt, but once Flynn and his daughter returned to California and she didn't have to see either of them all the time, she would figure out a way to go forward without them.

She would focus instead on the many things she had to look forward to—Christmas, the new book release, the movie production, a trip to New York with Hope to meet with their publisher at some point in the spring.

With a deep breath, she forced herself to stop. Life was as beautiful as a silky, fresh, sweet-smelling rose, even when that beauty was sometimes complicated by a few thorns.

She rose and headed to the bathroom, where she scrubbed her face in cold water before changing into her most comfortable sweats and fuzzy socks.

The mantra of her parents seemed to echo in her head, almost as if they were both talking to her like the angels Olivia had imagined. If they were here, they would have told her the only way to survive heartache and pain this intense was to throw herself into doing something nice for someone else.

With that in mind, she decided to tackle one more item on her holiday to-do list—wrapping the final gifts she planned to give her family members. It was a distraction anyway, and one she badly needed. She grabbed the gifts from her office and carried them to the living room, then hunted up the paper, tape and scissors. With everything gathered in one place, she turned on the gas fireplace and the television set and plopped onto the floor.

Lucy instantly nabbed a red bow from the bag and started batting it around the floor while Linus cuddled next to her. She had just started to wrap the first present when the little dog's head lifted just seconds before the doorbell rang.

It was probably one of her sisters checking on her after her abrupt exit from the dinner. She started to tell them to come in, then remembered she had locked the door behind her out of habit she developed while away at school.

"Coming," she called. "Just a moment."

She unlocked the door, swung it open and then stared in shock at the man standing on the porch. Instantly, she wanted to shove the door shut again—and not only because she must look horrible in her loose, baggy sweats, with her hair a frizzy mess and her makeup sluiced away by the tears and the subsequent cold water bath.

"Flynn! What are you doing here?"

He frowned, concern on his gorgeous features. "You didn't stick around the lodge for dinner. I tried to find you to give your coat back but you had disappeared."

"Oh. Thanks."

She took the wool coat from him, then lowered her head, hoping he couldn't see her red nose, which probably wasn't nearly as cute as Rudolph's.

Though she didn't invite him in, he walked into the living room anyway and closed the door behind him to keep out the icy air. She should have told him not to bother, since he wouldn't be staying, but she couldn't find the words.

"Are you feeling okay?" he asked.

Sure. If a woman who was trying to function with a broken heart could possibly qualify as *okay*. She shrugged, still not meeting his gaze. "It's been a crazy-busy few days. I needed a little time to myself to get ready for Christmas. I've still got presents to wrap and all."

She gestured vaguely toward the coffee table and the wrapping paper and ribbon.

He was silent for a moment and then, to her horror, she felt his hand tilt her chin up so she had no choice but to look at him.

"Have you been crying?" he asked softly.

This had to be the single most embarrassing moment of her life—worse, even, than crashing her bicycle in front of his grandmother's house simply because she had been love struck and he hadn't been wearing a shirt.

"I was, um, watching a bit of a Hallmark movie a little earlier and, okay, I might have cried a little."

It wasn't a very good lie and he didn't look at all convinced.

"Are you sure that's all?" he asked, searching her expression with an intensity she didn't quite understand.

She swallowed. "I'm a sucker for happy endings. What can I say?"

He dropped his hand. "I hope that's the reason. I hope it's not because you were upset at me for acting like an ass earlier."

She tucked a strand of hair behind her ear. "You didn't at all. You were worried for your daughter. I understand. I was frantic, too."

"Before that," he murmured. "When we were talking about Olivia's solo in the show. I was cruel to you, and I'm so, so sorry."

She didn't know how to respond to that, not when he was gazing at her with that odd, intense look on his features again.

"You were a concerned father with your daughter's best interests at heart," she finally said. "And you didn't say anything that isn't true. I *am* a small-town librarian, and I'm very happy in that role. More important, I don't have the right to make decisions for Olivia without asking you. I should have told you about her solo. I'm sorry I didn't."

He made a dismissive gesture. "That doesn't matter. While she was missing, I prayed that if we found her, I would drive her myself to acting lessons, singing lessons, tap-dancing lessons. Whatever she wants. As long as she's finding joy in the world again and I can help her stay centered, I don't care what she wants to do. She's not my mother or Elise. She's a smart, courageous girl, and I know she can handle whatever comes her way. These past few months proved that."

In that moment she knew Olivia would be fine. Her father would make sure of it. It was a great comfort amid the pain of trying to figure out how to go on without them.

"I realized something else while we were looking for Olivia," Flynn said. He stepped a little closer.

"What's that?" she whispered, feeling breathless and shaky suddenly. Why was he looking at her like that, with that fierce light in his eyes and that soft, tender smile?

Her heart began to pound, especially when he didn't answer for a long moment, just continued to gaze at her. Finally, he took one more step and reached for her hand.

"Only that I just happen to be in love with a certain small-town librarian who is the most caring, wonderful woman I've ever met."

Nerves danced through her at the words, spiraling in circles like a gleeful child on a summer afternoon.

"I... You're what?"

His hand was warm on hers, his fingers strong and firm and wonderful. "I've never said that to anyone else and meant it. Truly meant it."

She took a shaky breath while those nerves cartwheeled in every direction. "I... Exactly how many other small-town librarians have you known?"

He smiled a little when she deliberately focused on the most unimportant part of what he had said. "Only you. Oh, and old Miss Ludwig, who had the job here in Pine Gulch before you. I think my grandmother took me into the library a few times when I was a kid, and I *definitely* never said anything like that to her. She scared me a little, if you want the truth."

"She scared me, too," she said. *You scare me more*, she wanted to say.

He leaned down close enough that only a few inches separated them. "You know what I meant," he murmured, almost against her mouth. "I've never told a woman I loved her before. Not when the words resounded like this in my heart."

"Oh, Flynn." She gave him a tremulous smile, humbled and awed and deeply in love with him.

He was close enough that she only had to step on tiptoes a little to press her mouth to his, pouring all the emotion etched on her own heart into the kiss.

He froze for just a moment and then he made a low, infinitely sexy sound in his throat and kissed her back with heat and hunger and tenderness, wrapping his arms tightly around her as if he couldn't bear to let her go.

A long while later he lifted his head, his breathing as ragged as hers and his eyes dazed. She was deliriously, wondrously happy. Her despair of a short time earlier seemed like a distant, long-ago memory that had happened to someone else.

"Does that kiss mean what I hope?" he murmured.

She could feel heat soak her cheeks and all the words seemed to tangle in her throat. She felt suddenly shy, awkward, but as soon as she felt the urge to retreat into herself where she was safe, she pushed it back down.

For once, she had to be brave, to take chances and seize the moment instead of standing by as a passive observer, content to read books about other people experiencing the sort of life she wanted.

"It means I love you," she answered. "I love you so very much, Flynn. And Olivia, too. I lied when I told you I was crying over a television show. I was crying because I knew the two of you would be leaving soon, and I… I didn't think my heart could bear it."

"I don't want to go anywhere," he said. "Pine Gulch has been wonderful for Olivia *and* for me. She might have been physically wounded, but I realized while I was here that some part of me has been emotionally damaged for much longer. This place has begun to heal both of us."

He kissed her again with an aching tenderness that made her want to cry all over again, this time because of the joy bubbling through her that seemed too big to stay contained.

She didn't know what the future held for them. He had a company in California, a life, a home. Perhaps he could commute from Pine Gulch to Southern California, or maybe he might want to take Rafe's advice and open a branch of his construction company here.

None of that mattered now, not when his arms and his kiss seemed to fill all the empty corners of her heart.

A long time later, he lifted his head with reluctance in his eyes. "I should probably go find Olivia. I left her with Hope and Rafe at the lodge. I'm sure she's having a great time with the other kids, but I hate to let her out of my sight for long."

"I don't blame you," she assured him.

He stepped away, though he didn't seem to want to release her hands. "I doubt Rafe was buying the excuse when I told him that I needed to return your coat. Something tells me he knows the signs of a man in love."

She could feel her face heat again. What would her family say about this? She didn't really need to ask. They already seemed to adore Olivia, and once they saw how happy she was with Flynn, they would come to love him, too.

"Do you want to come with me to pick her up?" he asked.

She wanted to go wherever he asked, but right now she still probably looked a mess. "Yes, if you can give me ten minutes to change."

"You look fine to me," he assured her. "Beautiful, actually."

When he looked at her like that, she felt beautiful, for the first time in her life.

"But if you *have* to change—and if I had a vote—I'm particularly fond of a particular T-shirt you own."

"I'll see what I can do," she answered with a laugh. She kissed him again while the Christmas lights from her little tree gleamed and the wind whispered against the window and joy swirled around them like snowflakes.

Epilogue

"Are you ready for this?"

Celeste took her gaze from the snowflakes outside to glance across the width of the SUV to her husband.

"No," she admitted. "I doubt I will *ever* be ready."

Flynn lifted one hand from the steering wheel to grab hers, offering instant comfort, his calm blowing away the chaotic thoughts fluttering through her like that swirl of snow.

"*I'm* ready," Olivia piped up from the backseat. "I can't *wait*."

"You? You're excited?" Flynn glanced briefly in the rearview mirror at his daughter. "You hide it so very well."

Olivia didn't bother to pay any attention to his desert-dry tone. "This is the coolest thing that's ever happened in my whole life," she said.

Since Olivia wasn't yet a decade old, her pool of experiences was a little shallow, but Flynn and Celeste both declined to point that out.

The girl was practically bouncing in the backseat, the energy vibrating off her in waves. Celeste had to smile. She adored Olivia for the lovely young lady she was growing into.

The trauma of her mother's tragic death had inevitably left scars that would always be part of her, but they had faded over the past two years. Olivia was a kind, funny, creative girl with a huge heart.

She had opened that big heart to welcome Celeste into their little family when she and Flynn married eighteen months earlier, and Celeste had loved every single moment of being her stepmother.

Now Olivia breathed out a happy sigh. "I think I'm more excited about the Pine Gulch premiere of *Sparkle and the Magic Snowball* than the real one in Hollywood tomorrow."

"Really?" Celeste said in surprise. "I thought you'd be thrilled about the whole thing."

Olivia loved everything to do with the film industry, much to Flynn's dismay. Celeste supposed it was in her blood, given her mother's and her grandmother's legacies. Someday those Hollywood lights would probably draw her there, too—something Flynn was doing his best to accept.

"It will be fun to miss school and fly out and stay at our old house. I mean, a movie premiere in Hollywood with celebrities will be glamorous and all. Who *wouldn't* be excited about that?"

In the transitory glow from the streetlights, her features looked pensive. "But I guess I'm more excited about this one because this is our home now," she said after a moment. "This is where our family is and all our friends. Everyone in Pine Gulch is just as excited about the new Sparkle movie as I am, and I can't wait to share it with them."

Oh. What a dear she was. If the girl hadn't been safely buckled in the backseat, Celeste would have hugged her. It warmed her more than her favorite wool coat that her stepdaughter felt so at home in Pine Gulch and that she wanted all her friends and neighbors to have the chance to enjoy the moment, too.

"Good point," Flynn said, smiling warmly at his daughter. "The whole town has been part of the story from the beginning. It's only right that they be the first to see the movie."

"Yep. That's the way I feel," Olivia said.

Her father gave Celeste a sidelong glance before addressing Olivia again. "Good thing your stepmother is so fierce and fought all the way up to the head of the studio to make sure it happened this way. What else could they do but agree? They're all shaking in their boots around her. She can be pretty scary, you know."

Olivia giggled and Celeste gave them both a mock glare, though she knew exactly what he was doing. Her wonderful husband was trying to calm her down the best way he knew how, by teasing away her nerves.

She *had* fought for a few things when it came to her beloved Sparkle character, but wanted to think she had been easygoing. That was what the studio executives had told her anyway. She considered herself extremely fortunate that her vision for the characters and the story matched the studio's almost exactly.

A moment later, Flynn pulled up to the St. Nicholas Lodge, which had been transformed for the night into a theater.

Somebody—Rafe, maybe—had rented a couple of huge searchlights, and they beamed like beacons through the snowy night. The parking lot was completely full and she recognized many familiar vehicles. Unfortunately, they couldn't fit everyone in town into the lodge so the event had become invitation only very quickly. For weeks, that invitation had become the most sought-after ticket in town.

Though the official premiere the next night in California would be much more of a full-fledged industry event, a red carpet had been stretched out the door of the lodge, extending down the snowy walkway to the edge of the parking lot.

Had that been Faith's doing? Probably. Where on earth had she managed to find a length of red carpet in eastern Idaho? Their older sister was proud of and excited for both Celeste and Hope.

The past two years since they'd signed the contract licensing the Sparkle stories to the animation studio they had chosen to work with seemed surreal. Besides two more bestsellers, they now had a *second* Sparkle animated movie in the works.

Now that she was here, about to walk into the makeshift theater to see people enjoying *her* story come to life on the screen—and it would be enjoyable, she knew, given what she had seen so far of the production—Celeste felt humbled and touched. It didn't seem real that life and fate, her own hard work and her sister's beautiful artwork had thrust her into this position.

"A red carpet," Olivia squealed as she finally noticed—and caught sight of the people lined up in the cold on either side of it, as if this was the real premiere filled with celebrities to gawk over. "How cool is that? That looks like my friend Louise from school. Oh, there's Jose. And Mrs. Jacobs. My whole class is here!"

"I guess you can't escape Hollywood, even here in Pine Gulch," Celeste said quietly to Flynn as he parked in the VIP slot designated for them. "I'm sorry."

He made a rueful face, but she knew him well enough after these deliriously happy months together to know he didn't really mind. He had been her biggest supporter and her second most enthusiastic fan—after Olivia, of course.

"For you, darling, it's worth it," he replied. He tugged her across the seat and pulled her into his arms for a quick kiss. "I'm so proud of you. I hope you know that. I can't wait for the whole world to discover how amazing you are."

Her heart softened, as it always did when he said such tender things to her.

Two years ago, she'd had a pretty good life here in Pine Gulch—writing her stories, working at the library in a job she loved, spending time with her sisters and her niece and nephew and Aunt Mary.

But some small part of her had still been that little girl who had lost both of her parents and was too afraid to truly embrace life and everything it had to offer.

Flynn and Olivia had changed her. At last, she fully understood the meaning of joy. Sparkle might have his magic snowball that could save Christmas, but the true magic—the only one that really mattered—was love.

These past two years had been a glorious adventure—and in seven months, give or take a few weeks, they would all be in for a new turn in their shared journey.

She pressed a hand to her stomach, to the new life growing there. Flynn caught the gesture and grinned—a secret smile between the two of them. He pressed a hand there as well, then reached for his car door.

"Let's go meet your adoring public," he told her.

She didn't need an adoring public. She had everything she needed, right here, in the family they had created together.

* * * * *

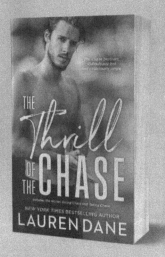 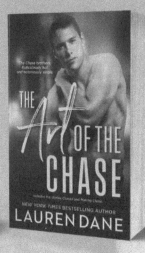